one last thing

A CONTEMPORARY ROMANCE

SEDDLEDOWNE SERIES
BOOK ONE

SUSAN HENSHAW
(CALLIE MAE SHAW)

FIREFLY FIELDS PUBLISHING

Copyright © 2024 by Susan Henshaw Auten

All rights reserved.

No part of this book may be reproduced in any form or by any electronic or mechanical means, including information storage and retrieval systems, without written permission from the author, except for the use of brief quotations in a book review.

Cover Design by Books and Moods

Edited by Emily Faircutler

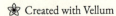 Created with Vellum

*For single moms and farm girls everywhere.
We all deserve a Silas.*

playlist

FOR ONE LAST THING

Find the playlist for Silas and Clementine's story on Spotify.

- You Belong With Me…Taylor Swift
- Marry Me…Thomas Rhett
- See You later (Ten Years)…Jenna Raine
- Don't Let Me Down (feat. Daya)…The Chainsmokers
- In The Stars…Benson Boone
- Before He Cheats…Carrie Underwood
- There She Goes…Benson Boone
- Always Been You…Jessie Murph
- A Little Bit Yours…JP Saxe
- Chance Wtih You…Mehro
- The Moment I Knew…Taylor Swift
- Shake the Frost…Tyler Childers
- Fallin' For You…Colbie Caillat
- Forever and a Day…Benson Boone
- Picture to Burn…Taylor Swift
- Here Comes Goodbye…Rascal Flatts
- Ghost…Justin Bieber
- I Get to Love You…Ruelle

- Grow Old With You…Brett Morgan
- If You Love Her…Forest Blakk
- I Guess I'm In Love…Clinton Kane
- The Good Ones…Gabby Barrett
- That Part…Lauren Spencer Smith

Dear Reader,

There is a **content warning** on the next page. If you don't want to read spoilers, skip directly to chapter one.

This is a realistic, contemporary, small-town, love story. **It is not a rom-com.** Hard things happen in this book. But you will also find happy, hilarious and heart-skipping moments too.

If you're okay with intense emotions, realistic situations, and swoony kisses, you're in the right place. Welcome. I'm so glad you made it!

All to pieces,

Susan

content warnings

Your mental health matters. For your information, this book deals with **infidelity, death, and a miscarriage.**

Heat level comparison: If you enjoyed the angst, mild swearing and spice in The Twilight Saga by Stephenie Meyer, you will love this book.

Now that we've gotten that out of the way, hold on to your cowgirl hats, 'cause Clem and Silas are waiting on the next page! Yeehaw! And move 'em out!

one

CLEMENTINE

Silas Dupree needed to stop glancing at me like I might break into a million pieces at any second. I wasn't going to break. Not in front of him. I wasn't going to shed a single tear. He hadn't bothered to call or text in more than eight years. Not even when I blew up his phone for weeks. Not even this past year, while his twin sister, my best friend, Sophie, was slowly dying. He didn't get to pretend he cared now. And the fact that he was trying to just made me mad. I needed to be strong for Sophie's daughter, Anna. I could cry once this graveside service was over, when I was alone and no one was watching.

Silas knew better than to have his eyes open while the Pastor was praying anyway. I mean, *my* eyes were open, but I didn't care about showing Pastor Allen any respect. He'd hellfire and damnation'ed Sophie right out of his church when she'd come to his office terrified and knocked up at the age of fourteen and a half. He should've preached love and acceptance and offered his assistance. Instead, he'd terrified her with all the ways God would let her burn for eternity if she didn't wrap herself in sackcloth, rub ashes on her head, and place that baby girl with another family through adoption.

I couldn't care less if he was the minister to marry Sophie's parents, Bo and Jenny, or that he'd baptized every one of their five babies—including the daughter they were laying to rest today. No, I wasn't closing my eyes and bowing my head for anything *he* had to say. Sophie wouldn't have wanted Old Fish Lips preaching her graveside service anyway. She wouldn't have let him set foot on Dupree land much less in their family cemetery. But Bo and Jenny never would ruffle feathers.

"And dear Lord," Pastor Allen's jowls hung limp like my momma's old basset hound, Buford. "Please forgive Sophie Ray Dupree for all her wrongdoings and mischief." Spit shot out of the side of his mouth and landed on an old lady I didn't recognize. She dabbed at her face with a handkerchief, but her eyes never opened. Silas should've taken note.

Pastor Allen continued, "Just like the Lord said of those two thieves on the cross, 'they know not what they do.'" Was he seriously comparing my best friend, single-mom extraordinaire, loyal sister, and loving daughter with the two thieves? My eyes narrowed, and I tried with all my might to burn holes into the scalp he was hiding with that pathetic wisp of a comb-over.

"Okay, boomer." Anna hissed next to me. "He's probably still mad about the time you and Momma made him a dating profile on Farmers Only. And everybody swiped left." I bit back a laugh and pulled Sophie's thirteen-year-old daughter against my side, enjoying a brief lift from the boulder of grief residing on my chest.

"Either that," I whispered back, "or the time we dressed up those chocolate-covered Brussels sprouts with Ferrero Rocher wrappers and gave them to him for Easter." Everyone knew Pastor Allen was "deathly" allergic to Brussels sprouts. Apparently, the covetous clergyman had snuck one of the "candies" between the Easter sermon and the potluck afterward. By the time the blessing on the food ended, his lips had swollen up to four times their normal size, and his nose ran like a firehose, dripping all over Momma's famous baked beans. Tragedy. But also hilarious. And also how he got his nickname, Old Fish Lips. Mrs. Allen had to rush him home to give him a shot with an EpiPen and pump him full of Benadryl. Said he didn't wake up for two days.

Oh, Sophie, I thought. *Will life ever be any fun without you?*

A sob rose up in my chest, threatening to crack my heart right in two. As if he could feel the impending rupture, Silas's gaze skittered to me. With the way the sun hit him right then, his gray eyes seemed almost translucent, especially against his chestnut brown hair. A muscle in his jaw flexed and his gaze narrowed, roving over my face. I held his stare, hoping he'd be uncomfortable knowing I'd caught him gawking. But he didn't show an ounce of regret. The man had a poker face like no one else. And it was infuriating. I tried to out-stare him but, like always, I was the first to break.

The petite blonde next to him doubled down on the death grip she had on his hand. The laser-beam glare she shot at me could rival the one I'd aimed at Pastor Allen. What was she even doing here? A funeral wasn't the time to meet your boyfriend's family. And it wasn't the time to be glowering at the deceased's best friend.

Apparently, Silas hadn't told her that I wasn't someone she should be threatened by. Maybe Si and I had been close friends through childhood and high school, but the minute he left for college, he dropped me hard, only exchanging the occasional greeting whenever he came home. Beyond that, the only connection we shared was a very inactive Facebook friendship. As far as I could tell, Silas never even logged on to his account. Or if he did, he never so much as liked or commented on anyone's status. And the past few years, up until Sophie got sick, he hadn't even come home. He'd flown his parents, Sophie, and Anna to him.

Oh, I still knew plenty about him—in a newish relationship with pint-sized Barbie, named Wyoming's Teacher of the Year last year, and had accepted a middle school assistant principal job starting this fall. But I'd learned all of that from Sophie or Bo and Jenny, who bragged about their kids every time they got the slightest chance. So, yeah, I may've known a fair bit about Silas, but Barbie over there could stop marking her territory. It was a waste of metaphorical urine.

Maybe if she realized that—even though this was a funeral and not a singles mixer—I was married, she might lower her hackles. I peeked over my shoulder, trying to locate my husband, Billy, at the back of the funeral tent, where he'd said he would be. Billy didn't do crying. Or getting up in his feelings. Or anything that forced him to pretend like he did. But a look over both shoulders told me no, he was not here.

He'd actually skipped out on Sophie's graveside service? I pulled my phone out of my jacket pocket.

> Me: Where are you?

A few seconds later, he replied.

> Billy: Emergency at the office. A girl needed stitches.

Billy was one of the doctors at the only clinic in town, so it wasn't unheard of...but he'd had an unusually high number of emergencies lately. It irritated me that he would let anything stop him from being here. Send them to urgent care, for crying out loud.

Just then, Pastor Allen must've said something else offensive because I'd never heard someone clear their throat in as threatening a way as Bo did just then.

"Amen." Fish Lips finished abruptly and scampered to the edge of the tent.

Everything went quiet. Anna nudged me. "Lemon, I think it's your turn."

Oh. Yeah.

The Duprees had asked me to give part of Sophie's eulogy during the funeral, but I knew my limitations. So we'd compromised, and I was supposed to say a few parting words now. As I stepped away, Anna walked across the tent and sidled up on the other side of Silas. He pulled her under his arm, blinking back tears and failing, and pressed a kiss to her head.

Sophie's mahogany casket had a spray of beautiful white lilies on top. I stood in front of it and turned to face everyone. All four of her brothers—Silas, Holden, Ashton, and Ford— were wiping their tears. What they say is true. Cowboys don't cry. Except at their only sister's funeral. And then they shake and whimper and blow their noses with the weakest of men.

Jenny and Bo sobbed against each other, still seated in the front row. Behind them, my momma pressed a tissue against her nostrils, her expression battle-worn. It's how we all felt. Too tired for whatever came next. A year of watching someone die will do that to a person.

I cleared my throat, my hands mangling each other, and began. "Sophie didn't say much about what she wanted at her funeral." I chewed my lip and shrugged. "Not too many twenty-eight-year-olds have their funerals planned out. And she never let us talk about 'what if.'" I cleared my throat and swallowed carefully. "Even when what if became when."

I made the mistake of looking up. There wasn't a dry eye in the house. It almost broke me.

I had to cheer them up. It was my responsibility. "Sophie

wouldn't have wanted this." I shook my head. "She'd shake her finger at all of us right now."

Someone let out a wet chuckle.

"She would tell us to get over ourselves and get on with it. And then she'd tell us to get some food in our bellies because everything looks better once you've had a nap and a snack."

A few more throaty laughs.

"She couldn't stand a hangry person. That's probably why she and Holden fought so much."

That did it. The group erupted in soft laughter. Especially Holden, the "third twin," the Duprees called him. He'd made an unplanned appearance eleven months after Silas and Sophie. And he was always hungry. Had the metabolism of a hummingbird. It had driven Sophie nuts.

"So that's what I think we should do right now. Go eat. Go tell some of our favorite Sophie stories—because there are plenty to tell. And let's celebrate the life of a woman whose presence will never"—I choked and recovered with a gulp—"truly be gone." I pointed to my chest. "Because she's right here. In all of us."

Nods all around.

I circled my arm in a lasso motion above my head. "Let's move 'em out."

Then I turned and headed for my truck. I needed a minute to pull myself together before I was bombarded with condolences at the potluck.

Anna jogged up to me, wet-cheeked but smiling. Oh, how I loved this raven-haired beauty—spitting image of her blond momma but with an Italian twist. She'd inherited it from her father, Gianni, the hot exchange student from Milan, who'd suckered Sophie out of her virginity and then taken off at the end of freshman year without a trace. "Is it okay if I ride with Silas to the church?"

I caught Silas's eye two cars over and nodded. Anna had

slept over at my place for the last few weeks while Sophie was in the hospital. But as soon as Silas showed up five days ago, she'd been glued to his side, even slept on the floor in his old room. I got it. He was Sophie's twin—as close to flesh and blood as she could get to her momma. If I were her, that's where I'd want to be too. You know, if Silas hadn't ignored me for the last decade.

My momma walked up and squeezed me against her. "How you doing, baby girl?" She'd always called me baby girl. I was the only baby she'd ever had. Something about having her arms around me almost did me in. I blew out my breath. She pushed my hair out of my eye and tucked it behind my ears.

I pasted a resolute smile on my face. "I've got this. I'll be okay."

"You have to be, for that girl." She glanced at Annaleise, who was getting into the rental with Silas and his girlfriend, whatever her name was. For the life of me, I couldn't remember.

"I know, Momma."

She patted my shoulder. "It was a beautiful service. You know Sophie loved a warm spring day. Couldn't have asked for better weather." She gave my hand a squeeze before she walked away.

"Lemon," someone hollered. I turned to see Jackie Shumaker, our nearest neighbor, jogging toward me. "BJ just called. You've got a cow out. Number fifty-six."

I swore under my breath, and my temper flared like a red-hot firecracker. Billy'd been promising to fix the fence on the south pasture for months now. I'd patched it a dozen times, but that section needed to be torn down and rebuilt. Not a one-person job. Fifty-six was the most trifling cow we had. If there was a weak spot in the barbed wire, she found it. Every. Time.

"BJ chased her back onto your land. He would've gotten her all the way, but he just had that knee replacement." She seemed annoyed that he'd done that much in his condition—and I couldn't blame her. "But you and I can probably get her back in together."

"No, it's okay." I wouldn't bother Jackie. She was supposed to help with the potluck. "You go ahead. I'll get her."

"You sure?" She asked to be nice, but I saw the relief in her eyes.

"Yeah." I shrugged like it was nothing. "You go."

I pulled out my phone, tempted to text Billy, but he would only remind me he had an emergency. Whatever he was doing always took precedence over the farm. And I was tired of asking. Tired of the lecture that he shouldn't have to do menial work now that he was a doctor, even though the cows brought in good money. I'd get the cow back in and arrive in time for a piece of pie. Easy-peasy. And tomorrow I would fix that confounded fence.

"Hey, need any help?" Silas asked, leaning over the top of the car. I hadn't realized he was listening. And I'd forgotten how deep his voice was. And when had he gotten so tall and broad shouldered? I couldn't even stand on tiptoe next to Billy without him getting mad. Forget about wearing heels. But dang. Silas had to be at least six feet four inches now. He'd finally gained some weight, too. No, not weight. Muscle. He'd been so skinny in high school it was painful. My daddy, rest his soul, used to tease Silas that one gust of wind would carry him away just like Dorothy in the Wizard of Oz. And of course, Silas took it straight-faced. Not even a grin or a scowl.

"Clem?" he asked again, and it sent a jolt up my spine. He was the only person on earth who called me that, besides Momma. When Anna was learning to say my name, she couldn't quite pronounce Clementine. Instead, she'd called me lemon-lime, which quickly got shortened to Lemon. It stuck. But Silas had never made the switch.

Did I want his help? Absolutely not. Did I need his help? Probably.

I was about to accept his offer when Girlfriend Barbie gave me a threatening look from the passenger seat.

My drama threshold was maxed for the day, so I shook my head. "I'll be okay. Should only take a few minutes."

He cocked his eyebrow as if he didn't believe me, but I didn't give him time to counter. If I could've gone anywhere right then, I would've headed straight to The Downward Dog, my yoga-barre studio. I needed the endorphins a good workout always brought. Instead, I slid into my dad's old truck and headed in the opposite direction of the church—home to Firefly Fields Farm. My personal piece of heaven.

two

SILAS

I was a discombobulated mess as I raced toward Firefly Fields. Where was freaking Billy? Why couldn't he get the cow in? No one would miss him at the church. And why was I even going over? And why couldn't I stop staring at her? Even with Christy right next to me, my eyes just kept flitting in that direction. I was pathetic.

I'd moved nineteen hundred miles to get away from Clementine. But Sophie's last words haunted me: *Make sure Lemon's okay. Please.* It's amazing the promises you'll make when your twin sister is hours from death. I didn't know exactly how to make sure Clem was okay, especially when I lived across the country. But I was here right now and I could help with this. And Clem belonged at the potluck. Sophie probably loved her more than anyone in the world other than Anna. If I didn't get her back there, Sophie would haunt me something fierce.

I punched the gas, trying not to think about how mad Christy looked when I dropped her and Anna at the church. But barring an outright miracle, Clem would miss the entire dinner trying to get that cow back in by herself. When I hit the gravel driveway, the road was so rough I bounced off my seat. I gently tapped the brakes. No time for fishtailing.

My eyes took in the farm and I couldn't believe what I saw. Sophie had told me how hard Clem worked to keep the farm up, but there were three hundred acres here. There was only so much one woman could do. Everywhere I turned, I saw signs of neglect. Thorn bushes and vines took over the high tensile fence lines. A corner of the tin roof on the hay barn flapped in the breeze. Most of the gates were rusted and barely held together—and rather than being hooked in place with a chain, they were tied with leftover bailing twine. If Clem's daddy, James, were alive, he would throttle Billy for letting the farm go like this. Then again, if James were alive, the farm wouldn't look like this.

A growl formed in my throat. If I'd been left Firefly, you could bet your retirement I'd spend every ounce of energy working alongside Clem to keep James's legacy alive. What had Billy been doing with all his time? I clamped my teeth.

Sophie had always hated Billy. Called him Billiterate, right to his face. Sophie wasn't afraid of anyone or anything. Said Clem had to write practically all of his papers in college and med school and that Billy wasn't good for anything. I didn't know if that was true. But if the state of Firefly was any indication, I'd say my sister hadn't been far off.

I rolled over the last hill coming down into the valley. And there was Clem, having a stand-off with the cow. Clem's high-heeled boots were covered in the red mud Seddledowne was famous for. She turned when she heard me pull up and I could already tell she'd had a doozy of a time trying to get fifty-six back in. Her bun was falling loose, letting strands of her copper hair poke out in all directions. And she had a smear of dirt on her left cheek. Clem had a way of looking soft and beautiful, even when she was a mess. I hated myself for noticing.

I pushed the door open and got out.

"I told you I don't need help." She tucked her bangs behind her ear. "You should be at the dinner with everyone else." But her expression couldn't hide the relief. I did the right thing in coming.

I shrugged off my suit jacket and tossed it into the passenger seat.

"So should you." I started rolling up the sleeves of my shirt. "Did you try grain?" Cows would usually follow you anywhere for a sack of sweet feed. As long as they weren't full on grass or hay.

She rolled her eyes but smiled. "I wasn't raised on a farm or anything." That was the Sophie coming out in her. My sister couldn't complete two sentences without one of them dripping with sarcasm.

It made me smile a little. I finished up my other sleeve and shrugged. "Had to ask."

She squinted in the sunlight. "You're going to mess up your Armani."

I actually didn't know what kind of suit I was wearing. Christy had picked it out. But I knew it cost a lot. More than I would've spent. "That's what dry cleaning is for."

"She doesn't want grain." Clem nodded to an open bag in the back of a side-by-side fifteen feet off. "Just wants to be a pain in my side."

"What about—"

"Mineral either." She nodded again to the side-by-side.

"What do you want to do then?" I mean, I knew what I'd do—but this was Clem's situation, and if I'd learned anything from Christy, it was that women usually didn't want you to come in and rescue them. At least, not strong-willed ones.

Clem inspected her muddy shoes. "Well, I've had enough running around for one evening. I was thinking of getting a rope from the barn."

My eyebrow lifted. "You finally learned to lasso?" Doubtful. I mean, I used to lasso anything that moved. My brothers, Sophie, Clem, Mom, the dog. A roping scholarship had paid my way through the University of Wyoming. But the few times I'd tried to teach Clem had ended in disaster. She wouldn't even try once we hit high school.

"We'll never have to find out now that you're here." She wiggled her eyebrows and if it had been any other girl, I'd have sworn she was flirting. Once upon a time, that would've made me way too happy, but I'd conditioned myself to ignore stuff like that. I'd been hurt too many times by this girl. She didn't know about any of them. But my heart sure did.

I gave her a brief, all-business smile. "Good thing I showed up, after all. Where are your ropes?"

"The red barn by my house." She nodded to the east like I didn't know where her house was. Growing up, we'd spent hours playing there in her Granny Eudora's musty basement. We'd build entire towns out of leftover shipping boxes. Of course I knew where her house was.

"Be right back." I hopped in my car and got back onto the gravel driveway.

In sixty seconds, I was there. Apparently, I had company. Right in front of the barn were two parked cars. A brand spanking new dually Ford F-450 diesel, still wearing thirty-day tags. I peeked inside. Leather everything, massive speakers, and a double sunroof. I whistled. Somebody had paid a pretty penny for that. The other car was a Honda Accord that was so old and beat-up it shouldn't have been on the road anymore. I'd seen better ones in the junkyard. It was a dull silver, all the shine worn off. The left side mirror was shattered, only there for appearance. One bumper was dark blue, mismatching the rest of the car, like they either couldn't find a matching part, or they were too trashy to care. And it had a single bumper sticker of a red slap button with the word "Easy" on it. Classy.

These two vehicles could not have been more contradictory if they tried.

There was the faintest sound of a love song coming from the barn. What in the...?

I opened the closest door and slipped inside. The bottom floor was empty. The noise was coming from upstairs, where there was a small room with a single bed. Another place we'd played as children. Before I could even think to look for a rope, a rhythmic banging stopped me in my tracks.

I stood there, not believing my ears, willing it to stop. There was only one thing in the world that made a sound like that. Flashbacks of my second year in college came rushing back. My dorm mate, Kinky Kenny, almost broke the wall between our rooms making that same sound.

A pit formed in my stomach as every possible scenario ran through my head. The only people that lived on this farm were Clem's momma—Miss Lisa—Clem, and Billy. Miss Lisa was a sixty-eight-year-old widow who was at the church, probably enjoying a plate of deviled eggs, ham, and baked beans. And Clem was out in the field. That left...

The banging continued, loud and aggressive.

I quickly texted Holden.

> Me: Any chance you know what kind of vehicle Billy drives?

My stomach twisted being in that building with whatever was going on upstairs.

I willed Holden to see the text. A few seconds later, his dots started moving, indicating he was typing.

> Holden: Oh, pick me, pick me. I know this one.

> Me: No time for jokes.

The dots flashed for what seemed like forever. "Faster, dude," I hissed at the phone. Was he writing a novel?

> Holden: Saw it last night at the viewing. A ginormous dually, Ford-F450. Because a 250 or 350 isn't big enough. Think he might be compensating for something? Man, you better hurry. Mrs. Allen's deviled eggs are almost gone. Nom, nom, nom.

I shoved the phone in my pocket and paced. This was the last thing Clem needed today of all days. What should I do? Run upstairs and beat the daylights out of Billy before Clem found out? Scream in his face that he was the biggest idiot on planet Earth? I didn't care who the girl upstairs was. She could not have held a candle to Clementine. Or maybe grab the rope, get the cow in and make sure Clem went straight back to the church without seeing this and break it to her later? I stood there trying to think of any way I would not have to be the one to tell her.

Too late.

The door flew open and Clem walked in, her hair wilder than before. She must've driven the side-by-side. I wrapped my arms around my head and turned away from her. *Cowboy up, wuss.* I dropped my arms and forced myself to face her. But I couldn't stop my expression from looking sick. I wasn't that good of an actor, even on my best day.

Her eyebrows drew together at the sight of me. "What's taking so long? Is Billy here? And whose car is that?" She scrutinized the ceiling. "Is that music?"

Right then the bed slammed against the wall so hard the floor above rained down dust. Her eyes shot upward.

I strode over and grabbed her arm. "You know what? I don't think we need a rope. I've got another idea." I pulled her toward the door. With all my heart, I didn't want to see the scene that was about to go down if she realized what was happening upstairs. I'd take her somewhere else and tell her, but she didn't need to find out like this.

She yanked her elbow loose and studied the ceiling, her nose scrunching up and her forehead furrowed. Watching the realization come over her was like watching a fatal car accident happen in slow motion. There was nothing I could do to stop the horror that would follow. Her face went slack. Angry tears filled her eyes. I cupped her face in my hands, forcing her to look at me. "Let's get out of here."

Another bang corresponded with a woman yelling, "Billeeee."

Any composure she'd had today drained faster than a broken hourglass. Her face went ashen, and she shot toward the stairs. I sprinted, catching her on the first step. I wove my arms around her waist, pulling her back.

She clawed at my skin, fighting to get free. I tightened my hold.

"Let me go!" She kicked like a caged wild animal.

The banging came to a crashing halt, and the music turned off. Finally.

"You don't want to see it, Clem. You think you do, but you don't." I pressed my face into her hair, wishing I could take her somewhere far away. To a different reality where this had never happened.

A sob ripped through her so hard and deep that I could feel the vibration in my own chest. It caused my grip to loosen ever so slightly. She whirled in my arms and shoved me away. I staggered back a few steps.

"I need to see!" The tears pouring over her freckled cheeks nearly broke me. I'd known Clem almost as long as I could remember and I'd never seen her this gutted. I wanted to take her in my arms and hold her so tight she couldn't hurt if she wanted to.

She bolted up the stairs, and I followed behind. I couldn't let her do this alone. I wouldn't. She threw the door open, and we came around the corner just in time to see Billy rolling off of a twig of a girl who couldn't have been more than twenty, both of them as naked as the day they were born.

The girl pulled an afghan up to her neck, her eyes bulging in fear. Billy cowered on one side of the bed, covering himself with his hands. His body was pasty white from his knees to his neck. I wanted to deck him. The girl wasn't attractive at all. Not even a little. And there was nothing in his stance to indicate that he felt the need to protect her in any way. I might've had an ounce of sympathy for him if he'd been stupid enough to let himself fall in love with someone else. But this? This was just Billy getting his jollies.

He opened his mouth to say who knows what, and I almost snorted. Dude probably hadn't done a push up or bench pressed a pound since high school. He definitely didn't deserve a girl like Clem.

Clem put up a hand to stop him. "Don't. There is literally nothing you can say to me right now that won't make it worse, so shut up, Billy." She looked over at me, her eyes blazing. "Can I have your phone? I left mine outside."

I didn't know what she was going to do with it, but I let the face recognition open the lock screen and handed it to her. She swiped to my camera. Oh crap.

"Stand up." She ordered the girl.

"Don't do it," Billy commanded, still cowering next to the bed.

"Get. Up!" Clem screamed, teetering on the verge of crazy.

"Settle," I said with a gentle warning. I needed to diffuse this before it got out of control.

"Oh, I'm plenty settled." But her shaking hands betrayed her and I could tell she was verging on hysterical. "What's your name, honey?"

"L-Lyla." The girl could hardly get it out.

"Lyla?" Clem let out a baleful laugh that was downright terrifying. "Drop the blanket!"

Lyla jumped out of the bed, tangled in the quilt, practically tripping onto the floor.

"My granny Eudora crocheted that blanket for my momma when she graduated high school and now I'm going to have to burn it," Clem said through gritted teeth. "Drop it, Lyla!" she screamed. This chick must be out of her mind. Didn't she know Clem was two seconds away from tearing her limb from limb?

As if someone finally plugged her brain in, Lyla threw the blanket like it was on fire.

As soon as it hit the floor, Clem snapped a picture of the two of them standing there naked together. Then she took two more, just in case. Apparently, that was enough. 'Cause she turned and handed my phone back. "Can you send those to me?" Then she bolted back down the stairs.

"What're you going to do with those pictures, Lemon?" Billy called out.

I shot him a warning glare. "I think you should count yourself lucky she left you with all your body parts."

"Lem, come back!" Billy yelled. "I messed up, babe! Let's talk about this?" He searched frantically for his clothes.

I bounded down the stairs to find Clem. When I got to the first floor, she was frantically rummaging through the drawers of an old desk. She'd yank one drawer open, rifle through it, slam it shut, and move on to the next. Black trails of mascara tracked all over her cheeks. With each drawer that turned up blank, her breathing got heavier and faster, her eyes more desperate. Whatever she needed, I had to get it for her, and fast —before she hyperventilated and passed out.

I placed a hand over hers. "What're you looking for?"

Her chest heaved a few times, and she gasped for air, her

eyes wild. She pulled her hand from mine and went through another drawer. She wiped her nose on her sleeve and tried another drawer. I'd never seen anything like this in my entire life. This depth of pain. It was worse than Sophie dying. Okay, not worse. Different. But heart-wrenching.

Sophie told me once that she'd tried desperately to talk Clem out of marrying Billy. Clem wouldn't listen. She was so sure that Billy was only going to get better with age. Up until the day she died, Sophie had nothing positive to say about him. Mom always chalked it up to jealousy. Thought that Clem marrying Billy gave Sophie less time with her. But maybe Mom was wrong. I mean, I'd never liked that viper, but I'd always thought it was because I was in love with his wife. Maybe Sophie could see this coming all along.

Clem's breaths were shallow and uneven now. She swayed.

I grabbed her by the shoulders. "Breathe. You have to breathe. Just a couple of breaths. *Please.*"

She shook her head, looking down at the ground. But she inhaled and exhaled deeply a few times.

I held her hands in mine and ducked so we were at eye level. "What do you need from me?" I asked in the most soothing voice I could muster.

She finally breathed out, "A pocket knife."

I was so relieved she said something coherent that I didn't even think. Just said, "Okay." I jammed my hand into my pants pocket, grateful I'd started the habit back when I was ten. Since the day my dad's hot-headed horse Trooper bucked me off. My foot had gotten tangled in her lead and she'd dragged me halfway home before I got loose. I slid it out of my pocket.

Something happened when I placed that knife in her hand. The tears stopped and her expression turned dangerous. What was she planning to do with it?

"Thank you." She flicked it open easily and studied the

blade for a second. "That'll do." *For what?* I wanted to shake her.

I was afraid she was going back up the stairs to shiv Billy and Last-call Lyla in the gut. But she turned and went the opposite direction back out into the sunshine. I almost exhaled until she walked right up to Billy's brand new truck, and that one Carrie Underwood song rang through my mind.

She wouldn't.

But her furious eyes said, oh yes, she would.

"Don't do something you'll regret," I warned. "No sense in going to jail for that prick."

"Oh, I'm not going to regret a thing." Then she bent over and stabbed the blade as hard as she could into his front left tire. The whistle the air made coming out was impressive. It reminded me of the bottle rockets we shot off every summer by the lake.

"Ho-ly..." I trailed off and blew out a bomb-whistle. This girl was unreal. "My dad always said you and Sophie would charge hell with a bucket of ice water."

"I'll take that as a compliment."

I might've tried to take the knife from her, to save her from herself, if I was confident she wouldn't come after me. I wasn't. At all. The craziness permeating from her was something that I'd never seen before and, quite frankly, I hoped I never saw again. Was it impressive? Absolutely. Hardcore? Undoubtedly. But this wasn't Clem, and the amount of hurt she must be going through to pull something like this out of her hat was unprecedented.

Once that tire was completely flat, she yanked the knife out, walked to the next tire, and shanked that one too.

Billy shot out the door in his tighty-whities and the white button-down shirt he'd worn to the funeral. His eyes flicked to me and then ricocheted, looking for Clem but she was on the other side of the truck, kneeling. "Baby, come on, let's talk about it. I messed up, okay?" His calling her baby made my fists curl and my chest tighten.

He saw the flat tires and ran around the front bumper. I headed around the back to protect Clem if she needed it.

"Are you crazy?" he screamed.

Hate burned out of her eyes. "What did you say?"

He backpedaled. "I'm just kidding. You know I didn't mean that."

"Oh, no. I am crazy." She sliced a five-inch gash into the first dually tire on that side. "But you don't get to call me that." She wiggled the knife free, ready for the next one.

"Lem!" He yelled and ran toward her.

I stepped in front of him. He dodged and tried a shake and bake to get around me. I stepped out and cut him off. He slipped, scraping his knees on the gravel. A string of curse words came out of his mouth that would've put a sailor to shame. He got up, gripping his thinning blond hair, gravel sticking out of his knees, and blood dripping down his shins.

Once that tire was completely flat, she walked to the last tire and sliced a five-inch gash into that one as well.

"I hate this truck," she said to me while she waited for it to deflate. "He ordered it three months in advance, custom made, and never told me. Just pulled into the yard one day, saddling us with eighty thousand dollars in debt, and never once asked what I thought about it. There went the home renovations."

I guess now that all the tires were ruined, Billy didn't see the need to placate Clem. That was a mistake.

"Do you have any idea how much new tires will cost us?" he screamed again.

She waved the knife at him. "*You*, buddy. How much new tires will cost *you*."

"You always did have a temper to match your hair. You are freaking crazy!" If I hadn't known he was stupid before, I knew it then.

She shoved the knife right in his face. "Don't you ever say that to me again!"

If she killed him, would I be considered an accomplice?

"Clem," I said in a warning tone, trying to get her to back down. At least a little.

"Don't worry, Silas," she said, never looking away from Billy. "I have never felt more clarity in my life." She waved the knife haphazardly until she had him backed up against the barn. Billy shrank down, sweat beading along his receding hairline.

"You're the one who's lost their mind," she hissed. "Throwing away a perfectly good wife on that trash." The knife was close enough to shave scruff, and I wondered if Billy's life was flashing before his eyes. I sure hoped so. "And don't even think of trying to press charges. I have pictures, remember? I will ruin you if you so much as say a word to anyone. Yours will be the deadest doctor's office in five counties."

Even backed up to the wall, with that knife practically in his sinuses, Billy didn't know when to shut up. His mouth started moving, but in an unprecedented turn of events, no words came out. He literally couldn't speak.

Clem's eyebrows kissed her hairline. "This divorce is going to be quick and uncontested. Got it?"

His only response was a whimper and a nod. Just then his co-adulterer came out the door fully clothed in baggy jeans with holes in the knees, and an oversized faded AC/DC T-shirt that looked like her grandmother had bought it at the band's first concert and hadn't washed it since.

"Now take your high school hussy and get out of here."

"I graduated last May," she had the nerve to say. This girl was even stupider than Billy.

Billy yanked her toward her pathetic car, his knees knocking as he got inside.

"I forgot my—" she protested. He reached over her and slammed the door shut. Then he punched the gas so hard he spun out onto the gravel driveway.

"Idiot," I muttered. It was the understatement of the century.

We stood there watching as he over-corrected, went into the ditch, and came back out again. Finally, those bald tires found some grip, and they sped down the driveway. Once they'd disappeared over the hill, I felt myself exhale like those slashed tires. Clem stood there, stone still, and I knew it would happen now. It was too much. The funeral and now this, both in the same day. It was more than any human could take.

But I should've known Clem was not any ordinary human. She was a freaking goddess. Because she never fell apart. At least not in front of me. She kept standing there, cemented in her spot, long after he was gone. Her hair was finally free from the bun, blowing out, fiery and unshackled in the breeze.

"Clem?" I stepped toward her, ready, and yet completely unprepared for whatever happened next.

That seemed to snap her out of it. She looked at me. I looked at her. Tear-stained, worn-down, and broken. And still the most beautiful girl I'd ever known.

"Clem. I'm so sorry."

"Don't be." She flipped the knife closed and handed it back to me. "Grab the rope. I still have a cow out."

three

CLEMENTINE

I spent the next few days crying with my head in Momma's lap. She said that was just fine and I could take all the time I needed. But by the evening before the reading of Sophie's will, even I was sick of my crying. If Sophie were here, she'd tell me to stop crying over Billy. He didn't deserve any more of my tears. She'd probably tell me Lyla had done me a favor too. But I wasn't there yet.

I was a quarter mile past the lawyer's office when I realized I'd missed my turn. I pulled the steering wheel hard to the left and swung a U-turn in the middle of the road. My brain couldn't hold my focus for more than ten seconds at a time lately. My phone dinged with another text from Billy. This had to be at least the fiftieth that day alone.

> Billy: C'mon, boo-thang. Just let me come over and we can talk.

I clenched my teeth. I hated when he called me that. So trashy. And he knew that. As always, Billy didn't give a crap about my feelings.

When I finally parked, I was late. I hated being late. It was so rude. But I took a second to respond to Billy.

> Me: No. Stop texting me.

I pressed send. And then sent him a copy of the naked picture of him and Lyla. For the twentieth time.

I left my phone in the truck and clicked the lock button. As I hurried up the sidewalk, I smoothed my jeans down my thighs. I'd never been to a will reading before. Was it even okay to wear jeans? I'd made sure to wear a button-down, hunter green, satin blouse and brown leather boots to dress things up a bit. And, of course, a pair of pearl stud earrings. I swiped on a quick layer of my favorite berry-colored lip gloss and headed inside.

As I came through the door, the secretary nodded me down the hallway. "First door on your right."

I was the last one to arrive. Everyone turned when I entered the room. My face flamed at my tardiness, though no one seemed the least bit ruffled. Anna sat closest to the door and reached out for my hand, pulling me into the seat next to her.

Immediately, she laid her head on my shoulder and snuggled against me. "I've missed you," she whispered, but the room was so quiet, no doubt everyone heard it. The mood was almost reverent, like in church.

"I missed you too." I smiled. I'd have to ask Jenny if Anna could have a sleepover at my house soon. It was so quiet without Billy there. It would probably be good for both of us.

The entire Dupree family was there—Jenny and Bo, Holden, Ford, Ashton, and, of course, Silas. I'd thought the brothers might've headed back to their various lives by now. Of all the five Dupree children, Sophie had been the only one to stick around Seddledowne once high school was over.

There weren't enough chairs, so Holden and Silas stood against the wall. They'd left the open seat for me, which made my heart a little gushy. Per usual, I could feel Silas's gaze on me. I hadn't seen him since the slashing of the tires and getting the cow back in. I'd had plenty of time in the last week to think about my reaction to Billy and Lyla. I didn't feel embarrassed that I'd lost my mind, just...a touch insecure. I'd kind of acted like a crazy person. I knew that. But even Momma high-fived me when I told her what I'd done. And if my momma—a proper southern lady—said my behave-yuh was justified? Well, that was good enough for me.

Did I regret doing it? No. Billy Eugene Adams deserved everything he'd gotten and then some. But it niggled at me that Silas might think less of me for it. I searched his face, hoping to find out. He had zero problems making eye contact, but as always, his expression gave nothing away.

Sophie'd been so expressive, full of life, and flat-out fun. Despite being her twin, Silas was her opposite in almost every way. Steady, quiet, and hard to rile, ruffle, or roughhouse with. At least with me. Had no problem being that way with his brothers or Anna. Something about being an uncle brought out the best in him. And Sophie had always said he was different when he was only with family. But whenever I was within ten feet of him, he was stiff and unreadable. It hadn't always been that way. But I couldn't help but feel like he'd purposely put up a wall to keep me out.

I chewed my lip and glanced away.

The door flew open and Arlo Llewellyn, the best and only lawyer in town, breezed into the room. He gave Bo a double-fisted shake.

Bo squeezed back. "Good to see you, Llew."

"Well, aren't you as pretty as a peach," he said to Jenny.

"Thank you, Llew. Please give Maggie my love."

"Of course." Mr. Llewellyn leaned against his desk, folded his hands in his lap, and grinned. "You're all probably wondering why we're here."

"Not really," Holden said. "This is a will reading, isn't it?"

"Holden." Jenny hissed and shook her head. Holden held his hands up like, am I wrong?

Anna snickered next to me, which made me snicker. Holden was the male version of Sophie. Blond and brazen. I gave him a beaming grin. He grinned back. Silas readjusted his position against the wall.

Mr. Llewellyn was not ruffled by Holden's honest response. "True. True. But you have to be wondering what Sophie would leave each of you."

"Darn right," Ashton piped in. "We all know that girl didn't have any money." She really didn't. She'd put everything she had into making a life for herself and Anna, but that was hard to do when you lived off of a teacher's aide salary.

Jenny tsked at him.

"Settle down," Bo warned.

"You're right," Mr. Llewellyn nodded. "She didn't have much. And what she did have has been put in a trust for Annaleise." He picked a manila folder up off the table and opened it, rifling through some papers. "Some of you might be disappointed that she didn't leave you anything."

Ford shook his head, always the grumpy one. The only time Ford smiled was when a guitar was in his hands. "Are you for real? I stayed an extra week for this and she didn't leave me anything?"

I shook with silent laughter. This family was the best.

Mr. Llewellyn held his hands up. "But she did specifically ask that you all be here."

Ford snorted in disgust.

Mr. Llewellyn picked up a baby-blue envelope, and I

smiled. Baby blue was Sophie's favorite color. She'd had those envelopes sitting around for years. Multiple times, I'd threatened to organize her junk drawer and toss them out, but she was confident she'd use them someday. Someday had finally come. Mr. Llewelyn sliced the envelope with a letter opener and unfolded a matching piece of stationery.

"She requested that I read this to you all today." He adjusted his glasses, cleared his throat, and began.

> *Dear family and Lemon,*
> *Lemon had better be there. If she's not, stop right now and go get her. This is not to be read without her present. Got it?*

We all chuckled.

"Bossy as ever," Ashton said with a shake of his head but a proud smile on his face.

Mr. Llewellyn started up again.

> *Now. If everyone is present, we can begin. I know what y'all are thinking: why is Sophie having a will reading when we all know she's broke.*

Ford guffawed.

> *But that's on Holden. If he wasn't so stingy he would've given some money to his dying sister and then I might have something to give y'all. So don't blame me. It's Holden's fault. Just like always.*

Holden shook his head, and Silas actually chuckled.

Holden was some kind of fancy lawyer up in DC. I wasn't sure exactly what he did, just that he made good money doing it. I also knew he'd paid some of Sophie's medical bills this last year. He and Sophie bickered like an old married couple. But I think he cried the hardest when she passed.

Momma and Daddy, I want to start by saying that I love you. I hope you know that.

Jenny was already crying, searching for a tissue in her purse. Mr. Llewellyn handed her one off his desk.

He peered at us over his glasses. "This next part is the meat of why we're here, so I ask that you let me read all the way through before you interject or ask any questions." He gave us a second, and when no one spoke, he continued.

Please don't be hurt by what I'm about to do— but I have to think of Annaleise above anyone or anything else.

My eyes widened. What did that mean? I saw Jenny and Bo exchange a confused look. Anna sat up straight, her hands twisting around each other.

And Anna, you may not see the wisdom in this right now, but you will. As for Holdie, Ashbucket, and Fo-shizzle—

Everyone laughed at that but Mr. Llewellyn pressed on.

This is not a slight to you three, but a mom

has to trust her gut. And my gut says y'all are definitely not it.

Holden and Ashton looked at each other, kind of hurt, kind of mystified. Ford just blew his bangs out of his eyes, annoyed.

Ready now? Here we go. Never mind. One more thing first.

There was a collective exasperated exhale.

To Annaleise, I bequeath Stella.

That was her white Honda CRV. She'd been so proud when she'd finally paid it off. It would be a good car for Anna when she got her learner's permit in a couple of years. We'd spent hours in there—the three of us—driving to the city to shop or go to the movies.

Don't wreck it.

Anna laughed but said nothing, obedient to Mr. Llewellyn's wishes that we stay silent.

And it does have four-wheel drive, but that is not—I repeat NOT—to be used for fun. Only for snow. Don't you dare take my car muddin'. Gramps will help you take care of it, remind you to get the oil changed, and teach you to change a tire. Won't you, Daddy?

He nodded and in a hushed, rough voice said, "Of course."

Mr. Llewellyn flipped the paper over.

"Sick," Anna barely whispered, and we shared a smile.

And if any of you have problems with it, you can kiss my deceased behind.

"Good grief." Ashton shook his head, laughing. My sentiments exactly.

The brothers all nodded their agreement, and it made my heart swell. Land got into your blood and there had been plenty of family feuds in Seddledowne over who was getting the farm some day. Their immediate acceptance of Anna as a landholder spoke volumes of their love for their niece.

Now that that's taken care of, we can move on to the other matter. The most important one.

Mr. Llewellyn took a deep breath as if he were gearing up for something, and I found myself doing the same. What was all of this about?

Please make no mistake, I was completely lucid when this was written. Mr. Llewellyn will attest to that. He watched me pen the whole thing myself. If you don't believe me, he has an identical typed-out copy of this letter which is dated, signed, and notarized.

Wow. This must be really serious.

Alright. Are you ready? Drumroll, please.

Ford made a *brrrrrrrr* sound, and Holden rapped his fists in the air.

I almost squeezed my eyes shut like you do right before the big drop on a roller coaster—I was so excited and afraid for whatever came next. But nothing could have prepared me for the next line of her letter.

Silas Dean Dupree and Clementine "Lemon" Laura Adams, to you, I leave Annaleise Nicole Dupree.

I don't know if anyone else gasped, but I did. I'd always planned to be as active in Anna's life as the Duprees would allow, but I hadn't expected this. Sophie never mentioned a word. I shook my head. What did this mean? Sophie left me Anna? Anna wasn't a *thing*. She was a person. Sophie couldn't just give her to me like a piece of jewelry. And how was I supposed to share her with Silas? He lived on the other side of the country. I tried to make eye contact, to see what he was thinking, but he was staring at the floor, stone still, a tiny pucker between his brows.

Jenny couldn't hold it in. "She had to be out of her ever-lovin' mind."

Mr. Llewellyn held up his hand. "Let her finish."

I know this isn't ideal, and it isn't going to be possible for you to do it long term. But for the next three months, I am requesting that the three of you reside together—Silas, Lemon, and Anna. To be a family. And Lem, I don't give a crap what Billy thinks. He can get over himself for three months. No outsiders allowed! Ninety consecutive nights of sleeping under the same roof.

My cheeks burned. Sophie couldn't have known Billy would already be gone. I made sure to keep my eyes on Arlo and not see if anyone had noticed me blushing. Over the past week, I had to have been a hot topic in the Dupree household.

I can't even imagine what Anna must be going through right now with me dead in the ground.

I winced. Sophie never did mince words, but geez.

But I know one thing—she needs all the love she can get, and she needs to be surrounded by it. Completely. At the end of three months, the three of you can decide how to proceed. But I'm asking that you take this seriously and do this one last thing for me. Please. Love my girl. All to pieces.

"All to pieces" was a Dupree thing. A ranch thing. Bo and Jenny had said it a lot when their kids were younger. We love you. All to pieces. Do the job and do it right. All to pieces.

It was the *please* that got me, and I didn't need to think about it for another second. It might be crazy and uncomfortable to live with detached, apathetic Silas, but if this was what Sophie wanted, then I would do it. Three months was nothing in the grand scheme of things.

Mr. Llewellyn paused to open a water bottle on the table

and take a gulp. "We're almost done." He swigged and replaced the cap.

> *Anna, your natural inclination might be to stay at Granny and Gramp's house, but let's be honest—you need young parents. People with enough energy to keep up with all the adventures you're going to have. College, world travel, marriage—parents who can love on your babies. And Uncle Si and Aunt Lemon will be there for every minute of it. They love you SO much.*
>
> *And so do I. All of you.*
>
> *Oh, and Ford, sorry I made you stick around for this. You'll get over it.*

Ashton snorted into his fist. Ford glared at him.

> *Mom and Dad needed you nearby this week. So thank you for staying.*

Ford caved at that. The corners of his mouth turned up almost happily, and his expression softened.

> *All my love,*
> *Forever,*
> *Sophie*

We all sat there for a few seconds, silent. I squirmed in my seat, a thousand thoughts in my head.

Finally, Jenny broke the silence. "I could've done that."

She blew her nose into the tissue.

Bo rubbed her back. "I know you could. She must have her reasons."

Mr. Llewellyn held up the letter. "That's it. That's all she wanted." Jenny reached for the letter. He handed it to her, and she started skimming. "Just to be clear. The ninety days begin today. It's May seventh. So, it will last until August seventh."

Mr. Llewellyn held his hands out. "I know you all have questions, and I've blocked out the rest of my schedule today to stay and answer them. But there's one more piece of unfinished business." He reopened the manila folder and pulled out two more envelopes identical to the first. "These are to be read three months from now only when the living period has been completed. She was very strict about that."

He handed the first to me. My name was swirled in Sophie's fat, perfect cursive:

She dotted the I with a heart just like she always did. Seeing my name in her handwriting made my throat close up, and I blinked back tears. He walked over to Silas and gave him the other envelope. Silas barely gave it a glance before his hand fell to his side. His cheeks were flushed and I couldn't tell if he was embarrassed, angry, or both.

"Can we talk now?" Holden asked.

"Please." Mr. Llewellyn nodded, opening the floor.

Holden talked at the ceiling. "Good grief, Sophie. Shoulda known you'd go out with flair."

Ashton went next. "Do they have to do it? What if one of

them just, I dunno, doesn't want to? I mean, how can Sophie dictate their lives for the next three months?"

"I'm in," I blurted. They could argue and complain and chalk it up to Sophie's hardheadedness, her need to boss everyone around—but for me, if it was what Sophie wanted, I could at least do this one last thing for my best friend.

"Me too," said Anna with a resolute nod. "It'll be fun." She turned to the final part of the equation, along with everyone else. "Please, Uncle Si?"

Silas pounded his fist against his temple. A vein bulged in his neck and he shook his head, looking livid. "Damn it, Sophie." His eyes slid sideways to me for a split second and then he strode out of the room, the envelope slapping against his thigh.

My cheeks turned hot, and I hoped no one noticed. He probably had a hundred reasons this inconvenienced him, a plethora of things to do in the next few months before he became assistant principal. But, and I knew I shouldn't take it that way, it felt kind of personal. Like he didn't want to do this...with me.

Ford bomb whistled. "Christy is gonna be ticked."

"Do you think she'll break up with him?" Ashton asked, the two of them gossiping like middle school girls. I guess I could stop calling her Barbie. Silas's girlfriend had an actual name. And I was with Ashton. She was going to be really upset. If she couldn't handle me even glancing at him, no way would she roll over at us living together for three months.

"Nah," Holden chimed in. "Hmm." He raised both brows. "But maybe. Seemed like there might be a Karen hidden underneath all that makeup and bleached hair. Like if you tried to pet her, she might take your pinky off." He made claws with his fingers and hissed like a cat being squeezed to death by a fur-obsessed toddler.

I covered my mouth to hide my laughter. Not a single class

I taught at the studio made my abs as sore as the Dupree brothers.

"This will be a test for them then, won't it," Bo said, finally standing and stretching.

He offered Jenny a hand, and she stood too.

Jenny seemed frazzled and heartbroken. I swear, she'd aged ten years in the last month. "But why? I don't understand. It doesn't make any sense."

Holden walked over and hugged her to him. "It's not a slight against you, Mom. Nobody could ask for a better granny." He opened his arm for Bo to join.

Anna jumped up and joined in, wrapping her arms around the three of them. "I'll come see you every day. Firefly Fields is only five miles away. Right, Lemon?" She craned her head to look at me. By then, Ashton and Ford were in on the hug.

I was afraid to speak. What if Bo and Jenny hated me after this? I wouldn't blame them one bit. My entire life, Jenny had put a knot in my stomach. She was perpetually on edge, making sure everyone and everything was perfectly in place. The last year had almost unraveled her, amplifying her need to be in control. But I forced myself to answer. "Of course. Absolutely." I desperately wanted in on that hug.

As if Bo could read my mind, he looked over the top of Anna's head and stretched his arm out to me. "Come here, you darling girl." That's all the permission I needed. In three strides, with my arms open wide, I pushed all my love into that embrace.

"It's gonna be all right," Bo said as the hug finally ended. "It'll all work out the way it's supposed to."

Ashton raised an eyebrow. "Of course it will, but can we all agree that Sophie was nuts?"

Everyone laughed.

Then Jenny asked the question I'd been thinking. "What if Silas doesn't agree?"

Mr. Llewellyn shook his head, glanced at Anna, and reluctantly replied, "You'll have to go before a judge, and they'll decide who Anna is going to live with. It will probably be you and Bo. But still, it will take some time and money to get it worked through. It would be much better if Silas did as Sophie asked." He shook his head. "I warned Sophie that it was a possibility that at least one party might be unwilling and she might want to consider a back up plan." He shook his head. "But she was determined."

"Wouldn't be Sophie if she wasn't," Holden said and then sighed. "I'll go talk to Silas."

four

SILAS

I sat on the hillside overlooking the high school baseball fields. The Seddledowne Stallions baseball team was in the middle of an after-school practice. The field was far enough away that no coach was going to think I was a creeper and not close enough that anyone would talk to me. I needed to be alone. Needed time to figure out what I was going to do.

The envelope Mr. Llewellyn gave me was already worn at the corners I'd handled it so much in the last fifteen minutes.

Sophie had even put a stupid heart for the dot over the I.

I slapped it against my palm, my jaw clenched. She never could leave me alone. Even dead, she was hounding me to do what *she* wanted. I gripped the envelope in both my hands, debating if I should just open it right now. Find out what her endgame was. Derail whatever plans she'd made. What was she going to do about it? Haunt me? Seemed like she already was. Besides, I knew what this was about.

Someone dropped down beside me and I looked over to see Holden staring at me with that dumb expression he wore when he thought I'd made a fool of myself.

"How did you find me?" I grumbled.

"Dude. Find My Friends. We've got the whole family on there. We can see each other at all times," he said, like I was an idiot.

I guessed I was. I hadn't used that app in years. Kinda forgot it was even a thing. It always felt like stalking to me.

"You didn't say goodbye to Ford and Ash."

I grunted. I'd left in such a huff I'd forgotten they were leaving straight from the lawyer's office to get back to college. Ford, the baby of the family, was catching a flight back to NYU, where he'd be preparing for finals, and Ashton was driving down to Virginia Tech, where he was enrolled in a master's program for English lit.

"I'll text them later." I bent the envelope in half and twisted it, frustrated at myself and at Sophie. And honestly, at Clem. Which was completely irrational. But kind of not. I'd spent way too much effort getting her out of my head and my heart, and now we were supposed to live together? Sleep under the same roof?

"I think I better keep that for you." He took the envelope from me. "Shy Si, huh?"

My childhood nickname. I hated when they called me that. I wasn't shy. Just choosy about who and when I talked to people. Massive difference.

I exhaled through my nose and hissed, "I know what she's doing."

"Who?"

I undid the knot on my tie, yanked it through the shirt collar, and tossed it in the grass. "Sophie."

"What's she doing?"

"She's playing matchmaker. Like she thinks she knows better than I do who I should end up with. Miss Freaking Know-It-All." I felt bad saying that about her. Especially since she was gone. I'd loved Sophie with a fierceness. Would've fought the entire world for her, though I'd had to do it long distance for the last decade. But right now it felt like she was going out of her departed way to make me miserable. And I couldn't even argue with her about it. My chest tightened, and I pinched the bridge of my nose.

Holden rubbed his stubbled chin. "Or." He held up a finger. "And this is just a thought—she might really want this for Anna. Three months of the three of you spending as much time together as you can? Seems to me she was legitimately worried about that girl. Think about it, man. If we'd lost Mom at her age, it would've killed us. We'd have all turned out like crap."

I threw my hands out. "And what happens at the end of three months? What do we do with Anna then? Fly her back and forth across the country to share custody? It's a terrible plan. And what about my job in Laramie? I'm supposed to be there all summer prepping my teachers, getting the classrooms ready. I have to administer a science exam to my sixth graders on Monday. And there's no way Christy is going to let me do this—"

Holden snorted. "Grow a pair, man. Get a sub." He may as well have clocked me in the jaw. He shook his head, disgusted. "Your sister—your *twin*—just passed away. She's asked you to do this for her. She's worried about her *orphaned* daughter. And if your girl can't let you do that—if she's so selfish that she doesn't get that you loved Sophie—then do you really want to be with her?"

When he put it like that...

I dropped my head into my hands, breathing it out, stalling. "I can't." I finally admitted.

"You can't, what?"

I pounded my forehead against my palms, and the words escaped. "I can't live in that house with *her* for three months." It killed me to say it out loud. I may as well have wuss written on my forehead in that red lipstick Clementine always had on her ridiculously perfect lips.

"And there it is," Holden said, wearing his usual smug smile. If it had been anyone else, I might've punched them in the gut. But Holden knew me. He was my best friend. The only person I really trusted with this stuff. Sophie would've been if Clem hadn't been in the middle of every conversation we ever had—even when we didn't bring her up at all. Clem was the elephant in the room. Always. And I could never open up to Sophie because of it. I hadn't brought Clem up to her in years. Wouldn't engage in conversations about her. Didn't matter. Sophie knew exactly how I felt, anyway. Called it twin-tuition.

I ripped a patch of grass from the ground and rolled a blade between my fingers. "I thought I was over it, you know? That time would kill it or something..."

"But it hasn't?"

I shook my head. "It's like the minute I see her, I'm twelve or fifteen or twenty all over again." I was so freaking weak.

He turned to face me. "This is your chance, man. Take it. She and Billy aren't a thing anymore. Finally. Sophie couldn't have orchestrated this better if she were God himself."

Oh, the irony of that statement. "Actually, Sophie couldn't have made a bigger mess if she tried." His head leaned, and I finally told the first Dupree, "Christy and I are engaged."

He eyed me like I'd suddenly grown an extra eye in the

middle of my forehead. "Seriously? You've been dating her for what? Five months?"

Saying it out loud sounded as stupid as Holden made it sound. I nodded, sheepishly. "I don't even know. One minute we were decompressing on my back deck with a couple of beers, and the next thing I know, she'd talked me into marrying her."

"She *talked* you into marrying her? Super romantic, bro." His eyebrows puckered. "Is that even what you want?"

I rubbed my forehead. "I want a family. I know that. I'm tired of dating. And I'm not getting any younger."

It seemed like he was in shock, sick for me. "This is the most depressing engagement announcement I've ever heard. You're tired of dating? That's nothing to base a lifelong commitment on."

He wasn't wrong. I'd kind of been thinking the same thing. But I didn't want to break up with Christy, either. And I'd given up the hope of ever feeling for another woman what I felt for Clementine. This was as good as it got for me. So why not settle down?

He guffawed. "Do you even love her?"

I sighed. "Yes?"

"Mmhmm. You've convinced me."

I threw my hands up. "It doesn't matter right now. There's no date picked out. There's not a ring yet. I can't think about that right now with everything with Sophie."

"And you told Christy that?"

"Yeah. I did. She wanted to announce it after the funeral and I shut that down. It was not the time."

"I'd say." Holden looked horrified that I was even entertaining the thought of marrying Christy. But I didn't care what he thought. Girls were easier for him. Fun even. Dating was the most exhausting game I'd ever played. The sooner I was out, the better.

I gazed at the baseball team. "They suck. You should go show 'em how it's done."

"Yeah, I should." His gaze turned wistful.

As much as I was a cowboy in my heart, Holden was an athlete. In high school, he'd been a triple threat: football, basketball, and baseball. A small private college had offered him a spot on their baseball team, but Holden laid down the glove to attend the pre-law program at the University of Virginia. Probably hadn't touched any kind of ball in years. But he made up for it with all the obstacle races he ran. Crazy man. He'd tried to talk me into doing a couple of them. No thanks.

I nudged him. "Can you believe you gave all that up just to become a big-wig shyster?"

He pursed his lips. "I'm not a shyster, Fartbox. I have ethics."

Nothing made Holden madder quicker than teasing him about being a stereotypical shady attorney. It was my favorite pastime.

We watched the pitcher throw a ball that landed two feet in front of home plate. The coach threw his hat into the dirt and stormed off. We both chuckled.

I studied the campus. Everything seemed neglected. "This whole place is a dump. Has the state stopped giving them money or something?" Had they failed accreditation? The entire building needed repainting. The athletics fields looked like they hadn't been fertilized since I graduated; the grass was a dead yellow. And the tennis court had cracks with two-foot-tall weeds growing out of them.

"You gotta tell Lemon how you feel," Holden said at the very moment I'd almost gotten Clem out of my mind—when my gut had settled for the first time in hours. "How you've always felt."

I huffed. "I almost did that once. Remember?" Probably

the second worst day of my life. Only topped by Clem's wedding day. It was the first varsity football game of our senior year. Clem and her boyfriend had broken up a few weeks before. Sophie had been building me up, saying how this was my chance to tell Clementine how I felt. She'd painted an idyllic picture of me and Clem going to prom together. Sharing all of our senior lasts. All I had to do was get up the guts to tell her how I felt. There was no way I could do it using my actual mouth, so I'd written it down. I'd spent hours on that letter. Probably crumpled fifty drafts. When it was finished, I folded it obsessively and stuffed it in my back pocket. Had it all worked out in my mind. After the game, I was going to walk up to Clem in her cute little cheerleading skirt, hand her the note, and walk away. It was in God's hands after that.

But there was a guy, a sophomore at the local community college—Billy Adams—who'd come home to watch his little brother, our starting quarterback, play. Johnny Adams threw three touchdowns that game. I still remember the scoreboard, forever etched in my memory. Seddledowne Stallions 36—Highland Hawks 7. And there, standing under the sign, was Billy asking out *my* girl.

The letter never left the back pocket of my Wranglers.

I spent the rest of senior year avoiding Clementine in every possible way. When the rodeo scholarship from The University of Wyoming came a month later, I couldn't sign fast enough.

I'd made the right decision then, and I was making the right decision now. I wasn't throwing Christy away on a minuscule chance that Clementine might want me. Heck, for all I knew, Clem would forgive Billy next week, and they'd be back together.

"Just do it, man. Tell her," Holden said.

"No." My jaw set. "I'm engaged to Christy."

"If you call that an engagement."

"Christy already told her family."

"Fine. But engaged is not married."

"Good enough." I shook my head, annoyed. "Maybe you're okay going around breaking people's hearts, but that's not how I roll. What we have might not be a fairytale kind of passion, but it's built on friendship and trust." I knew what it felt like to hurt. I wouldn't be that pain for someone else. Holden was a player. Jumped from one girl to the next before I could memorize their names.

He tugged on his collar. "I don't go around breaking hearts. It's called playing the field. I'm not settling until I know I'm with the right person. And you shouldn't either." His jaw was rigid. "Who lets themselves get *talked* into marriage? You should know without a doubt that you want to spend your life with her. Have babies with her. Grow old with her. You want to be lying in bed next to Christy in twenty years still thinking about Lemon?"

It was my worst nightmare. But I was already living it.

"I'm figuring it out, all right." I almost shouted. "But shoving me up in a house with Clem isn't going to help."

He scoffed. "Dude. It's exactly what you need to bring you to your senses."

I tugged at my hair. "What are you talking about?"

"You are delusional if you think you can keep ignoring this. You think you can feel this strongly about one woman and turn around and marry another and it won't come back to bite you in the butt? You can't ignore the splinter and think it's never going to fester." It was something Sophie used to say.

I shrugged. "Watch me." I'd been doing it for ten years. What was another fifty? Or sixty? Besides, I had a plan. Marry Christy, never come back to Seddledowne, and make Clem a distant memory—or at least shove my feelings to the very edges of my heart. It was a solid plan, and I was going to make it work. Just like I had with the rodeo scholarship, teaching, and now the assistant principal job.

Holden's lip curled. "You want to know what I think?"

"Not really."

"I don't care." His entire forehead wrinkled. "I think you're so in love with her that you can't handle it if she turns you down. It would *shatter* you. So you'd rather never know. You'd rather live a safe, passionless life with someone who will never reject you."

It felt like he'd sucker-punched me. Rage filled my chest, but I fought against it. If he came home with a black eye, Mom would never forgive me. I forced myself to take a couple of deep breaths. It felt like I'd spent my entire life either trying to get over Clem or putting on an award-winning performance so no one would know how deep this ran.

But with one sentence, Holden had metaphorically pantsed me.

I shot to my feet, about to leave. But Holden already thought I was a pansy. So I paced instead. I was so angry with myself. Why had I let this girl dominate my life? Why couldn't I let her go? She was just a woman. There were millions of beautiful women out there. Heck, I was engaged to one of them.

As soon as I thought it, I felt my insides turn to jelly. She wasn't just a woman. She was Clementine. Gorgeous, fiery, but somehow still sweet, hilarious, sexy like no other... Clementine. And there was no other woman in the world who made me feel what she did. Christy made me feel things. But they were different. Calmer and restrained. Whenever I was in the same room with Clementine, it felt like I was careening out of control—like at any second I might do or say something to give myself away and I was powerless to stop it.

I hated her for it.

And yet, I loved her desperately.

Truth was, Holden was right. With every fantasy I'd conjured up of a future with Clem—my arms around her waist, my lips on hers, whispering I love you before we hung up the phone every night—came the very real possibility of rejection. When I was a teenager, I'd let myself have a fake relationship with her in my mind, but in real life, I was hog-tied. Especially after Billy entered the picture. When she married that imbecile at the age of twenty, it had destroyed me. Cried so hard I puked.

But once I'd picked myself back up, I'd also been relieved.

I could finally get over this infatuation and get on with my life.

I thought I had my crap together when I came home that first Christmas. But there she sat at our kitchen table with Billy hanging all over her, big old diamond on her finger. And that old familiar beast raged in me just as fierce as always. It had taken every speck of willpower I could muster not to punch him right in his stupid, cocky face, drag her away, and tell her everything in my heart. That was the day I realized this love wasn't going anywhere. It would be inside me until the day I died. The best I could do was avoid it.

So I stayed away as much as I could after that. If I could talk Mom and Dad into coming to see me instead, I did.

My hands gripped the back of my hair. "You're right. I'm a coward."

He stood. "I'm not saying that. You're the opposite of a coward. I've seen you take down a raging bronco with a rope and your bare hands. It's just Lemon, man. You can't see straight when it comes to her." His tone was back to normal. Unfazed, unaffected Holden.

"Exactly. I have to stay far away from entertaining any kind of future with her." I was exhausted from all of it. Sophie's death, the new engagement, living with Clem. And on top of all that, now I had to be a dad to Anna. At least that one would be easier. Anna was so easy to love.

Holden put his hands on my shoulders. "I'm sorry for all the pushing. You've got a lot to think about right now."

I nodded, still coming down from wanting to break his nose.

Holden shook his head. "But you have to make a decision about Sophie's proposal quickly. Llew says that if you don't do the three months together, then it'll go to court. Some judge will decide what's best for Anna."

My eyes widened. "Seriously? Soph didn't have a contingency plan?"

"Nope."

I groaned. "Then I don't have a choice. I have to make sure Anna is okay." I shook my head, disgusted. "It's just like Sophie to pull this crap when she's out of reach."

"Or maybe she's doing you a favor."

I rolled my eyes. My sister could play cupid from the grave all she wanted, but I had control over how I reacted to it. And I wouldn't cave into the stupid, relentless feelings I had for Clem. I'd make sure of that.

"Ok. I'll do it."

five

CLEMENTINE

"You okay if we stop at the studio real quick?" I asked Anna as we headed home in my truck.

"Bet." Her eyes lit up. "Can I do the doohickey?"

"The inversion table?" I laughed. "Yeah. Just don't stay upside down too long or you'll make yourself sick."

She pulled her legs up under her crisscross. "Do you think Uncle Si will do it?"

"I don't know. He didn't seem too happy when he left."

She turned toward me. "I think he will."

"Why do you say that?"

"Because that's how Uncle Si is. It takes him a little while to warm up to something. You have to give him time to ruminate on the idea and then he comes around."

I laughed. "Ruminate?"

"I learned it in English class. I think it works here, don't you?"

I nodded, impressed. "It absolutely does. Ruminate."

She offered me a handshake. "Want to bet on it?"

This was a thing she'd been doing lately—betting on everything. From if there would be a snow day the next day to who would get the next text to who would win the next round of Uno.

"Sure." I shook. "What're the stakes?"

Her dark eyes lit up. "McFlurries. From McDonald's."

I shook my head. "You know I don't eat there."

She coughed the words "french fries" into her hands.

I laughed. "All right, all right. It's my occasional vice. Fine. If you win, you get a McFlurry. If I win, I get french fries." Either way, I'd end up buying. She was a broke thirteen-year-old.

"Deal." She bounced in her seat. "This is going to be the most epic sleepover of all time. Three months."

"If Silas says yes."

She smirked. "He will."

For her sake, I hoped he did. She needed this. Maybe if I could get him alone, I could help him see how important this was to Anna. I chewed my lip. No. I was the wrong person to talk Silas into anything. He always clammed up around me. I'd have to trust that Holden had done the best he could.

We rolled into the parking lot a few minutes later.

"I just love your studio sign." Anna's hands folded against her heart.

I smiled. "Your momma did good work, didn't she?" When I started the exercise studio two years earlier, Sophie had been right there with me. It was her idea to name it The Downward Dog. When I'd told Momma, she said it sounded like the name of a bar. But Sophie and I knew that anyone who knew anything about yoga would get it. And those were the people I wanted to attract. We were right. They'd found this place right away, and those who came were loyal. As we grew, we added classes other than just yoga. Actually, our barre classes were the most popular and my personal favorite.

I smiled up at the sign Sophie'd designed. A neon pink cord that spelled Downward Dog—but the letter N was a woman in yoga clothes in the downward dog pose. We'd converted half of an old warehouse into the most charming little gym around. The owner of the building, Mr. Greerly, an old retired veteran and machine shop owner, even let us paint our half Barely There pink. The other half of the structure was a plain white on the outside—the inside sat vacant, storing Mr. Greerly's old machine shop parts. My dream was to one day make enough to actually buy the entire building. Right now I could only afford to rent my half.

Anna was out the door as soon as I put it in park. She punched in the code and opened the door.

As she disappeared inside, I yelled after her, "The tension is still off. Be careful going backward!" Just another thing Billy had promised he'd fix.

I grabbed my purse and the packet of divorce papers Mr. Llewellyn's secretary had given me before I left his office. I'd discreetly asked for them, and she'd promised they always kept things confidential. I didn't know how I was going to afford Arlo if Billy went down fighting. But I wanted to get the ball rolling. I did not want to be married to Billy one minute longer than I had to.

Inside the studio was roasting.

"Are you kidding me?" I strode across the slip-control padded vinyl floor and punched the buttons to lower the thermostat. Peyton had left it full blast once again. I'd have to send out another message to all my instructors, reminding them to turn the heat down after their class unless there was another session coming up that day. If I singled Peyton out, she'd get her feelings hurt, and I did not have the energy for that.

"I bet she'd remember if I took it out of her check," I muttered as I walked to the hand-towel fridge. After each barre or HIIT class, we placed a chilly towel with a hint of essential oils on our clients' foreheads as they cooled down. If it was a slower yoga class, we'd give them a warm towel. It was a pain making sure enough towels were always ready, but these small touches kept people coming back.

I moistened the cloths under running water and rolled them up one by one.

Voices in the doorway caught my ear. "Told you we'd find them on Find My Friends."

I whirled at the noise and regretted it immediately. Everything went black, with the exception of some floating spots. I teetered and reached for the counter.

"Whoa." Someone caught me by the waist and steadied me. I knew it was Silas even with my eyes closed. I recognized that "whoa." I'd heard it hundreds of times growing up whenever we rode horses. "You okay?"

I forced an eye open and leaned against the counter. "Mhmm. Thanks." I smiled to show him I was all right. He stepped away, but his hands were still out in case I wobbled again.

That's when I noticed Holden was there, too.

"When's the last time you ate something?" Holden asked.

I had to think for a second. "Breakfast?"

"Are you crazy? The sun is going down," he pointed out, as if it wasn't obvious by the fading daylight. I'd honestly forgotten to eat. I did that when I got stressed, and I'd had plenty to be stressed about lately.

"Here." Silas led me to a folding chair someone had left out. "Do you have any food or—?"

I pointed at the basket on the counter full of healthy snacks. Clients who needed something after a workout could get one for a dollar. I wasn't making anything off of them, but they continued to snatch them up, so I continued to fill the basket. Anything to make my ladies happy.

Silas grabbed a banana, and I shook my head.

He put it back and picked up one of the Pink Lady apples Peyton had left. I crinkled my nose at that.

"But you love fruit," he had the nerve to say, like we were still friends. Like I was exactly the same person as a decade ago. Like I didn't have the right to change my mind when I became a full-fledged adult.

Okay. I did love fruit. Usually. Nature's dessert. What's not to love? But right then, I knew if I ate either of those, they might come back up. Was I getting a stomach bug?

He grabbed a peanut butter chocolate chip granola bar, and I nodded. "Thanks."

Anna yelped from the back room. "Lemon!"

I laughed, chewing on my snack. "I think she needs help getting out of the inversion table."

"What?" Holden's eyes widened. "You have one of those?"

I nodded and pressed a hand over my mouth. "Ughhh." I groaned. "I think this bar is expired."

Holden reached over, snatched it from my hand, broke off a piece, and chewed. "Tastes fine to me." He ripped another hunk off with his teeth. Okay. I guess it was his now.

Anna squealed again, laughing maniacally. Holden tossed the granola bar back to me and bounded out of the room, following her pleas for help.

Silas leaned against the wall and glanced around the room, checking out the studio while I attempted to eat more of Holden's granola bar. Sometime over the last hour, Silas had taken off his tie. His hair was mussed up too, like he'd been tugging on it or someone had put him in a headlock. I studied him, trying to figure out if he'd made a decision about Sophie's proposition. His expression was on lockdown. His phone must've buzzed in his pocket because he slid it out for two seconds and shoved it back in.

He glanced back at me, but said nothing. Just watched me eat.

I couldn't stand the silence. He always seemed so comfortable with it, but it made me twitchy.

"Crazy day, huh?" I said, my brows lifting.

"Yeah." He nodded and continued to watch me chew what was left in my mouth. A few seconds later, his head tilted, and he narrowed his gaze, studying me. My face overheated at the attention.

Holden screamed from the other room and Anna burst out laughing.

"I think I'm going to see what they're up to." I stood up slowly.

Silas took a step toward me. "Do you really think you should—"

"Yup." I made my escape. He was right at my heels, probably to catch me if I fainted.

"Help!" Holden hooted, his feet in the air and his head a few inches off the ground. "I can't...get up." He kept raising his head, trying to flip himself back up, but he was laughing too hard to actually rotate the machine. Anna was worthless—her head between her legs, gasping for air.

Silas snort-laughed as he walked around me. "Dude. You're such a dingus."

He grabbed Holden by the wrist and pulled him up enough that his feet swung back down to the floor. I giggled. I don't know why, but when the brothers called each other names, it always cracked me up.

Holden unclipped the foot latches, took one step onto the floor, and fell against Silas's knees like he was drunk. He rolled onto his back and moaned, lying on Silas's feet.

Silas stared down at him, nostrils flaring, his chest shaking with silent laughter. "What is wrong with you?"

"Uncle Si, you gotta try this thing," Anna tugged on his arm.

"So I can turn green like Holdie? No thanks."

She pressed her hands in a prayer pose, made her eyes

super wide, and poked out her bottom lip. "Please, for me, your only niece."

I fell for her Bambi eyes all the time. Silas must've been immune. He palmed her face like a basketball. I had not expected that. A laugh bubbled up in my throat.

Anna got him back by licking his palm.

He reciprocated by wiping his slobbery hand down the front of her face. This was the side of Silas I liked—where he opened up a little and had a good time. Why couldn't he ever do that with me?

Holden staggered to his feet, groaning. Which made me laugh harder.

Anna came up to me with that same sad puppy dog face. "You'll do it, won't you Aunt Lemon?" She tugged me toward the device. "C'mon. This thing is your favorite."

"Uh." I didn't want to be a party pooper, but if I flipped upside down, I might pass out.

Silas stepped forward. "It might help my back." He rubbed his lower spine. "It's been tweaked ever since Maisy tried to buck me off that one time." Maisy was one of the horses at their ranch. I doubted she'd ever bucked anyone off. She was the sweetest horse there. I was pretty sure Silas was saving me. Aww. My resolve to hate him softened.

Nope. Don't fall for it. He completely ghosted you, Lemon. Cut you out like a bruise on a peach.

"Aww, yeah." Holden squeezed Silas's shoulders. "That's what I'm talking about."

Silas stepped up into the footholds. Holden started latching his left foot and Silas swatted him away.

"Dude. I got it." When he was done getting his feet situated, he leaned over and the inversion table flipped too fast. Midway back, I realized we'd forgotten to adjust for his height. But it was too late. With the combined tension problem, Silas's head slammed into the ground with a thunk.

I clapped my hand over my mouth. That sounded really painful. He swore and tried to sit up, grabbing the top of his head. Anna and Holden doubled over each other, laughing. Fat lotta help they were.

"Oh my gosh," I ran forward and pushed his feet down, shooting his head up, again too fast. The stupid tension! His face went from beet red to ghost white in less than a second. His eyes did a weird roll, but then went back into place. That couldn't be good. While I undid the foot straps, he kept moaning.

"Oh, man." Holden wheezed between laughs. "You shoulda seen yourself."

I held Silas's hands as he stepped off the foot holds. I didn't want to let go because he was sheet white. But he yanked his hands out of mine as soon as his feet were on the floor. Then he bent over with hands on his thighs and…

Puked all over the carpeted floor.

Awesome. Just fantastic.

Holden and Anna were flopped over each other, gasping for air. Didn't even care that Silas probably had a concussion or that I now had a disgusting mess to clean up.

"You both suck." Silas stayed bent over, which was probably for the best.

They laughed harder, but Anna had the wits to hand him a tissue from the counter so he could wipe his mouth.

I stood there, looking at his puke, dreading the clean up. My already-touchy stomach wrenched, and I covered my nose.

"I'm so sorry," he said, standing up with a grimace. "Do you have something I can clean this up with?" I couldn't tell if his face was flushed because he'd vomited or because he was embarrassed. Possibly both.

I held up my hands. "I got it."

"Clem," he called, but I kept going. I was going to hurl if I stayed there.

No one with a concussion should have to clean up their own puke. So I hurried back to the big room and rifled through the cupboard above the sink. I didn't own any of that powdery stuff elementary school janitors used when somebody puked in the lunchroom. But Momma always said dish soap was a solid, all-purpose cleaner. It would at least work for tonight. I'd bring my carpet cleaner from home tomorrow morning when I came to teach my barre class. I hurried back down the hall with a handful of paper towels, a couple of wet cloths, and the bottle of soap.

But when I arrived, the mood in the room was totally different. There was no more laughter, only silent, vigorous scrubbing from all three of them. I didn't know what Silas had said, but somehow he'd put the fear of God into Anna and Holden. Someone must've grabbed some paper towels from the bathroom.

I knelt down to help, squirting soap onto one of the rags.

Silas held his hands up, his gray eyes drilling into me. "We've got it. You don't need to touch this." And I knew now that his flushed cheeks were because he was embarrassed. They were even redder than before—all the way to the tips of his ears. "Is there anything else you can do while we clean this up?" he asked in a tone and with an expression that screamed that he would pin me to the ground before he let me touch his vomit.

"Yeah. Okay." I hopped up and hurried out of the room as fast as I could, my cheeks smarting. Why did he have to be like that? What was it about me that made it so he couldn't relax? I looked around for something to do. Mirrors. I could clean the wall of floor-to-ceiling mirrors. I took my time spraying them and wiping them off. Who knew how long they'd be back there, but I wanted to be busy when they found me. If he'd decided to accept Sophie's proposal before, this had probably changed his mind. My stomach clenched, and I realized it had been in a knot ever since he'd entered the studio.

Silas must've wanted to be thorough because Anna brought the soiled cloths out and put them into a spare Food Lion bag. Then she grabbed a few more.

"How's it going in there?" I asked.

"Fine." She gave me a smile, but it was forced. She headed back to help some more.

Ten minutes later, they were finally done, and the mirrors had never been so clean.

Holden and Anna came out first. Anna was silent. Holden raised his eyebrows, but I could see a smile breaking through. "Good times," he said.

"I'm gonna check out Uncle Holden's new car for a minute," Anna said, still looking a little rattled. Silas had to learn to relax. He had no idea how tense he could be or how it affected everyone else.

"Okay. I'm just waiting for Silas so I can lock up."

I watched her get into Holden's fancy smart car and smiled. That would take her mind off things.

A solid five minutes later, Silas finally came out of the bathroom, his hands looking like he'd scrubbed them raw.

"Hey," he started. I expected him to apologize again but instead he said, "I have to grab some stuff from Mom and Dad's and then I'll be over. Do I need a sleeping bag or anything?" Oh. He was going to do it. "We're staying at your place, right?"

"Yeah. Of course. No, you don't need anything. It's a three bedroom."

"Ok. Cool." He stepped around me. "I'll see you there."

"Wait." I grabbed his elbow.

He turned, but kept his eyes hooded.

"Do you want me to call Billy? Have him check you for a concussion?"

His eyes flashed and his jaw clenched. "No. I definitely don't want you to call Billy."

Okay. "Well, do you at least want a ride?" I hated the way my voice was shaking. "You probably shouldn't be driving."

"I'm fine." He pulled his elbow out of my grasp and headed for one of the old ranch trucks.

My cheeks burned right along with my eyes. But I pushed it all down. In a little while, Silas was moving into my house. I had to give him some grace. Today had been a lot.

For all of us.

Six

SILAS

Mom kissed my cheek before she let me go. "It's a good thing you're doing." She smiled, but I wasn't convinced it was sincere. "I'm already seeing why Sophie wanted this. You'll be a great dad."

Dad. That was a terrifying title. I had no idea how to be anything but an uncle. Uncles were all fun. Dads had so much responsibility on them. I didn't know what Mom saw in me that made her think I could do this.

She patted my cheek like she could read my mind. "Parents don't know what they're doing. Just like anything else, fake it till you make it."

I gave her a half-smile. That I could do. It was basically my mantra.

I squeezed her into a hug before I turned and walked to Dad's old ranch pickup. Thank goodness for this old beater. Paying for a rental all summer would've made a painful dent in my savings. I was still living on a teacher's salary for a few more months.

I tossed my high school gym duffel onto the bench seat and revved the engine. A text appeared from Christy.

SUSAN HENSHAW & (CALLIE MAE SHAW)

> Where are you? Is everything okay?

I never ignored her texts. But I'd been ignoring them all afternoon since the reading of the will. They'd gotten progressively more frequent. I'd missed fourteen since our last call this morning.

I hugged the steering wheel and rested my forehead against it. If my gut was right, and it usually was, this was not going to go over well. Me, living with a beautiful, single woman for three months? Yeah, right. I'd made the mistake of telling Christy about my childhood crush back on one of our first dates. At the time, I never thought she'd end up meeting Clem. Or that things would go this far with us. And I didn't know back then that she had a memory like a steel trap.

I pulled out of the driveway and channeled my inner old-man farmer—taking the five miles of backroads between Dupree Ranch and Firefly Fields as slowly as I could get away with. Christy had insisted on coming with me when Sophie was passing. I'd tried to talk her out of it. Told her it wasn't the right time to meet my family, but she'd been unrelenting. And last week at the viewing and funeral, I could feel the hairs on her arm raise whenever Clem was around. Thought she was going to lose her mind when I helped Clem get her cow back in. Thankfully, Christy only stayed two days after the funeral so she could get back to her fifth grade class. It felt like I was walking a tightrope the entire time she was here.

I dialed her number.

"Hey," she answered on the second ring. Her voice was too cheery, and I could tell she was masking some worry.

"Hey. Sorry, it's been kind of a crazy day."

"That's okay." The tension in her voice lightened. If only it would stay that way. "How'd it go? Did your sister leave you something cool?"

I hesitated. "Cool? I don't know if you'd call it that."

She pushed. "She did leave you something, though?"

"Yeah," was all I said.

"Well, aren't you going to tell me what?" She sounded frustrated. It seemed that Christy was always frustrated with me.

"Anna," I said quickly.

She sighed. "What about Anna?"

"Nothing about Anna. Sophie left me Anna." I put my blinker on to turn left.

There was a long pause.

"Seriously?" I couldn't tell if she was mad or happy or what.

"Yeah."

"Wow." I could almost see her rubbing her neck the way she always did when she was thinking. "Well, I guess we'll make it work. She seems like a really sweet kid. We'll have to get her enrolled in school out here—"

"Oh, no, sorry. Anna's not moving to Wyoming." I wasn't doing this right. "At least...I don't actually know how that's going to work—"

"How are you supposed to take care of her if she's not in Wyoming? I don't—"

"Christy." I stopped her.

Silence.

I took a deep breath. "Sophie left Anna to both me and Clementine."

"I...I...don't understand."

"I don't really understand it yet either. It's going to take some time to figure out. I might be here longer than I planned."

"How long?"

I didn't want to say it. Really, really didn't want to.

"Silas?"

I gulped. "Three months."

Her reaction was immediate. "Three months?!" Her voice shot up an octave. "You can't stay there for three months."

"I have to."

"What are you talking about?" Her voice was downright shrill. And I knew some of that was my fault. I wasn't explaining it very well.

So I dove in. "There are stipulations I have to follow. And if I don't—if *we* don't—then the courts will end up deciding what to do with Anna. And I really don't want that to happen. I *can't* let that happen."

"Of course you can't." I heard her exhale. "I'm sorry. You're right. You have to get this figured out for Anna. It's okay. If it takes three months..."

I knew if I didn't plow through the next part, she might hang up or explode before I could finish. "There's something else. And you're not gonna like it, but it is what it is. The three of us have to *live together* during those three months"—she gasped, but I kept going—"before we can solidify a custody agreement."

"Are you pranking me right now?" I was fairly certain if she could have come through the phone and strangled me, she would've. "You have to *live* together? That is the most ridiculous thing I've ever heard." She scoffed. "No one does something like that in their will."

"I'm not pranking you. I can take a picture of the letter if you want to see it. This is the way Sophie set it up. Trust me, I've already banged my head against the wall all day."

Her laugh was bitter. "Let me get this straight. Your controlling sister is forcing you to play family with her best friend—your childhood crush," she spat. "And I'm just supposed to be okay with that?"

"Whoa, whoa, whoa. You didn't even know Sophie. She just wants what's best for Anna." I forced myself to be calmer, to see it from Christy's point of view. "You don't have to be okay with it, Chris. But yeah, that's pretty much what Sophie has done here. Trust me, I'm angry too."

"Really? 'Cause you don't sound angry."

I sighed and pulled onto Clem's driveway. "I already had it out with Holden about the whole thing. I'm too tired to be much of anything right now, anyway. I have a freaking concussion, okay?" The truck's front wheel hit a pothole and my head slammed into the roof. I swore.

"You have a concussion? What?"

I didn't want to tell her I'd been messing around on an inversion table when I should've been texting her. "It's nothing. I'm fine."

"Where are you right now?"

"Coming down Clem's driveway."

"You are not staying at her house, Silas," she threatened.

"I don't have a choice," I said, making my tone as soft as possible. Miss Lisa's lights were already off at the big house. I worried that I'd taken too long and was keeping Clem up waiting for me. I pressed the gas pedal toward Clem's. Potholes or not.

"You always have a choice," Christy said, but her voice shook and I could tell she felt helpless.

"Not if I want Anna to be okay," I said gently.

"Then I'm coming out there for the summer."

"You can't." That was the last thing I needed. I tried to hide how exasperated I was. "It's one of the stipulations. Just the three of us. No outsiders allowed. Those were Soph's exact words."

The first sob erupted.

Unlike Miss Lisa's house, every outside light was on at Clem's, welcoming me. "Oh, man, Christy, please don't cry." Crying girls would be the death of me. "It's going to be okay. Really."

I put the truck in park. Clementine bolted out the door with Anna right behind her.

I stomped the emergency brake with my boot. Clem and Anna jogged across the front lawn toward me. "Look, I've gotta go. I'll call you tomorrow. It's going to be okay."

"No, it won't." Her voice quivered, and she blew her nose. "You're going to cheat on me. She's all alone and vulnerable right now. Probably ripe for a rebound." She wailed, which made my headache even worse. "And she's so pretty." Another sob. "We might as well break up right now. Just get it over with."

Clem was almost to my door, a huge smile on her ridiculously gorgeous face. No human should be allowed to be that beautiful. My heart wagged faster than a puppy's tail when it got a treat. *It's muscle memory,* I thought. I'd have to figure out how to overpower my stupid, weak-willed body.

I held up a finger and Clem nodded. I turned away from the window and pretended to rifle through my bag so Clem couldn't lip read.

"We're not breaking up," I hissed into the phone.

"Do you still love her? If you tell me you don't love her, I'll believe you."

I squeezed my eyes shut and told my first fib. "I don't. I haven't talked to her in years. That crush is long gone. I love *you*, okay?" I had a feeling it was going to be a summer full of white lies and half truths. A summer of tightrope walking. I hated that, but it was a means to an end. I just had to get through the next three months and I'd never lie to Christy again.

The crying eased up. "You promise?" Her voice was hopeful.

"I promise."

"You're not going to cheat on me?"

"No. Not a chance."

She blew her nose a couple of more times.

"I have to go. They're waiting on me."

"Okay." Her voice quivered, but she sounded lighter. "I love you."

"I love you too." I hung up and tossed the phone in my bag, not ready for any of this. A couple of deep breaths and I forced myself to turn.

Clem yanked the truck door open, her green eyes sparkling. "You made it," she said like I'd hiked all the way from Egypt. And like she hadn't just seen me puke all over her studio carpet two hours ago. The sight of her—even with no makeup, wearing an oversized T-shirt that showed too much collarbone, pajama pants, and bare feet—made the breath catch in my throat.

Forget riding broncs, college exams, wrangling a class of middle school kids. At that moment, I knew I was about to begin the hardest test of my life.

SEVEN

CLEMENTINE

When Sophie had passed, it felt like part of me had been cut out. With Billy gone, I felt peace but deeply alone. My house and my life had slumped to dull and lifeless. Having Anna there brought the sunshine back. But when Silas rolled up, it was like a piece of Sophie was coming home.

Silas was rigid when he got out of the truck. He seemed exhausted, and it was obvious he'd just had the talk with Christy.

I put on the biggest smile I could, trying to erase any of the tension leftover from tonight at the studio. Clean slate starting now.

"Need any help?" I asked, as he gathered his things from the truck.

"No, I've got it." He slung a single duffel over his shoulder. Anna nestled under his arm and they walked ahead of me across the lawn. I felt a little left out and prayed that the whole summer wouldn't leave me feeling like a third wheel.

I let Anna have a few minutes to revel in Silas's being here. She threw herself on his bed in the guest room and talked his ear off while he unpacked. When he went to the bathroom to brush his teeth, she followed, giving him a play-by-play of her last rec league volleyball game. When he went back in his room, she trailed behind him and I couldn't help but smile. Anna loved her Uncle Silas. I gave her another ten minutes before knocking on his slightly open door.

I peeked my head in. Silas was propped against the headboard wearing an old blue Seddledown Stallions basketball shirt and black athletic shorts. The fact that his clothes were two sizes too small and completely faded hinted that they might be from our high school days—and since he hadn't anticipated a three-month stay, he was scrambling for things to wear.

"You really think I could be a setter?" Anna lay on her stomach, her chin propped in her hands, legs up, and ankles crossed in the air. When she noticed me, she patted a spot on the bed next to her. "Come sit."

"It's ten, sweetie. You have school tomorrow." The Duprees had given Anna a week off after Sophie passed. Tomorrow was her first day back. There were only two more weeks of school, anyway. But the principal and teachers had requested she come back to enjoy all the fun stuff they had planned, like field day and a cookout. They thought it might help to be around her friends. They were probably right.

"Just a few more minutes." She unleashed her doe eyes on me. I laughed, shook my head, and plopped down next to her. Silas folded his long legs up, giving me ample room. Anna started up again, telling Silas everything. "JV didn't win a single game last year, so Brooklyn and I are pretty sure we'll make the team."

"How's your serve coming?" Silas asked, folding his arms across his chest, his biceps popping. I looked away.

Anna glanced at me for help.

I bit my lip and answered for her, "We might need to work

on that." For Christmas I'd bought her a net she could keep up at my house. Since then, she'd spent hours trying to get the ball over with very little luck. And I'd spent hours trying to figure out exactly what she was doing wrong.

She groaned and bounced her forehead on the bed. "I can't get the timing right."

He cocked an eyebrow. "You sure it's not your skinny chicken arms?" He squeezed her nonexistent muscles. Jenny had handed me a three-page list of instructions when we picked up Anna's things. One of the items on Jenny's list was: *Make sure she eats at least 2000 calories a day. She's too skinny. We have to get some weight on her.* Anna had lost weight this year, with Sophie being sick. It was stressful watching your mother die.

Anna glared at Silas, which only made him grin. And I realized his smile was kind of dazzling. I don't know if he'd gained extra confidence along with those muscles over the years, but he was different than I remembered. He had those smile lines around his mouth some people have, like a set of parenthesis. His teeth had always been perfectly straight, no braces needed, but I'd never appreciated them before. And he had a really strong jawline, but in the best way.

Huh. I tilted my head.

His gaze skittered to me, his forehead furrowed. It took me a second to realize I'd been caught. I forced my eyes away, my face hot.

I smacked Anna's foot. "C'mon. Time for bed."

"Can I sleep in here?" she asked.

She'd slept in my bed leading up to her mom's passing. And Silas's floor every night since, according to Jenny. I really didn't want to let her make that a habit.

Gratefully, Silas helped me out. "You'll sleep better in your own space."

She hesitated.

"I'm not going anywhere." He promised. "I'll be right here when you wake up." Then he opened his arms for a hug. She flung herself into his embrace. He wrapped her up tight, his forearms flexing around her.

Once she had her light off, I headed to the kitchen to study Jenny's pamphlet of instructions.

-Don't let her get away without brushing her teeth twice a day. She'll try to weasel out of the nighttime brushing, but that's when the cavities are formed.

-She needs more protein. And Reese's don't count! She'll live off of them if you let her. Bo buys her one every day on the way home from school, no matter how many times I tell him not to. I don't even want to know how many cavities she'll have at her six-month checkup. Just another reason for the nighttime brushing.

Silas walked in. "Do you have any ibuprofen?"

"Of course." I walked over to the cabinet by the sink and pulled out a bottle, pouring the pills into my hand. While I filled a glass of water, Silas scanned the list.

I offered him the glass and pills and he set the list back down. He tossed the pills into his mouth and gulped until the glass was empty. Then he pointed to the fridge. "Is it okay if I grab something?"

I tipped my head. "Don't ever ask me that again. You don't need permission. For the next three months, this is your house too. What's mine is yours."

He held his hands up. "Got it." He opened the fridge and peered inside.

I went back to Jenny's list.

> -She can't have her phone in her room at night. I don't know why Sophie even got her that thing. She's too young.
>
> -For the love, please don't let her use all that ridiculous Gen Z slang. I need Google Translate just to have a conversation with her.
>
> -And try to get her to cut back on time spent with Brooklyn. They are so silly together. I think that's where she's getting all those ridiculous terms like "slaps" and "yeet" and "Gucci."

I got Jenny's frustration. Half the time, I didn't know what those two were talking about. I wasn't going to break up their friendship because of it. Their conversations were downright hilarious, even if I didn't always understand them. But they were committed to each other and loyal to a fault. Very reminiscent of Sophie and me at that age. Anna needed that right now.

Silas leaned against the counter a couple of feet away, Squirting a tube of bubble gum yogurt into his mouth. It was a snack I kept around for Anna.

His gaze narrowed. "You don't have to do any of that."

I gave him an "are you crazy" look. "Jenny gave me strict instructions to follow this exactly."

Before I knew what was happening, he reached over and crinkled the list into a ball. "You will make yourself crazy trying to do everything *Jenny* wants you to." He readied his arm for a free throw and launched the ball across the room, straight into the trash. "Nothin' but net."

I couldn't believe he just did that. "B-but—"

"Sophie didn't ask my mom to raise Anna. She asked us. And we get to decide what's best for her."

I stood there, frozen. It wasn't that easy. I already felt like I was in a tight spot with Jenny. If I ignored her wishes...

I walked to the trash and pulled the papers out.

Si caught me by the wrist. "Drop it." His laugh was light, but there was an edge to it.

I yanked my arm away and side-stepped into the living room with the paper behind my back. "I just want to see what it says."

He reached around me, smiling, but his eyes held a hint of seriousness. "I know how to deal with my mom. We don't need a list." His deep voice was soft, his arm around my waist was snug, and his bubblegum scented breath made my heart twitch a little. Weird, but I chalked it up to nerves. He peeled my fingers open and took the list back, looking down into my eyes. "Trust me." As soon as he had the paper in his grasp, he backed away.

I folded my arms. "You don't get it."

He stood all the way up, rolling his shoulders back, taller and more imposing than ever. "Try me."

I sat on the couch, leaned my elbows onto my knees, and dropped my head in my hands. "Your mom is going to hate me."

He plunked down on the opposite end of the couch and stretched his ridiculously long legs out in front of him. "Nah. She could never do that."

I leaned against the cushion and turned to face him. "Yes, she could. I'm taking her granddaughter away from her."

He shrugged. "So am I."

"But you're her son."

He sat up and leaned toward me. "She doesn't have it in her to hate you. I know my mom. She doesn't hate. Period." That was probably true. But I'd seen situations like this bring out the worst in people.

"Fine. Strongly dislike, then."

He shook his head. "Not possible. I don't think you know how much she adores you."

Jenny adored me? I mean, she'd always been kind and included me anytime I wanted it. And she'd never fussed or gotten annoyed even when I was younger and practically lived at their house. But adored?

"Even if that is true—"

"It is." He raised one eyebrow, daring me not to believe him. Then he lowered it, his gaze intense. "That girl is going through the worst trial of her life. I'm not going to run around making sure she's following a bunch of rules. If anything, we need to chill. Her life is going to be hard enough. We don't need to make it harder following some list we didn't even agree to. Sometimes my mom thinks she's helping when she's doing the opposite."

He was right. But I still didn't want to step on Jenny's toes. Anna wasn't the only one who'd lost Sophie. Jenny had too. We all had. "Don't you think it might be smart to try to uphold at least some of her wishes?"

"Fine." He unwrinkled the papers and smoothed them against his thigh. "Let me take a look."

Finally, he was seeing reason.

"I'll read my three favorites and you get to pick one." He scanned the first page.

He wasn't taking this seriously. At all. "One?"

"Yep. Just one." He rubbed his chiseled jaw, trying to decide. After a few seconds, his eyes lit up. "We've got a couple of winners here. You ready?" I could already tell from the way his lips were twitching that these were going to be the most ridiculous things he could find. *"Remind Anna to do her laundry every Saturday morning. If you let her wait, she'll put it off until Sunday night right before it's bedtime and then her wet clothes will sit in the washer all night long."* He lowered the paper and added sarcastically, "Because the world is going to end if her clothes aren't dried immediately. Nobody ever dried clothes in the morning before school." His jaw dropped and his eyes widened in mock horror.

I rolled my eyes, but a giggle bubbled up my throat. I didn't know what had gotten into him, but this was Fun Silas. And I liked it. "Next."

He looked back at the list. "Oh, maybe this one. *Please do not let her monopolize Buford. I don't think Lisa likes that she kidnaps her dog every time she comes over. Plus, he drools everywhere. It's gross.*"

Jenny wasn't wrong. Anna did indeed like to borrow Buford whenever she visited. She'd asked tonight if we could stop by and give Buford a pet. Unfortunately, Momma and Buford were asleep by the time we drove past their house. And okay, Buford did slobber all over everyone and everything. But Jenny was also wrong. Momma didn't care one bit if Anna shanghaied the basset hound. She thought it was cute. And she had her cat, Sunshine, to keep her company when Buford was away.

Si shook his head, adamant. "We are letting her spend as much time with that dog as she wants."

I relaxed a little. "Agreed." Si wasn't stressed about Jenny's list. Why should I?

"Last chance," he said with a mock-stern expression.

I adjusted in my seat. "Okay."

He searched the back of the first page and moved on to the next. "I've got it. This is going to be it right here." He sat up tall and cleared his voice. "*Please make sure Anna works on her embroidery for at least fifteen minutes each evening. I know you know how to embroider, Lemon, so this should be an easy one. She's almost done with a lazy daisy reel. Make sure she finishes, please. We don't want her to be a quitter."* He pointed to the paper. "She even put a smiley face next to it to make her appear less condescending." His hands flew out, and he slumped onto the couch. "A lazy daisy reel? What is this? A Jane Austen novel?"

He balled the list back up and hucked it into the open fireplace. He didn't know it never got used. For two years, Billy had been promising to get someone out here to clean the flue. I wouldn't dare light a match in there for fear we'd burn the house down.

I relaxed into the cushions. "You gave me terrible choices, admit it."

"It was a terrible list." He folded his hands behind his head. "Seriously though. Let me worry about my mom." He stared up at the popcorn ceiling for a few seconds. "We should do the phone thing, though. I do agree with that one."

"Yeah. Me too."

"And Sophie didn't get her the phone. I did. So she could text me this past year, if she ever needed anything."

My breath caught in my throat. I hadn't known that. I assumed Sophie got it for her. What else didn't I know about Si? Unlocking his mysteries was really satisfying. Like leveling up in a game. He was like one of those houses with twenty-seven different locks on the door. It felt like tonight I'd gotten a couple of them picked. Christy probably had the door completely open. I was a little jealous of her right then.

His brow furrowed and his eyes had glazed over, like he was thinking of her right then.

I nudged his knee with my foot. "Everything okay with you and Christy?"

He gave me a single nod. "Yup." His tone made it clear that, just kidding, all deadbolts were in place. He quickly changed the subject. "Should we be worried that Anna is doing so well?"

I'd thought the same thing for the last week. "I don't know. She seems really good, considering..." I couldn't finish the sentence. Considering Sophie was gone. Considering she's an orphan. Considering she will live the rest of her life never hugging her mom again.

I would never hug Sophie again.

Silas opened his mouth to say something.

But my stomach beat him to it, growling embarrassingly loud. I folded my arms across my belly, trying to shut it up.

Silas chuckled. "Have you still not eaten?"

"No, I did," I said sheepishly. When I took Anna for her winning McFlurry, the thought of a Quarter Pounder actually sounded delicious for once. So I let myself get one...along with a medium fry. But that was a couple of hours ago and apparently my body had already burned up every artery-clogging calorie I'd consumed.

"It sounds like you just ingested your spleen." He hopped up. "Want a quesadilla?"

My mouth parted. "I forgot about those. That actually sounds really good." He used to make them all the time when we were younger. It drove him crazy that every time he made one, Sophie got a hankering, too. But he'd make her one, anyway. And by default, he'd make one for me as well.

I followed him into the kitchen and opened my fridge to assess the tortilla situation. "Do you want corn or flour?"

"Corn. Of course," he said, a *duh* in his voice.

While I was there, I grabbed the butter dish and the cheddar cheese. By the time I turned around, Silas had already figured out the gas burner and had a cast iron pan heating up. I hopped up on the counter with my legs dangling over the side and watched him work.

It felt like high school all over again. His routine hadn't

deviated in the slightest. He dropped a pat of butter in the center of four tortillas and then sprinkled enough salt to cover the butter. He flipped two of them butter side down into the pan. They sizzled right away, and he turned the heat down a smidge. Then he carefully placed a calculated handful of cheese—not too much, not too little—on the tortillas. Once the last two tortillas were on top, we waited. Silas watched them studiously, as if they would burn the second he looked away. And while he watched them, I watched him.

This wasn't the Silas I remembered. Sure, he still pulled away from me if I touched him, and sure he was sometimes ridiculously awkward. But tonight, things were good. Almost normal even. Maybe this would be okay.

He handed me a plated quesadilla, cut into eight perfect triangles. Just like I liked it. How did he remember that a decade later? He watched as I blew on one of the slices and then popped it into my mouth.

My eyes closed, and I moaned without even thinking about it. "I'd forgotten how yummy these are," I said between chews. I got the strangest craving right then. "Oh, you know what would taste so good in these?"

He raised an eyebrow, chewing his quesadilla.

"Sautéed mushrooms." I closed my eyes, imagining it. Buttery 'shrooms with the salty cheddar cheese. Oh, man.

He made a gagging sound. "You hate mushrooms."

Again with the thinking I hadn't changed in ten years. Again, he wasn't wrong. I did still despise mushrooms, usually. What was wrong with my tastebuds today?

His gaze was scrutinizing, and I shrunk under it.

"Not anymore," I lied.

We stood there, leaning over our plates, contentedly silent —and I found myself watching Silas again. His Adam's apple dipped with each swallow. Why hadn't I ever noticed he was attractive before? I mean, I knew why. I'd only ever had eyes for Billy since the day he asked me out. And I was so in love that I couldn't see anyone else. Didn't want to see anyone else. Billy was all-consuming like that.

But knowing what I knew now, it was crazy that I'd spent countless hours with Silas and it had never occurred to me that he wasn't just...plain old Silas. He was much more. The one thing that hadn't changed was the peace I felt simply by being with him.

I smiled, watching him swallow.

"What?" His eyebrow lifted. "Do I have something on my face?" He ripped a paper towel off the roll and wiped his mouth.

"No." My nose crinkled. "I just...I think Christy is incredibly lucky." I shrugged. "That's all."

I may as well have taken a hammer to a glass vase. Because apparently things between us were that delicate. His face went beet red, and he stiffened. In three bites, he inhaled the rest of his quesadilla. Then he rinsed his plate and put it in the dishwasher—all in painful silence and all at breakneck speed.

Had he thought I was hitting on him? I wouldn't do that. He had a girlfriend. I was just being nice. That's all. Christy *was* really lucky to have such a great guy. Silas and I had always been friends. Just friends. Besides, I was barely out of a relationship that had gutted me. I wasn't even sure I ever wanted to date or marry again.

He eyed the pan nervously and I could see that he knew he should wash it, but he also wanted to disappear.

"It needs to cool down. I'll wash it in the morning," I offered, putting us both out of our misery.

"G'night." He barely made eye contact.

"Hey."

He turned and reluctantly met my gaze.

"Do you need me to wake you up every hour?"

His eyebrow lifted.

"You know, for the concussion."

He shook his head. "No, that's not a thing anymore." And then he hurried out of the room.

I googled concussions just to be sure, and he was right. Sleeping normally was totally fine.

I cut off the kitchen light and living room lights and made sure all the doors were locked. Thirty seconds later, when I passed Silas's room, it was pitch black.

I crawled into bed exhausted and fell into a peaceful sleep.

eight

SILAS

A scream pierced through the night, sitting me straight up in bed, my heart pounding. But then it stopped, and I thought I'd been dreaming. I rubbed my eyes, trying to remember where I was. The last thing I remembered was looking up at the ceiling and trying to figure out what Clem had been implying when she said Christy was incredibly lucky. Oh, I was at Clem's house. But why? I was too tired to care. I lay back down and closed my eyes again.

Another tortured shriek shattered the silence.

Anna.

I threw the covers off, flipped on the light, and bolted into the hall. Clem flew out of her room at the same moment. We shared a split-second gaze of terror. Clem yanked the door open to Anna's room and hit the light.

I didn't know how someone could gasp for air and scream at the same time, but Anna was doing it. Her body thrashed on the bed and I thought she might fall out. I rushed to the left and Clem went to the right. I knelt beside the bed and grabbed Anna's hand. Clem sat on the edge of the mattress and smoothed her bangs back.

"Anna," I shook her, trying to get her to wake up.

"No," Clem said in a hushed tone. "Don't wake her."

What? Didn't we want to stop this?

"She's having a night terror. She had them when she was little. We just have to make sure she doesn't hurt herself and wait it out."

Anna's bottom sheet had come loose and coiled around her legs. I rubbed my thumb over her knuckles, praying for her to stop.

"Mom! Mom!" Anna sobbed. "Where's my mom? Have you seen my mom? Sophie!" Her left arm flew up and Clem caught it before it smacked her in the face.

"Stop!" she screamed. "No! Don't do that," she mumbled. "She doesn't want you to put dirt on her. Stop it!" She tried to punch but her arms flopped down.

The funeral. She was freaking out about Sophie being in the ground. I willed her to wake up.

Of course Anna was freaking out. She would have PTSD for years. No thirteen-year-old should have to watch their mother die a slow, painful death. Or watch all their extended family sobbing over their mother's dead body. Or stand by helplessly as shovels of dirt are hefted onto their parent's casket. *I* couldn't think about Sophie being six feet under without fighting for air. No wonder Anna's body was overloaded.

I felt so helpless. Clem's eyes were swimming, but she stayed still, calmly tracing along Anna's forehead with her pointer finger.

"Mom, please," Anna cried feebly once again. Then her body went motionless. Her eyes flew open and everything was still for a split second. Was she awake? She looked awake. Clem glanced at me and nodded.

I got up off my knees and slid onto the edge of the twin

bed. "Hey, hey, sweet girl. It's okay." I used a gentle tone. "We're right here."

Her sobs shook the whole bed. When she realized who I was, she collapsed against my chest. Clem leaned back against the headboard while I held Anna, letting her cry it out.

"W-where's Aunt Lemon?" Her eyes darted around frantically.

Clem put a hand on her shoulder. "I'm right here."

Anna turned and reached for her, still holding onto me. Clem squeezed her hand. Anna pulled her against us. Clem slid one arm around Anna and the other around my waist. She leaned her head against Anna's. Clem's hair brushed my cheek and I could smell the scent of her shampoo. Roses. Heat spread through me, as longing pulsed through my veins with each heartbeat. I tried to focus on Anna.

I don't know how long we sat that way, huddled together, letting Anna cry—but it was long enough for my left leg to fall asleep and my hormones to melt almost all my willpower. Anna's breathing softened. Clem glanced down at her face and then back up at me. She was way too close. Like close enough for me to kiss her. I cut off the air in my nostrils because if I got one more whiff of the rose shampoo, I might do something stupid.

"I think she's asleep," she whispered.

Thank God.

Like literally. Did He think this was funny? Was He trying to break me? I didn't know, but it all felt like some kind of cruel joke. Like He wanted to dangle the world's biggest carrot in front of me just to see if I could handle it.

Together, Clem and I slowly eased Anna against her pillow.

"Do you think she'll remember in the morning?" I asked.

"I don't know. She hasn't had one in years."

Clem stood and carefully untangled the blanket from

between Anna's legs. We tucked the sheet back in and covered her up. Anna wiggled for a second and then went still. I needed out, so I padded slowly toward the door. Clem followed, both of us watching to make sure we didn't wake her. The floor creaked under my right foot.

Clem winced.

Anna sat up. "Don't go." Dang it. "Please. What if it happens again?"

I heard Clem sigh, but not in a frustrated way. More like in complete submission. She would do what needed to be done. Even if she got no sleep tonight. She walked back and slid into bed beside Anna. I didn't know if I had it in me to be stuck in this room with Clem a second longer.

"Uncle Si?" Anna held open the covers on her other side.

What else could I do?

I flipped off the light and crawled in next to my niece. It took a second to get situated. A twin bed is not made for three people. It quickly became apparent that the only way Clem and I were not going to fall out was if we reached across Anna and held on to each other—like some kind of balancing act.

I closed my eyes. Every nerve in my body was firing simply from Clem's fingers wrapped around my tricep and my hand pressed against the small of her back.

Yeah. It was perfectly clear.

At some point, somewhere down the line, I'd done something to make God really, really mad.

I probably lay there wide awake for close to two hours. Every time I moved, Anna sensed it. The moon was right above the house, its light falling through the sheer pink curtains and into my right eyeball. Combine that with my racing thoughts about the fact that I was sleeping in the same bed as Clem and, yeah…I was miserable.

Clem's finger traced the back of my arm, but in a twitchy way that told me she wasn't awake. Or was she? The thought that she might have done it on purpose caused an eruption in my gut. I was not getting any rest tonight. Not in this room, anyway. I had to go. I made a promise to another woman two thousand miles away, and I was going to keep it. And I couldn't do that if I was lying in a bed with Clem, even if Anna was between us. If someone sent a snapshot of my current situation to Christy, the why wouldn't matter. She would punch me in the face. Or worse. And I wouldn't blame her.

Anna let out a little snore, and I thought I might finally be able to get away. I carefully pulled my arm out from under Clem's hand. Hopefully Clem wouldn't fall out of the bed, but I couldn't care about that anymore. I couldn't be her protector tonight.

I slid slowly off the mattress. Anna rolled onto her stomach, taking up the space I'd been in. Clem seemed to sense there was room and rolled toward Anna, away from the edge. In my teenage years, I would've stood there and watched Clem sleep for a minute, creepy or not. I'd done it a couple of times when she and Sophie had a sleepover in the living room. Lying there, her eyes closed, her freckles begging to be touched, her long red hair splayed across her pillow—it was too beguiling. But twenty-eight-year-old, engaged Silas didn't have the luxury of giving in to temptation. I'd drawn a line, and I had to stay far, far above it.

I held my breath as I tiptoed out of the room. When the door was finally closed behind me, then and only then did I exhale.

Once in my own bed, I picked up my phone to check the time. 12:56 am. There was a text.

> Christy: How's it going? All settled in?

She'd sent it over an hour ago. Christy knew I wasn't a night owl, and we'd said our goodnight's earlier. She must've been feeling insecure. I doubted she was still up, but I wanted there to be a text for her when she woke up.

> Me: Hey. Rough night. Anna had a night terror.

I was about to set the phone down when her typing indicator started moving.

> Christy: Poor thing. Is she okay now?

> Me: Yeah. She's snoring away.

> Christy: Good. I'll talk to you tomorrow?

> Me: You bet. G'night.

Before pressing send, I quickly added...

> Me: I love you.

> Christy: Love you 2.

I set my alarm and laid the phone on the wicker chair next to the wall. Then I flopped back on my pillow and stared into the darkness. There were no doubts left.

God wouldn't put me in a situation where I'd end up in bed with the woman I'd loved my entire life. No. This was the work of someone completely wily. Someone who had endless time on their hands to cook up mischief.

The only being beyond this world who would find pleasure in torturing her sibling like this was Sophie.

nine

CLEMENTINE

I stood in front of the coffee pot, trying to force my eyes to stay open. At some point in the night, Silas had managed to get back to his own bed. But I'd conked out next to Anna and hadn't woken up until the alarm went off on my phone. My neck hurt from sleeping with only the corner of a pillow. It had taken all my energy to brush my teeth. I didn't have the motivation to even put on mascara. Or deodorant. Or clean clothes. Was it normal to be this tired after a bad night's sleep?

I glimpsed at my Apple Watch. "Anna," I called. "Twenty minutes."

My phone dinged on the counter and I groaned. Freaking Billy would not leave me alone.

> Billy: How's my girl today?
>
> Billy: Happy Wednesday, Sunshine. :-)
>
> Billy: Hello?

> Billy: C'mon, Lemon. You know we're meant to be. We always get back together. It's fate. Don't fight it, baby.

My molars clamped down. We'd broken up probably five times when we were younger. But we weren't kids anymore. I swear, Billy could sweet-talk a kid out of their Halloween candy. He did it to his nurses and patients all the time. And I was sick at how many times he'd done it to me.

I was about to pick up my phone and give him a piece of my mind when a noise made me jump. Oh, it was the side door entrance from the carport.

Silas came in fully dressed—in a pair of wranglers, work boots, and a long-sleeved, navy blue, button-down shirt. His hair was wet with product and he held my massive carpet cleaner in his arms. After worrying all morning that I was wrong, and that I really did need to wake him up every hour, it was a relief to see him alive and well. I hadn't even known he'd left. It took me a second to realize where he'd been.

"You drove to the studio?" I pursed my lips. "You didn't need to do that."

Silas wiped his feet on the doormat and put the cleaner down. "It was the least I could do," he said and I swear if he'd been wearing a cowboy hat he would've tipped it at me. He slid his foot into the boot jack and popped one shoe off and then the other. Then he rolled the machine into the living room.

While he was putting it away, I poured the steaming drink into my favorite mug. Sophie had given it to me. It was white with thin black lines forming a trendy arrow with three simple words underneath: You're My People. Once I'd added an adequate amount of cream and sugar, I wrapped my fingers around the toasty cup and closed my eyes, letting the aroma waft up my nostrils.

My eyes fluttered open to find Silas standing right in front of me. Less than a foot away.

My heart thunked hard against my ribs. "Geez. Are you trying to give me a heart attack?"

His gray eyes were particularly piercing this morning up against that dark shirt. He squatted down to eye level and narrowed them at me. "Do you really think you should be drinking that?" His tone held a rebuke.

My jaw dropped, and I snapped it shut. Had he been possessed? By my mother? She was always on my case about drinking too much caffeine.

"Excuse me? What is your deal? You don't go shaming a grown woman out of her Liquid Energy. Some of us need it to get through the day." I took a sip and sighed extra loud just to annoy him.

He didn't laugh—just intensified his disapproving stare. I fought the urge to squirm. He folded his arms across his chest. "It's bad for your adrenals."

I took another sip and wiggled my eyebrows, hoping to lighten his mood.

He shook his head, his lips pursed. Then he grabbed a mug and poured himself a cup. My mouth parted.

"Hypocrite much?" I scoffed. But I was kind of confused. He could drink coffee, but I wasn't supposed to?

"I'll quit if you do." He lifted his brows like he hoped I'd take him up on it.

"It's just coffee." I took another long sip.

He lifted the cup to his lips and swallowed, but his expression was...disappointed? Frustrated? Annoyed? Silas was confusing me already, and the day had barely begun.

Anna bounded into the room. "I think I forgot to pack socks."

"You can borrow some of mine."

She flitted back out.

I studied Silas over my mug. "How'd you get into the studio?" I hadn't told him the code.

"Peyton?"

My eyes went wide. "What time did you wake up?" She taught a five a.m. HIIT class, but she was gone by six fifteen. It was coming up on eight and he was just getting back? It shouldn't have taken Silas more than ten minutes to clean the spot from last night.

He shrugged. "I had some errands to run after."

My mug was empty. I could feel the octane hitting my bloodstream, but I had to have perfect cognition to lead a barre class. Another cup should do it. I reached for the pot.

Si stepped between me and it and pulled the mug out of my hand. "Why don't we get some real food into you?"

"I'll eat a protein bar on the way." I put my hands on my hips. "Now, can I please get to the coffee?"

"That's not real food. You go get ready. I'll make you something." And then he actually had the nerve to shoo me out of the kitchen to my room.

First of all, how did he know I wasn't ready? I sniffed my armpits, wondering if I smelled. And second, what kind of man liked to cook unless he was getting paid to do it? But I was curious enough—and hungry enough—that I obeyed.

The caffeine was hitting me full throttle now. A little bounce came into my step. Maybe Silas was right. Maybe I didn't need that second cup.

"Fifteen minutes," I reminded Anna when I walked by. I went into my room and shut the door.

Ten minutes later, I walked into the kitchen, teeth brushed, sporting a fresh layer of mascara, my hair pulled into a messy bun, wearing my favorite navy blue leggings and a gray, sleeveless, form-fitting top that said *Meet Me at the Barre*. I didn't know what Silas had cooked up but it smelled amazing. He was bent down, folding something. When he heard me walk in, he glanced over and his eyes widened—completely vulnerable for a split second—and I bit back a smile. He thought I looked pretty today.

A flush crept across his cheeks, and his eyes skittered away.

He handed me something wrapped in aluminum foil, his arm rigid and outstretched.

I grinned. I couldn't help it. Someone other than my momma had made food just for me. I couldn't remember the last time that happened. Certainly not the entire time I was with Billy.

"What is it?" I asked.

"Just scrambled eggs and fried ham between two pieces of toast. Nothing fancy."

"I think that's called a sandwich." I teased, hoping to get a smile before I left.

"Sure," he said, completely blank.

Anna walked out in a pair of gray leggings, a bright green henley, and fashionable leather-sheepskin slippers.

Silas's eyes bugged, and a vein bulged in his forehead. "No. Uh uh. Absolutely not. You are not leaving the house like that."

Anna's eyes widened, and she glanced at me for help.

I waved at her adorable outfit. "What're you talking about? This is how she always dresses."

"She's wearing *mascara*," he said like she'd committed the unpardonable sin.

Anna caved in on herself a little.

I shook my head and waved for her to stand tall. "And your point?"

He threw his hands up. "She's way too young for that."

I snorted and rolled my eyes. "Please. My momma bought me my first tube for my twelfth birthday."

Anna straightened and lifted her chin. "Momma let me wear it."

He leaned against the counter and rubbed the back of his neck. "She did?"

We both nodded.

I pulled my purse strap over my shoulder. "She's starting high school this fall, Si."

He pushed a hand through the front of his hair and left it there. "Sorry. You're just...you're too beautiful." He sounded defeated. "It makes you look way older. Like waaaay older."

Anna stood up really straight now, radiant.

I patted him on the shoulder. "If it makes you feel any better, Holden almost had an aneurysm the first time he saw her with makeup on."

I swiped my phone off the counter and said to Anna, "You ready?"

"Yup." She smiled, her backpack over her shoulders.

Si handed her an identical scrambled egg sandwich. She pushed up on her tiptoes and kissed his cheek. "Thanks." Then she disappeared outside.

"Oh," He rubbed his forehead, still looking a little sideswiped by Anna's glow-up. "I fixed the tension on your inversion table."

My hand pressed against my heart, and I almost went to hug him. But he was clearly struggling this morning. With everything. So I just said, "Thank you, friend." It seemed completely inadequate after months of trying to fix it myself. Carpet cleaning, cooking yummy food, fixing broken things...I had to step it up.

His eyebrow lifted. "I'll be at the ranch if you need anything."

"I won't. Have fun." I smiled and gave him the peace sign as I opened the door. He responded with a half-hearted wave and a typical Silas grimace. I pulled the door shut behind me.

Anna and I had a pact anytime we drove anywhere, and it was this: Crank the radio up as loud as possible and sing at the top of our lungs. Before I had my seat belt in place, one of Anna's favorite female singers—streaming from the bluetooth off of my phone—blasted through the speakers.

Another text from Billy interrupted our jam.

> Billy: I'm coming over tonight. We need to talk this out. What time works for you?

Anna's lips pursed. "Tell him I said he's a zero, and he's going bald. And to get some rizz."

I snorted but put:

> Me: How about never o'clock. Don't bother. The chain will be on the front gate. Stop texting me.

"Eh. It'll do." She shivered. "He's such an ick."

She wasn't wrong. I still couldn't believe I'd been married to someone that terrible as long as I had.

I put my phone on Do Not Disturb before he could text again. I'd need that on when the barre class started, anyway.

With one hand I drove and with the other, I stuffed the egg and ham sandwich into my mouth. Anna bit into hers at the same time.

She moaned and her eyes grew quarter-sized. "That is bussin'."

I groaned and set mine down on the foil wrapper. Something about the texture of the eggs was repulsive. I swallowed slowly, hoping it would get better once it was no longer in my mouth. Nope. Nausea churned in my stomach. But maybe it had just been the first bite and the rest would be fine. Si had made it for me. I had to eat it. I would be ungrateful if I didn't.

I jammed the sandwich into my mouth and took another bite. I was going to get this thing down, whether my stomach liked it or not. I plugged my nose as I chewed. Daddy had taught me that trick when Momma made me eat collard greens. Ticked Momma off, but I got them down.

Anna sniffed the air, searching for a bad smell.

My gut revolted at my attempt to overpower it, twisting and contracting in hard, powerful waves. Okay. That was stupid. I shouldn't have forced it. I set the sandwich back in the foil and balled it up, done.

"Lemon?" Anna whined. "I'm gonna be late."

I'd slowed to a crawl without realizing it. I punched the gas and focused on taking some deep breaths. My stomach was a rolling boil. I scanned the fence lines to distract myself.

It worked for a moment. But only because of the miracle spread out before me.

Like another little gift, it became glaringly apparent that Silas's "errands" weren't errands at all. He'd spent the morning fixing all the broken wire on the two fence lines straddling the driveway. Every last foot. My mind whirled along with my stomach. Sweat drops rolled down my cleavage. I turned the A/C up full blast.

"That's freezing," Anna shrieked over the diva's declaration of revenge. The overpowering base seemed to egg my stomach on.

I smacked the volume knob off and focused on breathing. Inhale and exhale. Four in, eight out. Just like we taught in our flexibility class.

Hot tears formed, and I wasn't sure if it was the overwhelming gratitude about the fences or the vomit that threatened to erupt into my esophagus like an angry volcano. *Distract. Distract. Distract.*

How did Silas know where the extra wire was? Or the crimps? Or the fencing tool?

But it was no use. My stomach cramped so hard it stole my breath.

I slammed the brake and put the truck in park. The seat

belt cut into my stomach. That did it. I barely had the door open before I projectile vomited out into the grass.

"Aunt Lemon?" Anna rubbed my back.

Her touch felt like an oven on broil. I stepped out of the truck and stood, fanning my shirt in and out. The cool morning air rolled over me. Maybe if I stood really still. Nope. I bent over and wretched again. And again—until there was nothing left.

Anna got out and walked around the truck. "Do you want me to call Uncle Si?"

"No." I shook my head. "I'm better. Let's get you to school." It had eased up a bit.

Anna didn't move, her eyebrows drawn together. "You're really pale. Are you sure you don't want me to get him to take me to school?"

I shook my head, adamant. "No. I'm ok. Let's go." I slipped back inside and shut the door, ending the discussion.

Once we were on the road again, I rummaged through my bag.

"What're you looking for?" Anna took it from me so I could focus on the road.

"A stick of gum." Growing up, Momma always made me peppermint tea when I had a touchy stomach. Spearmint gum was the best I could do at the moment.

Anna quickly found a piece and unwrapped it for me. I popped it in my mouth and chewed.

"You don't look so good," Anna said, her brows furrowed. She pulled out her phone.

"Who are you texting?"

"Uncle Si."

I put my hand on her phone. "Please, don't. I think it was the sandwich, and I don't want to hurt his feelings."

Understanding washed over her face. "Ah, got it." She nodded. "It'll be our secret."

ten

SILAS

"You've agreed to the job and signed the contract and now you're telling me you can't be here the entire summer to help get ready for the school year?" Mrs. Serafin, the principal I'd be working under, sounded like she might head straight to the school board office and petition for them to fire me as soon as we hung up.

I pulled onto the paved driveway of my family's ranch. "Look, I understand your frustration—"

"I don't actually think you do."

I may have been twenty years her junior, but I did understand the ethics of hard work. I'd grown up on a ranch, for crying out loud. I wasn't trying to get out of doing the work. From the beginning, I'd gotten the impression that either she resented that I'd gotten the position as young as I was, or she didn't believe I was capable of doing it.

I sighed and didn't care if she heard it. "If I don't stay here, the court will decide what to do with my niece and it might not turn out well." I repeated for the third time.

"So you've said."

I'd tried not to go the manipulation route but she left

me no choice. "Do you have kids, Mrs. Serafin?" I knew she did. A son in college and a daughter who was a sophomore in high school. Mrs. Serafin was beloved by all the people in Laramie and I was not ignorant to the amount of pull she had with the school board. I needed her on my side.

She said nothing.

I pushed on. "What if something happened to you? Wouldn't you want them to be taken care of? Sophie was my *twin*. I'm responsible for Anna now. I just have to fulfill the stipulations in the will and then I'll be back. And I'll be the hardest-working assistant principal you've ever had." The truck rolled over the asphalt easily, reminding me how bad Clem's driveway was.

Mrs. Serafin exhaled so hard it hurt my ear. "I have heard that you're a hard worker." She conceded thankfully.

"I admit, this is not the summer I had planned, either. But there's got to be a way we can make this work." I pulled up in front of the stock office and stepped out of the truck. The air was way too sticky for early May. I fanned the collar of my shirt. Man, I missed Wyoming. No humidity and hardly any bugs.

Just then, a call came through from Holden. I sent it to voicemail. He'd be down here any minute. He could talk to me in person.

"You're right. I apologize, Mr. Dupree. I could adjust some of my responsibilities and give them to you. Would you be able to go over the academic performance reports from this school year and present them to me over Zoom?"

I pounded my thigh in excitement. "You bet. Just tell me when you want it ready."

"We could have a check in next Thursday morning at nine?"

I nodded vigorously, even though she couldn't see. "That's

perfect. Yes. I can absolutely do that. And please send me as much work as you can. I have the time."

"Will do. But, Mr. Dupree?"

"Yes, ma'am."

"It would be really helpful if you could be here on July fifteenth for teacher training."

A text came through from Holden. I swore at him in my head and ignored it.

July fifteenth was twenty-four days before the ninety-day stipulation, and I may as well be upfront with her now. "I already know I won't be able to be there."

Her voice went shrill. "The lawyer won't let you leave even for that long?"

I rubbed my forehead, worried she was going to take back her decision to work with me. "Ninety consecutive nights under the same roof." I quoted Sophie's letter verbatim.

"Fine." She sounded completely put out. "But you have to be back here by August third. No excuses."

It was four days shy of the three-month stipulation period, but I'd pushed Mrs. Serafin as far as I could for one day. I'd worry about the rest later. Staying in Seddledowne for the entire summer was a once-in-an-adulthood thing. If I could just make it through, my career would stay on track. I did not want to step back down to a teacher position. I loved the kids, but I was tired of living paycheck to paycheck. It was time to put some money in savings and build a nest egg. Especially with Christy pushing for marriage.

So I made a promise I didn't know if I could keep. "I'll be there. You can count on it."

As soon as I pressed end, Christy texted. I swear she could sense anytime I had the slightest break. I smiled as I read her text.

> Christy: When are we FaceTiming tonight? I'm going to the gym right after school, but I should be done by 4:30. Is that too late?

She was two hours behind so that would be six-thirty Virginia time.

> Me: Could we do it a little later? Like seven your time? I promised Anna I'd watch a movie with her.

She responded immediately.

> Christy: Is Lemon watching it too?

I blew out my breath. I hadn't been here a day, and the questioning had already begun.

> Me: I don't know what her plans are for tonight.

> Christy: That only gives us an hour to talk.

That was true. But we texted back and forth every chance we got. Shouldn't an hour on FaceTime be enough? I took a deep breath and reminded myself that if she'd been living with her first crush, I'd be super insecure, too. Clem and Anna could watch the movie without me tonight.

Just then, my brother texted again.

> Holden: Stop playing footsies with Lemon and call me, doofus.

I texted Christy back.

> Me: No worries. I'll make it work. Talk to you then.

Then I dialed my butthead brother. "What do you want?"

"Why didn't you answer the phone, huh? You and Lemon sucking face?" I could feel his eyebrows wiggling through the phone. "Got the Do Not Disturb sign up?"

"No, moron." I snorted. "I'm at the stock office waiting on your butt to get here."

"Aw, is poor Si baby so sad because he had to leave his woman and do some real work?" he asked, like he was talking to a newborn.

I suppressed a laugh. He didn't need encouragement. "Do you want me to hang up on you? Why aren't you here yet?"

"Just waiting on Dad. He had to run to the feed store and grab a bag of grain." His voice dropped low. "Dude. Did you hear what happened at the high school this morning?"

I punched the code to unlock the office door. 1990. The year my parents were married. While I waited, I might as well get the computer on and pull out the needles and dewormer. "What high school?"

"Seddledowne." His tone was exasperated. "Dude, you've got to start checking the news. Or at least Facebook."

"Why do I need to do that when you'll just tell me?" I'd stopped watching the news years ago. It was depressing. And Facebook offered nothing but a temptation to stalk Clem. I'd learned long ago that being okay without Clem meant cutting her out of my life completely. Even on the internet.

"Ridiculous. Fine. Whatever." He grumbled. "You are not going to believe this. Apparently, the principal and the assistant principal were having an affair. They embezzled $250,000 in overtime pay from their teachers, maintenance funds, and from the student activities fund. Then they took off for Europe."

My jaw went slack. But then I snapped it shut. "You actually had me for a minute. Good one, Holdie. I think you need to hand in your library card." He'd been reading too much fiction.

"Okay, little boy. Don't believe me?" He sounded insulted, and I thought for a second he might be telling the truth. But, nah. It was too fantastical. Stuff like that didn't happen in Seddledowne.

Just then, a text dinged on my phone. He'd sent me an article in *The Washington Post*.

"Principal and Assistant Principal Charged With Embezzlement In Small Virginia Town. Manhunt Ongoing."

"Whoa." I sat down and propped my boots up on the desk.

"Yeah. You go ahead and let me know if you think it's real now."

"Shhh. I'm reading." It was only four sentences long because what Holden had told me was about all the info they had so far. "That is actually insane," I said when I finished. "That might be the first time we've made the Washington Post."

"Bro. You know what this means, don't you?" Holden's voice was over-the-top excited, like he was about to tell me we'd won tickets to the SuperBowl.

"No?"

"Seddledowne School District is going to be hiring."

"Um. Obviously."

"Si, you can live happily ever after with Lemon *and* have your dream job. You could stay in Seddledowne, and the three of you could be a family. Just think what this could mean for Anna." Holden was always looking for a way to capitalize on a situation. I couldn't believe he'd somehow thought this was going to benefit me or Anna. "Mom will be so happy you're living here, she won't know what to do. And you could help Dad with the ranch. And Firefly Fields would be yours and Clem's. Your own land, man. Think about it. You could get your own herd like you've always wanted."

Dad didn't need my help. He had Uncle Troy and two ranch hands. And I wasn't going to begin lusting over Firefly Fields. That would lead nowhere good.

I shook my head. "Earth to Holden. Life never works out that easily. This isn't a freaking Disney movie."

"Life *is* like that." I could hear the shrug in his voice. "If you're on the right path."

I snorted. "Then I haven't been on the right path my entire twenty-eight years."

"Exactly," he said in a Napoleon Dynamite voice. "And now you are. I'm telling you, our sister was a freaking genius."

If I could've rolled my eyes harder, I would've. But I still had a dull headache from the concussion. And this conversation was getting on my nerves.

"Clem and Billy are probably getting back together," I said, hoping to shut Holden up.

Yeah, I'd seen the texts Billy sent to Clem this morning. They were right there in my face when I grabbed a cup of coffee. And she hadn't shut him down in any way. Seemed like she wanted him to keep texting her. It was just a matter of time before he wormed his way back in.

"Uh, I know Lemon," Holden said, like I didn't. "She'd never go back with someone who cheated on her."

I shook my head and clamped my jaw. "You don't know the hold he has on her."

"Give her a little credit, man." He sounded annoyed. "Lemon is tougher than you think. She destroyed his ride."

I set my cowboy hat on the desk. "Temporary insanity.

"She's tougher than she used to be. You don't know her anymore."

I went rigid. "What does that mean?" Was he accusing me of abandoning her? Had Sophie put this in his head? She'd ripped into me more than once for not keeping up my friendship with Clem.

"Exactly what I said. You haven't been around her in years. She's been through stuff." Holden didn't know when to give up. "Si, I didn't call to argue with you. Just hear me out. You give things a little more time with Clem. Get settled in. Make her dinner all summer. Make friends with Miss Lisa. Bale her hay." The longer he went on, the more animated he became. "Compared to Billy, you'll look like Darcy from Pride and Prejudice. Women love that stuff. She will fall into your arms."

I scratched my jaw. "You done yet?" I could've bickered with him. Could've brought up Christy. But I didn't have to convince Holden.

It wasn't that I didn't want Clem to fall in love with me. That's all I'd ever wanted. I'd waited years for that. But loving Clem and not being loved back was soul-sucking. I was finally in a good place. A safe place. In the past couple of years, I'd finally hit a point where I wasn't so anxious that I couldn't eat.

I was happy too. And not the happy you fake for other people. The real kind. I'd be sitting with some buddies from my college days, talking about life, and suddenly I was bellylaughing. Shaking because I couldn't hold it in. There were years after Clem where I never laughed at all. The ache was so intense. I'd finally pulled myself out of that hole. And I would not go back to that dark place. If I entertained a future with her, and she chose Billy, it would break me all over again. And this time it wouldn't just be my heart she decimated. It would be Anna's too.

Holden didn't get it. He never would.

"Dad's here. See you in a few minutes." He paused and then said, "Don't outright dismiss it. Just promise me you'll think about applying. You know they struggle to get people to move here."

That was true. They hadn't been able to hire a Spanish teacher this school year. So even though Anna went to Spanish class every day, she was taught by a teacher from another school over Zoom.

I grunted a goodbye. Then I got back up and pulled the dewormer from the fridge.

But my mind was racing. It baffled me that people existed who only cared about themselves. People who would steal money from their co-workers and probably their friends. Without even thinking, I pulled the Seddledowne School District careers page up. There was nothing posted for the positions yet, but the teachers' salaries were listed and it wasn't anything to shake a stick at. Better than in Laramie. And they had decent insurance, retirement, and loan forgiveness— which would come in handy with the student debt left over from my master's degree program.

My brain jolted, like a wake up call.

Had I just thought the words *would come in handy*? Like I was actually contemplating this? I swore at myself. What a waste of time. I already had a job. And a girl.

Holden needed to get out of my head.

eleven

CLEMENTINE

By the time I made it to the studio, I knew I wasn't teaching anything. I had a stomach bug. I swiped open the app that clients used to sign up for classes and checked to see if any of my instructors were coming to barre. I tried Peyton first.

> Me: Any chance you can teach the 9 a.m. class? Not feeling great. Sorry for the late notice.

> Peyton: Sure thing. Pulling in now.

I glanced out the glass door to see her parking and quickly grabbed a mask from under the counter.

When she came through the door, bouncy little Peyton crossed her pointer fingers, aiming them at me. "Stay away." She giggled.

Peyton was a brunette with the body of a Dallas Cowboys cheerleader and the face of a makeup model. I didn't know how she'd made it twenty-four years without getting married. She was so gorgeous. Three years ago she'd been crowned Miss

Seddledowne and I couldn't think of another person in this town more fitting.

She dropped her hands and smiled. "Just kidding, you okay?"

"I think it's a stomach bug. I'm going home to rest. If you can cover barre, I can probably get Crystal and Blair to cover the others."

"Yeah. No problem." Then her right brow cocked mischievously. "If you'll do me a favor?"

I didn't feel well enough to do anything but I really needed her to teach. "Okay?"

She slapped her hands on top of the counter and leaned toward me, not caring that I would probably give her the pukes. "Tell me who the delicious Adonis was, that was in here cleaning carpets this morning?" Her eyes sparkled like she hadn't been dating Braxton seriously for the last six months.

Delicious Adonis? How much coffee had she drunk this morning?

I shook my head, relieved it wasn't a real favor. "Oh, that's Silas. Sophie's twin."

"Sophie's twin?" She tilted her head and thought for a second. "I could see that, I guess."

Sometimes it threw people off that Soph and Silas were twins. He had dark hair, and she'd had blond. She was loud, boisterous, and ready to fight at the drop of a hat, where Silas was...Silas. They may have shared fifty percent of their DNA, but they couldn't have been more different. Except for the eyes. Those were the same.

Peyton's nose scrunched. "Isn't that the one who lives in Wyoming?"

"Yeah. He's just home for a couple of months while we try to figure out what's going to be best for Anna." I could see the next question coming, so I went ahead and answered it. "We have joint custody, I guess." I chewed my lip. "So weird to say that out loud." My stomach had calmed down a bit now that Peyton had taken my mind off of it. But my knees trembled. I had to get some food in me. Food that I could actually keep down.

Peyton's face twisted in confusion. "You have joint custody and you're not married? Are you adopting her?"

"I'm not sure exactly how it's all going to work yet." I could already tell she was going to keep asking until I told her everything. So I gave her a quick rundown of what I did know.

Her eyes bugged. "That hottie is living with you for the next three months?"

Hottie? "It's just Silas." I snorted and reached for the mouse, so I could shut the computer off. "I've known him for forever. And he's got a girlfriend back in Wyoming."

"Good Lord." She fanned herself. "I'll tell you right now if he was living with me for three months, the first item on the agenda would be to break them up. Trick him into walking in on you in the shower. Go swimming in your cutest little bikini. You've got a hot body, Lem." She held her hands up in a *just sayin'* manner. "Touch him every time you get the chance. Heck, go crawl in bed next to him and blame it on sleepwalking."

If I told her I'd been in the same bed with him last night, she would've lost her mind.

She laughed and shrugged. "Don't tell Braxton I said any of that. Whew, I'm a sucker for the strong, silent type."

I was dumbfounded. To see one of the prettiest girls I knew fawning over Silas was...eye-opening. Sure Silas had a nice smile—I'd figured that out last night. And he'd finally stopped brushing his wavy hair, which had made it the texture of a used-up scouring pad. But she was talking about him the way my momma talked about Harrison Ford or Brad Pitt. Like she'd throw away every Christian virtue she'd ever been taught if she got a chance at him.

"You need to get ahold of yourself," I said. "He's just a guy."

She pretend slapped me. "Wake up, Lemon. He is not *just* anything. He's a ten, and he's got that deep, husky voice. Seddledowne doesn't normally breed men like that."

"If you say so."

"I definitely say so." She raised her brows up and down. "So? Are you gonna do it?"

"Do what?"

Her eyes widened, annoyed. "Break him and his girlfriend up?"

I pursed my lips. "No, I'm definitely not going to do that. Besides, I'm married, remember?"

She rolled her eyes. "*Please*. Everybody knows you and Billy split up."

My stomach dropped to my knees. As far as I knew, no one knew—except the Duprees and Momma. "Excuse me, what?"

She shrugged. "Yeah, he's going around telling everyone that you're a terrible wife. You haven't had sex with him in a year. You can't even make boxed macaroni without ruining it."

Honestly, at that moment, I wished those things were true. I wished I hadn't spent hours making him Food Network worthy dinners, ironing his shirts, working my butt off only so he could spend all our money.

But my biggest wish...

That I hadn't given him his way anytime he wanted it. I'd actually been stupid enough to believe if I kept him happy in the bedroom, he'd never go looking somewhere else. Even when I was flat out exhausted, I let him have his way. Every single time. Billy had drilled it into my head—that's what a good wife does. And I'd been so young and dumb when we got married that I'd believed him.

And he'd cheated on me anyway.

I was sick inside and not from the nausea.

My heart banged against my ribs and I felt light-headed. I held onto the counter. Why couldn't I stop blinking? "Where did you hear that?"

"Like three different people. Seriously, everyone's talking about it."

"Unbelievable." I bit my bottom lip and shook my head. "Funny how he won't stop blowing up my phone, begging me to let him come home. And I like how he left out the part where I slashed all his tires when I caught him cheating."

She gasped, then hooted and offered me a high five.

I left her hanging and crossed my arms. "So the whole town has been gossiping behind my back and you never thought to say anything? Or ask my side of the story?" I was probably more hurt about that than I was about Billy lying to everyone. I expected that from Billy. But Peyton? We'd been friends since before I opened the studio and spent countless hours working out together.

She finally noticed I was a person with feelings and came around the counter to hug me. "Oh, Lemon, I'm so sorry. I didn't say anything because I didn't want to upset you." She squeezed me tighter. "Don't worry about it. Nobody believes him. It's *Billy* after all," she said, like he was the biggest dimwit in the county. Had everyone known my husband was a narcissistic douche but me?

Sophie had always known. And Daddy. But he hadn't been around in the last three years to remind me every time I saw him. Oh, what my daddy would've done if he were here. My tire-slashing escapade would've looked like child's play.

I stood there as stiff as Silas, outta my mind, incensed, while Peyton laid her head on my shoulder, rubbing my back. I wished so bad that Sophie was here. She'd post the naked pictures on Facebook, Instagram, and TikTok. And then text them to every single person she knew. And she wouldn't care about the consequences.

But I would never do that.

Because while it might feel vindicating to humiliate Billy, it would also humiliate me.

Slashing Billy's tires would probably be the most fearless thing I ever did. They could etch it on my headstone if they wanted. But it wasn't who I was. It was something that I'd done. Once. On the worst day of my life.

I slunk out from under her hug. "I gotta go. I don't want to get y'all sick."

"Lemon," Peyton cried, but I didn't slow down. I stepped around her, ripped my mask off and threw it in the trash.

"C'mon, Lem. Don't be mad."

I pulled my phone out of my purse, my hands practically convulsing. As soon as I got in the truck, I was going to give Billy a piece of my mind.

One more step toward the door, my legs gave out and everything went black.

twelve

SILAS

I sat up in the saddle and straightened my back, trying to get the ache to go away.

"Dad," I hollered. "I really need to get back to Clem's and get some of that fence line cleaned up."

Dad had said we were tagging eleven calves but once we got going, he'd decided to brand them as well. I usually didn't mind working calves. But Dad had me on Fred, our old quarter horse, ready to rope any calves that got too testy or tried to make a break for it. So far, I'd had to rope just two. Dad and Holden were doing the dirty work, wrangling the calves to the ground, fighting their hooves off long enough to pierce the cattle tag into their ears. Searing their skin with the DR brand. That was the fun stuff.

"I have to get back to Clem's," Holden said in a high-pitched voice. "She's got you doing chores to earn your keep?"

"Shut it, Holey. She hasn't asked me to do a single thing." I growled. "Looks like Billy hasn't lifted a finger over there in years. I'm just being helpful."

He shook his head. "You've been there less than twenty-four hours and you're already whipped."

I was going to deck him if he didn't shut up.

Mom stood in the middle of the corral, keeping everything organized in a notebook. She'd type it into the spreadsheet when we were done. She raised an eyebrow. "Should we have a work day over there?"

"I'm outta here Sunday," Holden said, kneeling into a brown and white Hereford just enough to keep it pinned to the ground.

Dad slipped the ear tag applicator on and snapped it shut. The calf kicked and Dad and Holden jumped out of the way, letting it run back to its momma.

Just then, my phone rang. I pulled it out of my back pocket. I didn't usually answer numbers I didn't recognize, but it looked local and I wasn't doing anything else at the moment.

"Hello?"

"Is this Silas?" The voice on the other end was female and southern.

"Yeah. Who's this?"

"Peyton. We met this morning." She giggled.

Why was she calling and how had she gotten my number? "Okay."

"I'm calling because Lemon fainted, and she needs you to come get her."

Before I could respond, she hung up.

"I gotta go," I said as I jumped off Fred. "Clem passed out."

Mom called after me, but I didn't take the time to stop. I could update her later. Peyton had failed to include a lot of key information. If Lemon had regained consciousness. If they'd called for an ambulance. If they were at the studio or the hospital. I called back, but it went to voicemail.

Sixty seconds later, I had the gas pedal all the way to the floor and the truck still wasn't breaking fifty-five. From my parents' ranch to The Downward Dog was the longest eleven minutes of my life as I ran every worst-case scenario through my head.

So when I pulled into the parking lot and the only two vehicles were Clem's and what had to be Peyton's, and I saw no ambulance or emergency people of any kind, I headed into The Downward Dog full-on broody. The main room was dark and empty. I jogged down the hall to the back room.

Clem was lying on a yoga mat with an orange bolster under her head. Peyton, who I'd met this morning, was next to her.

Clem saw me first and smiled. "Hey." She sat up slowly, looking pale and weak.

Peyton stood. For the second time today, she eyed me like she was twelve and I was a member of her favorite boy band. It was weird. And annoying.

I walked over to Clem and squatted, resting my forearms on my thighs, studying her beautiful face. "What happened?"

Her green eyes were bleary, and she looked like she could take a four-hour nap. I wanted to reach out and touch her pale cheek, feel if she was cold. But I restrained myself.

"Can we talk about it in the truck?" She tried to get up. I put a hand on her shoulder, stopping her. She wasn't walking anywhere.

I scrutinized Peyton, expectantly. She shrugged, pursing her lips. "We were just chatting about Billy. She got really upset and tried to walk to the door and bam!" She smacked her hands together. "That's all she wrote."

"Like blacked out all the way?" I asked, trying and failing to mask my irritation.

"Like totally." She whirled her head around to mimic what Clem looked like on her way down.

I stared at her, incensed at her lack of concern for her friend. "Did you catch her?"

"No, sorry. I was in shock. But the floor is padded, so she's probably fine."

My face contorted. I couldn't stop it.

"I am fine." Clem tried sitting up again.

I shook my head. "You passed out. That's the opposite of fine."

My head cocked at Peyton. "And it didn't occur to you to, I don't know, maybe call for an ambulance?" I wasn't even trying now.

Peyton's head snapped back a little, and all the twinkle left her eyes. Fine by me. Her doe-eyed fangirling had gotten on my nerves, anyway.

"I told her not to," Clem said quietly. "Can we just go?"

I wanted to ask her why on earth she would do that. But the vulnerability in her expression told me that she didn't want to discuss this in front of Peyton.

When I scooped Clem up in my arms, she gasped. Peyton did too. I stepped past Peyton and maneuvered Clem out of the room.

"You don't need to carry me," Clem protested.

"Yes, I do." I strode down the hall and across the big room.

"Let me get her bag," Peyton said, running behind us. She grabbed Clem's purse from behind the counter and laid it in her lap as if she'd done something really important. I leaned against the door and shoved it open with my back. I didn't head for my truck. Clem's was newer and would actually reach the speed limit, so I walked around to the passenger's side, popped the door open, and set her in the seat.

Peyton met me at the front bumper. "What should I do about the ten-thirty class? And four forty-five?"

"I don't care." Then I got in the driver's seat and drove out of the parking lot before she could run around to talk to Clem. I didn't care if it was mean. Peyton could figure it out or text Clem in an hour or two after she'd recovered.

We rode in silence for a few seconds, my teeth grinding. I had a dissertation of things I wanted to say, but none of them were nice, so I kept my mouth shut.

Clem broke the silence. "Well, I think you may have shattered Peyton's perception of you. She actually called you a delicious Adonis." She made a strangled sort of cackle sound.

I scowled at her weird laugh, and the fact that Peyton had compared me to a Greek god. And I hated it when women talked about men like they were food. I wasn't a freaking Wagyu steak.

"I think she wanted you to be the father of her future children." How could she sit here and make jokes at a time like this? My knuckles were white around the steering wheel.

She threw her hands up. "Look, I'm sorry you had to come get me. But Peyton wouldn't let me drive, and I didn't know who else to call. Momma's in Honeyville bowling."

"You think I'm mad that I had to come get you?" I pulled into the Family Dollar parking lot.

"Aren't you?"

My mind was actually blown. "No, I'm...I just..." I pounded the steering wheel. "What were you thinking?"

"What...what do you mean?" She had her back against the door as far from me as possible. Like she was afraid of me.

Really? She was still going to act like I didn't know she was pregnant? I forced myself to count to five. "Why didn't you let Peyton call for the ambulance?"

She crossed her arms and lifted her chin like a defiant toddler. "Because I didn't want Billy all up in my business. And the town doctor would definitely find out about something like that."

I leaned my head against the steering wheel and focused on getting my temper under control. I hadn't planned on pushing Clem about the baby—it was her business, not mine—but she wasn't thinking straight. She wasn't thinking at all. She was in denial and I had to break her out of it. Her life, and the baby's, depended on it. Even if that meant Billy found out.

I glanced down, and that's when I noticed the sandwiches I'd made for Anna and Clem, barely touched.

I threw my hands up. "No wonder you fainted? Why didn't you eat the breakfast I made you?"

Clem pressed on her temples. It took her a few seconds to admit, "I took one bite and puked. I think it was the eggs. They hit my stomach wrong. I'm so sorry."

She was probably super dehydrated.

I pulled back onto the road.

"Home is the other way," Clem said, like I didn't grow up here and drive these roads every day of my childhood.

"We're getting some food in you. What sounds good right now?"

She bit her lip. "One of your quesadillas."

I'd make her those five times a day if she could keep them down. "Okay. When we get back. But we need to run an errand first and you're going to need a little energy. What can I get you right now?"

She seemed ashamed to admit, "A burger and fries."

"Done."

As soon as we tackled the immediate problem, we would tackle the bigger one. I could be patient a little longer. I drove toward McDonald's.

Ten minutes later, her hands still shaky, she lifted a Quarter Pounder to her lips. I was going to make sure she ate the fries and drank the strawberry milkshake, too. And the entire large-sized cup of ice water. Christy had texted me to find out when we were FaceTiming. I responded and then checked my email while Clem got some fuel into her system.

There was one from Mrs. Serafin, with an attachment of all the reports she wanted me to go through. I'd have to open it back at the house.

When Clem was almost done with the burger, I turned to face her. "Hey."

She glanced up at me, her mouth full of fries.

"You don't have to keep pretending, okay? I *know*." I said softly, but firmly.

She scowled and her nose scrunched. "You *know*?" She wiggled her fingers like I was the one being cryptic.

I threw my hands up. "That you're pregnant."

Her face blanched, aghast. "I'm not pregnant." Crap. She hadn't realized it yet. Man, I was such a prick.

I softened. "I think you are."

She scowled, not convinced.

"You love fruit, but suddenly it sounds gross. You couldn't eat a perfectly good protein bar. You almost passed out last night. You did pass out today. And you hate—absolutely *loathe*—mushrooms." I let out a shaky laugh. "So I kind of hope you are or maybe something worse is going on."

Her eyes grew bigger, and she looked like she'd swallowed a fuzzy caterpillar. "No!" She pulled up the calendar on her phone and sat there for a minute, staring at it. The blood drained from her face for the second time today. Her shoulders slumped and her chest rose and fell like she couldn't catch her breath. A hand went over her mouth and she squeezed her eyes shut.

She slipped her hands under her thighs and sat there for a long time. I didn't know if she was praying or just trying to process it. I wanted to touch her shoulder, but she was so rigid I wasn't sure she'd let me.

I leaned back against the headrest, staring at the ceiling, angry at the world.

Of course Clementine would be pregnant. I mean, it could've happened anytime in the past eight years of her marriage. But no. It happened right when I had to live with her. Karma may as well have put a big fat welcome sign on her front door. "Hey there. Glad you're here. Jerkface Billy knocked up the love of your life and now you get to watch her have his baby. Happy you came. Make yourself at home."

She peeked at me, shame in her eyes. And it broke me. I couldn't be mad at her. Not for getting pregnant, or puking up my breakfast, or being completely reckless with her health. She looked like she had the weight of the world on her shoulders and I was the only one who could lift it.

"Clem." I opened my arms, hoping beyond hope that she would accept my offering. She dove into me, sobbing, her left cheek pressed against my chest. I willed my heart to stop betraying me. There was no way she couldn't hear how fast it was beating. Or how hard. She slid her arms around my waist so tight. So I wrapped my arms around her back and ran my fingers up and down her spine. She snuggled in even closer like she'd been touch-deprived. Man, I would've given my roping scholarship back in the day to have held her like this. That rose shampoo wafted up my nose, causing electricity to sizzle all the way to my fingertips.

It wasn't even thirty seconds before she sat up, leaning back into her own space. Fury flashed across her face. "I'm going to kill Billy."

I raised an eyebrow. Had nobody given her the birds and the bees talk? She was a grown woman. She had to know it took two to make a baby.

She snorted. "He always threatened to cut holes in the protection. But I never thought he'd actually do it. Seems I underestimated him in more ways than one."

"Wh—are you serious? You think he did this deliberately?" I wiped a hand over my face. "You didn't want a baby?"

"No." She shook her head. "I mean, I want kids. A bunch of them. It's just...Sophie was sick and things with Billy..." She chewed her lip. "I didn't think we were ready."

I threw my hands up. "You've been married eight years.

Most women would've had three babies by now." It was none of my business. I should've shut up. Besides, I was glad she hadn't had any kids. I'd been holding my breath for years, waiting for the announcement that they were expecting.

"I didn't think Billy was dad material, okay? He has a foul mouth, drinks too much, and thinks it's funny to call me names. It's like he never aged past fifteen." Her voice shook. "And my kid deserves great parents. Plural. Not a great parent and a mediocre parent." Her hands balled up in her lap, and I had to stop myself from reaching out to hold one. "Momma said she and Daddy wanted to wait a year after they got married. But the minute they said I do, she loved him so much she wanted to have his baby." She pressed her hands to her cheeks. "I kept waiting for that feeling and it never happened. Billy got his way on everything—but not for a baby. I wouldn't budge on that."

I didn't know what to say. I'd always thought she was having fertility problems. It hadn't occurred to me that she was purposely holding off. Maybe Holden was right, and she was different. Maybe she wouldn't run back to Billy after all.

"If he did that...he's even more evil than I thought," I said. "Right?"

I turned the truck back on and pulled out onto the road.

"Home is still that way," she said,pointing behind us.

I let my jaw drop open in mock surprise. "You don't say."

She rolled her eyes but laughed. "Where are we going?"

"Grocery store."

"Why? We have food at the house."

"Does any of that food sound good to you right now? Besides quesadillas?"

She shook her head. "Point taken."

I pulled into a parking stall at Food Lion. "How about this? You pay your utilities and I'll buy all the food while I'm here."

Her eyebrows drew together. "I think I'm getting the better end of the deal."

"You're not charging me rent or anything. I'm definitely getting the better end." She rolled her eyes. I offered her a handshake. "So we have a deal?"

"Fine. Deal." She slid her hand up against mine and squeezed. I tried to ignore how someone touching my hand could put butterflies in my stomach. She was the only woman who had that effect on me.

"Stay." I pointed at her, my expression stern. "I'll be right back." I returned thirty seconds later with a shopping cart that had a seat for two small children. I pulled her door open. "Your chariot awaits, m'lady."

She laughed. "You cannot be serious."

I tipped the invisible hat on my head. "Never been more serious in my life."

thirteen

CLEMENTINE

Two weeks later, while Anna was watching a show and Silas was on his nightly FaceTime marathon with Christy, I drove to Momma's on the side-by-side to return Buford for the evening. I sunk into her couch and closed my eyes. Daddy said that couch was a trap. You sit on it for two minutes and you'll wake up two hours later.

"How are things at your house?" Momma asked, sipping her sleepy time tea.

I peeked an eye open. "Fine."

She set the mug down on the saucer. She was old-fashioned like that. Still used her wedding china for every meal. "Fine? All I've got to entertain me is a basset hound and a cranky cat. You've got an attractive cowboy living in your house and a brand new daughter. Spill some tea."

I sat up and crisscrossed my legs. "It's fine. Wish Silas wasn't in his room on the phone all the time, but when he is available, he's…"

"He's what?"

The last thing I needed was Momma reading more into

this than there actually was. I shrugged. "Silas is...nothing like Billy. That's for sure."

"Meaning?"

I chewed the inside of my cheek. "He's different than he used to be."

She smiled. "Happens to the best of us."

I shook my head. "Not like that. He's confident now. Comfortable in his own skin. Not like when we were younger." All the words Peyton had used to describe him rolled through my mind. *Adonis. Delicious. Hottie. Strong, silent type. Husky. A ten.* Ever since Peyton opened her big mouth, I hadn't been able to look at him the same way. Not only that, I was struggling to reconcile this new Silas with the boy I'd grown up with. And I found myself watching him constantly when he wasn't paying attention. When he unloaded the dishwasher. When he came out of his room, freshly showered. When he sat at the kitchen table helping Anna with Algebra. That one especially. Just like the old Van Halen song, I was hot for teacher. I giggled at the euphemism. But yeah, things that would've been ordinary a few weeks before suddenly seemed significant, exciting, or dead sexy.

"Ahhh." She laughed. "I see."

My face flamed. "No, it's not like that."

She peered at me over her glasses. "I'm pretty sure it's exactly like that."

"It doesn't matter, anyway. I'm not divorced yet, and he's got a girlfriend."

"True. True. But a summer can change a lot of things."

"Even so, I'm not ready for a relationship. I'm still getting over Billy."

She took her glasses off and laid them in her lap. "Sweetie, you got over Billy a long time ago. You just didn't know it."

I cocked my head. "What do you mean?"

"Over the years, that man has broken your heart in a

hundred tiny ways. It doesn't take something huge, like an affair, to kill the love you had for him." She lifted her chin. "I say if happiness comes, you take it. Don't you waste one more second thinking you owe Billy any more of your heart."

I leaned my elbows on my knees, my chin in my hands. "You really think I'm over him?"

She shrugged. "Do you miss him now that he's gone?"

"Not a bit." I laughed a little. I hadn't. At all. "If anything, I'm happier without him."

"That's because Billy took and he took and he took until he'd stolen all the love right out of you."

I shoved my hands under my thighs. "Huh. I never thought about it that way. But I think you're right." It was freeing to realize that. I thought maybe I was numb or broken and a tidal wave of grief would hit me later. There were a few leaks of pain here and there, but nothing that couldn't be plugged by belting a sad song, or eating a bowl of chocolate peanut butter swirl ice cream, or getting a hug from Anna. Maybe shoving a knife in all his tires had been more cathartic than I realized.

Momma smiled, her eyes warm. "Mommas usually are."

I still didn't think Silas was the least bit interested in me. He couldn't even stand being around me most of the time. Even now, if I got too close, physically or emotionally, he bolted or shut down. And clearly he couldn't get enough of Christy. Their FaceTime calls lasted at least two hours every night.

I closed my eyes again, so tired. This baby was sapping all my energy.

"You've been exhausted for a while now. You should go see the doctor." I hadn't told Momma about the baby. The minute she knew, she'd want to throw a parade and tell every one of her friends. I wasn't ready to celebrate yet.

I cocked an eyebrow. "You mean Billy? No thanks."

"Go over to Honeyville. They've got some great doctors there. Dr. Torres is really good. And I think they've got a nurse practitioner now."

"I'm just tired because of Anna's night terrors." She still had them most nights. Silas and I had started tag-teaming, though. No sense in both of us losing sleep. He'd tried to take all the nights so I could rest, but I refused.

Momma's forehead wrinkled. "She's still having those?"

I nodded.

"You need to get that girl into therapy."

"We've got her on a waitlist. But it takes at least three months to get an appointment. Or four." And that was only because this was a small town. Waits in the city were way longer. I'd checked.

Buford loped in from the kitchen and howled. "Arrooooo."

"Buford," I fussed, covering my ears.

Momma scratched him under the chin. "Buford just wants some attention, don't you, buddy?" He barked, slobber dripping out of the corner of his mouth. Momma sat up suddenly. "I have an idea that might help Anna stop having those terrible dreams."

"Really?"

"Why don't you let Buford sleep with her? She loves this dog."

I sat back and smiled, awed. "That's a genius idea." Why hadn't I thought of it two weeks ago? "You wouldn't mind?"

"Not a bit." She scrubbed him on the head. "He loves Annaleise, don't you, Bu?" His sad eyes peered up at her and he wagged his tail.

When I brought Buford back home and told Anna she could sleep with him, you would have thought I told her we were going to Disney World. For the first night since she'd been here, she didn't fight us on going to bed.

I pulled Anna's bedroom door shut, dreaming of how good I was going to sleep snuggled into my king-sized bed under my minky duvet, uninterrupted by terrifying shrieks. The only thing standing between me and bed was locking the doors.

"Hey." Silas walked out of his room wearing his typical evening scowl. I don't know what he and Christy said to each other every night, but it must've been heavy. He always came out of his bedroom more troubled than when he went in. He reached over and pulled his door shut. His bicep flexed ever so slightly and my stomach fluttered. I groaned in my head. *I hate you, Peyton.*

"Hey." I walked past him. "I'm going to lock up and then hit the hay."

"Hold up a sec."

I turned to look at him.

"You gotta take the test, Clem. It's time." He brushed past me—his hand accidentally skimming across my left thigh, sending heat down both legs—and into the bathroom. Then he pulled one of the pregnancy tests we'd bought at the grocery store out from under the sink. "You can't keep putting it off."

I crossed my arms. "But I like this place called Denial. It's comfortable here."

He gave me a small smile and his eyes crinkled at the corners. "Good thing I'm here to remind you, that you actually live in Reality." He held a finger up. "Hold on. I got you something."

"Okay." I chewed my lip, wondering what it could be.

He came out of his room with his hands behind his back. "Ta-dah." His palm opened to reveal a bottle of prenatal vitamins.

I looked at the vitamins and then back up at him. My heart swelled, and I stood there, staring at him, my mouth slightly parted. Billy never would've done something like that. It wouldn't have occurred to him. I couldn't remember the last time he'd been in a grocery store, much less bought something for me.

"You probably need some extra iron and folic acid. This stuff is supposed to make your hair and nails grow like crazy." He pretended to study the label. "Maybe I should take some of these." Nervously, he shifted from one foot to the other.

Our fingers brushed when I took the bottle out of his hands. He pulled back like I'd burned him. Why did he have to overdo every reaction toward me? I was starting to think he found me revolting.

"Thanks. That's really thoughtful."

He rubbed his neck. "You bet." Silas was so freaking confusing.

I sighed and took the pregnancy test from his other hand. I turned for the bathroom.

"Wait." He caught me by the arm. "Do you want me to wait with you, after?" Oh my gosh. His moods were giving me whiplash.

I swallowed and gave myself a moment, trying to shake off the confusion. "Sure. That would be great."

He leaned against the wall. "I'll wait out here."

I went inside and shut the door. My heart raced as I tore the box open, even though I knew what the result would be. I'd never gone this long without a period since I started back in seventh grade. And the morning sickness was still going strong.

The instructions said it would take one to three minutes before I would know. Once I'd peed, I laid the test on the counter and washed my hands. I purposely didn't look at the stick before I went into the hall and shut the door.

Silas and I sat down together. I set a timer on my phone for three minutes.

My hands twisted around each other.

"So, how was your HIIT class today?" he asked. I'm sure trying to take my mind off of thin pink lines.

"Kinda terrible. If my heart rate goes over one-fifty, I get lightheaded. I keep having to modify every exercise. The ladies have to be wondering what is going on."

He picked a piece of lint off of his shorts. Even his calves were ripped. "Well, once this is over, you can start telling people and they'll understand." Like it was as simple as that.

I shook my head. "No. I'm not telling anyone until I can't hide it anymore. Not even Momma."

"Clem," he chided. "Don't you think she deserves to know?"

The lecturing rankled me. He made it sound so simple. My situation was anything but. "The minute I tell her will be the last minute of peace I get. She'll want to go shopping and tell all her friends…"

He appeared flummoxed, like I was being unreasonable. "She's going to be a grandma. Of course she'll be excited. You should be excited too."

"Well, I'm not, okay? And I know that sounds terrible, but you don't understand what it's like for me. I don't have a husband or my best friend or anybody—"

"You have me. I'm your friend."

I wanted to smack the condescending smile off his face. Friend? We lived in the same house and he chose to be anywhere but where I was. We weren't friends. "For the next two and a half months, and then you're going back to Wyoming, and I'll probably never hear from you again."

He leaned away a little, probably getting PTSD flashbacks from my tire-slashing rampage. Well, good. I'd had about enough of stupid men.

He scratched his jaw. "You'll hear from me. We're sharing Anna. We'll have to talk. And I'm here right now." We'll *have* to talk? Could he hear himself? Did he actually think our current relationship was something I could lean on? This friendship was about as steady as a ladder with only one foot on the ground. And I knew he knew that. So what he was really saying was, I'll be here for you now and then I'm out of here. See ya, wouldn't wanna be ya.

And suddenly, I couldn't take stiff, standoffish Silas anymore. Didn't want to live with someone who cared so little about me. Didn't want to pretend for one more second that I hadn't noticed his ten-year sabbatical.

My fists curled up and my chest cinched. "You're not even here, anyway."

He sat there for a second, stunned. "What are you talking about? I'm right here, Clem. Living in your house."

I turned sideways to look at him. "Your body might be here, but your head and your heart are back in Wyoming. You're either on your computer doing work or in your room talking to Christy. I'm certain that isn't what Sophie had in mind when she set this arrangement up." His mouth hung open, like he didn't have a clue what I was talking about.

And it irritated me even more. "You're only here because you have to be. Stop pretending like you care about me. You haven't cared about me in a decade. So don't patronize me by saying we're friends. We are not friends." I threw out my hands, seething. "We haven't been friends since our senior year of high school. You got stars in your eyes when the Pokes came knocking on your door with that scholarship and you didn't care about any of us back here." I hugged myself, rubbed my shoulders and blew my breath out in an O, picking up steam. "You thought about what was best for Silas Dean Dupree and nobody else. Then you took off and never looked back."

The timer went off, and I punched the stop button. Then I chucked my phone down the hall.

fourteen

SILAS

Clementine could've slapped me, and I would've been less shocked.

She made no move to check the test, just sat there, her chest heaving, a shadow on her face.

I twitched, trying to shake off her words. "Is that what you think? That I didn't care about you?"

A coldness came over her that I'd never seen before. "I know it is." She stabbed her chest with a finger as tears spilled over her lashes. "I called you. I emailed. I texted. And you never responded." Her finger turned on me. "You didn't come to my wedding. I've been waiting three years for you to acknowledge that my dad died. That man loved you like his own son. He taught you to rope. And you couldn't even bother to post an 'I'm sorry for your loss' on my Facebook wall. That's not how you treat people you care about."

A tumbleweed of all the past hurts I'd suffered caused a frenzy in my mind. Of all the things I'd been accused of in my life, this made me angrier than any of them. Because it couldn't be further from the truth.

"I cared about you." I punched my fist against the carpet.

"You're the one who forgot about me—me *and* Sophie—as soon as Billy came into the picture." It was hateful to include Sophie in that. But it was true. Sophie had complained a lot that Billy monopolized Clem. And manipulated and twisted her into an emotional knot. The difference was Sophie stuck around to watch. But I couldn't. I was literally going to kill someone. Billy or myself. So I got out.

My voice turned vehement. "It was Billy this and Billy that. I can't. I have plans with Billy tonight. Sorry, Billy needs me to give him a ride. Oh, we were supposed to hang out? I forgot I promised Billy I would help him write his paper." I gripped my hair. "*Billy, Billy, Billy.*" I leaned closer and jabbed at the floor. "You wanna know how I feel about Billy? I *hate* him. I hated him then and I hate him still." Mom would scold me for using that word. She always said it was the strongest word in the English language and should be used with utmost caution. But it was exactly how I felt. To accuse me of not caring when I'd cared so much it had almost killed me was infuriating.

Clem shook her head, her eyes swimming. "If you'd met someone, I wouldn't have stopped being your friend. I would've made room for them." It was always about Billy.

She was obviously still in love with that window licker.

I glowered at her, my entire body tense. "I'm sorry I couldn't stand by while you made the biggest mistake of your life. You want me to feel bad that I took off so I wouldn't have to watch?" My voice was barely below a shout. "I'm not. I will never be sorry that I left! It's the best decision I ever made!"

I regretted it as soon as it came out of my mouth.

The saying "the tongue has no bones but it can break a heart" pounded in my brain. Because I was pretty sure from the look on Clem's face that I had just broken hers. Gutted, betrayed, crushed. I'd only seen her like this one other time. The day we walked in on Billy and Lyla.

Clem shot up and took off down the hall. And my heart threatened to stop.

I pushed up and sprinted after her. "Clem!"

She grabbed the truck keys off the hook by the door, and I panicked. What if she left and never came back? What if she got in an accident, and those were the last words I ever said to her? But the worst what if...what if she ran straight into Billy's arms, and I let him suck the rest of the life out of her?

Safe, comfortable future be damned.

I hooked my arms around Clem's waist and pulled her back from the door. "I'm sorry, I'm sorry, I'm sorry," I murmured into her hair. "I didn't mean it. Please forgive me. *Please.*"

We froze in place, our lungs rising and falling in unison. When I was sure she wasn't leaving, I guided her to the couch and into my lap. She curled up, her head against my shoulder, and we sat that way for like three minutes, catching our breath. Which was fine. I couldn't have said anything, anyway. My nerves were completely shot. Christy might've dumped me on the spot for the way this looked. I couldn't care less right then. I needed to comfort Clem. Needed to be the friend she didn't know I was. Clem was everything, and I'd only been fooling myself by pretending otherwise.

"Hey." I lifted her chin to look at me. Her tears had turned her eyes the same green as the fields outside. I pulled her face into my hands and pressed my nose against hers. The urge to kiss her pouty lips ripped through me and I shoved it down. "I have missed you. *So* much. You're right. We're not friends. And I hate it." I tapped my nose against hers. "I'm sorry, okay?"

She nodded, her nose brushing against mine. "Okay." I was afraid if I moved, it would break the spell. So I stayed perfectly still, nose to nose, breathing her in. If someone offered me a million dollars or a life where I stayed right here in this moment forever, I would've chosen this.

So when Clem slid off my lap, my eyes fluttered open and disappointment hit me square in the chest. It felt like when you're snuggled in front of the fireplace with a warm blanket and someone yanks it away. I wanted so badly to pull her back. She turned and her knee leaned on mine. It was something, at least.

"I'm sorry too." She wiped her cheeks. "I promise I don't usually cry this much."

I felt naked now without her against me. I didn't know what to do with my hands. "I promise I'm not usually that mean."

She rubbed my hand, and I hooked her pinky with mine.

She met my eye, her expression so vulnerable. "You've never—not once in my entire life—been mean to me." She traced a vein on my other hand. "That's why it hurt so much when you ghosted me." I wished I could take back her hurt. Thing was, I'd done what I had to survive.

Her hair fell, covering the left side of her face. "I miss her so much," she whispered. "I don't know how to do this without her."

I already knew she was talking about Sophie.

I tucked her hair behind her ear. "Have a baby?"

She shook her head, then corrected with a nod. "Any of it. All of it. She helped me bale hay every year after my dad died. Billy wouldn't take the time off. We were like the Sheroes of the Fields.

It was insane to me that Billy didn't care that Clem was out in the heat busting her butt with Sophie. I didn't know how it was possible to hate him even more, but I did.

"Dad and I will get your hay up this year, okay? And I can come back next summer and do it again if you need me to.

That's the great thing about being an educator. Lots of time off in the summer."

She nodded, then sniffed and twisted her lips, looking into my eyes. "Having you here has been like getting part of her back."

Well, dang.

For a second, I'd thought we were having a moment. Of course this was about Sophie. I couldn't blame her. I missed my sister something fierce, too. So I just said, "Yeah?"

"Yeah." She held out her hand for a shake. "Friends?"

I stared at her, scouring her perfect cheekbones, the delicate freckles, her lips, and those eyes that told you exactly what she was thinking. Friends was the last thing I wanted to be.

I shook. "Yeah. Friends."

She dropped my hand and looked around, like she'd heard a noise. "Listen."

I strained my ears for a moment. "I don't hear anything."

She nodded, grinning. "Exactly."

I laughed and rubbed a hand over my face. We'd had a knock-down-drag-out argument in the hall right by Anna's door and she'd slept through the whole thing.

That dog was magic.

"Shoot. The pregnancy test." Clem hopped up and raced down the hall.

I leaned my head back and closed my eyes. I was so in over my head here. There was no way I could keep walking this tightrope. I was going to fall off. It was just a matter of time, and I didn't know where I would land. But I had to be there for Clem. With Sophie gone, she needed me. And if I was honest, I needed her and Anna too. I made a decision right then—for the rest of my stay, I would be completely present. Then when this was over, I'd go back to Wyoming knowing I'd given it my all. But that meant making some changes with

Christy. No more holing up in my room all evening. No more constantly texting Christy, trying to appease her.

And no more holding Clem at arm's length. No more shutting her out. No more ignoring her feelings. I'd caused major damage while I was gone, and it was going to take this entire summer to repair that.

I'd been a fool to think I could give Christy my whole heart right now. Not with the promise I'd made to Sophie. Not with Anna needing me. And definitely not while I was sleeping across the hall from the woman who'd always held my broken, trembling heart in her hands.

fifteen

CLEMENTINE

The test was positive. Shocker.

The bigger surprise was Silas losing his crap on me. It was agonizing, revealing, and wildly exhilarating, all rolled into one.

He hated Billy? I mean, Sophie had, though she bottled it up as much as possible for my sake. But Silas had never acted like he cared one way or the other. The fact that he'd left after high school because of me only added to my list of regrets. Marrying Billy had hurt way more people than just me.

But the biggest thunderbolt of the evening had been that moment on the couch.

When he'd pulled me into his lap and, nose to nose, told me that he hated that we weren't friends. That he missed me... It was so opposite of all the times he kept me at arm's length, refusing to let me in.

The ache in his voice had been intense. I'd thought we were going to kiss—and good gracious, the smell of his aftershave, his strong arms around my back, his breath tickling my lips...

I'd waited for it. Yearned for it. But it didn't come. I

couldn't tell if he was waiting for me to initiate it, or if I was misreading him completely.

But then, as Anna always said, I checked myself before I wrecked myself. My marriage just ended. The divorce process had barely begun. I was nowhere near ready to be kissing someone else. Didn't even know if that's what I wanted. I hadn't unpacked these new feelings toward Silas yet. What if a week from now, I decided he wasn't all that and Peyton had just gotten into my head? I wasn't the kind of person to start things I couldn't finish. Especially with a guy I'd known my whole life.

And then I thought about Billy and how much his cheating had hurt me. And how I might respect Silas less if he cheated on Christy. My favorite thing about Si was his loyalty and goodness. Like a pillar I'd always been able to lean on. I didn't know how to face the future if he wasn't that guy anymore. And I didn't want to be the person who changed him.

And what about Anna? We couldn't be out here getting to first base on the couch while she was asleep down the hall. No, if I pursued something with Silas, I needed to be certain of my feelings for him. And right now, I couldn't be less certain if I tried.

So even though I'd wanted to stay safe in his arms, wanted to slide my fingers up into his wavy hair and push my lips against his, wanted him to love me, intensely, deeply, in a way Billy never had...

I made the decision for him and slid off his lap.

Something in his eyes changed when I told him that having him here was like having a piece of Sophie back. He seemed confused, but maybe relieved, too. Like now that I wasn't on top of him, he could think clearly again. And Christy was the future he really wanted.

These were the thoughts going through my head as I lay in

bed the next morning for more than an hour. When I heard Anna turn on a video game in the living room, I threw the covers off, pulled my robe around my pajamas and tied it at my waist, wondering how long I'd be able to cinch it this tight.

When I walked into the living room, Si was sitting on the couch, still in the same shorts and T-shirt, his hair poking out in the back, watching Anna play. Buford had his head in her lap and was snoring. Silas sat up and gave me a half wave, then he adjusted back in his seat like he wasn't quite sure what to do with himself. Maybe he had the same pit in his stomach that I had in mine. It felt like we'd broken through to a new level in our relationship and I couldn't let us regress.

So I smiled extra wide. "Good morning."

His eyes lit up, and he smiled back. "Morning."

I tousled Anna's hair. "Did you sleep okay?"

She beamed up at me. "So good. Buford kept the bad dreams away." The basset hound lifted his head at the sound of his name, his droopy eyes so sad. Basset hounds always cracked me up with how pitiful they looked, even when they were happy.

I squatted down and rubbed under his chin, right where he liked it. "Such a good boy. Yes, you are." I tapped Anna on the knee. She kept her eyes on the game but lifted her brows. "You hungry?"

"Yes." She squealed. "Please, can we have pancakes?"

I smiled. "Sure."

She leaned her whole body to the left, trying to get her car on the screen to turn that way. "Hey, is it okay if Brooklyn comes over in a little while so we can practice?"

"Sure. Will she be here for pancakes?"

"Let me call her." Anna dropped the controller and ran to the kitchen to grab her phone where she'd left it charging overnight.

Silas hopped up. "I'll help." He followed me to the kitchen

and watched as I flipped the coffeemaker on. I lifted a brow in a dare.

He grabbed two mugs from the cabinet. "I did a little research. You can have one cup a day."

I laughed, my nostrils flaring. "Oh, really. Are you going to be the warden of the coffee maker?"

"If I have to be." He shrugged, his chin dimpling as his lips pressed firmly together.

"But see, I'm still residing in Denialville. And I think that until I move away, I should get to drink all the coffee I want." I reached into the small pantry and pulled out the Bisquick.

"Denialville?" He sounded unimpressed with the name of my made-up town.

I tried again. "Denialshire." I shook my head. "Denialham." I snapped. "Oh, I've got it. Denialdowne. See what I did there?"

His lips curved at the corners, betraying the annoyance on his face. "You can call it whatever you want, but there's no more denying anything. You took a test. And it was positive." He whispered the last part.

I shrugged as I got a bowl out of the bottom drawer by the stove. "Could be a false positive. Happens a lot, actually." I tapped him on the chest, and his pecs flexed under his shirt. "G-google that." I'd meant it to sound sassy, but the hitch in my throat made me sound like a choking pubescent boy.

He rolled his eyes, shook his head, and gave up. "Do you want me to make some bacon?"

An hour later, when we'd stuffed ourselves and cleaned up the mess, I sat at the kitchen table, scrolling through The Downward Dog finances spreadsheet. Anna and Brooklyn were outside practicing their serves.

My phone chimed, and I picked it up.

> Jenny: I ran into your momma at Food Lion this morning and she said you're letting Anna sleep with that dog? Lemon, honey, that is a terrible idea. You're going to have fleas crawling all over my granddaughter. I'm sorry she's having night terrors again, but this is not the answer.

I pinched the bridge of my nose, my stomach cinching as I thought about how to respond. Jenny did this every few days. Found some reason to "check in" on my "parenting." I reminded myself not to be offended. Jenny was a controller. And when she couldn't keep a thumb on a situation, it made her a little crazy. But I hadn't heard about Silas getting these kinds of texts.

"What's this?" Silas took the phone from my hands. His eyes flicked to me, and his jaw clenched. I hadn't realized he was reading over my shoulder. He skimmed the text—his gray eyes turning stony—and pursed his lips, perturbed. Then he started punching a message back. I reached for the phone. He turned his back so I couldn't reach it, his broad shoulders a wall between me and the possibility of saving my relationship with his mother.

"Don't," I said, a knot in my throat at having my arm twisted around his rock-hard torso, as I grasped for the phone. "I can handle this. Give it back."

He spun around, inches away, grinning as he hit send.

I yanked my phone out of his hand. "Not. Cool."

I read the text he'd sent:

> Me: We've got it handled. Thanks.

I shook my head, not amused, and added: *Sorry. Silas commandeered my phone. Buford's been treated for fleas and we thought he might help with—*

Silas ripped the phone out of my hand before I could finish and held it high above his head. "If you cater to her demands, she will only demand more. You have to politely tell her where she can stick it."

He wasn't wrong, but I didn't appreciate him pretending to be me. I folded my arms across my chest and blew out my lips. "That wasn't polite. If you want to handle it like that, do it from your phone. Now she's going to think I'm rude. You're gonna tell her that was you." I raised my eyebrows, not asking.

He saluted, his lips curling as he tried not to laugh. "Yes, ma'am." Then he pulled his phone out and texted his mom.

I sat back at the computer and returned my focus to the spreadsheet.

Fully dressed now in jeans and a plaid button-down, he sat next to me, pulling his shoes on. "Whatcha doing?"

I scratched my forehead, wondering how much to tell him. "Just trying to figure out how I'm paying for everything without Billy's income."

He jammed his right foot into a boot. "You know you're entitled to half of anything he acquired during your marriage, right? He has to pay you alimony, too." Holden had probably told him that. Or maybe he'd read it on the internet. Silas was a researcher, I was learning.

I shook my head. "I don't want anything from him."

"But it's yours by law."

"All I want is the house and my truck. He can have everything else."

He yanked his other boot up. "You have to think further ahead than that. And what about bills? Doesn't he have student loan debt?"

"No. His grandparents paid for school."

His eyes widened, impressed. "Well, that's good. But what about insurance? I'm assuming you get it through his job."

Did he think I was naïve? "I know all of that. I've been

worried about it for weeks. I'm going to have to figure out another way."

"Hey." He put his hand on my knee, causing a surge of adrenaline. "Please take this the way I mean it, okay?" He tilted his head and spoke slowly and intentionally. "Don't let your pride right now screw you over in the long run. Think about your future. Raising a kid is expensive, even when you're living in Denialstead."

I put my hand over his and took a deep breath as I turned to him. "I promise that's exactly what I'm doing. The thing with Billy is, if you let his toenail in the door, he will worm his entire body inside. If I ask for alimony, he will throw that money in my face the entire time he's paying it. If I want him out of my life, I have to cut ties completely."

I let go of Si's hand and faced forward, intending for the conversation to be over.

He turned to face me now. "I hate to tell you this, since you're living in Denialborough and all—"

I fought against a threatening snicker.

But his eyes were solemn. "Billy is this baby's dad. He's going to be in your life whether you like it or not."

I exhaled. "I know that." I pressed my hands against the table. "But if he's going to be the kind of dad I think he will be, he won't be super involved. Billy always comes first, and that's going to work in my favor. If I demand child support, he'll use it as a way to get power over us." I sat up straight, determined. "If Sophie could do it, so can I."

Silas studied me for a moment before shifting his legs back under the table. His knee brushed against mine, shooting heat up my legs. He reached for the laptop. "Can I?"

I wasn't sure I wanted him up in my finances, but I searched those gray eyes and reminded myself that Silas was a good guy. He wasn't going to use any of this against me. He wanted to help. So I slid the laptop toward him.

I didn't have anything to hide—and the studio made a decent profit. It just wasn't enough. As he scanned, I studied him, gauging his thoughts. His brow furrowed in concentration, and I bit my lip when a muscle in his jaw flexed.

He pushed the laptop back in my direction and sat back. "You're solidly in the black. You just need more clients at the studio." He rubbed his calloused fingers across his lips, thinking. "How many monthly memberships do you have?"

"Forty-eight right now." But eleven of those hadn't attended classes in over six months. Eventually, they were going to cancel their memberships.

"You charge sixty-five a month?"

I nodded. Before he could suggest I raise my prices, I added, "It's less than memberships in the city, but this is a poor county. If I go any higher, I'll price out the clients I do have. Every week, I have potential clients telling me that if I charged half that, they would join. But I'm already paying my instructors pennies. Most of them do it for the free membership and because they love teaching. I can't go any lower."

"No, don't lower prices. If it's a priority, people will pay for it." He was right. I'd seen some of the complainers blow hundreds of dollars in the McDonald's drive through on soda and coffee every month. Or lotto tickets at the Fast Mart.

He nodded, chewing his bottom lip. "Seddledowne is a hard place to have a small business."

"Tell me about it. But I have to make this work or..." I pressed my forehead into my hand. "I'll have to go back to school and finish my degree." It wasn't that I didn't like school. I'd just figured out a long time ago that this is what I wanted to do for the rest of my life. And a business degree wasn't going to magically make my business more profitable. I might have to face facts. Seddledowne simply might be too small to sustain a business like mine.

He scrubbed a hand over his face. "Let me think on it.

There has to be a way we can bring in more revenue." His use of the word "we" made my heart quiver.

"And, hey." His voice was rough, like sandpaper. "I am sorry about James. I loved him too. He was one of the best men I've ever known."

I blinked. "Okay. Thank you."

He stood. "I'm gonna go smooth out your driveway. Are the keys in the tractor?"

I turned, my arm on the back of the chair. "Yeah. Momma will probably bake you a cake. She's been complaining about the potholes for months."

"I'm doing it for me more than anybody. Tired of hitting my head on the cab of the truck every time I drive in." He rubbed his stomach. "But you can tell Miss Lisa, pound cake is my favorite."

I laughed and watched as he sauntered his sexy long legs out the door.

If Silas could step out of his comfort zone and open up to me like he had last night, maybe I could be brave too.

I clicked on Google and typed *OBGYNs near me*, into the search bar.

sixteen

SILAS

"You're both being way too sweet." I palmed the volleyball. "That's a quality that will help you later in life, but not in this sport." I'd been to a few women's games in college. Those ladies were savage. "Is there a boy at school that drives you crazy? Like he's super annoying?"

Anna's face turned pink and Brooklyn giggled the name, "Deacon."

"Deacon?" I waited for Anna to acknowledge it. She nodded, her eyes on the ground. "What annoys you about him?"

She crossed her arms, anger flashing in her dark eyes. "He thinks he's all that, and he's not. Like he walks with this strut." She swung her arms and leaned back, mimicking this kid. "And he's constantly taking my lunch. Like on the last day of school, he swiped my bag of Doritos when I went to the bathroom for two seconds. They were half gone when I got back." Anna's words said one thing, but her eyes were shimmering, like someone had turned on a neon sign.

Brooklyn exaggerated her hands around her head in a mind-blown gesture. Her eyes were sparkling, just like my niece's. "And what about how he's always snapping and singing, 'Anna 1, Anna 2, Anna 1, 2, 3,' like he's about to break out into song."

"So annoying," Anna glared, but her lips curved up at the corners.

These two had misunderstood the assignment. I meant a boy that they honestly disliked, not someone they both had a secret crush on. Hopefully it would work anyway. I held the ball out and pointed to the middle. "Well, pretend the ball is Deacon's face. And he just ate your entire bag of Doritos."

I handed the ball to Anna and stepped out of the way. Her brow furrowed, determined. She dribbled the ball in a well-worn spot which was mostly smooth packed dirt, got her stance right, and tossed the ball up. When it came down, she hit it with an intensity that reminded me of Sophie. The ball zoomed across the grass court Clem had made for her and hit the top of the net, almost going over. It dropped back to the ground.

Anna groaned. "I'm never gonna get it."

"Yes, you will." I could tell her how many times I'd had to throw a lasso before I finally got it, but I thought it would discourage her. It was well into the hundreds. And she was already discouraged enough. "You're so close. This time, toss the ball a little higher and hit it a little sooner. Don't forget it's Deacon's head." I didn't want her to lose the intensity.

Determination stole across her face. She tossed the next one up and gave it a hard wallop. It skimmed across the top of the net and dropped to the grass on the other side.

Brooklyn screamed, "Yasss Queen!" and tackled Anna. They fell back onto the grass, laughing, and I grinned, pride swelling in my chest. But I couldn't help but feel a little sick at that moment. How many of Anna's successes had I missed by living across the country? And how many more would I miss when I went back? I loved this girl as much as I loved Clem.

Her enthusiasm and love for life were infectious. The thought of leaving her was wrecking me.

My phone rang.

Christy. A sick pang took up residence in my gut. I hoped with everything in me that today would be my lucky day and Christy would be uncharacteristically understanding.

"You guys keep working on it. I have to take this." I doubted they heard me over their celebrating. I strode across the lawn and answered the phone. This wasn't a conversation I wanted Anna to hear. "Hey. How has your day been?"

"Hey," Christy's voice was overly happy—a telltale sign she was anxious. The phrase "we need to talk" usually had that effect on people. "It's been good. Been working on my thesis like always. My brain is fried. I only need five more pages and I'll be done, but I feel like I'm already repeating myself."

Christy and I had met in the UW Masters in Education program. I graduated in December and she was defending her thesis in a couple of weeks. Normally, I would offer to edit for her. I'd spent hours brainstorming and proofreading. But I didn't know if she'd want me anywhere near her or her paper after today.

Brooklyn and Anna screamed and ran around the yard, pumping their fists in the air. One of them must've gotten another serve over. I gave them a thumbs up and turned around, looking out over Firefly Fields, giving Christy my full attention.

"We need to talk?" Christy's voice shook.

I sat on the edge of a wooden planter box and pulled newly sprouted weeds from the dirt, trying to calm my nerves. "I just...I think I overestimated how hard this situation was going to be—"

"Did you kiss her?"

Wow. Straight outta the gate. "No, I didn't." *But almost.* I pressed my forehead into my hand, rubbing one temple with my thumb, the other with my index finger.

"I hear a 'but' in your voice."

"But. Things are more complicated than I realized."

"What does that mean?" I could hear her struggling between being understanding and losing her crap. She never had patience with my tendency to beat around the bush. So I stopped beating.

"It means...I feel like there's a tug of war and I'm the rope. Sophie wanted me to be here for Anna—"

"That was a really selfish thing she did, forcing you into that agreement with Lemon." She sounded like she'd spit acid out of her mouth.

There was nothing that got my back up faster than someone questioning Sophie's character. Double that now that she'd passed away. "Sophie wasn't perfect, but she loved her family fiercely. And Clem was family to her." I threw out my hand. "Regardless of how you feel about it or if you understand why Sophie did it, I need to be here for Anna this summer. And honestly, Clem too. She's got some stuff going on and she needs a friend." I barreled on before she could react to that. "She was Sophie's best friend, and you know what Sophie made me promise on her deathbed." Christy had been standing right next to me when Sophie said it and, to be honest, I kind of resented Christy for it. I'd wanted that moment with my sister, alone. But Christy wanted to be there for all of it since she was "going to be family now."

"Make sure Lemon's okay," she recalled bitterly.

"Yes. And I am doing a halfway job of both things because I'm spending every evening on the phone with you—"

"You promised—"

"And the rest of my time with a knot in my stomach, waiting for you to get mad that I'm not texting enough or giving you enough attention." I hated putting that on her. I knew her worry was real. But... "I can't do it anymore."

There, I said it.

"You *promised* you wouldn't dump me." Her voice broke.

I tugged at the back of my hair. "I know. I'm...I'm really sorry." I was. I hadn't planned any of this. "I just...It's too much pressure. I'm not living like this all summer. I can't do it, and I'm sorry if you hate me, but this little girl needs me and my attention right now. She's got to be my top priority."

"Uncle Si, watch!" Anna yelled as she nailed one over the net.

"You're the GOAT!" Brooklyn bellowed.

I smiled and gave them a thumbs up. "Keep going!" I yelled across the lawn.

"Silas?" Christy scolded, proving my point. I couldn't keep her happy while I was here.

Big exhale. "Yeah."

"I didn't mean to put pressure on you." Her tone had lost all its fight. "Think if you were me and I'd left you for the summer to go live with some gorgeous guy."

The desperation in her voice was killing me and I almost took it all back. But then I'd be in the same position tomorrow and the next day. She'd painted me into a corner. And after what happened with Clem the night before, I didn't feel like I had a choice. If I wanted to keep my conscience clear, I had to do this.

"You're right. It would make me crazy. Do you like living like this? It isn't fair to you or to me."

We sat there for a moment, saying nothing. I didn't want to break things off. But I also didn't want to continue forward this way. It was a Catch-22 if I ever saw one.

"Are you still coming back at the end of the summer?" There was hope in her voice.

"Yes. I have a job there." I almost added, "and you're

there," but I didn't know if she even wanted us to be a couple anymore.

She sniffed. "What if...what if we pushed pause?"

"Pause?" I was afraid to get my hopes up. Christy was a pusher. Said she had to be as a woman or she'd never make it academically or professionally. But that tendency bled over into our relationship. She might dress this up like a break, but underneath it would be the same relationship with a different title. "I dunno..."

She must've heard my hesitation because she scrambled. "Okay, not a pause. A reset. We'll take this summer off and then, when you get home, we'll go back to how we were."

"Really?" My question was laced with disbelief. It seemed too good to be true. "You would be okay with taking the summer off?" I thought about the way things had been before I left. Christy was safe and comfortable and beautiful. And she loved me. I didn't want to lose that. We'd spent time building something. She was my friend and though I didn't know if I'd ever feel for her what I felt for Clem, I also knew Christy wouldn't break my heart like Clem had.

Could I do this? Could I focus on Anna—and Clem—and put Christy out of my mind all summer and then go back to Wyoming and start where we left off?

"If you make me one promise," she said.

Whatever it was, she'd want me to sign my name in blood. "What is it?"

"You have to promise not to kiss her. If you kiss her, all bets are off. Don't even bother calling me when you get back."

Fair enough. I'd already decided that I couldn't let something like last night happen again. Clem clearly didn't want it, and there was no point in humiliating myself or risking my relationship with Christy over it.

"Yes. Of course. I promise." So were we incommunicado for the rest of the summer? Was I allowed to feel whatever I was going to feel when Clem was around without a cloud of guilt hanging over me? Or would I be grilled when this was over? Put through my own personal Nuremberg trials?

I was about to ask, when a vehicle came flying up the driveway, way too fast. For a millisecond, I thought it was Clem coming back from the studio. But it was Billy's white Ford F-450. Crap. Clem must've forgotten to lock the gate at the entrance of the driveway. The truck fishtailed to a stop, spraying gravel onto the lawn. Anna and Brooklyn turned, both looking like they'd swallowed a rock.

"Uh, Christy, I gotta go." I hopped up and hurried across the yard.

Billy slammed the truck door, his expression dangerous. He took one look at me with the girls and must've decided he didn't care if minors were present.

"Where's Lemon?" he yelled, coming at me.

I motioned to where she usually parked in the carport. "Not here."

He stomped on the ground, his nostrils flaring, eyes drilling into me. "Well, where is that little witch? I am not signing those ridiculous divorce papers."

Deep breaths. I crossed my arms and stood up straight. "Anna," I said over my shoulder, "You and Brooklyn go inside."

Wide-eyed, they hurried up the porch steps and into the house. I breathed a little easier when I heard the deadbolt lock into place.

"You better tell me where she is right now!" Billy screamed like a two-year-old not getting the red firetruck LEGO his mom let him ogle for five minutes in Walmart before putting it back. I had to control the urge to laugh. Did he think if he threw a big enough tantrum that I'd give him what he wanted?

I shrugged, acting unfazed. "No. I don't think I will."

His chest started heaving and his glare narrowed. "I guess it's true then."

I wasn't going to ask what was true. That's what he wanted. And my main goal was to tick him off as much as possible. Childish, yes. But I felt good about it.

He laughed and shook his head. "She kicked me out so she could move you in. Guess I wasn't the only one cheating."

I continued staring him down, laughing in my head. Let him think what he wanted.

He roared at my silence and stomped up to me until his dress shoes were kissing my boots.

I lowered my eyes to look down on him. All I could see was his thinning hair. "You're getting some grays there, short stuff."

He turned red all the way up into his receding hairline. Then he stepped back, the corners of his mouth turning up into an evil smile. Oh, he was changing tactics. Got it. The spoiled brat angle hadn't worked, so that was probably a smart choice.

"You always did want Lemon, but you weren't man enough for her."

There was no way he knew that, nor had I ever done anything around Billy to make him think that. Until last night, I'd never, not once, slipped up and showed even a hint of my feelings for her. They'd always been completely under wraps. So this was just Billy building himself up.

I cocked an eyebrow, forced a yawn, and patted my mouth. "Whatever you say, Tiny Tim."

I had to give him a point—eh, a half a point. Aside from his nostrils barely flaring, he kept his calm after that one.

His eyebrows flicked up, and he wore the cocky grin that probably won Clem over in the first place. I wanted to break his face.

"Enjoying my sloppy seconds?" he sneered. "Is that whore keeping you satisfied? She never did me."

That did it. I clamped my hand around his neck, lifted him by the throat and sent him slamming onto his back. When he hit the ground, all the air wheezed out of his lungs like a popped balloon. I shoved my knee into his chest and hissed in his face. "Don't you ever talk about her like that again! You think you're a real man because you slept with the cashier at the Fast Mart? A real man doesn't cheat on his wife during the funeral of her best friend! A real man makes a commitment to love a woman and keeps it his entire life, you pathetic twatwaffle! The only real achievement you've gained your whole pathetic life was probably catching every STD in the county."

He gasped frantically, his eyes swimming.

I lifted him a few inches and slammed him back against the ground. His eyes widened, begging for mercy. He might get that from anyone else, but he wasn't getting it from me. I dug my kneecap deeper into his collarbone, to make sure we were clear. "You didn't deserve Clem when she married you, and you don't deserve the quick divorce she's trying to give you now. You *will* sign those papers or I will make sure she not only ruins your reputation, but takes half your salary for the next decade." I squeezed his throat, his eyes bulging out of their sockets. "Do you understand me?"

He nodded vigorously. A tear rolled down his cheek and into his ear canal.

I lifted the pressure on his chest a touch, but not enough for him to get up. "And if you trespass again, we'll get a restraining order." I had zero right to make any of these threats, but he didn't know that. I hoped he did think Clem and I were a couple now. Nothing could make me happier.

"Okay?" I shook him.

"Okay," he rasped.

I stood up, enjoying watching him squirm and puff until the air filtered back into his lungs. My dad always taught me to fight fair. That was hard to do with a coward like Billy. The least I could do was help him up.

I reached down to offer him a hand. "All right, then."

He shrunk back, suspicious and terrified. Then he rolled away, scampered to his feet, and tripped across the lawn until he got to his debt-mobile. As he drove by, his gaze flashed to me. I gave him a little wave and a toothy grin.

I stood there until I was sure he was gone, his taillights disappearing over the last hill as the sunset faded in the distance. Hopefully Clem wouldn't be mad. I was just keeping a promise to my sister.

Seventeen

CLEMENTINE

Silas held my hair back as I puked into the toilet. Super sexy.

Once I was done, I picked up the damp cloth he'd brought for me and wiped my mouth. "I really don't want you to watch this."

"You say that every morning."

I inhaled carefully, making sure not to jolt my stomach. "And I mean it every morning."

"You've seen me puke. It's all good." He grabbed the grape electrolyte drink from behind him, popped the seal on the lid, and handed it to me. I sat back against the wall and took a sip. Like it or not, Silas made sure I guzzled at least one every morning.

"You threw up one time," I said, once I was sure I could keep the liquid down. "Not every day for weeks." After the rampage my stomach had been on lately, I didn't have to worry about whether Silas wanted to kiss me. He absolutely didn't. There was nothing attractive about a hormonal, puking, sweaty, pregnant woman.

His knees folded up, and he leaned against the wall next to

me like he had all the time in the world. "Not every day. There was that one Monday, remember?" His head turned, rolling along the wall. His gorgeous gray eyes went grave. "Hey, something's gotta change. You can't keep this up or you're going to end up in the hospital. When's your first appointment again?"

"Two weeks from tomorrow."

"And you told them how sick you are?"

I nodded, my ponytail rubbing the wall. "They said they'll prescribe anti-nausea medicine at the first checkup. This is nothing new. They see it all the time."

"Yeah. Well. Sometimes doctors get jaded. If it gets any worse, I'm calling them. You need a break from this."

I put a hand on his shoulder, trying to stand. "What I need is to get my butt off this floor and go teach my barre class." My legs wobbled, and I fell back down.

"Yeah. You're not teaching anything this morning. I'll see if Peyton can fill in." A few weeks ago, he'd taken over finding a sub for my morning classes. Peyton usually covered. Sometimes Crystal would switch her four-thirty p.m. for my nine a.m., which worked. This was true morning sickness, and by one in the afternoon, I felt like a new woman. So far, we hadn't had to cancel a single class.

I closed my eyes while he texted Peyton.

"She's not responding," he said after a minute.

"Just cancel."

He grunted. "We're trying to build your business, not kill it. No worries. I'll figure something out."

I opened one eye and scowled. "Are you going to teach barre?"

He shrugged. "If I have to."

The thought of Silas holding onto the barre and showing the ladies how to plié made me giggle. "I'd like to see that. There's a lot of squeezing your butt cheeks and tightening your thighs around an exercise ball."

His smile went a little crooked. "I bet you would."

I almost swooned—like actually passed out from his hotness. Or possibly from my current state of dehydration. Probably a combination of both. I closed my eyes and simply breathed. My entire body jerked, and I realized I'd fallen asleep for a few seconds. "I need to lie down."

Silas hooked an arm around my waist and lifted until he'd set me on my feet. Funny how my mouth could taste disgusting, I could be drenched in clammy sweat, and yet his touch left me tingling and wanting him.

As the morning sickness had intensified, so had my internal reactions to him. Every look, every touch, caused some kind of electric jolt. I was on emotional and physical high alert constantly. No ebbs and flows. Just consistently, deeply attracted to this man living in my house. I couldn't even close my eyes and get away from it. His baritone voice made my stomach twist and yet calmed my nerves in a way nothing else ever had. Not even yoga. It was addicting and euphoric. And ever since he'd stopped spending every waking moment texting or FaceTiming Christy, it had only amped up. I didn't know if they'd broken up or what. But I found myself hoping, wishing, praying that they had.

"Hey," he said, too close to my ear, sending shivers down my neck. "Anna's supposed to go shopping with my mom this morning to get a new swimsuit for beach week."

"But it's still weeks away." I'd been to beach week with the Duprees every year since I turned eight. But never without Sophie and never as Anna's guardian. The fact that Jenny was in preparation mode put a knot in my already strung-out stomach.

So far, Silas had managed to swat away her constant invitations to dinner. Yeah, he and Anna went over to visit often, but he was keeping me out of it. He didn't say he was outright protecting me from his mom, but some things don't have to be said. The thought of being in close quarters with her for a week left me jittery. If Sophie's proposal wasn't so specific about us sleeping under the same roof, I would've bowed out this year.

"You know Jenny. Couldn't squelch that Type A personality if we tried." He shifted his arm, his strong fingers gripping my waist. "I really think we should take you up to sit with your mom. I'm not comfortable leaving you here alone."

I tried to speak, but my nerves were a tangled mess with him so close. "Y-yeah. Okay." It took major effort to force those words through my windpipe.

He'd worn me down on telling Momma. I hadn't done it yet, but I knew it needed to be soon or she'd be hurt. The thought of Momma taking care of me at that moment sounded like heaven.

He gave me a sideways glance. "Maybe today's the day?"

I nodded. "Yeah, I think so."

His mouth split into a grin. "Miss Lisa's about to have her world changed forever." The words barely registered. I was so delirious by the way his lips framed his perfectly white teeth. "Clem?"

I shook my head to clear the cache of my weak-willed brain. "Yeah. Mhmm. World changed. Forever."

"Anna," he called as he practically carried me across my room. "Anna, I need you to get moving."

I pointed to my dresser. "I need to change my shirt. Can you grab the red one?" He pulled the drawer open and moved clothes around until he found the one I wanted. We had a routine down. If I got vomit on my clothes, he'd get the ones I needed and then leave so I could change. He'd offered to help once, but I drew the line at him seeing me naked.

His left eyebrow drew into a stern upside down V. "Call me when you're done and I'll help you up."

Ten minutes later, the three of us were in the old ranch

truck, with Silas in the driver's seat, Anna in the middle, and me on the passenger side. Buford was in the truck bed, licking the back window, trying to eat his way through the glass to get to us.

As Silas revved the engine, Anna glanced over at me, worry in her eyes. She squeezed my hand. "Are you okay?"

I nodded, but it clearly did nothing to alleviate her apprehension. Silas watched out of the corner of his eye, concern etched in the lines of his face. Retching in the bathroom every day, spending half my life exhausted on the couch—it wasn't normal and Anna knew it. When she asked if I was okay, I knew she was really asking, "Are you going to leave me too?" Maybe it was time to tell more than just Momma.

"Shoot." Silas had barely gotten the truck in reverse. "I forgot my hat." He put it back in park.

I pursed my lips and said to Anna, "A cowboy will die if he goes anywhere without his hat."

She played along. "No cows will be roped, the grass will stop growing, all the equipment will break."

One half of Silas's mouth curved up. "Shut it, you two." He hopped out of the truck and closed the door.

"Arooooo!" Buford barked.

Anna waved at him. "You're okay, Bu. We're going to Miss Lisa's right now to take you home."

He yipped and his tail wagged.

"Hey." I poked Anna in the side, causing her to giggle. "You wanna know a secret?"

She sat up and turned to face me, her eyes dancing. "Yes."

I pressed a hand against my stomach. "I'm going to have a baby. That's why I've been so sick."

Her mouth dropped and her eyes got huge. "Seriously?" She squealed when I nodded. "Oh my gosh, I can't believe it, Aunt Lemon. That's so awesome!" She squeezed me so tight I almost couldn't breathe. "We'll be a real family. I'm going to have a brother or a sister. Wait until I tell Brooklyn." She pulled out her phone.

A real family? "Wait." I placed my hand over hers, stopping her from sending out the text. "I'm not telling anyone yet. Miss Lisa doesn't even know. I'm telling her next, but probably no one else until after the first trimester. Can you keep it a secret?" I should have asked that first. "You can't tell anyone. Not even Brooklyn." The last thing I needed was a giant Seddledowne-wide game of telephone to get things all jacked up. I'd tell Billy eventually, when I absolutely had to. Hopefully once the divorce was final, if he'd go ahead and sign the dang papers. But I'd do it on my own terms and not through the grapevine.

Anna bounced in her seat and locked her lips with an imaginary key. "Oh my goodness, this is the best news ever. You, me, Uncle Si, and now a baby."

What did that mean? Did she think it was Silas's baby? I scowled.

Her nose crinkled. "I guess Billy will be around some too. It's his baby."

I exhaled a little. At least she got that part. "It's going to be harder than you think. Babies cry a lot. I mean, you did anyway." I pinched her nose lightly. "Your momma and I were so exhausted. But babies are cute, so it makes up for it."

"It's okay. Between you and me and Uncle Si, we'll take turns. You know what Granny always says. 'Many hands make light work.'"

I didn't want to kill her elation. I really didn't. But somehow she'd gotten the idea that Silas was hanging around. Either that or she and I were moving to Wyoming. I wasn't sure. I just knew she was deeply confused or misinformed. And the longer she carried those ideas around, the harder it would be when Silas left.

"Hey," I said more seriously. "You know it takes nine months for a baby to be born, right?"

"Bruh. Momma gave me that whole birds and the bees talk back in sixth grade, remember?"

I tilted my head. "Then how do you figure that your uncle will be here when the baby is born?" She knew he had a job in Laramie. He talked about it all the time. Incessantly and annoyingly.

She bit her lips and covered her mouth, her eyes wide, looking ridiculously guilty.

"Anna?"

Her hands fidgeted in her lap. "I maybe, possibly, might be praying every single night for you and Uncle Silas to fall in love."

I gasped. What?

A slow smile spread across her face. "And wish on the first star every night. And all the dandelions Brooklyn and I can find. And every coin I toss in a fountain. And the other day when there was a rainbow." She began ticking the wishes off on her fingers. "Every ladybug that lands anywhere near me. Whenever you or Uncle Si gasses it through a yellow light. Whenever the time is one-eleven or two twenty-two or three thirty-three. You get the picture."

My mouth parted.

She shrugged. "Then there's all the four-leaf clovers in the yard. They're more common than you think. We really need to put down some weed and feed." She looked up at the ceiling of the truck, thinking for a second. "Whenever Brooklyn or I find an eyelash on the other's cheek." She let out an exaggerated exhale, her shoulders lifting and falling. Then she remembered one more. "Oh, and fireflies. Every one that we can catch."

"Wow," was all I could say, half impressed, half horrified by the energy and aspirations of a thirteen-year-old with her heart set on something. She was going to be one disappointed girl at the end of the summer.

Anna sat up straight, beaming. "With all that good juju, it's got to happen." She elbowed me in the ribs. "I mean, Uncle Silas is pretty cute, don't you think? He's got that great hair and his smile. Oh, and his really deep voice." She wiggled her eyebrows. "Admit it. You think he's sexy."

I gasped. "You are way too young to be using that word."

She rolled her eyes. "Fine. Hot. You think he's hot, don't you?"

"No. Pfft. He's just...Silas. He's too tall." And it was so freaking attractive. "And kinda skinny." At least he used to be. "And he wears that dumb hat." Which I'd come to adore.

She pursed her lips. "The lady doth protest too much, methinks."

My jaw dropped. "Did you just quote Shakespeare at me?"

"It's kinda sus, not gonna lie."

My mouth fell open even more. Shakespeare to Gen Z in less than ten seconds. This kid.

"Picture it, Aunt Lemon." She held her hands up as if they were framing something. "If you married Uncle Silas, he could use that dreamy voice to whisper sweet nothings every night until you fell asleep. Just think about that."

Oh. My. Word. Where was Silas? It couldn't take this long to find a hat.

"I'm not too worried about him," she continued. "You're gorgeous. Like *gor-geous*. All my friends at school dream of looking like you when they grow up. And you're a freaking Girlboss. Literally. Yeah, Uncle Silas doesn't stand a chance." She shrugged one shoulder. "Besides, he already looks at you that certain kinda way whenever you're in the room."

"Excuse me." My laugh came out shaky. "He doesn't look at me any kind of way."

She shrugged, full shouldered this time. "Brooklyn sees it

too, so I know it's not just me. Because Brooklyn always tells the truth about everything. Like she'll tell me if I'm stressing too much about my outfit or if one of my eyebrows is wonky. You know what I mean? And she says you and Uncle Si got this chemistry going on. It's just a matter of time till you're couple goals."

But my brain was stuck way back at *he looks at you that certain kinda way*. I wasn't going to hang my hopes on the intuition of two thirteen-year-olds, but it made me wonder. *Was* Silas attracted to me? I tried to think back through the years. Was the way he looked at me now different from when we were younger? I almost shook my head, chiding myself for even entertaining the thought. No, that look was the same one he'd given me when I was twelve. Anna's hopes were addling her head.

She grabbed my hand and squeezed. "Brooklyn thinks you should go for it—lay one on him and see what he does." Her eyes were full of longing, like I obtained some kind of tantalizing seductress kissing skills that would make her every wish come true.

"I think that is a terrible idea."

She slumped and poked her bottom lip out. "I told Brooklyn you'd never do it. You're way too proper." She said it as if being proper was the dullest quality in existence.

I scoffed. "I am not too proper. I am the exact right amount of proper, thankyouverymuch." My phone chimed. "Hold on. We're not done here." I mindlessly pulled it out of my purse with every intention of seeing who it was, ignoring them, and then giving Anna a lecture on how you should save your kisses until you were sure about a guy.

But it was Mr. Llewellyn, my lawyer.

> Arlo Llewellyn: Don't ask me how, but you got a miracle today. Billy signed the papers.

I stared at the message, rereading it over and over again, waiting for Arlo to rescind his words. Was he kidding? Was this a really late April Fool's joke? Had someone stolen his phone and pranked me?

> Me: Are you serious?

> Arlo: Yes, totally serious. I'm not sure what happened. Last time I talked to his lawyer, he was going to fight to the death. Then this morning I got word that the papers were signed. Go celebrate. You're a free woman.

I sat there, stunned, unable to speak.

Anna took the phone from me, scanning the words. When she laid it back in my lap, she gave me a matter-of-fact expression. "After Uncle Si scared him witless? I'm surprised it took this long."

My head snapped around. "Um. What?"

She cocked her head, puzzled. "Didn't he tell you about the day Billy came over—you know, when Brooklyn was here and we ate all those pancakes?"

I shook my head. But I was surprised *she* hadn't told me. Then again, Anna and Brooklyn had the attention span of whatever reel they were currently watching on TikTok.

Silas finally came out the side door, hatless, a frustrated look on his face. He walked around the carport, picking things up to check underneath.

"Spill it, sister," I hissed. "Tell me everything."

"Yeah. It was *insane*." She said the word in a sports announcer voice. "Billy acted all crazy, screaming that he wanted to know where you were. I mean, Uncle Si made me and Brooklyn go inside, of course, because Billy was being a psycho. He probably thought we couldn't hear, but we cracked the window open."

Silas popped open the door of my truck, still in the carport, and leaned inside.

I motioned for her to go on. "And?"

"He even accused you and Uncle Si of having some sleazy affair. Uncle Si was really calm until Billy called you some bad names." She shook her head, her eyes holding a touch of shame. "Like really bad." No surprise there.

Silas stood up, plopped his hat on his head, and shut the truck door.

"As soon as that happened—"

"Quicker, Anna."

Her words gained the speed of an auctioneer. "He grabbed Billy around the throat, body slammed him to the ground, and screamed in his face to never talk about you like that again. Told him to sign the divorce papers, or he'd make sure you took him for all he's worth. Then he told him never to trespass again, or you'd get a restraining order put on him. I thought he might kill him, honestly. I've never seen Uncle Si like that. You shoulda seen Billy high-tail it out of here. Big yikes." She slapped her thigh, laughing. "I'm telling you. Uncle Si is the GOAT."

Silas pulled the door open and slid inside. "Sorry, I guess I left it in your truck."

Anna pressed her hands together. "Guess what, Uncle Si." She didn't wait for his response. "Aunt Lemon's having a baby."

Silas's head snapped back, clearly not expecting that. He nodded, his brows raised. "I guess a lot happened while I was looking for my hat."

Anna snickered. "No, silly, she and Billy made a baby a while back. Before...*you know*." She was referring to the barn incident.

He nodded, glancing at me like, wow. "You don't say."

"And guess what else?" She bounced on the seat like it was a trampoline. "Billy signed the divorce papers. So Aunt Lemon is *siiin-gle*." She sang the words right next to his ear, and I wanted to die. Just turn to salt like Lot's wife. "I guess you really shook him, didn't you?"

Silas's gaze skittered over to me, scared he'd done the wrong thing, but kinda proud of himself, too. For once, I proudly and confidently held his gaze, my eyes burning with the heat of everything he'd done and been for me since he got here. What I wanted to do was kiss him right on that sexy mouth, just like Brooklyn suggested. But I reminded myself that I was a proper woman and mouthed the words *thank you* instead.

He tipped his hat and winked.

And I can't believe I ever thought cowboys were anything but dead sexy.

eighteen

SILAS

As the weeks went by, Mom hounded me to bring Clem over to the house. I put Mom off until the last week in June, but by then she'd declared she would lose her ever-lovin' mind if the three of us didn't come over for dinner after church on Sunday. Especially because Holden had driven down for the weekend. And Ashton was home from school for a few days. So the three of us climbed into my truck and headed for Dupree Ranch.

Clem was going to chew her bottom lip straight off if she didn't stop stressing. She'd banished us from the kitchen and refused all offers of help. She was so anxious about getting her layered cornbread salad and baked beans just right. Baked beans "utterly repulsed" her in her current state. But she knew my mom, and Holden, loved her momma's recipe.

Clem's arms encircled the salad in her lap, as if protecting a priceless artifact from attacking invaders. She'd given Anna a two-minute lecture on how to hold the beans just right so they didn't slop over the sides while we drove.

I slid my arm behind Anna's head and squeezed Clem's

shoulder. Our eyes locked, and I smiled. But I thought she might throw up. And not from the morning sickness.

"I can't wait to see Holden and Ash." Anna wiggled in her seat.

Clem's left hand shot out to steady the beans. "Anna, please be careful."

"Sorry." She smiled sheepishly, but then she sloshed them again as she turned to me. "Do you think Holden will let me drive the smart car around the ranch?" Clem squeezed her eyes shut for a moment and kept a hand on the casserole dish.

I laughed at Anna's exuberance. "I wouldn't get my hopes up. The ranch is probably not the best place for a smart car."

Her shoulders slumped and her bottom lip poked out. I squeezed her neck and smiled. "But I think the two of us could gang up on him."

I'm not sure Clem took a full breath until we parked in front of my parents' house.

Holden and Ashton rushed out the door to meet us. Clem tensed back up like there was a tidal wave coming straight for her. I mean, there kind of was. Holden yanked her door open and Ashton ran around to my side.

Holden hugged her and pulled the salad from her lap. "I'll take that." He tucked it under his arm and wrapped the other arm around her as soon as she was out of the truck.

She almost reached for the salad but pulled her hand back, forcing a smile. She took the beans from Anna. She was taut and seemed like she was about to have a real-life nervous breakdown. I would have to stay on top of Mom the entire time to make sure she didn't pressure Clem, especially about Anna. Human shield engaged.

I stepped out to be immediately tackled by my little brother. We pounded each other on the back. "Dude." I laughed. "You're almost as tall as me. How are you still growing?" He was twenty-three now.

"I'm not. You're just so freaking old, you keep forgetting how tall I am." His dark blonde hair flopped into his eyes and he shoved it back.

I put him in a head-lock and nougied him. "Mom give you crap about your hair yet?"

I let him go, and he stood up, running his hand through the tangles. "Pfft. You think Mom could not give me crap about my hair?" No doubt she'd already offered to pull out the clippers at least once.

He stood next to me, lifted his chin, and pushed up on his tiptoes. "You only got a half-inch on me. We should make everybody call us the Towering Twins." The word twins croaked in his throat. I looked at the ground and back up, forcing a smile. His cheeks flushed. "I got a better one." He snapped twice. "The Altitudinous Amigos."

I laughed. "Altitudinous? Do we have your fancy master's in English lit to thank for that?"

His eyebrows raised. "Obviously. Gotta give Pops his money's worth."

"Pshaw. That's about the only thing that degree's gonna be good for."

"Ha. Ha." He rolled his eyes. Ashton was the least cowboy of us Dupree boys. All guy, but he loved books as much as I loved Clementine. More than once, we'd joked that he'd been switched at birth. But he looked too much like Mom and Sophie, for there to be any doubt. Best thing about Ash was, he didn't care what people thought of him. He was who he was, and I loved him for it.

I smiled. "It'll really tick off Holdie and Ford. Let's do it."

As soon as I stepped away, Anna launched herself at him. He spun her around like he had when she was a toddler and she threw her head back, giggling.

I caught up to Holden and Clem right as they were going through the front door. Now Holden had her beans and her salad. Clem's empty fists balled, pinching the sides of her purple church dress. I slipped my right hand around her left and gave it a quick squeeze. Her wide green eyes held my gaze long enough to see me mouth, *I got you.* Then I pressed my hand against the back of her silky dress. She unexpectedly leaned into me, causing all kinds of chaos in my gut region. I wrapped an arm around her waist, pulling her tighter. If that's what she needed, then I would give it to her. Happily.

Mom walked out of the kitchen, wiping her hands on her floral apron. Holden, still carrying Clem's salad, disappeared into the kitchen, probably to snitch some food. Holden consumed about six thousand calories a day because he was always training for some kind of obstacle race.

Mom saw my hand on Clem's hip and frowned. Clem leaned away, looking embarrassed. I dropped my arm, heat rushing to my face—not because of my mom's reaction. But because I'd tried to do something to make this better for Clem and I'd made it worse. Maybe it was a mistake to let Mom talk me into bringing her.

Dad walked in from the den. Mom had probably marched in there, shut off whatever football game he was watching when we pulled up, and demanded he come be social. Typical Sunday stuff.

"Glad you could finally make it." Mom smiled in our general direction, but there was a bite to her voice.

Clem's neck turned pink. "Um, sorry, I j-just…it's been really busy at the studio."

There was a beat of awkward silence while I stared my mother down. She refused to look directly at either Clem or me though, so she didn't see it.

Dad strode over to Clem and wrapped her in a big hug. "Hey, shugga. You want a glass of lemonade? Just made it fresh." He swept her away to the kitchen.

Mom stepped in front of me, waiting for a hug. I pulled

her in close. "Be nice. Or we're leaving," I whispered. I didn't want to hurt her, but I wasn't going to let her hurt Clem. When I leaned back, Mom's chin was quivering. I kissed her cheek. "She's just really nervous to be here, okay?"

Mom shook her head, her teeth clamped. "She used to come here all the time. What's different now?"

"Everything. And you know that." I gave her shoulders a small shake. If I didn't make this all about the fact that Sophie had left us Anna, hopefully Mom wouldn't either. So I spun it in a different direction. "Sophie was her sidekick, her comfort zone, and she's lost without her. She's trying to sort it out, just like the rest of us. Throw a divorce in the mix and it's a lot. It's not personal. Just show her that you're the same loving second mother you've always been and she'll loosen up. You'll see."

Mom nodded, staring at my collar.

I hugged her again, pulling her tighter this time. "We're happy to be here. I promise. Let's have fun. Enjoy the evening."

She sniffed and smiled a little. "Okay. I'll try."

Anna and Ashton burst through the front door, tripping over each other to get inside first. Ashton had only been ten when Anna was born. They were more like brother and sister than uncle and niece. Anna elbowed him in the gut and shot out of his reach. He doubled over, groaning, and fell onto the couch. When Anna crossed under the doorjamb to the kitchen, she shoved her fists in the air and screamed, "I am victorious!"

Mom rolled her eyes but laughed. She missed having everyone at home. Said the quiet made her restless. She lived for this craziness.

Ashton moaned again and reached out, laughing. "Help me up, Mom."

She pulled the dishrag off her shoulder and twisted it, a smirk stealing against her lips. "I'll help you all right."

Ashton shrieked as she snapped the rag at him. He covered his butt with his hands and bolted out of the room.

Dinner was good. The food. The conversation. The teasing. Once, Clem laughed so hard she cried. When Holden told the worst dad joke of all time—*How do you know when a clock is still hungry? It goes back four seconds*—I had to laugh, just because she was. Her smile was infectious.

"You look real pretty in that dress, Lemon," Dad said, smiling at her. He had a soft spot for Clem. Always had. Probably would even more with Sophie gone.

"Thanks," she said, barely above a whisper. She blushed and looked down at her lap, her dark lashes brushing against her pale skin. Right then the sunlight came through the kitchen window lighting up the freckles on her right cheek and it stole my breath—just like the time in eighth grade when we toured the Smithsonian art museum and I saw a Frederic Remington painting for the first time.

Clementine was fine art.

I caught her gaze and held it for a few seconds. I should've glanced away, but I really didn't want to. Dad was right. She was stunning in that dress.

Holden cleared his throat loudly. Clem looked away, and I glanced over to see him scowling at me, shaking his head like I should know better. I frowned. What was that about? I thought he wanted things to work out between me and Clem. He'd badgered me about it up until a few weeks ago. Even offered to pay for cruise tickets for the two of us. He was positive she'd see me in a different light if we were sipping margaritas and lying in the sun in our bathing suits all day. No joke. When I reminded him that we had to live under the same roof with Anna for ninety consecutive days, he blew me off. Said he'd come stay with Anna and cover for us with Arlo if need be.

Mom walked around collecting plates. When she got to

Clem's, she stopped. "Lemon, you didn't even touch the egg salad. What on earth? You love my egg salad."

Clem stiffened and sat up straighter, her hands gripping the seat of her chair. She still couldn't tolerate eggs in any form. They came right back up. "Sorry, I ate too much of your delicious ham."

Mom acted like she hadn't even heard the compliment. "I'll have to give it to the pigs now, I guess." She huffed, like we were in a recession and Clem had wasted our last farthing. Mom had always been intense about food. Once I'd poured way too many Lucky Charms. She was so mad, she saved the soggy cereal and made me eat it the next morning.

Clem's gaze skittered to mine, pleading to be rescued. I'd told her before we came, just to take a little of everything and push the stuff she couldn't stomach around her plate to make it look like she'd eaten it. My plan had failed her and now I had to fix it.

I reached for Clem's dish. "I still have room." I really didn't. Was stuffed to the gills. But I shoveled that egg salad in anyway. Ashton must've noticed I was turning green because he pulled the plate between us and helped me out. He was the most perceptive sibling I had—always knew when one of us was sad or angry without us saying a word—and I was grateful at that moment.

Dad stood and took the dishes from Mom. "Holden and Silas'll get the cleanup. The rest of us are checking cows." He took the rag from Mom's shoulder and tossed it at Holden.

"I'm driving." Anna jumped up and ran out.

"Hey," Holden complained, holding his hands up. "What if I want to check the cows?"

Dad scoffed. "You been trying to get out of checking cows since you were ten. Don't act like you like it now." He grabbed Mom's hand and guided her away.

"I guess so," Holden scoffed. "Back then, we had to saddle

up the horses. Now you got that fancy side-by-side that seats six. Why can't Ash-hat do the dishes with Si?"

"Cause I want to show him the new Highland cows we got. You've already seen them." Dad cuffed Holden on the shoulder as he walked Mom out. "It ain't gonna kill you to get your hands dirty, city boy."

Ashton guffawed and wiggled his fingers in a wave as he backed out of the room. "Heh. Have fun, suckas."

Clem pushed back from the table. "I'll help."

I smiled. "Nah. It's okay. We got this."

Her expression was tense. I understood. Being around my mom made her insecure. But Dad would be there and he could tell Clem was nervous. He'd make sure she was all right.

"Go. It'll be fun. The Highlands are really cute." Holden might ask for my man card for using the word cute, but there wasn't a better way to describe them. And Clem loved "cute" farm animals.

"Okay." She turned and walked out of the room, her heels clicking against the wood floor.

As soon as the screen door shut behind her, Holden started whining. "I freaking hate the dishes. I'm twenty-seven. I shouldn't have to do stupid chores anymore."

"Are you sure you aren't five? Do you think Mom should have to do all this?" I blew out my lips, annoyed at his current mood. Holden was always over-the-top cheerful. Said it was all the endorphins from working out so much. Maybe he hadn't hit the gym lately. "I'll wash, you dry?" I sprayed down the sides of the sink and plugged the drain. Then I walked back and helped Holden collect the remaining plates and silverware.

When the water was ready, I grabbed a sponge from under the sink, jammed my hands into the suds, and started scrubbing. Holden was quiet, and he's never quiet. Dad always said he talked more than three tweenaged girls combined. And he wasn't wrong.

I glanced over to see my brother glowering at me.

I cocked an eyebrow. "Dude. What is wrong with you today? Did you and Ford trade bodies or something?"

Ford came out of the womb grumpy, also according to Dad. And if we ever caught him smiling, which was about once a year, Mom tried to get a picture before he realized what she was doing. She'd succeeded probably less than five times in his whole life.

I ran a plate under clean water.

"Shut your piehole." Holden yanked it from my hand.

I glowered at him like he was asking for a scuff on the shoulder. "Did you get dumped? What is your problem?"

He rubbed the dishtowel over the plate so hard he was going to break it. "What is wrong with *you*, mouth-breather?" We called each other names all the time, and it usually resulted in us laughing or wrestling until we wound up laughing. But today he was angry at the world about something and his name calling held a twinge of vitriol.

I raised an eyebrow. "Bro. What's up? You can talk to me."

He pulled the cup out of my hands before I was done. It still had a piece of lettuce stuck to the back, but I'd let him figure it out. "What are you doing looking at Lemon like you want to drag her down the hall and jump her on Mom and Dad's bed or something? You shouldn't be doing that."

I let my hands sink in the water and my mouth parted slightly. I mean, yeah, I was struggling to take my eyes off of her, but it wasn't like that. "Weren't you the one badgering me to confess my feelings for her?"

His shoulder twitched. "Yeah. But then I started thinking." His tone was calmer, more careful.

I started washing again. "About?"

"I dunno." He shrugged. "Christy."

I stopped and turned. "*Christy?*"

He held up his hands. "She messaged me on Facebook,

okay? Sent me a friend request when you two decided to do a *reset.*" He said the word like it was the most idiotic thing he'd ever heard. And he looked a little guilty that they were social media friends and he hadn't told me. "And Instagram."

"Dude. It's fine. You can be friends with Christy. Not a big deal." I went back to scrubbing. "So, you've gotten to know her and finally realized she's a human with feelings."

He cocked his head, his tongue running over the front of his teeth. "Yeah, I have. Have you?"

I grabbed the nozzle and sprayed a cucumber off of a bowl, tempted to spray him. "I'm the one who didn't want to blow her off on the possibility that Clem might like me, remember? I'm very aware of Christy and her feelings."

He bristled, scrubbing the cup too hard. "I saw the way you were looking at Lemon tonight. It's not right. Don't you think Christy deserves to have someone look at her like that?"

I exhaled hard through my nose. "Yeah, I do. But I can't force what I don't feel. It was probably too soon to be talking about marriage. I dunno." I pulled my hands out, dried them off, and leaned backward against the sink. "That's why I told her I couldn't keep going on the way we had. I'm trying to do right by her. But I can't worry about it right now. I can only worry about Anna."

His eyebrows flicked a few times, and he snorted. "But you're going to head straight back to Laramie in a month and pretend like you weren't lusting after Lemon all summer, aren't you?" His voice was acid and his jaw pulsed.

Okay. I was done. "Dude, I have no idea what's up with you. Are you ornery 'cause they went to see the Highlands without you?" He glared like he wanted to throw me over a bar counter. "I'm not going to waste anymore time defending myself or vacillating between guilt and a fear of rejection. I already did that, and it sucked, and I'm finally in a good place with Clem." I stepped away from the sink. "I think you're forgetting that I didn't volunteer for any of this. I was voluntold by my deceased twin that this is how I would spend my summer. I'm making the best of a ridiculously complicated situation." I held my hands up, arrested-style. "And you're being more hormonal than a girl on her period. When you're done here, I suggest you go slip one of Mom's valiums. I'm going to find Anna and Clem." It was misogynistic and insensitive. I knew that. But it was a lot nicer than what I wanted to say. Waaaay nicer.

There was still a pile of dishes, but I couldn't care less. I let the screen door on the front porch slam behind me. Mom would've beaten my butt if she'd seen.

Then I hopped on the four-wheeler and took off for my little temporary family.

nineteen

CLEMENTINE

Even though Silas ordered me to stay home and sleep off the exhaustion from my morning round of worshipping the porcelain God, I got up and met him at the studio. If I waited for him to come all the way home after class, we'd have to rush to the city for my first prenatal appointment. This way, we could take our time.

When I pulled into the studio lot, my mouth parted and my eyes widened. There had to be fifteen cars parked there. Was something wrong? Had there been an emergency? We hadn't had that many people show up for a class since opening day. I jumped out of the truck and jogged inside. The bell over the door jingled, announcing my arrival. Every head turned, and I almost ducked back out. There had to be twenty people crammed in there. But there was no emergency. They were... working out.

I saw a bunch of new ladies I hadn't seen before, but also five guys. *Guys.* At my women's gym.

Everybody went back to what they were doing almost instantly. Burpees. Lots of burpees. But burpees weren't a barre thing.

Huh.

Silas jogged over to me, his expression apprehensive. "Hey." He scratched his forehead.

"What is this?" I asked incredulously, pressing my hands to my cheeks.

"Oh, man." He scrubbed a hand over his face. "I'm so sorry. I should've asked first. It's just that a couple of ladies' husbands came out when they found out a guy was teaching the class. But then they wanted something with more cardio. So I started doing a Bootcamp style class." He offered me a weak smile. "I thought with you trying to build up the business—"

I grabbed his arm and shook it. "Silas." I grinned up at him. "This. Is. Amazing."

I swear he sunk down three inches with relief. He laughed and put an arm around my shoulders. "Oh, good." He exhaled long, like he'd been holding his breath since I walked in. "I thought...I thought maybe I'd overstepped. I was going to tell you on the way to the appointment."

I stood there, in awe, watching as my packed little studio, muggy and hot from all the body heat, pulsed with the happy endorphins you get from a good workout with friends. Silas's arm was still around me and I slid mine around his waist. I didn't even care that he was sweaty. Peyton saw me from across the room and waved. Her eyebrows wiggled at the sight of me against Silas's side.

I rolled my eyes but laughed. "Looks like you won her over again."

"Who?" Silas's forehead crunched in confusion. Then he realized. "Oh. Yeah. Peyton and I came up with an unspoken truce. As long as she doesn't undress me with her eyes, she can come to my class."

I snorted.

He squeezed me closer and whispered into my ear. "You have ten new memberships this month."

My head snapped back. "Seriously?"

He nodded. "I think you just needed some testosterone in here. The guys in Seddledowne need a place to workout too. Knox over there..." He pointed to Knox Freeman, a guy we'd gone to high school with. He was cheering on one of the ladies now that he'd completed his round. "He says he's sick of driving to Honeyville. Gas is too much, and he'd rather support a local business. He never came because he didn't think men were allowed."

My forehead crinkled. "How are they here at nine a.m. on a weekday?"

"Well, Knox is a firefighter in the city. He works a twenty-four-hour shift and then has two days off. So he can't come to every class, but he comes as often as he can. The others mostly work from home or they're ranchers." Silas shrugged. "They fit it into their schedules. But I've had some of them ask if we could have a boot camp class in the evening." My stomach fluttered at the word "we." But I forced it to settle. Silas was just excited. He wouldn't even be here four weeks from now. That thought made my stomach do the exact opposite—a rock replacing the butterflies.

Silas dropped his arm. "We're almost done. I need to cool them down and then we can take off."

He walked back to the front of the class. I may or may not have appreciated the way his short-sleeve compression top showcased the muscles in his shoulders. And there were plenty of them to appreciate.

The idea of letting men into the gym was crazy. The entire reason I'd started the studio was because women kept reaching out to tell me how they wanted a place to get fit without the scrutiny of judging or creepy men. So I'd given them what they wanted.

Or what they thought they wanted. But these ladies didn't seem to mind this group of guys. As a matter of fact, all my regulars were pushing themselves harder than normal.

My mind was blown and spinning a hundred miles an hour with the possibilities.

Peyton literally bounced over to me as everyone was putting their weights away and rolling up their mats. "I saw your arms around each other," she sang.

"Okay, Peyt." I patted her arm. "We're just friends."

"Mmmhmm." She pursed her lips. "Well, you shouldn't be. If I had a guy like that look at me the way he looks at you..." She barely pointed her finger at Silas who was looking at me right then. His eyes skittered away, and he turned, giving all his attention to Knox and two other guys chatting with him. "We would not be 'just' anything. We would be definitively, unquestionably, ex-clu-sive."

Just then, the three guys who had been talking with Silas walked over and swarmed me and Peyton.

Knox—tattoo sleeves on both arms and a thick, perfectly manicured beard to match his glistening black hair—offered me a fist bump like we saw each other all the time. I legit had not set eyes on this man in at least five years. "Great place you've got here, Lemon. Thanks for letting us come."

I nodded, my mind still in a flurry. "Absolutely. So glad you like it."

A guy who was about five inches shorter than me, but solid muscle and probably three percent body fat, stuck out his hand. "I'm Wayne Robbie. Live over on Junction Road." He squeezed my hand so hard one of my knuckles popped. "We were wondering, hoping actually, if you'd let us start an obstacle race group. We could meet in the evenings after most guys get off work." His hands moved faster than his words. "Everyone would get a membership, of course. We already have about twenty of us that work out, but it's in my garage and it gets frigid in the winter. And your speaker system is far superior to mine." He glanced around. "This would be ideal."

My head bobbed in a circle, not able to decide if I should nod or shake it in disbelief. "Oh my gosh. Yes. I love that idea."

Peyton gaped, her eyes flashing like she was seeing Times Square for the first time. "You guys have done those obstacle course races? Those look so fun."

The guys nodded.

"Yeah. They really are," Wayne said.

"And challenging," Knox added. "If that's your jam."

"Could I join your group?" Peyton's eyes were full of hope.

"Yes," Wayne said so fast that I almost snorted. He shrugged, his voice suddenly cool. "I'm sure the guys would be okay with that." I'd already caught Wayne discreetly looking her up and down, so it was no surprise that he'd take the 'guys only' sign off their door for her.

Silas sidled up to the group, dressed in jeans and a T-shirt now, listening quietly. Really, I could get rid of my TV, internet, and radio, as long as he was around. All the entertainment I would ever need would be Silas entering the room wearing something different than he had a few minutes before. Didn't even matter what it was. It always made my pulse race, my gut flip backward, and my breath catch in my throat. His eyes sparkled, and he was biting the insides of his cheeks to keep from grinning.

The third man broke in then—a tall, lanky guy, who might've just graduated from high school. "I wish this place was bigger, though." He spoke to the other two guys. "We need access to some weight machines if we want to bring our game up to the next level." He looked at Knox. "I know you're trying to move up to Elite class. That ain't gonna happen if you stop going to the gym in Honeyville."

Like a true curmudgeon, his words took a bit of the excitement out of the air. The rest could join The Downward Dog, just not him. Kidding. The Downward Dog was an equal-opportunity gym. We welcomed all kinds. Even killjoys.

Silas rubbed a hand over his stubble, but he was still grinning, unlike the rest of us. "We gotta git." He nodded toward me. "But we'll try to come up with a solution. See you guys Friday?"

"You know it." Knox and Silas did the bro hug with the back slap.

Then Silas ushered me out the door. He held the passenger door of my truck open and shut it when I was settled inside. Chivalry was so shmexy, and this man could give classes on it. Then he hustled around the front of the truck and got into the driver's seat.

He grinned. "Kinda cool, huh?"

I shook my head in awe. "Unbelievably cool."

He pulled out of the parking lot and onto the road, leaned back, his arm outstretched, resting on the steering wheel. Somebody going the opposite direction passed, and he gave them a one-fingered wave. I chewed my lips, fighting against the smile that was trying to betray how adorably hot I thought that was.

He ran a hand over his hair. "So, I had an idea about how you could expand your studio and make more money."

I turned to face him. "More than a bunch of new guys forming an obstacle race group?"

"Yeah. I mean, Jonathan basically said it back there." Oh, Gruff had a name. "I can't take all the credit. But what if you talked the owner of the building into selling it to you? The whole thing. You could keep the studio, but turn the other half into a full gym with weight machines, treadmills, ellipticals...you get the idea." His thumb tapped the steering wheel. "The other side's just storage, right?"

I frowned and blew out my breath. "Yeah. But that's...that sounds like...I'd be way in over my head." The thought of trying to run something like that, along with the studio and managing the farm by myself, made my chest tighten. "And how would I pay for all of that? It would be a huge investment."

"I'm not sure about the finances, but I think it would be easier to run than you think. You get everything set up and we can install a swipe system. They have them at the gym I go to in Laramie." He adjusted in his seat. "Everyone downloads an app and when they approach the building, the app signals the door to unlock. People can come and go as they please, twenty-four-seven. Just get a couple of employees to man the front desk—a few high school kids for the evenings. Then you hire someone to clean." He clicked his tongue. "The place practically runs itself."

I tilted my head. "There's no way it's that simple. What about when a machine breaks down? And do you think it would make enough money to pay back the loan on the building and all the equipment?"

He nodded confidently. "I do. I've been thinking about it for a while, actually."

My eyes widened. "You have?"

"I called around to some gyms in nearby towns around the same size as Seddledowne. Some of them have as many as a thousand memberships a month. In the city, big gym memberships are peanuts. But farther out, you can charge more. Not as much as the studio, but you wouldn't have to. You're not paying instructors." He nodded. "Apparently, this is a big thing with this generation of teens right now. The gym is their hangout."

"Really?"

"Yeah. Holden detests going to the gym in the evening

because it's overrun with cocky, pubescent boys trying to show off for their girlfriends and using it as a hookup spot. Says he has to go early before work or it takes two hours to get his workout done. Kids sit at a machine on their phones for twenty or thirty minutes before he can get to it." Silas flipped the blinker to turn left. "And you'd need a good repair guy on speed dial. Didn't you say the guy who owns the building used to run a machine shop or something? He's probably good at fixing stuff. Some retired guys are itching for something to do."

My insides were settling, but Silas tended to have that effect on me in general. And I didn't want to confuse that with genuine peace. Was this something I could actually do? Or would I be hurtling myself, warp speed, toward financial ruin? What I didn't want was to screw over the studio for the sake of trying to make more money.

I opened the calculator app on my phone. "So, if I charged, say, forty-five dollars a month, per member and…let's be conservative…got six hundred memberships…so, for a year…" I plugged in the calculation. The number on my screen was massive. Like too big for me to fathom.

He chuckled. "You got really quiet. Everything okay?"

I turned the screen toward him so he could see the dollar amount.

His face broke into a cocky grin, forcing my pulse into a gallop. For a split second, I forgot what we were even talking about. "You would make more money than Billy. And that's at six hundred memberships—think if you really did get a thousand."

I couldn't. I could not wrap my head around the number on my screen right now. I laughed. "Why hasn't someone already done this?" But immediately, I started second-guessing the idea. Nothing in my life ever fell into place that easily. "I don't know. It's a huge step. I'm not sure I can do it on my own." I chewed the inside of my cheek. "Maybe if Sophie was here. Or my dad."

I glanced over at him and I couldn't hide the longing. *Or you*, I thought.

If Silas stayed, I could do anything.

twenty

SILAS

Clem lay on the exam table, her fingers trilling against her thighs as we waited for the doctor to come in. She kept glancing at me nervously. "I wish Momma could've come." Her hands lifted. "I mean, I'm so glad you're here, but..."

I got it. Sometimes a woman just wanted her mom. And the first time listening to your baby's heartbeat was one of those times. "She'll be here when you find out the gender." Miss Lisa hadn't been able to find someone to fill in for her at work. But she swore she'd be here for the twenty-week ultrasound if she had to quit her job to do it.

Clem nodded and her fingers went back to trilling. The longer she lay there, it seemed, the more antsy she got. I reached out and ran my fingers through her thick red hair, tickling her scalp. She and Sophie used to do this all the time. I'd walk into the living room before bed, and they'd be snuggled on the couch, in their pajamas, watching whichever reality competition show they were into that season. Inevitably, one of them would have their head on a pillow in the other's lap, getting "head tickles." That's what they called them. I used to tease them about it. Only girls could get away with that. If you walked in on two guys running their fingers through the other's hair...well, they either needed to come out or hand in their man card.

Clem's gaze shot up at my touch. I stopped. She wrapped a hand around my wrist. "No, don't stop. It's helping."

So I went back to drawing twirls with my fingertips. She stared up at me with her big, green, unguarded eyes. My heart thundered in my chest.

She bit her bottom lip. "I have a confession...and it's kind of terrible."

I offered her a gentle smile, still tickling. "I won't judge. I promise." There couldn't possibly be anything she'd say that would make me think less of her.

She reached up and grabbed my forearm, pulling my hand out of her hair. Her palm slid against mine and she spread her fingers open, pulling mine in between. My knees buckled, and I covered by sitting on the side of the table. Her ginger locks were splayed across the crunchy crepe paper beneath her. She reminded me of Snow White lying there waiting for the prince. I wished I was Prince Charming right then, and that she was asleep and I could get away with kissing her.

I'd gotten the feeling lately that she might be okay with that. I wasn't sure, though. Just little glances, or the way she would shudder whenever I touched her. Then again, the shuddering could be because she found me disgusting. Gah. It was all so confusing. I simply wasn't sure. And the longer I stayed in Seddledowne...the longer I stayed with Clem...the less sure I became.

She squeezed my hand tight. "I'm terrified there won't be a heartbeat...and I'm terrified...that there will." She covered her face with her other hand, ashamed. "I mean, I want this baby more than I ever thought I would. But..." I pulled her hand away from her face and stared down at her with a soft smile. She didn't need to hold back with me. Not anymore. She grabbed that hand, now holding both of mine, her body lying between them. "I don't want him or her to have to have Billy as a dad. And he doesn't deserve to be rewarded with a kid when he tricked me into making it with him."

"No. It's okay. I get it." I ran my thumb along her knuckles, forcing myself to ignore the heat that hit my bloodstream. "Let's make a deal."

Resolve entered her face, and she nodded. She didn't even know what the deal was, but she trusted me enough to make it anyway. Man, that felt good.

"Let's put it in God's hands," I said. "If there's a heartbeat, this baby is meant to be yours regardless of how it got here. It'll be an unexpected gift. Just like Anna was."

She nodded, but her expression held a hint of fear. "But if not?"

"Then He might be taking it away to ease your worries. And you'll get the chance later with someone else." I'd made the words up as they were coming out of my mouth. But they felt right.

I'd tried not to think too much about the fact that the woman I loved was having another man's baby. There wasn't a single thing I could do to change it. And I wouldn't take this away from her even if I had that kind of power. This baby was half Clem's. I would love this little boy or girl like crazy for that reason alone. Even if I had to do it from two thousand miles away. Even if it killed me that it wasn't mine.

I kept running my thumb over Clem's knuckles, hoping to get the worry lines between her eyes to lessen. "Remember how heartbroken and livid my parents were when Sophie told them Gianni had gotten her pregnant?"

Clem smiled. "I will never forget. It's seared into my memory."

Mine too. "Sophie sat on my parents' bed, sobbing, practically hyperventilating. And my dad wouldn't stop shouting about how her life was ruined now. I remember your face as you sat next to her, holding her hand. You looked terrified, sick, and like you wanted to take a hot poker after him all at once."

"Your dad was being such a..."

"Butthead?" I said it for her.

"Yeah."

"Remember how stunned my mom was? She was actually speechless."

"First and last time that's ever happened." She covered her mouth like she'd said something scandalous.

"Facts." I agreed, using an Anna-ism. "And then my dad went for his gun, saying how he was going to shoot that horny Italian for stealing her virginity."

Clem snickered. "And how deflated he was when Sophie told him that Gianni was long gone, back in Italy already. Because she'd hid the pregnancy for six months." Clem shook her head, making the paper crinkle beneath her. "I still don't know how she did that as skinny as she was. How did your parents not notice when she went from wearing midriffs and tank tops to your oversized T-shirts?"

I laughed. "No idea. They were so oblivious." Sophie had confided in me almost as soon as she found out—second only behind Clem. It had been an anxiety-ridden five months, keeping that secret. Knowing, inevitably, it was going to hit the fan. Watching my parents' every move to see if they'd figured it out.

Clem's expression went solemn. "And then they kicked her out." But then a smile played at her lips. "But I told her not to worry. We'd have the world's longest sleepover. My parents said she could live with us. But then, a couple of weeks later, you fought your dad and fixed the whole thing."

I shook my head, still ashamed. "I didn't *fight* my dad."

She scoffed. "You screamed in his face that you were going to quit school and get a job and take Sophie and the baby far away and he'd never see any of you again." Clem told it like she'd been there. She hadn't. Just my mom and Holden. But she'd heard the story a hundred times. Sophie had loved telling it, always with pride in her eyes. "And then you pushed him down on the bed, drove to my house, got Sophie, and took her home." Her expression was incredulous, like after all these years she still couldn't believe I'd done that.

I lifted my hands, and hers came with them. "Well, he wanted to place Anna through adoption just because Pastor Allen told him Soph wouldn't go to heaven if she had a baby out of wedlock, as if adoption canceled out 'sin.'"

"Pfft." Clem rolled her eyes and laughed. "Old Fish Lips. I still can't believe your parents let him preach at her funeral."

"Comparing Sophie to one of the thieves on the cross... what in the world?" But I was getting off topic and there was a point to the story. "Remember the first time we held Anna, though?"

"Annaleise Nicole Dupree." Her eyes danced. "Nothing else like it in the world."

It was one of my favorite memories. Clem, Dad, and I spent all night in the hospital waiting room while Mom was in the delivery suite with Sophie. At one point, Clem had nodded off and fallen asleep on my shoulder. I didn't take another deep breath until she woke up a couple hours later when the nurse ran out to tell us the baby was finally here. Best. Night. Ever.

"Remember how tiny her fingers were?" I asked.

Clem was looking at me funny now, like she was seeing me differently than ten seconds before. "What I remember most was *you*."

My body wanted to squirm, but I held still.

Her evergreen eyes were so earnest, burning into me.

"When the nurse put Anna in your arms, you got all choked up, and the way you looked at her was like she was the best thing in the whole world. And then Sophie hollered from the bed, 'What do you think of her, Uncle Si?'" My cheeks were on fire because I knew what she was going to say next. "And you tried to talk, but you couldn't. It took like thirty seconds for you to get the sentence out. "She's the most beautiful thing I've ever seen."

It was one of the most vulnerable moments of my life. Anna captured my heart from second one and she'd had it ever since. "But remember my dad?" I asked. "How he'd been all prideful and grumpy the entire pregnancy—"

Her nose crinkled, and I wanted to kiss it. "But the minute he held her for the first time, he broke down sobbing. Like convulsing. Snot everywhere." We laughed. "And the nurse tried to take Anna because she thought he might drop her. But he curled Anna against him like a quarterback holding a football and sat in the chair, dripping tears all over her blanket. Nobody was getting that baby out of his arms." Her eyes were dancing. "And he's been treating her like a princess ever since. You'd never know he had such a struggle to accept her existence." She shook her head, awed. "I've never seen your dad cry like that again." Her voice broke. "Until Sophie passed."

But I didn't want to go there. The point of the story was to focus on the happiness a baby would bring. I pushed her hair back off her forehead. "If there's a heartbeat today, promise me you'll try to let go of the hurt Billy caused you and accept this for the incredible gift that it is."

She smiled, looking more at peace. "You're right. Of course you are."

The doctor finally knocked on the door and popped her head inside. "Mrs. Adams?"

Clem started to sit up, and I put a hand behind her back to

help. "Ms. Shepherd," Clem corrected. "Sorry, I need to change that."

"What?" My head was spinning. "You're going back to your maiden name?"

She smiled and nodded. If someone had given me a brand new thoroughbred quarter horse, I couldn't have been happier. She wouldn't be walking around wearing Billy's last name anymore. Halle-freaking-lujah.

The doctor shook her hand. "It's so nice to meet you, Ms. Shepherd." She turned to me and we shook. "And you're the father?"

I opened my mouth, but no words came out.

Clem rescued me. "No. The father won't be here today. This is my... Silas."

"My Silas." The Doctor smiled. "I like that." So did I. "I'm Dr. Gregory. Nice to meet you both. Sorry I'm running so late. It was a full moon last night and I swear every woman anywhere close to their due date went into labor. I delivered three babies this morning already."

"No worries," Clem and I said in unison. Apparently, living together under the same roof made your minds sync up.

The doctor glanced between us, and I could see the wheels turning. But she said nothing. Only opened her laptop and started reading Clem's chart.

"Nurse Angela already sent in a prescription for anti-nausea medicine, but if it doesn't help or completely take it away, please don't hesitate to call and let us know."

She ran down a list of questions—like other medications Clem was on. What the date of her last period was. Any additional health issues. Thankfully, Clem was perfectly healthy and had nothing to report on that front.

"We're going to draw blood today to check your iron and folate levels, that kind of thing. Is there anything else we need to test for?"

Clem shook her head. "No, I'm good."

My head tilted. "Are you sure?"

The doctor's brow raised. Clem scowled.

I didn't want to overstep but... I leaned down by Clem's ear and whispered, "Don't you want her to test for STDs?" Clem stiffened and from the look on her face, I think it was the first time the idea ever crossed her mind. "Sorry. I just want to make sure you and the baby are safe." We'd never talked about it, but we knew nothing about Lyla's other partners, and it was entirely possible that she wasn't Billy's first indiscretion.

Her face softened, and she nodded. "It's okay."

Dr. Gregory must've heard everything. Not gonna lie, it's hard to whisper with a voice as deep as mine. "Is there a reason you would need to be checked for sexually transmitted diseases? Have you had questionable partners?"

Clem blanched at the plural use of the word partner. The room went silent and then Clem quietly said, "My husband had an affair. So yes, it might be smart to check."

Now the doctor was the one to blanch. "Well, he's an idiot. Because you are lovely and darling and seem wonderful. Some people are just stupid." It was the most honest thing I'd ever heard a doctor say. It was refreshing, and I decided I liked her.

"All true," I said, causing Clem to blush. "Especially the idiot part."

Dr. Gregory's mouth turned up at the corners in a half-smirk, but she quickly slipped her professional hat back on. "Are we ready to hear this baby's heartbeat?"

Clem hesitated. I mouthed the words, *a gift*. She nodded. "Yes. Let's do this." She squeezed my hand so tight, my knuckles rubbed together.

The doctor had her lie back on the table and pulled her shirt up, tucking it under the bottom of her bra. I didn't know what the tummy of a woman who was eleven weeks along should look like, but I thought Clem's was entirely too flat. Hopefully it was because she'd lost weight with the morning sickness and not because there was a complication with the pregnancy.

"This might be a little cold." Dr. Gregory squirted gel on the handheld Doppler device.

When the gel hit her skin, Clem flinched. "Yeah. A little cold." Her grip tightened even more.

I thought it might take a few seconds to find the heartbeat, but almost instantly, the most beautiful sound entered the room. A fast whooshing that reminded me of galloping horses.

Clem let go of my hands to cover her mouth, her eyes twice as big as normal. The whooshing continued on, strong and quick.

"Sounds like a perfect heartbeat," Dr. Gregory said. "Congratulations, Momma."

Clem was quiet but happy as we left the exam room. No doubt she had a lot on her mind. Back outside, the heat was sweltering and the air thick with humidity.

I opened the door for her to get in the passenger seat, then I walked around to get in my side. But when I opened my door, Clem wasn't sitting on the passenger side. She was in the middle, slipping the seatbelt over her waist.

I scooted in next to her, not sure what was happening. Her elbow rubbed against my side and electricity jolted through my veins. She never rode there. It was Anna's seat, even when Anna wasn't with us. My hands fumbled, and I dropped the keys. I swore, but picked them up and quickly started the truck.

I glanced over at her, trying to smile, but I'm sure it came out as more of a grimace. Why couldn't I breathe right now? We'd been holding hands in the exam room and I was okay then. But I knew why. That was me comforting her. She needed that a few minutes ago.

But right now, there was no reason for her to sit in the middle. None. Why was she doing this? Home was an hour away, and I wasn't going to make it that long with her this close. *Chill the frick out!* I forced myself to exhale slowly as I put the truck in reverse. But then I realized my problem. I had to turn to look over my shoulder. Turn in her direction. Usually, I put my arm across the middle seat to make that a little easier. I didn't know how to back up like this. We sat there for a second, not moving. *Get your crap together, man!*

Finally, I stretched my arm behind her head so I could see what I was doing. And dang if she didn't take that as an invitation to lean into my side. That rose shampoo went straight up my nose, hitting me with pheromones like a baseball bat smacking a grand slam. My heart thunked in my chest so hard, I was sure she could hear it. Or feel it. It felt like it was shaking the entire truck.

She seemed totally zen, like this was the most natural thing in the world. And I was the opposite—a freaking tornado of hormones and heart palpitations, my thoughts racing headlong toward cliffs that were downright precipitous. I couldn't even inhale correctly.

Once I finally got turned around, I pulled my arm from behind her and gripped the steering wheel for dear life. But she still snuggled up against me, a slight smile on her lips. Then she actually leaned her head on my shoulder. Was she trying to break me? Give me a heart attack? Short-circuit all my nerve endings?

Well, it was working. All of it.

"Si?" She slid her hands around my bicep. I quit fighting and dropped my hand to my thigh. What was even the point? She slid her palm against mine, interlocking our fingers. Oh, good grief. "You're my best..." I thought she was about to put me squarely in the friend zone and I didn't know if I could handle it. Not with her all smashed up against me. But then she amended, "You're my favorite person. I'm really glad Sophie did this. I missed you so much while you were gone. And I want this baby to grow up with you in their life. They're going to need an example of what a good man looks like. And I can't think of anyone better than you." She released a blissful sigh. "I really wish you didn't have to go back to Laramie."

I was her favorite person? My heart couldn't even comprehend it. She'd always been mine. Did this mean that she felt the same way about me that I'd always felt about her? Thoughts. Hormones. Cliffs. Precipitous.

Rein it in, dude.

But I couldn't. I didn't even want to anymore. I completely gave up and sank down in my seat until it felt like the cushions were part of my body, melting against her. I leaned over, inhaling the clean, floral scent of her hair freely and without reservation. And then I pressed a kiss onto the top of her beautiful head.

"Me too, Clem. Me too."

twenty-one

CLEMENTINE

The closer we got to the ninety day finish line, the faster time went. And the faster time went, the more I wanted it to slow down. The anti-nausea meds worked right away, and I was back to teaching in no time, though Silas kept the nine a.m. class, which was still gaining new clients steadily.

I contacted Mr. Greerly, the owner of the building, to inquire about possibly buying it. It didn't take much to get him to agree, especially when I told him I'd need an on-call machine repair guy. Said his wife would be thrilled—apparently she'd been hounding him to sell it for years. But I was honest and told him it was only a possibility. I hadn't decided. Wasn't ready to commit quite yet, especially with Silas leaving. He assured me he was ready to sell whenever I made a decision and just to let him know.

Two days before beach week, on Anna's fourteenth birthday, I found myself up at Momma's, going through my old baby clothes. I wasn't convinced anything twenty-eight years old would be in any condition for a new baby. But Momma was insistent.

"Oh my goodness, look at this one. I remember when you wore this." Momma held up a white-footed pajama set with pale yellow ducks all over it. "This would work for a boy or a girl." She handed it to me to put in the keep pile.

The attic was dusty and humid and the last place I wanted to be on a scorching July day. I fanned my sleeveless shirt and took a swig from my water bottle. Then I stood and unbuttoned my jean shorts. With the nausea gone, I was gaining weight finally, all in my stomach. At least the fatigue had tapered off. I walked around the attic, trying to get closer to the vent going outside. Maybe I'd catch a breeze.

There was barely an aisle to walk down. My parents had kept anything and everything they'd ever acquired. And I mean everything. I was more of a minimalist myself, probably because of this attic. More junk equaled more clutter. And clutter gave me anxiety. But I think it had the opposite effect on Momma. She and Daddy had been convinced that every item up there might be useful someday. Daddy had even saved his dad's old helmet and uniforms from World War II. And Momma had a stack of afghans Granny Eudora made forty years ago or more. I reached down for a leather-looking scrapbook I'd never seen before and opened the cover.

Huh.

There was an article that someone had printed off the internet with a picture of Silas, in full cowboy dress, on a horse, roping a steer. The headline read, "Pokes Take It All." My eyes devoured the words. Silas's team had won the Central Rocky Mountain Men's Regionals.

I flipped through the book, absorbing the articles. Each one about Si and his roping career at UW. There were a few cards for Daddy's birthdays. Just a pre-printed greeting with some sappy sentiment about what a great guy my dad was. But each one had Silas's almost-undecipherable signature on it.

"Momma?" I walked back through the clutter and squatted next to her. "What is this?"

She stopped sorting. "Oh, your daddy kept every news clip he could find about that boy. You know how proud he was when Silas got that scholarship."

I shook my head. "Proud enough to make a scrapbook?" Was there a scrapbook of me in here? Actually, yeah, probably a couple. But Momma had put them together. The fact that Daddy even knew what a scrapbook was blew my mind. "Did he print these articles?"

She tsked. "You know good and well that man didn't know how to turn on the computer. Made me crazy, getting me to scour the internet every time he knew that boy was competing. I printed about half of those." She folded a onesie with stains on the front and put it in the keep pile. I'd toss it later when I took it home. "Silas printed the rest and sent them to him."

I sat back on the floor, stunned. "Silas sent him these?"

"That's what I said, honey." She cocked her head at me. "Why are you so surprised?"

"I just...I didn't realize they kept in touch after he left." I couldn't be jealous of my dad. I was happy for him. Silas was the son he never had. But part of the hurt I'd held toward Silas wasn't just that he'd left me—he'd left Daddy too. I'd walked around thinking that for years. And now, come to find out, it wasn't true. I mean, yes, he physically left, but I was the only one he'd cut out of his life. The hurt smacked me right in the heart and left my cheeks stinging. "Unbelievable."

"What are you talking about?" Momma asked. "You're mad that Daddy was proud of him, or that Silas kept in contact?"

"Momma," I said, knowing I sounded like a selfish brat, but not caring. "He completely ghosted me after he left."

She stared blankly. "I don't know what that means."

"Broke all contact. Amputated me from his life."

"Of course he did," she said, tapping her finger against my forehead like I was thick-skulled. "He was in love with you. And you broke his heart when you chose Billy."

My entire face twisted in shock. "He was not in love with me. That is the most ridiculous thing I've ever heard." It really was. Silas had always been withdrawn and standoffish. He hadn't acted anything like a boy in love. More like a boy who wished I'd disappear.

"Don't you question me, Missy." Her tone got sharp. "A Momma knows when a boy is in love with her daughter."

"Okay." I held up my hands. "Believe what you want. But he didn't even contact me when Daddy died. Never said I'm sorry or anything. That's not how you treat someone you're in love with."

Momma gawked, like I'd grown tentacles out of my neck. "He came to the funeral. Is that not enough for you?"

My head fell back. Now I was the one looking at her like she was some kind of alien. "No, he did not. Do you have dementia? Should we get you checked for Alzheimers?" I reached up to tap her forehead like she'd done mine. She smacked my hand away. Hard.

"That is so disrespectful. I'm old, but I'm not that old. And your daddy only died three years ago. I remember very clearly that Silas was there. Don't believe me?" She stood up, towering over me.

"Sorry, Momma, but, no, I don't. I was there too. I think I would've seen Silas if he'd come."

She swished her way to the back of the attic where I'd been when I found the scrapbook. A minute later, she came bustling back up the aisle with a white book in her hand. The funeral guest book. She flipped through, her gaze following her finger down the lines, searching for his name. But she wasn't going to find it because it wasn't there. I didn't know what event she was confusing Daddy's funeral with, but I knew Silas hadn't attended.

Until she laid the book in my lap, her finger pointing right at his chicken-scratch signature. The same one on Daddy's birthday cards.

I gasped. Silas had come?

She stood over me, her arms folded, looking smug. "Don't question your momma."

I stared at his name, so confused. "I never saw him."

She sat down facing me, her legs criss-crossed. "I don't think he wanted you to see him." Her tone was softer now. "I think he stood at the very back, away from his family, and he slipped out before it was over."

My face twisted up, trying to understand. "Then how did you see him?"

She sighed. "I didn't see him at the funeral. But I knew he was going to be there. He told me." She squeezed my knee, giving me a pity look. "He stopped by the house the night before and tried to give back the rope your daddy taught him to rope with. He thought I'd like to have it. But I wouldn't accept it, told him James would've wanted him to have it." Her stare pinned me. "He loved you, Clementine. And he loves you still." She patted my cheek. "You weren't ready to hear it back then. Maybe you're still not ready."

I was dazed, unable to process any of it.

She caught the time on her watch. "Oh, we'll have to finish this later. We got to get up to your house and get everything done before Anna gets back."

Silas and I had planned out Anna's party. Jenny had taken Anna shopping all day and out to a movie. Bo and Si left before dawn to pick up a new bull in North Carolina, but he promised he'd be back at seven with Brooklyn and the cake and ice cream. Momma and I only had to decorate.

I held the book up, completely shook, as Anna would say. "Can I keep this for a little while?"

"Of course, baby girl."

My thoughts were a raging cyclone as we hung streamers and blew up balloons. Silas was in love with me? Why hadn't Sophie ever mentioned it? And why hadn't she told me he came home for the funeral? And if Silas had those feelings for me, how could I not have known? And why hadn't he said anything when we were younger?

Actually, I was glad he hadn't. Momma was right. I wasn't ready back then. If he'd told me I would've ruined him—cracked his ribs right open, yanked his heart out, and left it pulverized on the ground. But I wasn't that girl anymore. I was a woman. And I'd been through hard things. With Sophie dying and Billy's affair, I was well acquainted with heartbreak, too.

The difference was, someone else had broken me. Someone Silas despised. Someone I never should have chosen. Regardless of all that, Silas had come charging in on his white horse, scooped me up, and put all my broken parts back together again.

And what had I done for him?

Absolutely nothing. I was disgusted with myself. Entirely. All I'd ever wanted was to be loved, completely and unconditionally. And he'd been there all along, quietly waiting. I'd seen the quiet patience as weakness or indifference. In actuality, Silas was probably the strongest person I knew. If he did love me, I didn't deserve it. He was so far above me, it was embarrassing. And to think only a few months ago I'd still seen him as...just Silas. Momma had been right. It was crazy what a summer could do.

The sound of an engine and crunching gravel brought me back to the present. I ran to the window to see Silas pulling up.

"Momma, they're here."

"Perfect timing." She tied off the last balloon and stood back. We'd picked the Happy Birthday sign up at the craft store. Momma had brought the rest from the attic. Anna would love the pink and green balloons and streamers. They were her favorite color combination.

I looked down at my clothes—sweat-stained and dirty—and peeled a cobweb off my leg. "Shoot." I ran to the bedroom, suddenly hyperaware of my appearance. In thirty seconds, I had a sundress on and was back in the living room right as Silas came through the door with Brooklyn and his dad.

"Hey." I walked up to him and took the cake, my pulse skipping every other beat. He smiled, crow's-feet barely appearing at the corners of his eyes. And I let myself believe what Momma had said. Silas loved me. Right?

Like he could read my thoughts, his smile broadened, his gray eyes burning into me in a way Billy's never had. Not even in the beginning. And everything in me screamed that Momma was right. I wanted to kiss him right there, in front of everybody. Just grab his shirt in my fists, yank him as close as I could, and smash my mouth on his. But it would have to wait.

First, we had to celebrate our girl.

twenty-two

SILAS

I'd never been more excited about a gift in my entire life. But I waited patiently through the cake and ice cream, and the birthday spankings. Dad wouldn't stop grinning, looking at me every couple of minutes. My palms started sweating, worrying he would let it slip. But he didn't.

Clem didn't know about the extra gift I'd gotten Anna. But I couldn't help myself. I'd seen it online and knew it had to be hers. So Dad and I made up a story about going to pick up a new bull. Really, we'd driven to Nashville to get Anna's present.

Clem walked over to Anna, barefoot, her sundress showing off her perfectly toned shoulders. Her eyes had been flicking over to me all night, and I loved how excited she was to celebrate Anna. She handed Anna a small package wrapped in pink and green birthday paper.

"Oh my gosh, I love this paper. Thank you, Aunt Lemon. I'm going to save it." She took her time peeling the tape off carefully so as not to rip it. Inside was a bright blue jewelry box. I knew what this was. Had paid for half of it. Anna slowly snapped the lid back and choked on a squeal.

Brooklyn shrieked with excitement, "Pop off, Sis. It's gorgeous."

Anna carefully lifted the gold locket out of the box.

"There's a picture inside. It's tiny, but...you'll see," Clem said, her knuckles against her mouth.

Anna slid her fingernail between the front and back and pried it open.

"Oh." She covered her mouth and then squeezed her eyes shut. I couldn't see, but it was a picture of Sophie. Clem and I had picked it out together. It was a snapshot from two years ago, at beach week. Ashton had just dumped our cooler full of ice water down the back of her shirt. Sophie was laughing, face up toward the sky, so happy.

Anna pressed her hands over her eyes, sobbing. Clem glanced at me, sick. That wasn't the reaction we'd hoped for.

"Hey." I knelt next to my niece. "It's okay."

"It's my first birthday without her." She hiccuped. "I miss her so much."

Mom knelt on her other side and pulled her into her arms. "Oh, baby, we all do."

Clem squatted down in front and lifted Anna's chin. "Your momma might not be here, but we are." She glanced around at each person in the room and Anna followed her eyes. "And we always will be."

Anna nodded and wiped her eyes on her sleeve. "You're right. I have the best family." She smiled at Brooklyn. "And friends." She fanned her face for a second, then studied the picture of her mom in the locket. "It's the best gift you could've given me." She hugged Clem. "I love it so much. Thank you."

"It's from Uncle Silas too."

Anna threw her arms around me.

I squeezed her tight. "Love you, sweet girl."

Once the gifts were opened, Anna sat on the couch,

looking overwhelmed in a good way. "Thanks, guys. I love them all. Like really."

Brooklyn nodded, straight faced and emotionless. "Highkey the best presents ever."

Mom rolled her eyes and pursed her lips.

I held up a finger. "Hold on. There's one more. I'll be right back."

Clem's forehead furrowed, and she tilted her head at me, puzzled. I went out the front door and jogged across the lawn to the bed of the truck. Then I flipped the tailgate down and pulled a cardboard box toward me. Hefted it in my arms, and strode back across the lawn.

Anna was sitting on the couch still, looking perplexed. I put the ordinary brown box on the ground in front of her.

Anna peered down. "What is it?"

I bit my lips to keep from grinning while I untucked the corners where Dad and I had folded them so they wouldn't come open. "I thought Miss Lisa might like Buford back."

"Oh, no, I don't mind at—" Miss Lisa protested.

But before she could finish, I had the box open. Anna peered inside and then up at me, not believing her eyes. She dropped to her knees and reached inside, pulling the tiny basset hound puppy out of the box.

"Are you kidding me?" The pup had slept most of the way home. He was still a tiny thing—barely weaned from his mom. We'd fed him right before we got here. Apparently, with a full belly, he didn't want to wake up and play.

"A new bull, my eye," Mom said and everybody laughed.

Anna lifted the pup up, checking out his face, his ears, his feet—her cheeks bursting with a smile.

"OMG, he is the cutest thing ever." Brooklyn sat next to her, stroking a single finger down his back.

Then and only then, I glanced up at Clem. "If you don't want to keep him at the house, Mom and Dad already said he can stay with them and they'll bring him over every night."

Clem looked at me like I was nuts and also the most wonderful person in the world. "Um, no way. He's staying here." She knelt beside me, one hand on my thigh, the other rubbing the puppy's head.

He opened one eye and then the other. "OMG, OMG, I love him already." Anna glanced over at me. "It's a boy, right?"

I nodded.

"You can tell right here." Brooklyn pointed to his boy parts, and we all laughed. Leave it to Brooklyn to keep it real.

"What're you going to name him?" Clem asked.

"Oh, I already know this. Huckleberry. Huck for short." She nodded decisively.

"Huckleberry," I repeated. "I like it."

After Brooklyn's parents picked her up and everyone went home, Anna and Clem sat at the kitchen table, Huckleberry in Anna's lap, playing the new board game Holden had sent her for her birthday. Clem was still wearing her sundress, and my eyes kept roving over her. The way it hugged her waist and dipped down in the back to show off her shoulder blades. For the hundredth time that night, she glanced at me, a slight blush on her cheeks. Something felt different between us, more intense.

I shoved a hand in my hair, frustration spilling over me. Staying in the house, with her constant glances, with the way I felt, was a terrible idea. I went out onto the back porch and sat down on the top step, overlooking the yard, the fireflies dancing in the dark, the bullfrogs croaking in the river bottom, the smell of sweet honeysuckle tinging the air. My time in Seddledowne was almost up. And for the first time in ten years, I didn't want to run back to Wyoming. I wanted to stay right here. With these two girls I loved so much.

Getting on the plane in a week and a half was going to be

the hardest thing I'd ever had to do. Like a dead man walking to his execution. How could I leave them? How could I go back to Christy? Christy, who I'd barely thought of in weeks. This reset felt more like a breakup. But my life was no longer stagnant. For the first time, I was really living.

I was no longer an imposter in my own body. I'd laughed and teased, protected, and opened up. I'd given it my all. The possibility that Clem was falling for me had even entered my mind. I couldn't go back to Christy anymore. My heart wasn't in it and it never had been. Not really. I knew that now.

But I couldn't stay here for a possibility. I couldn't leave Mrs. Serafin hanging after I'd given her my word.

Could I?

The sliding door rolled open. Clem walked out and sat down next to me, her shampoo tickling my nose.

She closed her eyes, listening to the bullfrogs. "That is my favorite sound in the whole world."

I studied her, taking in every feature, trying to burn the way she looked at that moment into my memory. Her perfect cheeks, her barely upturned nose, her pouty bottom lip and, man, that hair.

"Si?" she said, her eyes opening. "I wanted to talk to you about...Anna." She turned, her knees touching my thigh.

I turned too, leaning in, gazing into her eyes, hoping to work some magic spell that would make her fall in love with me. Conjure some kind of feelings in her so that we could stay together and the three of us could be a family. But thoughts like that were hazardous to my health.

I blinked. "Yeah?"

"We've been skirting around it all summer, but I think it's time. We need to figure out what we're doing." Her finger traced a tulip on her dress. "And..." She stopped, and chewed her bottom lip, her forehead furrowing. Then she stared into my eyes with such longing. Like she wanted something from me. Yearned for something. "Actually...there's something else I think we should talk—"

The door slid open, and we turned. Anna walked out in her pajama shorts and one of the T-shirts she liked to wear to bed. She squirmed between us, pushing us apart—but then hooked an arm around each of our elbows, pulling us back in.

The three of us sat there watching the fireflies before Anna broke the silence. "I made a wish tonight when I blew out my candles."

Clem sat up straight, leaning away. "Anna." Her voice was tight with a warning.

"Don't worry, Aunt Lemon. I can't tell my wish or it won't come true."

I raised an eyebrow, giving my niece the side-eye. Then I peeked over at Clem. But for the first time tonight, she wouldn't meet my eye.

"Then why bring it up?" I asked.

Anna shrugged. "Because when it comes true, I'll remind you of this moment and you can thank me."

Clem groaned and stood up, blushing. She shook her head and mumbled, "I'm going to finish the dishes." Then she escaped inside, sliding the door closed behind her. The energy of a few moments ago deflated.

I glanced at Anna so confused. "What was that about?"

Anna seemed completely unruffled. "Aunt Lemon's just flustered."

"About what?" Girls were so confusing. Young or old. Fourteen or Twenty-eight. They were a conundrum.

"My wish makes her nervous." She sighed. "And before you ask, I can't tell you my wish from tonight because that's the rule of birthday wishes. They don't come true if you spill them. But I've made the same wish a bunch of other times and I can tell you those."

"Okay?" This was such a weird conversation.

She took a big breath. "I've been wishing the same thing all summer. And it is...that you and Aunt Lemon would fall in love and we could be a real family."

Had someone shoved a boot in my gut? Had Anna read my mind? 'Cause we had the exact same wish. I looked over my shoulder, watching Clem through the kitchen window, her head down, muttering to herself as she scrubbed a dish.

"Does Clem know about your wish?"

"Yeah. I told her a while ago."

My body tensed, but I had to know. "And what did she say?"

She pursed her lips. "Basically that I shouldn't get my hopes up."

I slouched down, feeling like a fool. All the looks, the imagined tension...I'd been living a fantasy, pretending, just like in high school. It had been fun while it lasted, but it wasn't real. We'd just been playing house. Apparently, some of us more than others. *Idiot.* Would I ever learn?

"But you know what?" Anna said, her voice shaky. "I can't stop wishing it." She looked up at me, her brown eyes turned down. "With Momma gone, you and Aunt Lemon are my best shot at a real family. I don't want to fly back and forth. Spend the school year here and the summers out there. I know that's what you guys are planning. Aren't you?"

I sat there, speechless. That was my plan, exactly. What other option was there?

She threw her hands out. "Shouldn't I get a say in what happens to me? Why do the adults get to decide when they're not the ones who have to live it?"

Oh, man.

She was absolutely right. Everyone she loved was here in Seddledowne, except me. I may not be able to give her the happily ever after she'd hoped for Clem and me, but I could make it so she didn't have to split her life down the middle.

I rubbed her head and pulled her against me. "Yeah. If anyone should have a say, it should be you."

For the first time, I really considered the what-ifs of staying in Seddledowne. Would it be hard to live here and see Clem all the time? Yeah. Would it suck to give up my new job and let Mrs. Serafin down? The thought was sickening. I always followed through. Always. But looking at Anna, her pleading face, her guileless desire to have stability and be surrounded by family…I had to follow through for her.

Clem or not.

Jobless or not.

I needed to stay in Seddledowne for good. Man, these next hurdles were gonna blow.

Anna hopped up and went back inside. I pulled out my phone and found Christy's name way down my message list. She'd been true to her word. The only noise coming from her direction had been crickets.

For the second time that summer, I texted her the words:

> Me: We need to talk.

twenty-three

CLEMENTINE

I woke up the next morning before the sun, determination pulsing through me. Bo and Jenny were coming to pick up Anna and Huckleberry to go to Honeyville to buy a crate, collar, leash, and who knew what else. Tomorrow morning, we were all heading to Sandbridge for a week at the beach. Holden, Ashton, and Ford would be there too, which meant chaos and hilarity, but zero chance to be solo with Silas. If I wanted to talk to him alone and uninterrupted, today was the day.

No. Not if. Today *was* the day.

Waves of nervousness rolled through me all morning no matter how much relaxation breathing I did. I took a shower, spent extra time shaving my legs. I even exfoliated. Then I gave myself a blowout and perfected each lash with mascara. If Silas turned me down, it wouldn't be for lack of effort.

As I was dressing in a green v-neck T-shirt and my best-fitting cutoff jean shorts, Silas's deep voice resounded from the living room. Bo and Jenny were leaving with Anna. When I heard the front door shut and the house go quiet, I checked myself one more time in the mirror. I grabbed the scrapbook off the top of the dresser and took a deep breath before walking out of my room.

Silas was on the couch, putting on socks like he was about to leave. He looked up, expressionless. "I'm going to spray weed killer on the fence lines so the vines don't grow back."

I walked over, sat next to him, and placed a hand on his arm. His gaze dropped to the scrapbook and back up to me. He didn't know what was inside. I could see that on his face.

"Can I talk to you before you go?"

"You bet." His words were flat and lifeless.

Sigh. Something had happened last night, but I didn't know what. I'd planned on talking to him before I went to bed. But when he and Anna came in from outside, Silas was stiff and standoffish again. I'd let my doubts get the better of me—maybe Momma was wrong. Maybe he hadn't been in love with me after all. Maybe he was still so hung up on Christy that he couldn't see past her. And I'd chickened out.

Then I lay in bed half the night running through all the things Sophie would've said if she were here. Cowgirl Up. No pain, no gain. Go big or go home. This is where the rubber meets the road. She also said stuff like, "It's never too late to give up" and "The light at the end of the tunnel might be an oncoming train." But I was choosing to believe she'd go with a motivational cliche at the moment. She had a hundred of them and the knack for pulling the perfect one out at exactly the right time. And the courage to execute them. Sophie wasn't afraid of anything. Not even the cancer that killed her.

What I needed right now was to channel my best friend's tenacity.

I bit my lip, determined. I couldn't let Silas's and my relationship regress. I was going to take this bull by the horns and wrestle it to the ground. Wherever I landed when it was over was up to Silas.

I scooted closer, and a breath hitched in his throat. I

gripped his elbow, pulling him farther back onto the couch. Then I turned, purposely resting my knee on his thigh. He scowled, but I didn't let myself analyze it.

My gaze locked with his as I picked up his arm and put it around my shoulders. His frown deepened, but he didn't pull his arm back. I snuggled in as close as I could get until our sides melded together, then I laid the book across our laps. "I found this in Momma's attic yesterday." I flipped the cover open.

He leaned forward, eyes narrowing. "What is this?"

Deep breath. "It seems that my daddy took up scrapbooking when you were in college."

He glanced at me, his gray eyes so vulnerable, and then back to the book. I turned the pages, letting him take them all in. There was no surprise on his face as he studied them. Why would there be? This was a documentation of his life. He'd already lived it.

"Why didn't I know you came to my dad's funeral?"

He stared at the book, but he wasn't actually looking at it. "I didn't want to see you with Billy. So I stood in the back and slipped out before the prayer ended."

I'd expected it, but it didn't make the punch hurt any less.

He flipped another page.

When we got to the end, I pointed to the date of the final article. "Why does this stop during your junior year? Did you not compete your last year in school?" The question had niggled at me since yesterday.

He pulled his arm from around me, flipped the book shut and scrubbed a hand over his face. Then he leaned his elbows on his knees, eyes on the floor. But I was running this meeting. Not him. And quiet, closed-off Silas was not on my agenda. So I set the book aside, pushed his knees apart and slid onto his lap.

He was tense, wary, and I hated that we were back at this place.

I trapped his face between my hands. "Talk to me. No more of this holding back nonsense." Then I took a page out of his book and pressed my nose up against his, our lips millimeters apart. "Please tell me what happened."

He shook his head, but I held on tight. A vein in his jaw twitched beneath my fingertips.

"Silas," I breathed and my lips parted. Then I did the most terrifying thing of my entire life. I stepped off a ledge, no parachute, and smashed my lips against his.

His lips were warm and soft. But they were statue still. Not a single hint of returning my affections.

My stomach started a thousand-foot drop, but I pulled it back. I was not giving up that easily. I wanted this too much. For me. For Anna. For all of us.

"*Please.*" I clenched his shirt in my fists, pulling him closer, trying anything to gain entrance. Still nothing. I pushed harder, begging, my lips urgent against his. But he was Fort Knox on complete lockdown. He wasn't going to kiss me back. The realization sliced right between my ribs and into my heart with a hard twist. And like a dying person barely hanging on, my heart stopped—started—then stopped.

This summer, Silas had single-handedly put me back together piece by piece. But with this one moment of rejection, I was fragile glass all over again.

I was making a fool of myself, but I decided to go for broke. "I love you," I exhaled against his mouth.

Still nothing.

Splinters cracked, shooting down every vein in my body.

"*Don't you care that I've fallen in love with you?*" It came out in complete desperation.

He grunted. But that was all. I'd bared my soul and he couldn't even bother to speak a single word.

And I shattered. If Billy's betrayal had broken me into a thousand pieces, Silas's rejection was a hundred million more. And I knew I would never be whole again. There wasn't a man on earth who could put me back together now.

I guess mommas don't know everything after all. At least not mine.

twenty-four

SILAS

She was in my lap, kissing me like I'd always dreamed. And like an idiot, I couldn't move. Couldn't breathe. Couldn't believe it was real. Was this some kind of cruel joke? I'd never wanted Clem to know why I'd stopped roping. It was too revealing and raw. Would she do this just to get me to talk? No. She wasn't that person. Or maybe she was, and I didn't know her anymore. I couldn't think straight, needed air to process what was happening. But I couldn't get any because the little I had, she kept stealing with every kiss she placed.

"I love you," she said, and my brain refused to comprehend. I must've misunderstood. It was the fantasy I'd played out a million times when I was younger. It wasn't real. My head was playing tricks on me.

"*Don't you care that I've fallen in love with you?*" she begged, her chin quivering against mine. The desperation in her voice hooked me in the heart and yanked me to the surface. This wasn't a trick or a test or any kind of manipulation. She'd meant that.

I knew it in the deepest parts of my soul.

In less than a second, my heart, which had been lifeless, barely existing for years, burst into full bloom. A shot of adrenaline tore through me, making me dizzy. I couldn't take a full breath. The ecstasy was all-consuming. I tried to speak, but only a grunt came out. Oh, good grief. *Pull it together, man.*

I got my arms to move, lifting them to pull her tighter. But before I could slide my hands around her middle, she shot up off my lap. She took a step toward the hallway and I knew if I let her get out of that room, she might never give me another chance.

I reached out, my fingertips catching her by the waist. She stopped, frozen. So I wound my arms around her, pulling her back to the couch and into my lap. Her eyes were closed, like she was afraid to open them. Afraid of what was coming.

I cupped her porcelain cheeks in my hands. *"Clementine,"* I murmured, so relieved to finally be moving and talking again. An intoxicating rush surged through me and I kissed her with a fierceness I didn't know I possessed. Every kiss from the past was dilapidated and sputtering compared to this. My lips and hers were one—searching, exploring, demanding. All pistons firing. She parted her mouth, letting me in. I groaned, trying to get closer, deeper. But it wasn't enough.

She pulled back, fingers curled in my hair. "I love you, Si. It's okay if you can't say that to me yet, but I have to say it because you're..." her breath hitched. "You're everything to me."

I pressed my forehead against hers, breathing her in. She was wearing a new perfume today—it was sunshine and daisies and it couldn't have matched the moment more completely. "I love you too. My whole heart is yours. It always has been. I was stupid to ever think otherwise. Please." I tapped my nose gently against hers. "Please, don't break it. I'm not sure I could handle it again."

She smiled against my lips. "Never. I promise. Your heart is safe with me." Then she pressed kisses all along my jaw, up the bridge of my nose, and across my forehead. But she was getting carried away, taking too long. My lips hummed, pulsed along with the rest of me, needing to show her that I meant what I'd said.

I gripped her wrists, stopping her. It was my turn. I growled into her neck and she tipped her head back, moaning, giving me full access. Goosebumps broke out on her skin and it thrilled me that I'd caused that. But then she slid her hands back into my hair, gave it a tug, and pulled my lips back to hers.

Suddenly, I wanted—no, needed—to bare my whole soul. Every desire to hold back, to keep her at a safe distance, had taken flight—and the urge to tell her everything took over all the newly vacant spots.

I searched her bright eyes, cradling her perfect face in my hands. "I need to answer your question." Her cheeks were flushed and her supple lips slightly swollen—but her eyes were frenzied, overjoyed. "I quit roping because I lost my scholarship."

The joy slipped away, and she scoured my face. "I never knew that. No one told me."

My right thumb traced her bottom lip, dragging it open just barely. I said the next part slowly and carefully. She needed to understand precisely how deep my love for her ran. "You got married, and it almost killed me. Literally. I couldn't eat, I slept through my classes, couldn't get out of bed to go to practice. I almost failed out of school. Finally, Mom threatened to come get me and make me come home. It worked when nothing else did. Because the only thing worse than you being married to Billy was me having to come back to Seddledowne and watch from a front-row seat." I lifted her palm and pressed a kiss against her fingertips. "So I got my crap together. My teachers let me make up my work. But the scholarship was gone. They'd given my spot to someone else by then."

Her eyes turned down, ashamed.

I lifted her chin, forcing eye contact. "Hey. It's not your fault. You made your choices—you're allowed to do that—and I did a crap job of coping with them. That's on me."

She shook her head and I could see I'd done nothing to convince her.

"Hey," I said again, softer. "It's okay."

She met my eye, biting her bottom lip. "I'm so sorry. For everything. I didn't know I was hurting you. I hate that I caused you so much pain."

I pressed my lips to hers for a moment, trying to assure her. "It doesn't matter anymore. Don't you see? We're here now. Whatever we had to go through to get to this point was worth it."

She slid her hands around either side of my neck. "I wish I hadn't been so stupid when we were younger. Why couldn't I see how perfect you were? It would've saved me—you—us, so much heartache.

I tangled my fingers in the ends of her silky hair. "You know what Sophie would say?"

"You can be bitter or you can be better," we said in unison.

We both smiled, and I pressed my forehead to hers. "I'm staying in Seddledowne. With you and Anna. I want to marry you." I put a hand on her barely protruding belly. "Be this baby's dad. And I'll wait however long it takes for you to be ready to marry again. A year. Two years. Ten." Her face dropped, and she looked down at her lap. I scrubbed a hand over my face. "I didn't mean it like that. I want to marry you. Right now. Like today. But if you're not ready..."

She kissed me and then smiled against my mouth again. "When everything first happened, I never wanted to get married again. Why would I want to jump back into something like that? It brought me nothing but heartache. But these past few months, living in the same house..." She squeezed her eyes shut for a second. "I've known you my whole life. I've seen you at your worst, and even at your worst, you're...amazing. You're the only man I would ever trust enough to try again. But I do." The tip of her nose brushed mine. "I do trust you and I'm ready." Her eyes went worried. "But what about your job?"

I shook my head, in absolute wonder that she saw me that way. "I'll get a job here. I checked last night. The high school has the principal and assistant principal jobs open still. Something will work out."

Her forehead wrinkled. "How do they still have those openings when school starts in a few weeks?"

"They had some enormous scandal earlier this summer. Holden told me about it. They must be struggling to fill those vacancies. Here, I'll show you." I leaned sideways, holding her so she wouldn't fall off my lap, and pulled my phone out of my back pocket. With her between my arms, curled up against my chest, we read the most recent articles about the scandal. They'd finally found the couple in France. One of them had stupidly posted a picture of them eating croissants in front of the Eiffel Tower.

Clem wrapped her arms around my neck. "Won't the school board in Laramie be angry? Will they give you a good reference?"

"I think I can get Mrs. Serafin and the board to see reason. At least I hope so. They have a few weeks to find someone else if I let them know soon."

Her eyes darted over my face. "Am I completely selfish to

let you do that? Maybe you should stay there this year, complete your contract, and then move back."

I pecked her on the mouth. "It's not your choice. It's mine. And that's what I'm doing. I'm never leaving you again."

She tipped her head back, laughed and pumped her fist.

I laughed with her, my mind still trying to catch up.

An alarm went off on her phone and she groaned. "I have to run to the studio and teach the ten a.m. class."

I pressed my forehead against hers. "No worries. I'll be here when you get back. I'm not going anywhere." I tapped my nose against hers. "Ever again."

It was agony letting her walk away to change into her gym clothes. As I walked her to the truck and kissed her goodbye, I couldn't get the stupid grin off my face. I stood there, hands on top of my head, watching her truck head down the hill, past the barn—the love nest, as she jokingly referred to it now—and over the hill. When she was out of sight, I hooted as loud as I could and punched my fists in the air like Rocky.

Last night, I'd called Christy and told her that I wasn't coming back to Laramie. After a string of swear words—calling me every derogatory name she could think of—and promising we would never, ever speak again, she'd hung up on me. So twelve mere hours ago, I'd been certain of what I thought was my reality: I would live the rest of my life alone, loving Clem from afar.

And I'd accepted it.

Now, my mind was boggled. How could a life completely change in half a day? It seemed impossible. Surreal.

What if this day had never happened? What if Clem had never sat herself in my lap and forced me to see the truth? What if I'd spent decades wishing, never knowing everything I'd ever wanted was on the other side of a kiss?

My chest tightened and I couldn't breathe, thinking about

it. Holden was right. I'd been a coward. So afraid of the what-ifs that I'd held back. I made a promise to myself at that moment: I would never miss out on loving Clem again because I was afraid. I would fight dragons—no—entire armies if I had to.

Now that I knew she loved me too, there was nothing in this world that was ever going to keep us apart.

twenty-five

CLEMENTINE

That ten a.m. barre class was the longest hour of my entire life. And then, when it was over, two new ladies wanted to purchase memberships so they could attend "that hot guy's class," so I had to stick around to sign them up. By the time I walked back into the house an hour and forty-five minutes later, I figured I was overdue a kiss by at least an hour and a half.

I slid through the side door ninja-like and snuck up behind Silas while he loaded the dishwasher. I curled my arms around his chest and pressed my cheek against his back. He turned, and I went up on my tiptoes to give him a quick kiss. But when I tried to pull away, he gripped my face, trying to inhale me. His lips were insistent and his hands traced across my shoulders and down my back, drawing curlicues.

I shuddered, stepping away. "I'm so gross. Let me take a quick shower."

There was a hungry, devious look in his eye. "No." His hands were on my hips, his steely gaze pinning me. "I'm not waiting another minute. It's sexy when you're all flushed like that." His mouth crashed against mine. He cupped the back of my thighs and hiked me up to waist level. My legs wrapped around his hips. I sucked his bottom lip between my teeth and he stumbled forward, catching us against the counter. He slid me onto the formica, his lips roving greedily. His hands were on my ribs, all over my back, up in my hair, everywhere at once. Granny Eudora would die all over again if she saw what we were doing in her kitchen.

He pulled back, blinking. "How soon can we get married? Like, can we just elope?" His eyes bore into me. "I *need* you."

I threw my head back and laughed. Having this effect on him was intoxicating.

"Clem?" His voice was husky and impatient, his expression dopey-drunk.

I pecked him on the lips and then held him there, smiling against his mouth. "Let's figure it out after the beach."

I lifted the bottom of his shirt, running my fingers up and down his warm back as we got lost in each other's eyes. He dove back in, kissing me so hard my back arched. I moaned, welcoming it.

"What in the Sam Hill do you two think you're doing?"

Silas whirled around so fast I almost fell off the counter. I caught myself against his back. It took a second for my vision to clear and my brain to catch up. But when I peeked over his shoulder, I saw Jenny and Anna right inside the doorway, gaping at us. I sucked in my breath, too loud.

Jenny's arms folded across her chest, disapproval etched in every line of her face. "Are you out of your ever-lovin' minds?"

Anna, on the other hand, was bouncing on her toes, Huck asleep in one arm, a smug smile splitting her face. "Aw, yeah. That's what I'm talkin' 'bout. I knew all that juju I put out into the universe would work." She hula-hooped her hips.

"Anna, go to your room," Jenny ordered, furious.

"But Granny." She punched her free hand at us. "YOLO."

"Now!"

Anna humphed and hurried herself and Huck out of the room.

Jenny took a step toward us with the glower of an angry prison guard. "You think because you're over here playing house that you can just do the hippity dippity for fun? Both of you were raised better than that."

Hippity dippity? My face burst into flame and I cowered behind Silas, wishing there was some way to escape without having to walk past her.

"Mom," Silas said, his tone abrupt. "The 1950s wants its euphemism back. And that's not what this is, so stop. We love each other."

She guffawed. "I don't care if you do. You're raising a fourteen-year-old girl here. You can't be going at it like feral rabbits on the kitchen counter. You shouldn't be touching at all. This is not the time for that."

Hot shame rolled over me in flames. She was right. What had I been thinking? This isn't why Sophie put the three of us together. This was supposed to be about Anna and Anna alone.

I was acutely aware that I couldn't keep hiding behind Silas. But I wanted to. Oh gracious, how I wanted to. But Jenny wasn't going to stop as long as I was pressed against his back. So I slid off the counter onto my feet and moved away from him.

He reached for me.

I wrapped my arms across my stomach and took another side step. "No. She's right."

"No. She's not." Silas scowled, throwing his hands out. "Clem."

I shook my head.

A vein in Jenny's forehead protruded. "Well, I'm glad someone isn't letting their hormones run the show."

"Mom." Silas clenched his jaw, his fist punching his thigh. "Shut. Up. You don't know what you're talking about."

Everything was silent for a split second.

The only time I knew of Silas disrespecting his parents to their face was that night he pushed his dad on the bed and brought Sophie home. He didn't respond this way unless he felt there was injustice that needed defending. I felt sick that I'd done anything to lead up to this.

"I am your mother and that girl's grandmother." She jabbed her finger toward Anna's bedroom. "Don't you ever talk to me like that!" She was coming unhinged, and I thought she might slap him. I couldn't be here to see it if she did. I had to go. I walked quickly across the kitchen.

"Clem, come back," Silas called.

I shook my head and disappeared into the hall. Call it cowardly, but I loved him too much to witness anymore. I hated myself at that moment. This was my fault. All of it. Jenny was right. I shouldn't have initiated things right now. In a week and a half, I would've been free to do that. Why couldn't I have waited? I was so selfish and stupid.

"Mind your own business!" Silas shouted as I closed the bedroom door behind me.

Anna hadn't gone to her room. She was here, sitting on my bed, wide-eyed but beaming. She launched herself into my arms and whisper-squealed, "I'm so freaking happy right now. Wait until Brooklyn hears about this. We're going to be a real family."

I lowered myself to the edge of the bed and put my head between my knees, trying to get my breathing to slow down.

"Aunt Lemon." Anna rubbed her hand over my back. "It's gonna be okay. Granny will get over it. She always does." Her voice cracked and I could tell I was scaring her.

So I sat up and nodded. "Yeah."

She bounced on the bed, turning to face me. "Tell me everything."

But I couldn't. The rock in my gut was tugging, trying to exit through my back as the argument in the kitchen intensified.

"Okay. I get it. You're shook." She grabbed my arm, her chocolate eyes disco balls of excitement. "You don't have to speak. Just nod or shake your head. Do you love Uncle Silas?"

A shaky laugh threatened to erupt, but I bit it back. Silas and I were...a couple. I was still reeling from it all. And, wow, the chemistry. If kissing were a hotel, I'd been living at a cockroach-infested, charge-by-the-hour, hookup motel for the last decade. And for the first time, someone had taken me to a penthouse suite at The Four Seasons.

And I was never. Ever. Going back.

But of course Silas was five stars. Why was I surprised?

"Aunt Lemon?" Anna asked again.

I touched my lips—remembering the heat of a few moments ago—and nodded.

"Yes!" she shouted. "I knew it! I knew it, I knew it!"

I put a finger to my lips. "Not right now."

Jenny and Silas's quarrel was raging, a hailstorm of words rumbling through the drywall.

Anna and I strained to hear.

Silas: "Mom! I'm grown! She's grown! We don't need your approval. You don't get a say and I'm sorry if you can't handle that. But that's your problem."

"Oof." Anna winced.

Jenny: "How long have the two of you been fooling around? Huh? Wait till Arlo hears about this. He'll probably call off the whole thing."

Anna shook her head, lips pursed in a line. "Oh, Granny. Pulling out the lawyer card."

Silas: "You'd be that petty? If you call him, you can forget about beach week because we won't be there."

Anna did a dramatic reach for the door with one hand and laid the back of her other hand against her forehead. "Oh, beach week, how I will miss thee." Oh my word. She was Sophie reincarnate.

"Shhh." I snickered.

Whatever Jenny's response was, it was too low to hear, but it must've been terrible because Silas exploded. "You're acting like a jealous toddler. You've been doing it all summer and I'm embarrassed for you. You're not allowed to talk about her like that ever." I cringed. It had been about me. "Do you understand me? Get out! Now!"

Anna's eyes bugged and all the Sophie-like commentary ceased. I held my breath, waiting for something to signal it was over.

Jenny roared—actually roared—like a deranged lunatic. I strained to hear what sounded like heavy stomping. Then a door slammed so hard a picture fell off the wall in the hallway.

Anna covered her mouth, shaking with laughter. "Ho-ly. Crap. Granny is pissed."

I scowled, amazed she could laugh at a time like this. She really was Sophie's kid. "Don't use that word."

She held up her hands, biting her lips closed. "Sorry. Irate, incensed, a raging inferno."

All the air trapped in my lungs over the past few minutes started to release and I felt my heart rate drop at least twenty beats per minute.

The door flew open and Silas rushed in, haggard. He knelt in front of me, his eyes wild and desperate. "I'm so sorry." He pulled my forehead to his. "Please don't listen to her."

I sat there, stunned. That had been horrible. But Silas had defended me. Kicked his own mother out for talking badly about me. Billy chose his mother over me every single time. I didn't even know someone could love me like this.

But I had to pull myself together. Things had gotten out of hand way too fast. I gripped his wrists, placing them back at his side. "Hey. It's okay, I'm okay."

He looked hurt that I would push him away, but I'd made a decision in the last few minutes. I wouldn't be the reason something like this happened again. There were some lines we needed to draw, starting now.

I desperately wanted to kiss him one last time. Instead, I laid my hands on my lap. "Your mom's right—"

"No. She's not." He shook his head, so defiantly I wanted to kiss his adorable frown lines. But I wouldn't be doing that anytime soon.

I held up my hands to stop the barrage he was about to begin. "Silas. The ninety days are almost up. We're going to the beach with your family—"

"No. I'm not taking you anywhere she'll be."

"Yes. We are. I'm not going to be a wedge between you and your mom. If you think she's struggling now, think how she'll feel if I let you guys miss vacation. We're going. And we can wait for this." My finger metronomed between us. "We've waited this long. Twelve days will fly by." His expression said he wasn't so sure. I looked directly into his eyes. "I. Love. You." His breathing was finally calming. "A week and a half is not going to change that."

He reached for me, but I dodged him and jammed my hands under my thighs. "No. No more touching." His cheeks flamed. I locked eyes with him, willing him to understand. "If you so much as graze a finger against me, I am going to cave." I ignored Anna biting her fingers to keep from squealing like this was a climax in some romcom. "I never, ever want to witness a scene like that again. Because if I do, I'm going to say some things to your mother that will not be kind. And she's already having a hard enough time with me as it is. I don't want to give her any more ammo. Do you understand?"

His outstretched hand fell, his fingers balling into a fist at his side. He slumped in defeat and groaned. "I've waited my whole life for you. I don't want to wait another minute."

"Awwww." Anna pressed her hands over her heart. "Uncle Silas, you are a romantic."

He pursed his lips at her before drawing his focus back to me. "Clem." His tone was pleading.

"Twelve days," I reminded him. "Please. *You* can do this. *I* can do this."

"*We* can do this!" Anna shouted. "I'll help. I'll be the No Touching Patrol. I have a whistle and everything." She straightened her arm out, flipping her palm down. "Put 'er right there. Team Simon on three."

"Team Simon?" Silas frowned.

"You shipped us?" I choked, laying my hand over hers.

"Oh yeah. Me and Brooklyn. Months ago." She shrugged. "But if Simon isn't your vibe, we can always do S'lemon."

Silas snorted. "You're a part of this too. How about... Lem'anna'las."

"Nope. Uh uh." I shivered, it was so bad. "I don't think the shipping thing works in a three-way. How about...Team Trifecta?"

Anna nodded slowly. "Yeah. I like it." She looked to Silas for approval.

His gaze burned into me, begging me not to make him commit to this.

"C'mon. Take one for the team," I said, Sophie style. "I believe in you."

"Fine." He huffed, but he clearly wasn't going to be happy about it. He went to lay his hand on mine but stopped. Then he slipped his hand under Anna's, taking the touching thing as literally as I'd meant it. That was the best thing about Silas. When he committed, he *committed*.

Anna led us out, jouncing our hands. "One. Two. Three."
"Team Trifecta!"

twenty-six

CLEMENTINE

Again, Silas tried to talk me out of teaching the ten a.m. class. Told me to ask Peyton. Even offered to stay behind to ride with me. But I told him to go ahead and have fun. There was no sense in missing half a day in the water when I'd be right behind him.

Truth be told, I was dreading this beach trip. Being in close quarters with Jenny all week already had a knot in my stomach. Add the absence of Sophie and I didn't know how I was going to do it.

I'd had too many firsts without my best friend in the past three months. Some hard, some amazing. The beach trip had always been my favorite week of the year. But this summer Sophie would be in every room, every memory, every board game we played, without being there at all. It would be low-level torture. I knew that.

Silas and Anna left at five a.m. Silas drove his truck to the ranch, and they rode down to the beach with Bo and Jenny. I thought I'd sleep in, but I lay there staring at the ceiling, wide awake. Recently, the fatigue had completely disappeared. It made sense, I guessed. I was entering the second trimester. So I got up, fed the chickens, gave the cows a bag of mineral and grain, grabbed my suitcase, and headed to the studio.

When class was over and I got back in the truck, there was a text from Silas.

> Silas: We made it. Hurry and get your cute butt down here, you beautiful woman. But don't drive too fast. I need you to arrive safely. Love you and can't wait to ogle you from across the room.

Then he sent a separate eye roll emoji.
I giggled.

> Me: Ogle away…but only when your mom's not looking. Eleven days. We got this. Love you too, cowboy. On my way.

My emoji blew him a kiss.

He'd also left a pin for the location of the house.

Two hours into the drive, Momma called. "Don't forget, I'm in Atlantic City with the girls." Like I had short-term memory loss or something. The girls were her book club ladies. They hadn't actually read or discussed a book in years. Book Club was now a cover for going shopping, going out to eat, bowling, or to bingo night. It really depended on the mood they were in. A couple of times a year, they took a "big" trip to Gatlinburg or Nashville—somewhere crowded and touristy. This time it was New Jersey.

"I know, Momma."

I had run up to her house after the Jenny incident to let her know about me and Silas before she left. To say she was thrilled was an understatement. Said Dad was probably doing a happy dance on the other side. I'd wondered if Sophie was too—or what she thought about the whole thing.

I left Jenny out of it. After her breakdown yesterday, I realized Sophie had left a hole in her heart as big as the one she'd left in mine. But Jenny wasn't handling it so well. I needed to give her extra grace.

"And Buford is boarding at Bow Wow Bungaloo. So don't worry about him."

"Okay, Momma."

"Well, if you need me, just call."

I wasn't sure why I would "need" her or how she would help even if I did. They'd purchased spots on a charter bus. They weren't coming back till that trip was over.

"I'll be fine. I have Silas if I need anything."

"All right." I could hear the smile in her voice. "You give him a hug for me, and Anna, too."

Technically, I couldn't hug him, but I said, "I will. You have fun and don't be coming home with a new boyfriend yourself."

She scoffed. "No, thank you. I spent forty-five years training your daddy. I'm finally retired from that job. This is me time now."

I laughed. "Okay. Whatever you say. Love you."

I ran through the Chick-fil-A drive thru in Williamsburg, fully intending to get nuggets, fries, and a cookies and cream milkshake. I'd come to terms with my fast food cravings. But when I got there, a grilled chicken salad and a light lemonade sounded divine. I smiled at my stomach and patted it. "Thank you, little one." It was nice to eat healthy again. As I cruised down the freeway, enjoying my salad, I reveled in my life now. Anna, this baby, and now Silas? I was finally getting the life I'd always wanted.

Somewhere between the Bay Bridge tunnel and the beach house the Duprees rented every year, my stomach started hurting. I guess I shouldn't have ordered the salad after all.

When I parked in front of the house, there were three cars in the driveway. One was Jenny's minivan. Another was Holden's car. I didn't recognize the other. Maybe Ashton got a new car? As I grabbed my suitcase out of the bed of the truck, Anna flew out the back door, wearing a tank top and board shorts. Her hair was wet and her tan cheeks had a hint of sunburn. She must've spent the day in the water. Good for her.

"Aunt Lemon." Her voice was hushed and anxious like something was wrong. My mind immediately went to Huckleberry. Had something happened to him? He was still so tiny.

I set my suitcase down on the asphalt. "What's wrong?"

She shook her head, lips pressed into a thin line. "It's not good. It's really not good." Was it Silas? Had he gone body surfing and drowned in the undertow? Did Bo have a heart attack like Daddy? Bo ate entirely too much red meat. It wasn't out of the realm of possibility.

I gave her a little shake. "You're scaring me. Spill it."

She eyed the house like a bad guy was coming after her. "Christy is here," she whispered.

"What?" That was the last thing I'd expected to hear. But at least no one was dead. "Why?" As far as I knew, Silas and Christy had broken up a long time ago.

"'Cause she's freaking crazy. Why else?"

"Where's Silas?" Shouldn't he be the one meeting me at the truck, warning me about this? My touchy stomach twisted hard, and I winced, my abs contracting.

Thankfully Anna was wigging out too much to notice. "He left an hour and a half ago with Uncle Holden and Ashton to pick Ford up from the airport. I tried calling all the brothers, but no one answered. Silas left his phone on his bed. I heard it ringing."

I ran a hand across my brow, not sure what to do. "She showed up after he left?"

She nodded, her eyebrows drawn tight.

Jenny waved from the back door. "Come on in here, you two. We've got dinner ready."

I popped the handle up on my suitcase and whispered into Anna's ear, "Does Christy know?"

"About you and Uncle Si?" She shook her head. "Definitely not. She thinks they're still a thing."

What? How was that even possible? None of this made any sense.

"She's inside being Granny's sous chef. So cheugy."

"Let's go!" Jenny's waving was getting bigger, more animated. "You're letting all the heat in."

Anna and I shared a tentative glance and walked to the door. Jenny hugged me like yesterday hadn't happened and I didn't know how to take it. Had she known Christy was coming? Had she invited her—to *beach week*—to get back at me? No, Jenny wouldn't do that. Was this hug her trying to smooth things over?

Bo pulled me into a hug, but his smile was nervous. "Here, I'll get your bag. You and Anna are sharing the Flamingo room." Sophie and Anna had always shared that room. My heart panged at the thought.

I followed Jenny and Anna into the kitchen, my body a stiff board. When I came around the corner, there Christy was, mixing a large tossed salad in a glass bowl, barefoot, wearing an apron like this was completely normal. She looked up and smiled, her Bambi eyes nervous but excited to be here. Her hair had grown a couple of inches since the funeral and she'd had her blond highlights recently touched up. She really was pretty—cheekbones that could cut glass and almond-shaped eyes. I could see why Silas had picked her.

A punch of insecurity hit me square in the chest. I shoved it off. Silas loved me. He always had. There shouldn't be any doubt in my mind after the past couple of days. Christy was confused or grasping at straws. But this was only going to end in heartbreak for her as soon as Silas got here. If I was kind, it might soften the blow.

Faking confidence, I lifted my hand in a small wave. "Hey. It's good to see you again."

Anna, Bo, and Jenny all glanced at me with varying degrees of discomfort.

Christy smiled. "You too, Lemon." She handed the bowl to Jenny. "I think we're ready." Then she untied the apron and laid it on the counter, revealing a darling sundress that hugged her curves perfectly. If Sophie were here, she'd say, *Love the dress. Hate her.* That's what she always did when she saw a woman that she thought was pretty.

Anna stuck to my side, and we walked to the small, round dinner table together. Christy sat next to Jenny on the other side with Bo between us. I wasn't sure where the guys would sit when they got here, but that was the least of my worries.

No sooner had Bo finished a blessing on the meal than the back door opened.

"We're baaaack. And we brought Grouchy McPoutyface." Ashton's sing-song voice floated into the room.

"Okay, AshyKnees." That was Ford. "You're just jealous I'm so much better looking. Everybody knows that's why you and Holden are so chipper. You're trying to make up for your ugly mugs."

Ashton snorted. "Whatever you say, Crankenstein."

My brain registered that I should laugh. Normally I would have. The Dupree Brothers could start their own comedy act, in my opinion. But I couldn't make myself right then. Because Christy had actually stood up, smoothed her dress and smiled into the doorway like June Cleaver waiting for Ward to come home after a long day of work. Anna wasn't lying. She really, truly thought she and Silas were a couple.

Anna pressed her knee against mine, gripping her chair. I gripped mine.

Ashton walked past Jenny, glancing at Christy sideways, confused. "Hey, I didn't know you were gonna be here," he muttered.

Ford came in next, straight-up scowling as he peeled his guitar strap from over his head. For a split second, it struck me how much he took after Silas. Same color hair, same face, different eye color—a little shorter and more baby-faced. But there was no doubt they were brothers. A shadow crossed his face when he saw Christy. But that was just Ford. He didn't even say hi when he walked past her. Just grunted.

Silas stopped in the doorway, and my stupid heart actually whooshed at how handsome he was in his board shorts and slim-fit T-shirt. He stared at Christy, then at me, and back at Christy, wearing that poker face he did so well.

Right then, Holden bounded into the room, running straight into Silas's back. Silas stumbled forward, right into Christy's open arms.

The room was pin-drop silent. Anna squeezed my knee. I couldn't take a full breath. Why was he still letting her hug him? His hands were stiff at his side—but why hadn't he stepped away?

Oblivious, Holden pounded Silas on the back. "Oh, sorry, dude. Not looking where I'm going." He took a step back when he realized who was hugging Silas. "Christy?"

"Hi." She beamed and offered them both a little wave. She was the only person in the room smiling.

Silas finally spoke. "Uh...what're you doing here?" But then he just stood there, dumbly, like he didn't know what to do, his eyes shifting between me and her.

Christy cocked her head, her eyes following Silas's gaze each time it fearfully ping-ponged to me. Jealousy flashed across her face. She shot me a glare right before she went up on her tiptoes and pecked him on his lips. The same lips I'd been kissing yesterday. My breath hitched, and a gasp came out that I wished no one had heard.

Anna squeezed my hand tighter. "Oh, no she didn't," she growled.

"What're you doing?" Silas stepped back this time.

The discomfort in the room was thick. I wanted to crawl out of my skin and run as fast as I could away from here. My stomachache had heightened, and I curled in on myself as another cramp hit.

Christy put a hand on her hip. "I'm here to surprise you, silly. I know our conversation the other night was...less than ideal. But I wanted to make it up to you."

Um. What? The other night?

Silas's nostrils flared. "Less than ideal? You cussed me out and told me you were never talking to me again."

I put one hand to my mouth, and the other lifted in a stop motion. "Hold up. I thought you two broke up a long time ago." Was I a rebound?

Christy scowled like I smelled bad and rolled her eyes. "No. We definitely did not."

"Yeah, we did." Silas appeared dumbfounded. I knew I was. Was he acting?

I stood up, every eye in the room volleying. "Wait. So you didn't break up?"

Silas tilted his head, silently pleading. "Yes, *we did*."

Christy's body went tense and her voice a little shrill. "No. We were on a pause. We were taking the summer off. That's all."

Silas opened his mouth, but I cut him off. "Okay. Enough. When did this pause happen?" I needed exact dates. Had he been playing me or her? Or both of us?

"Clem." Silas took a step toward me.

Christy yanked him back by the hem of his shirt. "What has she got to do with anything? This is between me and you."

Anna shot up. "No." She pointed between me, herself, and Silas. "We're Team Trifecta. You're just Christy. You are not part of this." Her voice cracked, which could only mean one thing. Tears were coming. I put an arm around her, pulling her against my chest.

"Team Trifecta?" Christy said like she'd eaten something bitter. Then she aimed herself at darling Anna. "Silas and I are engaged. So I'm definitely on the same team as him, whatever any of that means."

My mouth fell open.

Silas's face crumpled.

It felt like I'd coughed up my heart. "You're engaged?"

I may as well have been standing in a cave because my words immediately echoed around the room.

"Engaged?"

"You're engaged?"

"Nobody said anything about y'all getting married?"

Every single person flinging a similar question in their direction.

Except for Holden. He sat there, his chin in his hands, looking unsurprised by the announcement but sick to his stomach. I caught his eye, trying to see if he knew about me and Silas, but his gaze brushed over me like my pain meant nothing and Christy's meant everything. So it was true. Christy wasn't making it up. And Silas had told Holden about their engagement, but nothing about us.

"We're not engaged!" Silas finally shouted. A deafening silence permeated the room and, for a split second, I thought he was about to make everything right. I was sure of it. Right until he said, "I mean, we were, but we're not anymore."

"Were?" Christy choked. "You told me we were pausing." Her voice was semi-hysterical. Those weren't crocodile tears falling down her face. She was as broken by this as I was. "That we would reset as soon as you got done with this little pretend family thing you were doing and we would make it official."

Jenny jumped up and slapped the table. "You were engaged to Christy and—"

Anna's sob ripped through the air, flash-freezing everything—the chaos, the yelling, the accusations. Silas's gaze skittered over, taking the two of us in, his face full of guilt, shame, and...admission.

Christy was telling the truth.

"I knew this would happen," Anna cried. "Everyone I love leaves me. My dad. My mom. You said we would be a family!"

"Anna. It's not like that." He took a step toward us, begging with those eyes. "Just let me explain."

I shook my head, somehow managing to keep the tears inside my eyelids. "No. *I've* got her." Pulling Anna toward me, I turned her around, catching Holden's expression as I did. He looked pained, like he was holding back from comforting Christy. I didn't have time to ponder that.

"Clem, come back." Silas's voice was desperate, but I wouldn't believe it. Apparently he had some hidden acting talent I'd never known about. And, apparently, he was the worst kind of cheater. The kind that played with your heart so hard that you'd tie yourself up and repel over a thousand-foot cliff, fully believing he had you. And as soon as you were over that ledge, he would cut the rope and watch you fall to your death, all for kicks.

I'd thrown myself at him. Had he seen an opportunity and taken it?

Christy balled her fists and stomped her foot. "Why can't you call her Lemon like everybody else?" It came out in a half-crazed shriek.

I stood frozen in disbelief, my chest heaving for two seconds. Other women might've gotten a kick out of witnessing the downfall of their rival, but I found no joy in another woman's scorn. Christy was completely wrecked. And I knew that feeling all too well. If she'd been anyone else, and if my heart and Anna's hadn't been bleeding out onto the floor, I probably would've tried to comfort her.

I hurried Anna out the other side of the kitchen, across the dark living room and down the hall, trying to get her out of earshot. Jenny's muffled voice was the last thing I heard before shutting the door of the Flamingo room.

We collapsed onto the queen bed, and Anna buried her face in my shoulder. Huckleberry, who'd been napping on the pillow, waddled over and laid his head on her thigh.

I tried. I really did. But the tears were torrential and I couldn't stop them.

The person I thought I could trust more than anyone in the world was a liar and a cheat.

Just like Billy.

I couldn't breathe. I was sobbing so hard.

"Lemon, it's okay." Anna gulped, smoothing her hands over my hair. "Aunt Lemon."

"You're scaring her," Jenny said, suddenly there. She pressed a hand against my arm. "Lemon, you have to get yourself together."

I made the mistake of making eye contact. Jenny didn't have to say a word for me to know exactly what she was thinking. Sophie should've left Anna to her and Bo to raise from the get-go. I wasn't mature enough to handle this, and neither was her idiot son. And this summer-long experiment had done nothing but prove her right.

I nodded, wiping my face. "I'm okay. I'm okay." I managed to get out. But I couldn't have been further from okay if I tried.

"I've got her," Jenny said. "I'll take her to my room so you can have a minute."

I nodded again, shifting Anna into her arms. Anna

glanced back at me, unsure, and I don't know how, but I pasted a smile on my face. "I'm okay. You go."

As soon as they were gone, I pulled my knees to my chest and buried my face in my hands.

For twenty consecutive years, that beach house had brought me nothing but happy memories. Card games, board games, Spoons, late-night snacks, fish fries, Ford's moonlit guitar sessions, and more laughter than one person deserved. And in one afternoon, those memories were wiped out and replaced with this disaster. And it was no one's fault but my own. Well, I wasn't going to hang around to ruin any more. The Duprees deserved better than that. Well, most of them did.

I grabbed my purse and my suitcase off the floor, carefully popped the door open, and tiptoed myself right out of that nightmare.

twenty-seven

SILAS

I yanked my arm from Christy's grasp and put my hands on my thighs to stop the earth from flipping backward.

A couple of minutes ago, I'd been positive this was going to be one of the best weeks of my life. Early morning sunrises with Clem. Late night walks along the beach under the stars. Even if I couldn't touch her. Just knowing she wanted me to...

And now, somehow, Christy was in our vacation rental, glaring me down like an angry heifer whose calf was being threatened. Had Holden invited her? Or my mom? Or had she invited herself? And how had she found the house?

"I've got the girls. You handle this mess." Mom nodded at Christy, clearly referring to her as the *mess*. Then she stalked out of the room.

Everything in me screamed to go after Clem—to lay it all out and make her see the truth, the same way she had done for me. And not to leave her side until she did. But the determination on Christy's face told me that if I didn't set things straight with her first, she would follow after me, causing an even bigger train wreck.

I grabbed Christy by the elbow and marched her past my brothers and my dad, out the front door of the beach house and onto the screened-in porch. The ocean waves, which normally relaxed me, were loud and annoying.

I'd spent the entire summer trying not to hurt Christy. When she cussed me out and hung up the other night, I was relieved. Even more so after Clem kissed me. I'd thought I would never have to tell Christy the truth, and she'd move on none the wiser. I'd told myself I did it for her. But I'd taken the coward's way out. I could see that now. Christy was going to get hurt no matter what I did.

I let go of her hand and stepped back. Christy was a tinderbox, and while I should take my time, I didn't have that luxury.

I held my hands up before she could talk. "Clem and I kissed. A lot. Intensely." I didn't know a quicker way to clear things up than that.

Anger flashed in her eyes. "You're a freaking cheater, Silas."

I blew out my breath. "If that's what you want to think. But it's not true. It just happened yesterday."

"Oh, so technically you didn't cheat. You know, if you want to be the technicality guy." She laughed bitterly. "Did you even love me at all?"

"I thought I did. But I can see now that I've never given you my whole heart. I don't want to hurt you. But this is the truth: I love Clem. I always have. And I had no business trying to make things work with you when I felt that way about someone else."

Her bottom lip quivered. "Does she love you back?"

I scrubbed the top of my hair, looking at the ground. Anything to avoid the pain in her eyes. "She does. Or she did until a few minutes ago. I have no idea now." And the longer I stood there, the less certain I was. I needed to get inside and find Clem.

I glanced through the window back into the kitchen. Dad and Ashton were talking, both glancing out at us. Ford was listening intently, frowning. I hadn't told Holden about me and Clem—looked like I wouldn't have to. Dad was doing it for me by telling Ashton right in front of him. Holden had been such a douche the last time he was at the ranch that I didn't feel like I could. Why did he look so sideswiped, listening to Dad's explanation? He knew how I felt about Clem. I burned a hole into the side of his skull, trying to get his attention. His head snapped around, and I widened my eyes at him, pleading for help. He stood up so fast, his chair fell backwards.

"I need to hear you say the words," Christy said, bringing me back around. "I need closure."

I bit my lips and sighed. Okay. "It's over between us. I'm sorry. I really am. I didn't mean to hurt you."

Christy stood there, hugging herself, tears streaming down her cheeks. A decent person would've hugged her, but I wasn't touching any woman other than Clem ever again. Especially right now, with the chance that Clem could walk in and see it. The door opened and Holden walked out.

He offered me a sad smile. "I've got her. You go."

"Christy." I gave her one last look. "I really am sorry."

She collapsed in Holden's arms, sobbing into his neck. I'd never been more thankful for my brother than I was right then.

If I could've cloned myself for a few minutes, I would have taken the time to make sure Christy was okay. But the more time that ticked by, the bigger this would build up in Clem's mind. That was human nature.

Dad and Ashton's conversation hushed when I walked in. I jogged through the kitchen and down the hall. "Clem," I called her name. The flamingo room was empty. "Clem." She wasn't in my room either. "Clementine!" My chest tightened. Why wasn't she answering?

I thought of running to the master suite but didn't think she would've gone into my parents' room. I took the stairs to the second floor three at a time and opened the door to the big bonus room, with the ping-pong and pool tables. Dead empty. "Clementine!" My voice was getting louder, more frantic each time I called her name. I raced back down the stairs and this time I did go to the master suite.

I flung the door open and stopped. Anna was curled up against my mom, with Huck in her lap. The TV was on and they were watching one of those cheesy teen dramas. Clem was not in the room.

Anna sat up when she saw me. "Uncle Si?" I was relieved to see she'd stopped crying. It killed me that she'd had to witness that. Anna had already been through way too much. I'd been such a tool, thinking I could contain this situation and it would never touch her. I had to do better from now on.

"Hey." I rushed over and knelt in front of her. She wrapped her arms around my shoulders and pressed her cheek to mine. "I'm so sorry," I said. "But don't worry. I'm going to fix this. I meant what I said. We are going to be a family, okay?"

She sat up, her hands on my shoulders. "You promise?"

I looked right into her eyes. "Absolutely. Team Trifecta all the way."

She smiled, hope returning. "Team Trifecta."

"Don't make promises you can't keep, son." Mom pursed her lips. "You're missing part of your Trifecta, if you haven't noticed."

I didn't have time to let that get under my skin. I spoke to Anna and Anna alone. "As soon as I find Clem, we're going to work this out. It'll be fine. Don't you worry."

Mom shook her head, lips in a straight line. "I think she's gone. I'm pretty sure I heard her truck leave a few minutes ago."

I ran to the window, separating the blinds with my fingers. Mom was right. Clem's truck wasn't parked where I'd seen it less than twenty minutes before when I walked inside. My hands went numb. She actually left?

I swore. I shouldn't have taken the time to break up with Christy. Clem should've been my priority. I slid a hand into my back pocket to grab my cell, but I realized I was wearing board shorts. No back pockets.

"Where's my phone?" I grumbled to myself. When was the last time I had it? We'd spent the afternoon at the beach. I left it inside so it wouldn't get wet or covered in sand.

"I saw it in your room," Anna said.

I raced across the hall and found it lying on the bottom bunk of the bed I always slept on. I flipped it over and pressed call on Clem's name. While it rang, I paced. She didn't answer and her voicemail was full. I hung up and dialed again. Again, nothing. Two more times and she still didn't answer.

I switched to messaging.

> Me: Hey, please come back. Let me explain exactly what happened. It's really not what it looks like. I'm so sorry.

I gave her thirty seconds and when she didn't respond, I tried again.

> Me: Christy and I were kind of engaged at the beginning of the summer, but the longer I was with you, the more I realized that you were the one I loved. Maybe I didn't handle it perfectly, but I was trying not to hurt her. And I never meant to hurt you. I love you, Clementine. Please believe that.

I set the phone down and told myself I wasn't allowed to text her again for two minutes. She was probably driving, not looking at her phone. I tugged at the back of my hair, wearing a line in the carpet. I only made it another thirty seconds before sending another text.

> Me: Clem, please let me explain. Just tell me where you are and I'll come to you.

I sent five more, much the same, and then I sat on the floor, my back against the wall, panic trying to drown me. Had she left for good, or was she just driving around the block for a bit? Why wouldn't she answer or at least text me back?

I pounded the side of my fist against my forehead and groaned.

"Mom said Clem took off," Ashton said, suddenly standing in front of me.

I banged the back of my head against the wall. "Yeah. And she's avoiding my calls and texts."

"Just go to her, man."

I scowled. "I would if I knew where she was."

He shook his phone at me. "She's on our Find My Friends group, remember? I see her on there all the time."

Somewhere in the recesses of my mind, I vaguely recalled that. Freshman year of college, I'd checked her location incessantly. That's why I hadn't used that app in years. It was just another part of the Cutting Clem Out Of My Life plan.

Ashton pulled the app up and clicked on her name. "Sometimes it takes a minute to load."

Off in another room, Ford started in on his guitar, playing a soft country ballad, his quiet tenor filling the house. Ford's answer to anything resembling a battle was to hole up in a room, strum his guitar, and sing until the mortar stopped falling. Oddly, it usually worked, like petting a purring kitten. I closed my eyes, trying to let it soothe me.

After a full sixty seconds, Ashton said. "It says no location found. Do you think she would've turned her location services off?"

I tapped the back of my head against the wall. "I think she turned her entire phone off. Either that or she's blocked me and any way of me finding her."

"Do you think she went home?"

I pressed my hands into the floor beneath me and pushed to a stand. "Probably. If I'd been caught in the middle of this mess, that's exactly what I would do. You think Holden will let me take his car?"

Ashton's eyebrow raised. "Back to Seddledowne? It's four hours away, man." He stood too.

"I don't care. I have to fix this."

He tipped his head, his forehead crunched. "You really love her, don't you?"

"Obviously, Einstein. I always have."

"That's what Dad said." He laughed. "Then I guess you better go after her. But Mom is going to be so salty that you're skipping beach week."

"Yeah. Well. Sorry, not sorry. An eternity with Clem or making Mom happy for two seconds?" I balanced invisible scales with my hands.

Holden was in a surprisingly generous mood, and minutes later, I had my duffel hung over my shoulder and his car keys in my hand.

"Where are you going?" Mom met me in the hall.

Here we go. "I think Clem went home. I gotta go make this right."

"Silas. The three of you have to sleep under the same roof tonight or the ninety-day agreement is ruined." It actually shocked me that this wasn't about the fact that I was ditching family vacation.

"I don't know what you want me to do. Clem left and she

won't answer her phone." I could drag Anna along, with the hopes that we found Clem before the night was over, but there was no guarantee.

Mom just stood there, lips pursed, shaking her head, like I should've been capable of working miracles. And like I was becoming a perpetual disappointment to her.

Anna appeared behind her, her bag over her shoulder. "I'm coming. Team Trifecta isn't going down that easily."

"No, ma'am," Mom said. "You are not missing beach week." Mom's expression told me she was not going to relent.

I walked over and wrapped my niece in a hug. "It's okay. You stay here. Team Trifecta will be fine. As soon as I find Clem, we'll be back. Even if I have to drive all night to get here before the sun comes up."

She stuck her pinky out, her eyes worried. I hooked it and squeezed.

I didn't know how I was keeping it, but I had to try.

twenty-eight
CLEMENTINE

I wiped the tears off my cheeks as soon as the truck door was closed. I was done crying over stupid, douchebag men. I gassed it around the corner and didn't breathe until the house was out of sight. Then I pulled over long enough to block Silas and turn off my location services. The last thing I needed was for him to track me on that stupid Stalk My Friends app Sophie had added us all to years ago. And I definitely didn't want his empty apologies. Then again, maybe he wasn't even trying to contact me to apologize. For all I knew, he was walking happily ever after up the beach with Christy right then.

A rogue sob escaped at that thought, but I shut it down. I blew my breath out in a hard O. This stomach ache was getting worse. I gunned it, beach houses getting smaller in my rear-view mirror. By this time in the evening, the tunnel traffic was super light. Once I was past Richmond, my cell rang. I gritted my teeth, tempted not to look. Silas had probably borrowed someone else's phone to get through. But I had to be there for Anna if she needed me. So I pulled it out of my purse.

Momma.

"Hello?" I answered, trying to hide the anguish I felt. She was on vacation, after all.

"Honey." The way she said that one word, dripping with pity, told me Silas had called her. "Clem, sweetie, you need to call him. He's desperate to talk to you."

My jaw clenched. "Momma, you weren't there. He led both of us on. He's not who I thought he was. He's no better than Billy." I slapped the steering wheel. "And he shouldn't have bothered you on your trip." I bent over, barely keeping my eyes above the dash, my abs contracting so tight I thought they might tear.

She sighed, and I prepared myself for a lecture on how things aren't always what they seem. She'd given it to me many times in the past, and usually she was right. Not this time.

"I don't know all the details, but I know one thing. Love is messy sometimes. You know that thing Shakespeare said, 'The course of true love never did run smooth.' Well, he was right on this one." I'd been quoted Shakespeare twice now this summer, pertaining to my love life. I used to like the man. But I was seriously rethinking him now.

Another call came through. Ford. Nope. I wasn't falling for that trick. I sent it to my full voicemail. Silas could enjoy a second rejection there.

"Momma. Th-this is not a play. This is r-real life. And I've had enough. I took a chance, I decided to trust a man again, and that was my m-mistake. From now on, I'm a party of one. Gah!" It felt like I was being punched from the inside. I eased over onto the side of the freeway, cars and semi trucks flying past, shaking my truck.

Ashton's name came up on the caller ID. I didn't even send Silas to voicemail that time, just straight cut him off.

"Lemon, honey, why are you breathing like that?"

I leaned my head against the steering wheel. "I think the salad I had earlier was bad. My stomach is killing me."

"Are you nauseous?"

"No. My muscles keep cramping. It's been going on for a couple of hours now."

Momma went silent, and that was okay. I could barely carry on a conversation anyway.

"What pregnancy symptoms have you had lately? Are you still tired?"

"No."

"Nauseated, food aversions?"

"Nope." Mushrooms sounded disgusting again.

Mushrooms sounded disgusting? Salad sounded good?

No.

Oh no.

"Oh sweetie." She said it at the same time I realized. "Clem, baby, listen to me and don't panic. I think you might be having a miscarriage. I need you to check."

Her words grew massive fists that curled around my heart and squeezed as hard as they could. *No. No, please.* I closed my eyes for a moment and then looked down. I didn't even need to unzip my pants. Warm blood had leaked through my shorts and was staining the cloth on the bench seat of Daddy's old truck. I'd been so distracted by my breaking heart that I hadn't noticed.

I whimpered. "I-I think you're right."

"Listen, how far are you from a hospital?"

I took a moment to get my bearings. "St. Joseph's is a few miles ahead."

"Can you drive there, or do you want me to call for an ambulance?"

I shook my head even though she couldn't see. "No, I can make it." I didn't know how I was paying for this. I'd just been dropped by Billy's fancy insurance plan. My new coverage was something affordable, but it came with high deductibles and co-pays when it came to hospital stays. There was no way I could cover an expensive ambulance ride, especially if I was thinking of buying Mr. Greerly's entire building and converting it into a larger gym.

"I'm so sorry I'm not there, baby girl. You need someone with you. Let me call Silas. Or Jenny at least."

"No. They're too far away and I don't want them here anyway. I'll be fine."

"You're not fine, Clementine." She sounded as broken as I felt. "You need someone to hold your hand and be with you afterward. You're not doing this alone."

I wiped the tears off my lips, my hands a shaky mess. "I'll call Peyton."

"Pfft. Peyton is not—"

"I don't care who you call!" I didn't mean to yell. I simply couldn't handle any more. "Just don't call the Duprees. Please. Anyone but them."

"Okay. I'll figure it out. You focus on you."

"I'm sorry, Momma." I meant for the yelling—but also for not being able to carry her future grandchild to term. I felt like I'd failed her. And myself.

"Don't apologize. This isn't your fault. Sometimes these things just happen. And Clem?"

"Hmm."

"You're not a party of one. You never have been. Too many people love you for that to be true. You will find happiness and love again. It will work out in the end. You know how I know?"

There was a clump in my throat and I couldn't push anything past it.

"Because if anyone deserves it, it's my Clementine."

We hung up with a promise that Momma would be on the

next charter home. But it didn't matter. She was more than six hours away and who knew when the next bus would leave. There was no one here to help me with what I had to face next.

As I'd been reminded repeatedly since the day we laid Sophie to rest, I was on my own.

twenty-nine

SILAS

I gave my family strict instructions to call the minute Clem got back. *If* she came back. On the way, I must've called her at least ten times and texted twice that many. I kept the locater app reloading. But it kept coming back inconclusive. So I continued heading home, farther from Anna and the beach and closer, I hoped, to Clem.

Lisa had been tight-lipped when I called her the second time. She'd talked to Clem but wouldn't give me a bit of info.

"I'm sorry, Silas. I can't take sides. Just give her some time," was all she'd said. It stung that she wouldn't go up to bat for me. If James had been here, he would've had my back. And Sophie. Actually, Sophie would've smacked the back of my head and told me to fix the unmitigated disaster I'd single-handedly made. I would've deserved it.

The ride back was the longest four hours of my life.

The gate at the end of Firefly Fields was closed and locked. It didn't mean that Clem wasn't here. Just that possibly she'd come through and chained it behind her. It looked like I was hiking a half-mile to the house. I parked in the grass and got out.

"Nobody's home," BJ Shumaker called from his porch.

"Clem didn't come through here this evening?" I had to be sure.

He shook his head. "Just got done checking their cows and feeding Lisa's cat. The farm is locked up for the night." He walked down off the porch, across his lawn, toward me. "Lisa won't be home for a couple more days and Lemon's on vacation too, I think Miss Lisa said."

"Yeah. Okay." I pretended to know none of that. The last thing I needed was to have to explain to BJ what a jackwagon I'd been. "Thank you."

He scratched his forehead. "I thought you were living here. Do you want the key?"

It was tempting. I could go to the house and wait for Clem. Park my rear on her porch, so I was the first thing she saw when she pulled up. But with her ignoring all my attempts at communication, I was pretty sure it would do more harm than good. I couldn't take that chance.

I waved. "No, that's okay. I'm going to head over to my parents' house. Thanks." What I wanted was to wait in the car at the end of her driveway in case she did come by. But with BJ playing neighborhood watch, that wasn't an option.

BJ still looked befuddled, but I had bigger fish to fry. What if I'd driven all this way, and she was still near Sandbridge somewhere, processing? Or maybe she had stopped in Richmond—done some retail therapy, as Sophie always called it, drowned her sorrows in a good meal—and was on her way. Or possibly she was back at the beach house and they'd forgotten to call.

I rang Ashton.

"Still not here," he said without a hello.

"Anna hasn't heard from her?"

"No, man. None of us have."

We sat there in silence. I chewed my lip. BJ was still watching me from his rocking chair.

"What're you going to do?" he asked.

I put the car in gear and flipped a U-turn. "Go sleep at the ranch and check again in the morning. Not sure what else to do."

"Mom's freaking out about the ninety-day thing. She's scared of this going before a judge."

I rubbed my forehead. Normal people might be tempted to lie to Arlo. I mean, he'd never know if we didn't tell him. But Duprees were Boy Scouts when it came to honesty. Do What's Right, Even When No One's Looking was literally our family motto. It's one reason I'd tried so hard not to deceive Christy or Clem this summer. Even if I had failed miserably.

But any hope of finding Clem was fading with the sunset to the west. "Hopefully Arlo will understand." It was a weak answer, but it was the best I had.

"Christy's calmed down," Ashton said. "Spent the entire evening with Holden on the beach."

"She's still there?" I kind of thought she'd leave once I was gone. Hoped anyway. I wasn't trying to be mean. I just didn't see how she'd be comfortable there now. I guessed she and Holden were better friends than I'd realized.

"Sounds like she's heading out in the morning."

"All right. Thanks, Ash."

"No prob. I promise I'll call if Lemon shows up here."

That night, I lay down on my old bed, but I hardly slept. I texted Clem a few more times, but she didn't respond. The longer I lay there, staring into the darkness, the higher the boulders of anxiety piled on my chest.

I'd messed up. Royally. The day Clem and I got together, I'd been so certain. We were going the whole eight seconds. Me, Clem, and Anna. We hadn't even made it to one. In hindsight, I knew my mistake. I'd nodded too early. I'd always been a roper, but I'd attempted bull riding a few times in my life. When you're in the chute, atop an angry bull, waiting for the ride to start, you signal for the gateman to open the chute with the bob of your head. But I was never any good at bull-riding, and I'd had no business digging my spurs in until I'd been completely straight with Christy. My only hope now was that Clem would give me a re-ride.

If only I could find her.

I'd like to say I woke up with a plan, but I didn't. I got up with the sun and headed back toward Firefly Fields. The wide-open gate was the happiest sight I'd seen in the last twelve hours. I leaned forward, scanning the glorious green fields. The driveway was smooth now and the fence lines in perfect condition. I hoped James was smiling down on the efforts I'd put in over the last three months. If nothing else came out of this, I was at least proud of that.

My stomach was in a hooey knot as I came up the hill in front of her house. The knot tripled and tightened when I realized that, yeah, Clem was there...

But so was Billy.

His gargantuan truck was parked in my spot in the carport.

First thing in the morning.

The boulders were back, tenfold, and I felt myself crumbling, darkness closing in. Right back where I'd been in front of that scoreboard and on her wedding day. I wiped a hand over my mouth, staring at the house. Even if this meant what I was pretty sure it did, Clem still needed to know how sorry I was for the way things went down. She had to know that my heart never had been Christy's, even if she never gave me hers again. Whatever it took, I wasn't leaving until she knew that.

Stress and no sleep were giving me a migraine, so I rubbed

circles on my temples before getting out of the car. I took my time coming across the yard, ambling up the stairs and onto the porch, trying to get my hands to stop shaking. Billy yanked the door open before I had a chance to knock.

He was fully dressed, in khakis and a rumpled polo shirt, his blond, thinning hair a greasy mess. He'd definitely slept over.

He eyed me up and down with a scowl, then straightened, lifting his chin to appear taller. "What do you want?" But his eyes were swollen and bloodshot, like he'd been crying. Looked like Billy's night had been as rough as mine. I didn't let myself deliberate on what that meant. The last thing I needed was to get my hopes up.

I took a step toward him, trying to get inside. I couldn't be bothered with his little-man syndrome right then. "Where's Clem?"

"She doesn't want to see you," he growled, like he had a right to be her gatekeeper. She told him what happened? A stab of betrayal hit my chest, but I humbled myself real quick. If Clem had run back to Billy, it was only because I'd propelled her there. Whatever had happened here, this was on me.

I leaned over him and poked my head in. Everything was in shadows, the early morning sun the only light in the room. When I saw a pillow and a blanket on the couch, along with Billy's shoes on the floor, relief washed over me like a tsunami.

Billy puffed out his chest. "You need to leave. Now. Before Lemon wakes up."

"Not until I talk to her." My voice came out rough, gravelly, and I hoped he wouldn't turn this into a thing. But I wasn't leaving until I saw her. Even if I had to body slam him to the ground again.

He glanced over his shoulder, toward the hall, and then back at me. "She lost the baby last night," he hissed. "This isn't the time."

My mouth parted slightly as my heart fell out of my chest and onto the floor.

"She lost the baby?" I said, barely a whisper. No wonder she hadn't responded yesterday.

"Yeah." His voice cracked. He'd been crying a lot. Well, look at that. Billy had a heart, after all. He tilted his head in disbelief. "You knew and you let her keep it from me?"

A minute ago, I would have given him a sarcastic reply about how Clem could keep him in the dark for the rest of his life for all I cared. But now, I didn't have it in me. I couldn't kick a man when he was down. I just shrugged.

Maybe the baby hadn't been mine, but it had been Clem's, which was enough for me. When I'd told her I'd be this baby's dad, I'd meant it. Fully. Gotten my heart set on it. Hearing the news gutted me and it was trying to come out through my tear ducts.

"Billy?" Clem's voice trembled from the hall. "Who's at the door?"

I straightened, praying to get a glimpse of her. "Clem, it's Silas. Can I talk to you for a minute?"

"I told you to leave." Billy tried to shut the door on me. I jammed my shoulder in the way.

"Stop it," Clem said forcefully, standing ten feet behind Billy. "Let him be."

Reluctantly, Billy stepped back, holding his hands up.

I pushed past him and in two strides I was to her, arms open, ready to be whatever she needed at that moment. Ready to grovel, crawl across hot coals. Any of it. All of it.

"Don't." She stepped back, her expression a three-way split between betrayal, loss, and fierce determination. She looked at Billy. "You need to give us a minute."

He raised his brows at me in a threat. "I'll be in the guest room, right around the corner." Like I didn't know where it was and like I hadn't been sleeping there all summer. Like my stuff wasn't still in there at that very moment.

She closed her eyes and took a deep breath. "Billy, just go."

Once he was gone, I took a long look at her. Hair tousled, baggy sweats, and an oversized T-shirt hanging off one shoulder. Like Billy, her eyes were swollen and red, not a trace of makeup anywhere. She brushed her hair out of her face and I wanted to trace my fingertips over her cheekbones. Even standing here, as broken as she must've been, she was the most beautiful thing I'd ever seen.

My hands folded behind my neck so I wouldn't reach for her. "Clem, I'm so sorry—"

She shook her head, biting her bottom lip. "I can't do this, okay? You shouldn't have driven all the way back. You should be with Anna. She's going to need you now."

My forehead furrowed and I slouched. "She's going to need me now?"

"I know you came here to apologize, beg me to forgive you, or whatever—"

I cut her off. Whatever I came here for, she trumped that. "Clem, the baby, I'm sorry for—"

"It's not your concern. You're with Christy." Tears leaked out, and she squeezed her eyes shut, trying to stop them.

My hands flew out, frantic. "Christy and I are over. I never should have agreed to the pause/reset thing—"

"No." Her jaw pulsed. "That's what I'm talking about. It doesn't matter anymore."

I tilted my head, eyes narrowing. "Why doesn't it matter?"

She gazed out the window past me, a distant look in her eye. Then her expressive green eyes flashed back, piercing like a dagger. "I thought I wanted to be in a relationship with you, but this whole thing made me realize..." She looked at the floor, a slight shrug. "I just... don't."

My shoulders rounded as if she'd sucker-punched me. I couldn't speak. I could barely breathe. I glanced down the hall where Billy was probably eavesdropping. Were they back together?

She must've read my mind because she said, "It's not about Billy either. He's just helping for a bit until Momma gets here and then I'll be sending him on his way, too."

I didn't understand any of this. "Clem, please," was all I could say.

She wiped her cheeks. "Don't go beating yourself up. It's not you. It's me. I'm broken, okay. I'm never going to be able to trust a man again. It's just the way I am now. The damage is too extensive," she said, like a doctor breaking the news to the family of someone who'd just died in a tragic accident.

I stood there in shock.

"Hold on." She walked out of the room and down the hall. She must've gone into my room, because Billy's muffled voice sounded through the wall. Then it went quiet. A couple of minutes later, she carried out a big box.

She held it out for me. "It's over, Si."

I stared at my belongings and back up at her.

"Please, just take it and go." Her voice quivered. She shoved it against my chest.

I stood there, staring at her, not wanting to believe it, the box rammed between us. I finally got my hands to raise, to hold the bottom of the cardboard. She gave me a little push, trying to get me out the door, but I couldn't. My legs refused to move.

"Go," she cried. "*Leave.*" Her hands pressed against my chest with a shove.

I stumbled backward and finally got myself to turn. The door shut behind me, as soon as I was over the threshold.

In a daze, I walked to the car. I don't even remember

getting in but somehow I must've. I held it together until I was over the first hill. Then I had to stop the car because my eyes were drowning and I couldn't see the road. I tipped my head back against the headrest. A groan broke free from the deepest recesses of my soul and I let the waves of grief crash over me.

thirty

SILAS

That familiar darkness wrapped around my chest, squeezing, trying to get me to cave in. To return to the murky state I'd existed in for years, where I was numb, only half alive.

And then I saw Sophie's light blue letter out of the corner of my eye. It was tucked between my cowboy hat and a pair of jeans Clem had folded.

Shy Si

It had only been eighty days, but I didn't care. Everything was ruined now anyway. I tore the envelope open, chest heaving with anger at my sister. I hoped she at least apologized for the misery she'd put me through. And maybe I could find something in her words that would help me understand this and go back and fix the mess I'd made.

> *Dear Silas,*
> *The Hansel to my Gretel. The Luke to my Leia.*

I pursed my lips, disgusted. Sophie knew I hated it when she called us that.

> *The Abel to my Cain. Stubborn, strong-willed, emotionally constipated Silas.*

Did she seriously just compare my lifelong struggle to adequately communicate my feelings to a clogged bowel movement?

If she hadn't been dead, I would've burned the letter on the spot. But she was. So I read on.

> *Remember when we very first met? We were in a pretty tight spot.*

I rolled my eyes.

> *Okay. Okay. Enough with the twin jokes. I'm going to run out of room so I'll get to the point. And here it is.*
>
> *Please, please, please tell me you didn't bungle this, Spare Parts. You may be three minutes older, but let's be real. I've always been the wiser twin. At least on the things that really matter. Except that one time I got myself knocked up. I mean, I couldn't be perfect all the time or I'd make you look bad. And*

we got delightful Anna out of the whole thing. Our adorable plot twist.

Anyway. I digress.

Silas. I bought you three months with Lemon. What did you do with it?

My hope is that you're sitting next to each other right now, reading your letters together, shaking your heads at me and laughing. That you spent your days falling head-over-heels, crazy in love. That you couldn't keep your hands off each other. And you stole a thousand kisses when Anna wasn't looking. And hopefully a few when she was.

Yeah. The three months were definitely about my girl. But I never doubted for a second that you and Lemon would love the heck out of her. You already do. My fear is that you won't see this time for what I meant it to be: a gift.

Si. You have a hard time going for it. You start, stall, reverse, second-guess yourself into a tail-spin until it paralyzes you. If you're with Lemon now and you two are at the beginning of your happily ever after, then my work here is done. The silver lining to dying at twenty-eight will be that it finally got the two of you together. But if you spent the summer under the same roof and you never let yourself open up to her, then I failed. And I think that might kill me more than actually dying IRL.

What I'm saying is this: you deserve happiness, wonderful brother. You are a good, loyal, respectful, kind man. You've finally grown into that gangly body *and you got hot. Own it. But you're not just any man, Silas. You're the man who loves, desires, and craves Lemon. All the way down to your cowboy-studded soul. And she deserves to be loved like that. I need you to love her like that.*

Please make her see sense. You have to talk her out of Billy. Every day that she's with him, she's wilting. He is sucking the life out of her and if she makes it up here to heaven earlier than she should because he broke her, it will kill me all over again. First thing, when I get up to those pearly gates, I'm heading straight for the Big Man himself to see what I can do about getting her away from him.

I chuckled and shook my head. With the way Billy and Clem's marriage had blown up the day we buried Soph, maybe she really had gotten "The Big Man" involved. It would be true Sophie style, indeed—barreling into heaven, ready with her list of demands.

Lemon needed to be near you this summer so she could see, front and center, what being loved by a real man looks like. I'm hoping it will be enough that she'll be able to break free. But even once she's out, she's going to need you. It will take years of someone loving her, and all her broken pieces, before she'll see that she was worthy of it all along. And you're the one, bro. It won't be easy. She doesn't think she deserves better. Billy did that to her. But you're a little broken too because you don't think you deserve her.

You're both wrong.

What's that horrible phrase people say to be mean? You deserve each other?

But this time, it's true. You do deserve each other. In all the best ways.

I need her to be okay, Silas. <u>Please make sure she's okay.</u>

I sucked in air at that line. That's what she'd meant when she made me promise on her deathbed. It wasn't a vague request. It was code for *make sure Billy doesn't destroy her*.

But Si? Don't think this is all about Lemon. I need you to be okay too. Cause right now, you're not. Oh, you think you are. But you still don't know true happiness. And you won't until you recognize that you're always going to love her and you do something about it.

I need you to fight, Si. With everything you've got. Fight for Lemon. But fight for yourself, too. Whatever it takes. All to pieces.

I couldn't have asked for a better brother. Heck, I got the four best on the planet. But you're my twin. I can't imagine I made it easy on you. But you were the right person for the job, and I'll never, ever forget how much you loved me.

Enough of the mush. I'm sure you're squirming in your seat.

She was right. I was. Eyes were burning too.

> Give Anna lots of hugs from me.
> See you on the other side, Bestie from the Nestie.
> Forever and always,
> Sophie

I set the letter in my lap and closed my eyes.

So she had done this for me and Clem to get together. I'd been right about that. The part I got wrong was that Sophie wasn't trying to boss me around from the grave or have one last laugh. She knew me. She knew what I needed to be happy, and Lemon, too. And she'd facilitated a plan to knock us both off our axes, and give us the time to set them aright, together.

I cruised the winding, hilly back roads of Seddledowne for hours, mulling over Sophie's letter, over Clem, over the botched ninety days with Anna—trying to figure out what to do. By the time I headed home, it was well past lunch. My stomach was reciting an oral presentation about it.

There are five residences at Dupree Ranch—my parents' house, Sophie's small cottage, two tiny ranch hand trailers, and all the way on the other side of the five hundred and twenty-two acres, Uncle Troy and Aunt Wendy's house, the original homeplace. Sophie's was the first one you passed once you crossed onto Dupree land. I hadn't been inside since the day after she died. And I'd left that day, hyperventilating. It was vacant now, and my parents hadn't made plans for anyone to move in.

So when I drove by and saw a car parked in front, I made a three-point turn and pulled into the driveway.

It was a standard, nondescript gray sedan. With a rental company sticker on it.

Christy.

It was her rental. I'd seen it for half a second in the driveway at the house in Sandbridge.

Had she driven here from the beach? She must've come looking for me and thought this was my parents' house. I didn't want to do this with her, but I couldn't really avoid it if she'd come all this way.

I got out and jogged to the house.

But I never got off a single knock on the front door.

Because there, on Sophie's couch, framed by the picture window like something on a Christmas card, was my brother and my ex-girlfriend, arms wrapped around each other, sucking face.

My hands gripped the sides of my head and a sound I'd never made before exploded out of my lungs—part shocked snort, part incredulous laugh, part expletive. I stumbled backward off the porch and onto the grass.

Holden jerked back, his eyes flashing to the window. He jumped off the couch and raced over to the door.

My head gave a small shake, reeling. "I can't...wow. Unbelievable."

The weird laugh-snort kept repeating in my throat and I couldn't stop it. Didn't have a name for it. I'd never walked in on my brother kissing my very, barely ex-fiancée before.

I was pretty sure Holden was experiencing feelings he couldn't name either. Because Holden had dated probably a hundred girls over the years and never felt a bit of shame in the way he necked with Julie one night and went out for a drink with Jocelyn the next. Discomfort, guilt, and self-doubt were not emotions he possessed when it came to the female sex. But they were on his face now, in every tense, taut muscle of his body.

"Si, I'm sorry, man. I didn't mean—"

Christy bolted past him like he wasn't there—her eyes desperate. "It was nothing, Silas. It was a mistake."

Holden's head snapped back like she'd elbowed him in the nose.

I put my hands up for her to stop before she got any closer. "Doesn't look like nothing to him."

She glanced sheepishly at Holden. Then she turned back and reached for me. I took another large step back, shaking my head.

"Silas," she hiccuped, wrapping her arms around herself.

I finally got my jaw up off the ground. "It's whatever. Really. I just can't believe the scene you made at the beach, probably completely ruining any chance I had with Clem—and you've been macking on my brother this entire time."

"No, dude, it's not like that," Holden started.

"It wasn't premeditated. It just happened." Christy added.

"Maybe not for you." I scoffed in Holden's direction. I really couldn't care less who Christy made out with. I wasn't jealous. It was Holden. For him to be so skeezy...I mean, he'd always handled females differently than me...but I was his brother. His flesh and blood.

I had a lightbulb moment and aimed myself at him. "So this is why you got all huffy that one day in Mom and Dad's kitchen. Ah, it all makes sense now. You were falling in love with Christy."

Holden opened his fat mouth to explain, but I cut him off.

"I literally don't care." I turned to Christy. "We were done long before this, but just to be clear, we are completely over." I shook my head, disgusted. "You wriggle your way into my family and wreak full-blown havoc on my life, and then top it off with this." I did a slow clap. "I honestly don't know if I've ever met anyone more selfish." She was silently sobbing now.

"Hey, that's enough." Holden stepped up next to her. His expression said I was out of line. *I* was out of line.

I aimed my parting words at Christy. "You know what? It's fine. You deserve someone who loves you enough that he'd stab his own brother in the back. You do. I can't blame you for that. You truly deserve each other." Sophie probably would've put her boot up my butt for flipping her words around.

I turned to my brother, hands in my pockets. "And Hobags, well...I'm sure Savannah stopped rolling over in her grave long ago at the list of women you've blown through. Probably nothing you do shocks her anymore. Too bad you can't just let her rest in peace."

Holden crumpled, his hands folded up behind his head, the shock landing like an invisible punch to the jaw. I threw my hands out in spectacular jackass fashion and took a bow. It was probably the most hateful jab I'd ever taken in my life. We didn't talk about the girl whose death had shattered Holden's life. Ever. Holden wouldn't allow it. But at that moment, I didn't care. Holden had been my safe place in the last year while Sophie was dying. And now that was riddled with buckshot. I pulled the car keys out of my pocket and tossed them to my normally loquacious brother who suddenly couldn't find a single word.

Christy stood there, hugging herself, mortified.

"Good riddance." I turned and walked away, laughing in disgust. Why were they even here? Holden should've been at the beach and Christy on a flight home. I flung myself over the fence and cut across the field to Mom and Dad's, not even caring.

Well, one thing was for sure, I wouldn't spend anymore time feeling bad about breaking Christy's heart. Looked like my brother had patched her right up.

thirty-one

CLEMENTINE

It had been eleven days since the beach house. Eleven days since I'd lost my baby. Anyone watching from the outside probably would've thought I was handling things well. My body had healed, and I was already back teaching at the studio. But my heart still had a long way to go.

I'd barely begun to get excited about the prospect of being a mom when the miscarriage happened. At least, I'd barely begun to let myself admit my excitement. Truth was, I'd gotten attached to the little human growing inside of me. I'd made big plans for us and Anna, of course. And then Silas.

The past week and a half, alone in my house again, had been harder than right after Sophie died. With Anna and Silas, it had brimmed with happiness, laughter, sarcasm, teasing...all the good and wonderful things about life. I felt their absence keenly.

The hardest part of losing the baby was the not knowing. Would I ever get the opportunity to try again? And if I did, would I lose that one too? The doctor said there wasn't anything wrong with the fetus. Sometimes it just happens. But the worry was still there, a constant fear in the corner of my mind.

I headed for the guest bedroom to do some tidying. It was time. Silas's bed was still haphazardly made—a reminder of how he and Anna had rushed off to the beach so early. I pulled back the blankets, yanked the sheets off, and piled them onto the mattress. Granny Eudora's old alarm clock, the kind that flipped a new number every minute, was still on the nightstand after all these years, and I noticed the date.

The ninety days was up. Yeah, we'd failed. This wasn't a new realization. I'd known it since I left the beach in the dust. The loss of Anna was tightly tangled around the loss of the baby. And Silas. I didn't know how to unwind any of it. It might take me months or years to figure out how.

I hurried to my bedroom to retrieve Sophie's letter. I'd stuffed it in the top drawer of my walnut dresser. Sitting on the end of my bed, I tried not to think about how these would be the last words my best friend would ever say to me.

Lemonlime

I tore the envelope open. When I slid the blue stationary out, an additional letter fell onto my lap. I picked it up and smiled. It resembled our notes from middle school, back before we'd given up paper for texting. The note was folded carefully into a perfect rectangle with a triangle tuck holding it together. The paper was lined, probably torn out of a school notebook, and it had yellowed over time. Was this an actual letter from when we were kids?

I opened the stationery letter first, in case.

A sentence was underlined at the top of the page:

SUSAN HENSHAW & (CALLIE MAE SHAW)

<u>*Read this before you read the note.*</u>

Ok. Good choice. I took a deep breath and began.

> *Dear Lemon,*
> *Hey, my sister from another mister. First, let me apologize for dying. I'm really sorry. Sometimes life be like that. What're you gonna do?*

I shook my head and laughed. Oh, Sophie.

> *Please don't hate me for saddling you with a summer full of Silas. I know he's stiff and emotionally caged and a bit trust-challenged. And it takes about a thousand picks to break through his ice. Lord knows I wouldn't want to live with him again.*
> *But I hope by now you've realized Billy is not who you're meant to be with, Lem. It's Silas. It's always been Silas. And it always will be.*

I paused. Sophie knew?

> *He's loved you since the moment his body thrummed with hormones. Maybe even before. But not just loved. Ached. Yearned. Lived for. You get the picture. And no, he's hardly mentioned you since high school because, again, emotionally caged—but a twin doesn't need words to know what her other half is feeling. He didn't move across the country just for a roping scholarship. He ran from his feelings for you. And anytime he came home for a visit,*

his heart would break all over again. So eventually, he stopped coming.

I reread the last paragraph. It was exactly what Silas had said. And Momma. So maybe he hadn't been playing me after all. Maybe he'd just gotten himself snarled up in a relationship with Christy that he didn't know how to get out of. I'd done the same with Billy and it had taken years to cut myself loose.

Listen. I didn't do this just for Anna. I'm sure Mom's been all over you both about taking care of her and getting everything right. Mom's just hurt that I didn't leave Anna with her. She'll get over it eventually—when she sees Anna thriving again. I'm sure mistakes have been made and will continue to be made. Heck, we both know I made plenty of them. But I want you to forgive yourself, Lem. Anna will be okay. She's got the two of you.

What must Sophie think of us now that we'd lost Anna? But I couldn't think about that or I'd never finish the letter.

And, if you fell for my frustrating, pig-headed, devoted, adoring, handsome brother, just know that Jenny will get over that too. I'm the one who died, and this was my evil plan all along. Not dying. Just using it to get you and Silas together. What I'm saying is, you've got my blessing all the way from heaven. If Mom gives you any lip, remind her you two have the endorsement of a verified angel. That trumps any and all of her opinions.

I chortled, wet-cheeked.

In all seriousness, I hope you did, Lemon. I hope you fell so hard that you'll never recover. Because I know if you've allowed yourself to do that—there's no doubt Silas has loved you back even harder.
And if somehow you fell in love and you've lost him—though I don't think that's possible—you have to fight for him. Fight hard. Harder than you've ever fought in your life.
Fight like a girl.

She drew the breast cancer symbol next to the motto we'd all lived by the last year of her life.

Fight better than I did. Because Silas really does love you.
He always has. And so have I. All to pieces.
Forever.
Until we meet again,
Soph

This had been her plan all along? Why was I surprised? It was so...Sophie. My chest broke into a shaky laugh and I sat there for a moment rereading it.

On the third run through, I noticed an arrow under her

signature, pointing to the back. There was more. I flipped the page over.

> *P.S. Silas almost told you how he felt once. The folded note is his, from high school. He was going to give it to you at the beginning of our senior year, right after The Fated Football Game—as we Duprees like to call it. But Billy got to you first.*

My trembling hands struggled to untuck the corner of Silas's letter. I smoothed the creases against my leg.

Clementine,

I've tried to write this letter at least fifty times and I can't get it right. So this is the last time. However this comes out, it is what it is. I'm gonna go whole hog over here and hope I don't get my heart broken.

I'm crazy about you, Clem. Like weak-in-the-head in love.

There I said it.

Sophie just read over my shoulder and said it's too cowboy, and maybe it is. But like I said, I'm out of paper.

> I'm not sure what to do next. I don't
> know anything about girls or
> relationships. I just wanted you to
> know. And if you hate me now, I hope
> we can still be friends, at least.
>
> Sincerely,
>
> Silas Dupree

I snorted at his last name. As if I wouldn't have known who he was if he hadn't specified. As if he hadn't been one of my best friends in the whole world. Silas always had been a man of few words. But I was beginning to learn there was always a story behind his silence. I folded the note as easily as if we were sitting in seventh grade. Muscle memory, I guessed. Then I chewed my lip, regret enveloping me.

I had broken his heart. Probably a hundred times over. But I didn't have to hurt him anymore. This could be a new beginning. One where Silas didn't associate Clementine Shepherd with gut-wrenching heartbreak. One where my last name became Dupree and I loved him so hard that all the past hurts became nothing but pinpoints of light that had led us to each other.

Hope filled my chest for the first time in a week and a half and after a few seconds of letting that feeling settle, peace spread through my entire body—from the top of my head to the tips of my toes. A peace I'd never known until that moment. Call it a sign. Call it Sophie's presence. All I knew—all that I was certain of—was that Sophie was right.

Silas and I belonged together.

I picked up my cell and scrolled to his number. I

unblocked him and almost pressed call. But it would be better if I did this in person. You can't pepper kisses all over someone's face, neck, and jaw over the phone. Or shove them up against a wall, jamming your body as hard against theirs as you could get, while running your hands down their muscled chest. And I wanted to do all of that and more. I opened the Find My Friends app, my fingers tapping on my knee as his location updated.

But then my stomach took a large dip.

I wouldn't be kissing him today. Or possibly ever.

He was two thousand miles away.

A bright blue pin sat right over the bottom border of Wyoming.

Silas had gone back to his life out west. Back to Laramie.

Back to Christy?

thirty-two

CLEMENTINE

It looked like I wouldn't get a lick of sleep before my red-eye flight.

I'd taken so long deciding what to bring that by the time I fell asleep, it would be time to get up again. My carry-on refused to zip. Clearly I'd over-packed. But taking a trip to a place you've never been, not knowing how long you're staying, calls for a selection of outfits. Peyton and Crystal vowed to cover all classes until I returned, whenever that might be. And Knox, who was turning out to be a champion of my small business, promised that he and the guys would make sure the studio was tidied and locked up every evening.

The beach disaster and miscarriage had been in my rear view for seventeen days. Three days ago, I'd pulled a Christy and bought a one-way ticket to Laramie. Thankfully, I'd googled and found Silas's address. His location pin had disappeared altogether after the one time I saw he was in Laramie again. No one close to the Duprees knew what I was doing, except Momma. And she vowed not to say a word. I was honoring my best friend's last wish and, as Silas would say, going whole hog. Making the grand gesture. I'd thought of telling Anna. Had even seen her for a few minutes when she got Jenny to stop by the studio long enough to give me a hug a couple of evenings ago. I hadn't given up on getting Anna back. Not at all. But *if* I could fix things with Silas and get him back to Seddledowne before the court date, even better. But I didn't want to get Anna's hopes up in case the trip came to nothing.

I leaned all my weight onto the bag, finally getting the zipper around the corner. My body should've been exhausted, but the anxiety of the unknown was pulsing through me, a steady stream of adrenaline. Which was a good thing since I still needed to stop by the studio on my way out of town. The app clients used to sign up for classes had gone haywire this evening—because of course it had. You would think clients would be ok to struggle through till I got back, but I'd lost more than one client in the past to janky apps. People, I'd learned, liked things to be smooth and easy or they went somewhere else.

At twelve-thirteen a.m. my cell rang. It was Jenny. In my entire life, I'd never seen her stay up past ten. Even when her kids were younger and out for the evening, Bo handled all the waiting up. And the only contact I'd had with a Dupree since the beach was Anna. I'd called Jenny a few times to see if I could pick Anna up to go to McDonald's and she'd ignored and never returned my calls. So Jenny calling me now was unusual, to say the least.

"Hello?"

"Lemon." Her voice was distraught and weary. "Sorry to bother you so late—" An all too familiar shriek cut her off.

My chest tightened. "Anna's having night terrors again?"

"Yeah. It started at the beach and it's happened every night since. Bo and I are at our wits' end." Her tone was defeated. She hated that she was calling me. That she, Anna's grandmother, way older and wiser than little old Lemon, needed my help, desperately.

"You're letting her sleep with Huck?"

"Mhmm. Every night. But when the screaming starts, he scampers onto the floor and hides under the bed."

From the sound of hysteria currently happening, I couldn't blame him. And from Jenny's voice, it sounded like she wished she could do the same. "I know it's the change of not having you and Silas nearby." It sounded like it killed her to admit that. "Could you possibly come over and see if you can get her calmed down?"

I pulled the bag behind me as I came down the hall, turning off lights as I went. "I really wish I could, but I'm headed out of town as we speak."

"At this time of night?" It sounded like someone had made a fist around her vocal cords.

"Yes. Right now."

"You can't leave right now." Her voice was panicky and annoyed with a touch of desperation, like she might come over and try to stop me.

"I'm really sorry, but I'm on a flight in a couple of hours. I have some things I need to take care of." Like making up with your son. "It took Silas and me a bit to figure it out, too. I know you must be exhausted. The hardest part is patiently waiting it out—when you just want to wake her up and stop it. It's the opposite of what your instincts tell you to do. But it's the only thing that works."

There was an uncomfortable pause. I was about to say goodbye when she asked, "When will you be back?"

I grabbed the truck keys off the hook by the door. "I'm not sure."

Silence. You know, other than Anna screaming bloody murder in the background.

"Hey," I said gently. "Do whatever you have to for now?

Sleep next to her, or let her sleep between you and Bo. She feels safe tucked in between, like a cocoon." Letting kids sleep in her bed went against everything Jenny stood for. Allowing Huck on the bed had probably been a huge concession already. "Her first therapy appointment is next week, which will help. And when I get back, if it's still happening, I'll come help out. Just hang in there."

"Yeah. Okay. Be safe."

"Will do."

Once I was on the road, I sent a speech-to-text message to Anna so she'd see it first thing in the morning.

> Me: Hey, sweet girl. Heard you had a rough night. I'm so sorry. I'm going on a little trip but I'll have my cell at all times if you need me. Get ready for souvenirs because they're definitely headed your way. Love you so much.

The studio parking lot was pitch black, as it should've been at that time of night. The only light was the neon lettering on the sign. But as soon as I stepped out of the truck, blaring country music hit my ears. It sounded like it was coming from inside. Maybe Knox and the guys had forgotten to turn the speaker off? I quickly punched in the code and the door unlatched. One step inside and I realized it wasn't from my studio. Someone on the other side of the warehouse was jamming out though.

I scowled. And then winced. I liked country music as much as any other resident of this small southern town. Growing up on a farm, working cows, picking acres of corn, manure stains ruining every piece of clothing it ever touched... it was in my blood. But this...*song*...if you could call it that, was awful. Twangy, sappy, depressing. Whoever was listening must've been really low—drowning their tears in a trough full of beer, dog dead on the side of the road, fishing boat sunk at the bottom of a lake, wife run off with their best friend and she ain't never coming back. It was that bad. Only the most yee-hawin' of cowboys would enjoy this.

I flipped the computer on, trying to focus over the assault of the cacophony. But then some high-powered saw turned on, amping the discord level even higher. What in the world? The saw turned off. Turned back on. Turned back off. But another horrible song was on now, equally bad with an accent even worse than the one before. I widened my eyes and let myself shiver my nerves out.

But then—and this was the final straw—whoever was on the other side of the building started singing. Loud, off-key, and so, so drawly. I couldn't. I just couldn't. Admittedly, the edge-tipper was probably the fact that my body was already overloaded with pre-trip jitters. I had to stop this sound pollution nonetheless. Hopefully the wannabe country star would cease their one man karaoke night—at least until I was gone.

I walked down the hall, past the room with the inversion table, and up to the door that separated the two sides of the building. I hardly ever went in there since it didn't belong to me—so it took a second of fumbling on my tiptoes to find the key on top of the doorjamb. But I finally retrieved it and opened the door.

The barrage of noise was twenty times louder now that there was no wall muting the sound.

I covered my ears to prevent future hearing damage and looked around the huge, open warehouse. This was not the way I remembered it. Before, it had been full of junk—old machines that did who knew what, a couple of half-built classic cars, rusty scrap metal, and VHS tapes, of all things.

But this was a completely different room. Talk about a transformation. All the junk was gone—completely cleaned out. The oil-splotched concrete floor was covered up with a fresh layer of padded gray rubber. Gone were the rusty off-white walls. The entire inside, floor to ceiling, was painted a nice matte black, giving it a modern feel. There were snacks littered against the far wall and a sleeping bag.

The culprit of the terrible voice—a tall man in jeans and a cowboy hat, of course—was still belting out the song, his back to me, on the other side of the vast room. I strode across the floor, determined to talk some sense into him. He was standing on a short ladder, nailing a two by four over a brand new entrance. It looked like he was about to install a massive all-glass sliding door, which was leaning against a nearby wall. Like a new business was being opened in here.

I stopped dead in my tracks. Had Mr. Greerly sold the building out from under me? It hadn't been that long ago that we'd discussed my possibly buying it. And he'd seemed fine with letting me take my time deciding.

Just then, the off key voice belted a line so loud and so bad —*and he knewwwww, if he couuuld, do it all over again, he'd love her the saaaame as he did back thennnnn*—that a snort-laugh erupted from the bottom of my lungs. I was unable to contain it. I flat out guffawed—nostrils flaring, belly shaking, not even trying to be nice.

The man whirled on the ladder so fast it toppled over. Cowboy hat sailing through the air.

I screamed. Not simply because his feet flew above his head and he landed smack on his back on the newly padded floor—though it was scream-worthy. And hilarious.

No.

Because the person plummeting to the ground, The Off-Key Cowboy, was none other than Silas Dean Dupree.

Here.

In Seddledowne, Virginia. Not Laramie, Wyoming.

He was right *here*.

Turning this warehouse into a gym.

"Oh my gosh." I sprinted the rest of the way across the huge room. "Are you okay?" I slid to a stop on my knees, next to him.

He stared up at me, his beautiful gray eyes dazed and apprehensive. I should say eye. His wavy, chestnut hair covered the other one.

"Hi," was all he said, never breaking eye contact, looking like he was afraid to even gulp.

I pushed his bangs back so I could see his entire, dashingly handsome face. My eyes drank him in. "I can't believe you're here. I thought you went back to Wyoming. I looked on that stupid app and it said that's where you were."

He blinked a few times, still flat on his back, looking as surprised to see me as I was to see him.

"No. Nope. Definitely not in Wyoming." He pushed up on his elbows and I leaned back, letting him sit up. "I mean, I was for a few days."

My head gave a little shake, still in shock. "I don't understand. What are you doing in here?" I waved at the room.

He leaned against the wall, scrubbed a hand through his hair, wearing a sheepish expression. "Building you a gym." His shoulders slumped, and he glanced away, at the new door, the ceiling, anywhere but me. "As soon as I'm done, I'll sign it over. But it's yours, bought and paid for. The equipment is coming next week. It should bring in plenty of money, give you a nice life." He dared to look back at me. "I thought you could call it The Upward Dog. Get it?"

That was actually...perfect.

But.

It sounded like he wasn't staying. Like he was only here to make sure I was taken care of. My mind was blown at the gift. Exploding like a fireworks finale.

But I wanted *him*. Not the gym.

I sat back, my hands catching me. "Wait. How did you pay for this?"

He slouched like he wished he could sink through the brand new floor. "Dad and Uncle Troy bought out my share of the ranch."

I held up my hands in disbelief. "You gave up Dupree Ranch for this?"

He ducked his chin into his shoulder and nodded.

My mouth wouldn't shut, just hung open, waiting for all the bugs in Virginia to fly in. "Let me get this straight. You're a landless cowboy now and you took time off work right before school's about to start to come back here and build this gym for me, all so I would be financially secure?"

"Clem." His gaze pinned me. "I didn't take time off. I quit. I'm staying in Seddledowne for good."

My joy shot upward like a bottle rocket. I leaned forward, bouncing on my knees. "You're staying?"

He swallowed and his Adam's apple bobbed. My heart did a little dip. "Yeah. I need to be here for Anna."

Oh.

I felt my face fall, and I looked away, pretending to check out the gym so he wouldn't notice. But I could feel him watching me, his gaze drilling a burn mark into the side of my cheek. I dared to look back at him.

His eyes narrowed and then flashed with determination. "I am here for Anna. Absolutely. But I also came back for *you*." It came out in a breathy gush, like it had taken all his air. My heart melted into a puddle. "I love you, Clem. And I'm going to fight for you. For us. Whatever it takes. All to pieces. I won't quit."

All to pieces. The Duprees' saying. And the fighting for me? That was Sophie. It sounded exactly like what she'd written to me. My cheeks were melting off my face at the way he was looking at me. Like his whole world hinged on my response.

I willed myself to keep eye contact, even if his gray eyes left me a pile of sizzling ash. "And here I thought *I* was making a grand gesture." I took in the room, digesting the fact that this was mine. That he'd used up his inheritance on a woman who'd given him no guarantees. To be loved by Silas Dupree was unlike anything I'd ever experienced.

He leaned toward me, his hands shaking a little. "What do you mean, you were making a grand gesture?"

I hooked him with my gaze as I slid onto his lap, facing him. I straddled my legs around his waist. His breath hitched, and I bit back a smile. I gripped the front of his button-down shirt in my fists, tugging him toward me until we were nose to nose. I caught a whiff of musky aftershave. Whew. He was not making this easy on me, wearing that stuff.

I nibbled my lip and lifted a shoulder. "I have a plane ticket. I'm leaving. In three hours."

He looked dejected, like maybe I was just playing with his heart. "Yeah. My mom said you were going out of town."

"Wow. News travels fast." His eyes dropped, and I lifted his chin, forcing them back up. "Looks like I'm going to eat the cost of that ticket." I burned my gaze into his. "Because I was going to Wyoming. To see *you.*"

There was a beat of silence where it felt like everything hung in the air. Our past, this summer, whatever the future held. Then his hands wrapped slowly around my wrists, causing my entire body to crackle with electricity. I looked down at his calloused fingers, possessively holding me in place. Then I closed my eyes, smiling, breathing in the peace. How could I have not known all along?

He tipped his forehead against mine.

"*Clementine.*" It came out in hushed reverence, his breath

a perfect mix of dark chocolate and mint. And it didn't matter that he was an absolutely terrible singer, because my name on his tongue, baritone, husky and rough, was the most beautiful sound I'd ever heard.

I slid my hands up both sides of his stubbled jaw. "I love you too, Si. All to pieces."

Neither of us kissed the other first. It was completely, flawlessly, harmoniously mutual. The perfect amount of delirious, heady desire intertwined with gratitude and finality. We'd made it. At last.

He outlined my top lip with the tip of his tongue, causing blood to thrum in my ears. His hands found mine, twining our fingers tightly. He tugged them behind me, trapping me, a prisoner in his arms. And I was here for it. All of it. Whatever he wanted. He trailed kisses down my throat and along my collarbone, the hairs on my neck standing on end and goosebumps springing up everywhere. He chortled, giddy at the effect he had on me. He pecked me on the mouth and then held me there, smiling against my lips, my pulse racing.

I smiled back. "You think you're really something, don't you?"

"Let me have my moment. I've had to work hard for it."

And he had. So I let him perform his little science experiment. His nose ran up my jawline, up to the back of my ear, and my entire body purred. His thumb traced across my cheekbone and I shuddered. I was powerless. Complete putty in his hands. Ravished by the mere touch of his fingertips.

"Clem?" He broke away after another round, his forehead to mine.

"Yeah?"

"Marry me?"

I sat unmoving, taking it in for two breaths. The boy who was once one of my dearest friends had grown and deepened into the man of my ultimate dreams. And he wanted me to be his wife.

"I don't have a ring yet. I've been too busy doing this." He waved around the room. "I didn't know if it was false hope to think you'd ever say yes—"

"Yes. Absolutely, yes." I peppered kisses up the bridge of his nose, along his forehead. "Ring-shming. I just want you. Everything else can come later."

He kissed me harder, with a touch more lust and a little less respect. He growled into my neck. I moaned and my back arched involuntarily.

He swore and slammed a fist against the floor, frustrated. I threw my head back and laughed.

"When?" His question came out in a rush.

"When will I marry you?"

"Yes."

I cupped his wonderful face in my hands. "Yesterday, Silas. Tomorrow. A month ago. You name it. I'm there."

He grinned. "Can we seriously elope? I mean, is that a possibility? Or do you want a big wedding? I honestly don't care about any of that."

I tilted my head and shrugged. "I think we should at least invite our parents. And Anna, of course."

"Yeah. Of course, Anna."

We stared at each other for a second and I knew he was regretting losing her, just like I was. But somehow I knew it would be okay. As hard as we'd fought for each other, we'd fight for Anna.

I pecked him on the mouth. "But yeah. Eloping. I'm here for it."

His expression dropped. "I'm sorry about the baby. Sorry I w-wasn't there"—his voice broke, but then he recovered—"for you when you needed me. Can you forgive me?"

"Yeah." I pressed a kiss on the tip of his nose and nodded.

The edge of the hurt threatened to pull me over. But I didn't want to do that right now. Tonight was for the happy stuff. "Hey." I chewed the inside of my cheek. "So, I read your note finally."

He raised a dark eyebrow. "My note?"

"You know, the love note you almost gave me in high school, right after The Fated Football Game. But Billy got to me first." I quoted Sophie's words.

His expression turned guarded for a second. Habit? Then he lowered his force field, probably when he remembered I was his now. His eyes narrowed. "How did you get that?"

I lifted my shoulders in awe. "Sophie. She tucked it inside her letter. I guess she had it all this time."

His mouth parted and I could see a decade's worth of light bulbs coming on. "Are you kidding me? I lived in fear for months after that went missing. Freaking thief." His jaw clamped and his nostrils flared. "I'm gonna ki—" The words died in his throat.

I smiled into his wonderful, apologetic eyes. "You were gonna say kiss her, weren't you? When you see her again? She deserves a big, juicy one, on each cheek, from both of us." I shrugged. "Because if it weren't for her..."

He nodded, his eyes turned down, a little sad. "Yeah. If it weren't for her." He pulled me closer, forehead to forehead again, closed his eyes as if he was going to pray, and whispered reverently, "Thank you, Sophie."

My best friend had been the best there ever was. I'd known it when she was here and she'd left no doubt now that she was gone. There was no battle she would not run into for someone she loved. And she'd loved me since the first day of Pre-K. I would miss her with all my heart. But I could do this. Because she'd given me the best gift of all. An unsurpassed legacy of friendship and a love that would last me the rest of my life and beyond.

She'd asked us to do this one last thing for her. But in truth, she'd done one last thing for us. And I would never stop being grateful.

I tapped my nose against Silas's.

"Amen."

epilogue
SILAS

I blew out my breath. "Wish me luck?"

Clementine scoffed. "Baby, you don't need luck." She leaned over, slid her hand up into the back of my hair and pecked me on the mouth. "You've got me."

I grinned against her lips. Nine days since the night she'd thankfully stumbled upon me in the gym and we were still riding the new-couple high. I hoped we never came down.

Her thumb traced along my jaw. "And if you don't get the job, we still have a house, a farm, a small herd of cows, and a new gym that's almost open. So, no stressing."

She was absolutely right. My worst-case scenario was better than a lot of people's best. I laughed and inhaled her flowery scent. Oh, I shouldn't have done that right before I walked into the closed Seddledowne School Board meeting. Being near her like this made my brain fuzzy, and I needed to be able to answer whatever questions they threw my way. Smart Silas would've pulled back.

But Love-drunk Silas let my hand run along her spine and nuzzled her neck. "What about food?"

"Eh. Who needs groceries when you're living on love?"

"True." I pressed my lips against hers. "Still, it might be nice to have some rice and beans occasionally."

She ran her tongue across my bottom lip, melting me, making me even less clear-headed. "Momma has a five-gallon bucket of twenty-year-old instant potatoes in the attic. I'll sneak it out next time I'm up there. Probably feed us for two months."

I fought back a laugh and gave her one more kiss. "Sounds delicious."

Someone pounded on the window, and I jumped, bumping Clem's teeth. I whirled, ready to cuss. But it was Anna, standing next to Brooklyn, both grinning, their backpacks over their shoulders.

I wound the window down, biting back all the comments I wanted to make about how Anna had on too much makeup and her shirt was too tight. She didn't, and it wasn't. I just didn't like that my niece, who I'd helped raise from infancy, looked like she could own any boy in this school with one toss of her dark hair. Did not like it one bit.

"Told you they're adorable," she said to Brooklyn.

I beamed. "Yeah. We are." My eyes danced to Clementine. "Some of us more than others."

She shook her head, blushing.

I looked back at Anna. It felt wrong that she wasn't living with us and we only saw her here and there. Clem and I kept finding reasons to go help at the ranch, just to get a few minutes with her. We'd taken her out for ice cream when she and Brooklyn made the JV volleyball team a week and a half ago. But every time we dropped her at my parents' and returned to Firefly Fields, it felt like someone was missing. The two of us were happy together. Ridiculously. But without Anna, we were incomplete.

My throat closed up, and I cleared it. Then I tugged at the collar of my dress shirt. "Aren't you two supposed to be in class?" They weren't. We'd heard the class-change bell ring a few minutes ago. I was just giving them a hard time.

Clem leaned across my lap. I rested my hand on her waist, still not used to the fact that I could do that now. Whenever I wanted. "How's your first day of high school?" She wiggled her eyebrows. "Any cute boys?"

Anna stepped closer, gripping the open window ledge, her eyes gigantic. "Lemon," her voice was barely a whisper, as if my truck might be bugged and her words might be broadcast over the loudspeaker to the entire school. "Blue Bishop is in my second period class. And he is hot." The t was more of a tuh.

I snorted. "Somebody named their kid Blue?"

Clem pursed her lips at me, but she was hiding a smile. She put a hand over Anna's. "Spill the tea."

Anna bounced on her tiptoes. "He's the JV quarterback. Tenth grader. Light brown hair, like five eleven. But it's the dimples for me." She fanned her face and her chest shook with a fake cry. "And when he looks at you, it's like he knows something about you that nobody else does."

Brooklyn's head bobbed. "The boy is a delicious snack."

Anna closed her eyes and exhaled. "No. He is the entire meal. And a piece of warm, gooey chocolate cake for dessert."

"Drippin' the rizz." Brooklyn nodded.

Anna's eyes sparkled. "It's sending me." Her hand cut through the air like a paper airplane plummeting over a cliff.

I gaped at them. Horrified.

Clem laughed so hard at my expression that it shook my ribcage. Which made me smile. If she was smiling, I was smiling. Even if these two teenagers were discussing a boy like he was food at a cheap buffet.

Clem squeezed Anna's hand. "Sounds like a cutie. We'll have to go to a game. Let Uncle Silas give him the once over and"—she pointed at Brooklyn —"make sure there are no pink flags."

"Yasss." Brooklyn said, impressed with Clem's mastery of their foreign language. "But you better hurry." She made duck lips. "With the way he kept glancing at her in Personal Finance, I give it two weeks before they're in a situationship and having a DTR."

I was so lost. "Situationship?" My eyebrow raised. "No ships allowed. Of any kind. Anna can't date till she graduates. College."

Anna tilted her head, not amused. I wasn't kidding.

The one-minute warning bell blasted.

"Gotta go." She leaned through the window and hugged Clem and me at the same time. With our heads smashed together, she whispered, "Don't worry about tomorrow. We've got this. Team Trifecta to the very end."

I gulped, wishing I had her confidence. Her custody hearing was tomorrow afternoon. And while we'd prepared as best we could, Clem and I knew it looked bad that we hadn't made it the ninety days.

Anna stepped back, gave me a quick up and down, and flicked her hand like I'd burned it. "Sheesh, Uncle Si. You should wear a suit more often."

"That's what I'm sayin'," Brooklyn said with zero expression. They waved and walked away.

Clem looked at me, brow lifted. "Did you understand all of that?"

I pinched my fingers almost together. Then I exhaled, facing facts. "It's time."

She pressed her hand against the lapel of my suit jacket, her emerald eyes softening. "You clean up nice, cowboy." She smoothed out my collar one last time. "Don't sweat it. You've got this."

"Yep," I said. "Because they're desperate at this point."

As I stepped out of the truck, she smacked me on the rear end, making me laugh.

She slid into the driver's seat and leaned out of the open window. "Text me when you're done and I'll be here in five."

A nod and one more kiss to her supple lips. And then I turned and walked into Seddledowne High School.

I tried to ignore the students side-eyeing me as I ambled up the inclined hallway. This building had seemed oversized and looming when I'd attended. But now, as a full-grown adult, with a decade of life, loss, and love behind me, I no longer felt like a terrified teenager waiting for whatever the universe threw at me. Surreal was this right here. Being back in Seddledowne, trying to get an assistant principal job at my old school. It was the stuff bad dreams were made of. And yet, it was exactly where I wanted to be.

"Mr. Dupree." A squat lady with curled, short black hair about the same age as my parents greeted me as I came toward the auditorium doors. Her blue eyes sparkled. "When they told me it was little Silas Dupree we were meeting today, I couldn't believe it."

I squinted, and recognition hit me. "Mrs. Travers?" My third-grade teacher.

She twinkled. "You remembered?"

I squeezed her outstretched hand. "Of course. I couldn't forget you. You're the reason I became a teacher." It was true. She and Mr. Montrose, tenth grade, accounting. They were the standards I held myself to every day.

She put a hand over her heart and I thought she might cry. "Well." She rubbed a spot on her chest. "Let me be the first member of the school board to welcome you as the new assistant principal of Seddledowne High School."

I got the job? My eyes widened, but I quickly recovered. "Oh. I thought there was another interview."

She shook her head, a pleased expression taking over. "No. No need for that. We all know who you are and what kind of family you come from." She leaned closer and whispered, even though her mouth only hit halfway up my bicep. "Personally, I think you should've gotten the principal job and not the lady. A Seddledowne graduate or an outsider? Shouldn't have even been a discussion. But nobody listens to me since it's my first year on the board." She shrugged. "But, she did apply two weeks ahead of you. And, well, when the principal in Laramie was on the phone..."

She didn't need to finish. Let's just say Mrs. Serafin hadn't taken the news so well. I was lucky Seddledowne even considered me after Serafin got done.

I waved my hands. "No. This is perfect. I'm happy to be here. I'm so grateful you all are taking a chance on me. I'm putting down roots. I'm committed to Seddledowne and I'm excited to jump in with both feet. Whatever is needed."

She patted my arm. "That's exactly what I told them." She smiled up at me. "You always were a good boy. All you Dupree boys were." Her voice turned solemn. "And Sophie. I'm so sorry about that."

I dipped my chin. "Yes, ma'am."

She sighed and straightened as she peered through the glass on the double doors. "Looks like they're about ready for you." Her hand curled around the push bar. "It's so crazy that you and Principal Thornbury are both University of Wyoming graduates. The exact same master's program. What're the chances?"

She pushed the door open, but I stopped dead, completely rattled.

Thornbury was Christy's last name.

There was no way. Christy wouldn't move two thousand

miles from her family to take a job, even if it was a principal position. Her entire family lived in Laramie.

Mrs. Travers turned to see why I wasn't following. With a tiny shake of my head, I stepped forward, my jaw clenched, eyes trained on Travers's black pumps. It all played through my mind quicker than a movie montage on fast forward.

Christy hadn't left the beach immediately, like I thought she would. And then she'd driven all the way here, to my hometown, with Holden. Had she come out for a job interview—as well as a Holden hookup? Had she applied before we even ended things? And when I ended it, had she taken the job just to spite me? To have some kind of power over me now that Clem and I were together? Or maybe she thought she could worm her way back in and break us up?

I willed my hands to relax. Because it didn't matter. Even if it was true and it ended up being the school year from hell, I refused to let it bring me down. I had Clementine. And hopefully after tomorrow, we'd have Anna too. They were all I needed. I took a deep breath and forced my head up, dreading the confirmation. Sure enough, standing at the head of the table, with her back to me, was the frame of a familiar petite blond—a size zero, as she liked to remind me.

I knew Christy. She was terrified right now. Her shoulders sort of curled over, like she was struggling to stand upright—and there was the tiniest twitch in her hands. She was trying to stop them from shaking.

What a joke this was going to be. Christy knew less about administration than I did. Was two years behind me in teaching experience. Her plan had been to teach another full year before she even applied for an assistant principal job. How in the world she'd convinced them she could be a principal was beyond me. The board must've been desperate. Seddledowne had no idea what was about to hit them.

But I knew one thing. I was going to be the best freaking

assistant principal this town had ever seen. If this ship went down, I was not going with it. Because the difference between me and Christy was, this was *my* town. I had a place here. A future. And I was going to make it work, by whatever means necessary. She could crash and burn on her own and start over somewhere else next year. But this was it for me.

"Miss Thornbury?" Mrs. Travers said when we got to the top of the stage stairs. "I'd like to introduce you to your assistant principal."

Christy rolled her shoulders back and turned, her eyes bulging like she'd swallowed a boiled egg still in its shell.

"Hey, there. Silas Dupree," I said, pinning her with my gaze. She offered me her right hand to shake.

But that's where she got it wrong. I might be forced to work under her this year. She could give me every menial task, every delinquent student she didn't want to deal with, every overbearing parent. She could make my life purgatory if that's how she wanted to play this. But there was one thing she had zero control over.

I didn't give her my right hand.

Instead, I gave her my left.

She corrected, switching hands, sporting a tiny scowl.

I made sure to keep my palm down, over hers, so she couldn't miss my ring finger—the one donning the shiny gold wedding band that Clementine had slid over my knuckle last weekend up in the Blue Ridge mountains—where we'd said our vows in front of our parents, Anna, and Ashton, who'd somehow gotten himself ordained as a minister from a website on the internet. The ring finger that helped steer my truck to a quaint little cabin on the Skyline Drive, overlooking the breathtaking Shenandoah Valley—where I'd made sweet but intense, knee-trembling, gasp-inducing love to my wife for the next three days. Many, many times.

And planned to many more. Like as soon as we were done here.

"Nice to meet you." I squeezed as she looked at the ring, aghast.

She glanced up at me, wide-eyed, like she might've made the biggest mistake of her life taking this job.

I grinned. "It's going to be a fantastic year."

Not ready to leave Seddledowne?

Read Not A Thing, Book 2 in the Seddledowne Series today!

Read All to Pieces, Book 3 in the Seddledowne Series after that.

Would you like to read the prologue for One Last Thing? It's the scene of the Fated Football Game back in high school where Silas almost gave Clem the love but Billy got to her first. Click here to read The Fated Football Game.

Is Facebook your thing? Come join Susan Henshaw/Callie Mae Shaw's Southern Charm Readers Group, and discuss all things Dupree, as well as future projects.

Want to read snippets from future books, see cover reveals first, and keep up with what I'm working on now? Sign up for my newsletter at
www.calliemaeshaw.com

Do you love playlists? Find the playlist for One Last Thing on Spotify.

Rate One Last Thing on Amazon, Goodreads, and Bookbub. Follow me on Facebook, Instagram and TikTok.

CHAPTER 33

from not a thing

CHRISTY

My head fell onto the wooden desk with a thunk.

Silas was married.

A half-crazed cackle teased my vocal cords. I stifled it. Of course he was. He and Lemon had only been together for a total of...I actually didn't know. According to him, he and Lemon had kissed the day before Beach Week began. So, less than a month.

Who drops the anchor that fast?

No man I'd ever known.

I groaned, lifted my head a few inches, and let it crack against the desk again.

A man who'd been pining over a woman his whole life, that's who. Two people who'd known each other for years and already lived together for three months, that's who. A couple who couldn't wait to kick the bedroom door closed whenever they wanted, *that's who!*

I was such an idiot.

My phone rang, and I lifted my head to see who it was. I squeezed my eyes closed for a second before putting it on speaker. "Hi, Mom."

"Hello, Christianna. How did your first day go?" she asked, but not in the concerned or hopeful tone of a normal mother who wants her oldest daughter to succeed at her new job. Though I'm sure a tiny part of her wanted that. My mother loved me. I knew that. But right now, she was still angry that I'd taken a serious detour from her life plan for me. If I replied that there had been four fights, three drug busts, and the entire school had burned to the ground, she would've given me a fat "I told you so," and a "that's what you get for leaving Laramie," and hopped on the next plane to pack me up and move me home.

I pressed my palms against the cool wood of the desk and ran my hands over the top, trying to calm myself. "It was fine. Everything's great. The teachers and staff are very welcoming." I left out the part where the cafeteria oven had caught fire, burning the pizza that was supposed to feed every kid on the first lunch shift. And I skipped over the two boys who'd been caught smoking weed in the bathroom during second period. I'd had to expel them. On my first day.

"And Silas? How'd he take the news that you're his boss?" Her tone was a touch proud that somehow I'd wrestled the job out of the school board's hands before he could get to it, and a touch hurt that the cowboy she'd grown to love was not going to be her son-in-law. I actually hadn't confirmed that yet. Only that our relationship was on the rocks. And technically, I wasn't his boss. The Seddledowne School Board was. But there was no point in arguing with her.

"It was okay...I think. His first day isn't until Monday. But he seemed fine with it." It was a lie. I mean, yes, he'd acted unruffled. But there was a terrifying fire in his expression too.

"Maybe now that he sees you're a force to be reckoned with, he'll come to his senses." It was almost a question and I hated the hope in her voice. "Tell him your dad is still willing to cut him in on the ranch if he'll reconsider."

I rolled my eyes. Mom could've lived in the eighteenth century, no problem. Love? Romance? Sure, if you happen to find that, great. But to her, marriage was a contract. A negotiation where two people used each other for whatever they most wanted. For her, it had been children. For my father, it had been a ranch.

My mom's family, the Lawsons, owned more land in Wyoming than the next three richest families combined. More than five hundred thousand acres broken up into three parcels. Yup. I was Laramie royalty—if that were a thing. Silas could've been a proprietor in one of the biggest ranches in Wyoming. As a matter of fact, my dad had tried to basically bribe him into the family the first time I brought him home to meet them. Because no way could Christy land a decent man without some kind of strings attached. Silas had simply lifted an eyebrow, slid his arm around my waist, and said, "I'd live with Christy in a trailer by the creek." Then he'd shrugged. "My family has a ranch in Virginia." It's one of the things I loved about him.

Had loved about him. I rubbed my temples. Silas was past tense and the sooner my brain remembered that, the quicker my heart could do the same.

"Christianna?" Mom nudged.

May as well swallow the bitter pill. "Silas is out of the picture for good."

Mom scoffed. "Surely, you can work things—"

"He's married," I yelped and barreled on before she could comment. "He and Lemon are together now. And he looks really happy." He had. Even after finding out that I was the principal, there'd been a gleam in his eye that I'd never seen before. A sparkle that said he'd live in a trailer by the creek with Lemon if he had to. If this job didn't work out. No. He'd live in an un-air-conditioned tent.

Lemon had gotten my "trailer."

I resisted the urge to crack my forehead on the desk again.

"Miss Thornbury?" A teenage girl called from the main office adjoining my smaller one. School had ended an hour and a half ago. The only people left in the building were the janitors and the girls' volleyball team.

"Principal Thornbury?" A second female student called.

"Mom, I have to go." I pressed end, knowing she'd shoot me a text telling me how hurtful I was being. I may have been avoiding her more than usual since I left Laramie.

I walked to the door and poked my head out. Oh, it was Anna, Silas's niece, and another girl about the same age.

I waved even though they'd already seen me. "I'm here."

I smoothed my hands down the front of my faux leather pencil skirt. Normally, I wouldn't be nervous about two teens approaching me, but I'd practically had a nervous breakdown in front of Anna at the beach. There was no telling what she'd told her friend. Or what they'd spread to other students. So yeah, my nerves were on high alert.

Anna strode through the office with more confidence than I felt at that moment. More confidence than I'd possessed as a freshman in high school. If there were any residual hard feelings from the beach, she hid them well.

"Hi, Anna," I offered her a gentle smile.

She studied me for a moment with a quizzical brow, as if my presence answered a question for her. I'd seen her earlier in the cafeteria, but I was pretty sure she hadn't noticed me. At what point in the day had she realized I was the new principal?

Gathering from both of their tiny, tight spandex shorts, they were on the volleyball team.

"I'm Principal Thornbury." I offered my hand to Anna's friend.

She eyed it like I might give her some kind of disease, but gave me a dead-fish handshake. "Brooklyn."

Okay.

Anna's phone was in her hand and she glanced at it as if to gain courage from something on the screen. "I think we have a problem," she said. Then she brushed a stray piece of mocha-colored hair out of her eyes. This girl was the kind of pretty I wish I'd been at her age. Heck, the kind of pretty I wished I were now. Sophie had been a blonde with blue eyes. But Silas had said Anna's father was Italian. I could see Sophie in her—the cheekbones, the smile. But her complexion was tan, and she had dark eyes with lashes most women would kill for. If she never put on a speck of makeup, it wouldn't matter.

I offered her a gentle smile. "What's going on?"

Her chocolate eyes were wide and worried. "Ms. Whorley, our coach, just quit. Like walked right out of practice."

My forehead crunched. "Why would she do that?"

Brooklyn let out a loud sigh. "Because she does nothing. She's the definition of mid. Told us to play Queens and sat on her phone for the first hour and a half of practice. Just like every other day. So when Coach Byrd—"

"That's the varsity coach," Anna interjected.

Brooklyn plowed on. "Got fed up with it, he started coaching—"

Anna lifted a hand but didn't wait for her friend to stop. "Because we're his future pool of talent, you know? In a year or two, we'll be his varsity team."

Brooklyn continued, a geyser of monotone words. "That got Whorley off her phone real quick. But she still didn't start coaching. Instead, she glared at Byrd for like ten minutes. Like how dare he. And of course, he ignored her because, like I said," she shrugged, "she's mid. So then she told him she did not have to be treated this way. She did not get paid enough for this. And stormed out of the building." Brooklyn made duck lips. "Lame AF."

I snapped two fingers and pointed at her. "Watch it. I know what that means."

Brooklyn shrugged. "Sorry." She didn't look sorry though and I couldn't tell if she was an apathetic punk or if it was her personality to be this vanilla.

Whatever emotion Brooklyn was lacking, Anna made up for it—evidenced in every line of her worried face. I couldn't blame her. I knew Silas had worked with these two all summer, trying to get them ready for tryouts. I could imagine the heartbreak, after all that preparation, to think your team was now going to fall apart.

I offered them an easy smile so they'd know I wasn't ruffled. Hopefully, they'd feed off of my energy. "Are you girls alone in the gym?"

Anna shook her head. "No. Coach Byrd is still there...for today. But the rest of the team is freaking out because we don't have a permanent coach. And our first game is Monday." Her eyes darted around my face, hoping for a miracle. Brooklyn still looked unfazed.

"Where's Mr. Alvarez?" This was more of an athletic director situation. I handled the academic side of things. Sports weren't part of my contract.

"Sksksk." Brooklyn fake laughed and immediately went straight-faced again. "Out with the football team, as always. He doesn't care about girls' volleyball."

We stood there for a moment—Anna watching me and Brooklyn staring off into space—and I had to wonder. If the varsity coach was there, why had Anna come to me?

As if she could read my mind, she glanced at her phone screen once more and said, "Silas said if anyone could fix this, it would be you. Because you're really capable and stuff."

I swallowed the lump in my throat and fought back the urge to wrap her in a hug. And Silas too if he'd been here and wasn't newly married. The fact that Anna was willing to overlook, even momentarily, the beach incident, and give me a chance, was more than I could've hoped for. And the fact that, apparently, Silas, only hours after learning I was here and he'd be my right-hand man, had encouraged her to come to me, was boggling. Then again, Silas was a classy guy. Even if he had broken my heart, I could still admit that.

I bit back the grin that wanted to take over my face. "No worries, I got you. We'll figure it out. We'll make sure you ladies are ready for the game. I promise." It was probably just a misunderstanding.

Anna slouched in relief and smiled.

"Let's go see what's going on." I led them out of the front office. As we trudged down the hall, Anna and Brooklyn whispered to each other behind me. I wasn't sure what they were saying, but the tone seemed hopeful. I'd take it.

I pushed open the door to the gym and the three of us stepped inside. Coach Byrd, one of the twelfth-grade history teachers who I'd met for the first time a week ago, was indeed trying to coach both teams. My high heels clacked against the glossy polyurethane floor and most of the girls turned. The bleachers to the left were pulled halfway out and it looked like the parents were beginning to trickle in for the meeting that I knew was scheduled to begin in a few minutes.

Coach Byrd peeked over his shoulder at me, then looked back at the girls and yelled, "Butterfly drills. JV this side." He pointed across. "Varsity on the other. Jasmine and Ming, take charge."

He stepped back to join me but continued watching the girls' progress.

"Coach Whorley quit?" I asked.

"Yup." The P popped. He shook his head. "And before you ask if I can coach both teams, I already tried last year and was told no by Alvarez."

That had been my next question. "There were problems last season?"

His eyes were trained on the drill as he spoke to me. "Whorley coached JV last year, and it was a nightmare. Same thing as now. No coaching, just wasting time. She only cares about the paycheck. The girls and their parents"—he waved toward the adults on the bleachers—"were extremely frustrated. But Whorley is the only teacher in the county besides me who knows anything about volleyball and no one else applied." He shrugged. "Halfway through the season, they hadn't won a single set." He cocked an eyebrow. "Do you know what a set is?"

I nodded. "They play three sets every match. Whoever gets to twenty-five first wins a set." One of my best friends in high school had been the captain of our varsity team. I'd been to some games.

He nodded, pleased. "Yeah, for JV it's something like that. Varsity plays best three out of five. Anyway, JV hadn't won a single set, which is ridiculous. They have talent, just no direction. So I told Alvarez I'd coach both." His jaw clenched. "He said cool, but I'd only get paid for coaching one team since we practice at the same time." He snorted. "That's not right. Varsity football alone has five paid coaches. There's a lot that goes into coaching that doesn't happen during practice. Games, for one. Besides, I went to college like everyone else here. I'm worth more than that. And I'm not talking just money." He rubbed a hand over his jaw. "But as a matter of principle, I told him to forget it. I thought with all the parent complaints, he'd try harder to find a better coach." His lips were pursed, disgusted. "Nope. Just kept Whorley." He threw his hands up. "And now we have no JV coach at all."

I scanned the moms and dads on the side. Some were wearing looks of concern and I wondered if they'd witnessed Whorley's adult temper tantrum. "What about a parent?

Could one of them do it?" These girls hadn't made the team without their parents' involvement and understanding of the sport. My guess was that most had at least been in rec volleyball, if not club or travel, in the past. There had to be at least a couple of adults here that knew the game.

He shook his head. "Has to be a teacher or staff of Seddledowne School District per Virginia State High School rules, according to Alvarez." His hands moved to his hips. "But that's not true. The next county over has a guy who's coached for twenty years and he's a logger. They just won state. Alvarez is just stubborn. Likes to throw his weight around. But he won't listen to me. Trust me, I've tried."

My lips twisted as I thought about what to do. Technically, this wasn't my problem. But emotionally, as a principal who wanted to know these kids—to care about what they cared about—it completely was.

"I'll try to talk to Alvarez." Coach Byrd eyed me, and I could tell he was unconvinced that it would make a difference. They needed a solution. Now. So I lifted my hand like a schoolgirl ready to answer the question. "And I'll help out for the time being."

Byrd snapped around, facing me now. "You'll coach JV?"

That's not what I said. "I don't know a ton about volleyball. I'm more of a soccer girl myself. But I could—" I was going to say fill in until we found someone.

A grin split his face. He slapped my back like I was one of the guys. "Great. Why don't you stick around for the parent meeting? I'll introduce you." He glanced back at the players. "Good work, ladies. Shag 'em up!"

I grabbed his arm. "I will *help*. I do not have the time to coach this team by myself the entire season." I widened my eyes. "I'm the *principal*." In case he'd forgotten. It was probable since I was at least twenty years his junior.

He nodded, his excitement waning a bit. "Okay. Understood. We'll take what we can get for now."

As long as we were clear on that.

The girls scattered in all directions, scooping up balls and dropping them into the ball cart. To collect them as quickly as possible, a few girls popped one or two under their shirts, like a pregnant woman. I gulped as I walked toward the parents. I'd never coached a sport in my life.

And then I gulped again.

Because sitting there, in the middle of the group, was Silas's super hot younger brother Holden. The one I'd kissed right after Silas broke my heart. And he was scrutinizing me with his honey-brown eyes. I swear if a gaze could burn, he would've scorched two iris-sized holes right through me. He leaned back and folded his arms across his chest, a slight smirk at the corners of his mouth. I should've looked away, but he was wearing dark slacks and a light blue slim-fit business shirt that hugged his muscled chest just right. I knew it was muscled because I'd run my hands all over it when I'd kissed him. And let me tell you, abs for days.

His dark blond hair was perfectly coiffed in the front as if he'd just walked out of the barbershop two minutes ago. He had the chiseled jawline of an underwear model, and his eyebrow cocked, like, are you going to look away or what? A muscle in his jaw pulsed, hinting irritation at our little interchange, but his lips looked kind of happy about it. Either that or they'd like to take a bite out of me. Heat prickled my cheeks, and I quickly sat on the front row, turning my back to him. But my mind was ablaze, knowing he was in the same room. My hands wouldn't stop mangling each other.

Holden was...my friend. Or, he had been. I'd turned to him during Silas's and my "reset." What had been a moment of weakness on my part had morphed into nightly phone calls, *The Office* watch parties, and truth sessions that had pulled some of my darkest secrets out of obscurity. Like how I was a disappointment to my mother for letting both of my younger sisters find husbands before me. Or how I'd failed to claim the valedictorian spot in high school by two-tenths of a point. Or how I couldn't run for crap because my lungs seized, and I always ended up with my head between my knees, wheezing for air. I told him things that would've made the polish peel right off my mother's manicured nails. "Put up your best front always," Mom said on repeat. "You never know when a man will look at you as something more." And yet, Holden kept coming back every night for weeks.

Yeah, I'd kissed him out of desperation. My heart had felt like it was on the edge of the world, about to drop off into a dark, bottomless abyss. But something unexpected had happened during that kiss. The way he'd touched me, gently but with a torrent of underlying desire. How he'd looked at me between carefully placed pecks on my mouth like I was the most beautiful woman he'd ever seen. The patient slowness of the movement, like he'd stay there all night if that's how long it took to make that kiss perfect. The heat that had hit in ways it never had with any other guy. How my heart had swollen so big I couldn't take a full breath.

I wanted to fan myself just remembering it.

Hands down, it was the best kiss of my life. Not a runner-up in sight. Top of the medal stand, totally alone.

Until Silas showed up and made me feel like a cheap floozy. And I'd played the part just how he wanted me to. Taken all the blame and then turned, tail between my legs, and bolted for my motel room. With weeks to reflect, I shouldn't have done that. Maybe I had kissed his brother, but he'd broken my heart. We were even.

I glanced back at Holden, whose massive biceps were now locked around adorable Anna, listening intently as she animatedly told him, I don't know, probably about her first day of high school. My chest tightened, and I exhaled. Good gosh, he was even more attractive when he was being sweet and interested in his niece.

My heart panged hard. If I was being honest, I missed him and his friendship. Achingly. He was smart, kind, and hilarious. And yes, I could've reached out. I could've apologized for going after Silas instead of standing firm next to him. I'd started to text him multiple times.

But I wasn't going to.

Because the thing I'd had to remind myself hourly, no minutely, was this...

Holden was a big, fat player.

Silas had told me that, and Holden had admitted it in one of our first conversations. He'd dated over a hundred girls. Well over. To the point that he'd stopped counting. But I felt confident in labeling him a serial dater. So, no wonder the kiss had been so incredible. He had a PhD in perfectly placed hands and the right amount of pressure needed to induce a moan, or how to use those warm eyes to elicit certain emotions...

But it hadn't meant anything to him.

The entire reason I'd first gone out with Silas when he asked wasn't because I was super attracted to him. Even though I'd grown up in Wyoming, cowboys weren't my type. Nope. Players were. Good-looking, cocky ones, just like Holden. In high school and college, I'd been naïve enough to think I could tame a guy like that. Had even brought one home to meet my family once.

But I'd realized after having my heart obliterated that maybe some girls were capable of conquering a ladies' man—like my little sister Gabby—but I wasn't one of them.

So, while Holden might be dreamy and swole—as I'd heard two teenage girls say today—and his rose petal lips might induce a full-body tremble, weaving an exhilarating spell around your heart—one thing was perfectly clear.

I needed to stay far, far away from Holden Dupree.

Find out if Christy can stay away from Holden (spoiler alert: she can't) in Not A Thing, book two of the Seddledowne Series. Available in Kindle Unlimited, ebook, and paperback!

thank you

Thank you for reading the first book in the Seddledowne Series.

When I sat down to write Clementine's story, all I knew was that she would (soon) be single, broken from her best friend's death, and taking care of her family's farm on her own. I knew Silas had been in love with her his entire life. And I knew they were going to have a happily ever after, but I had no idea how they were going to get there. Along the way, I fell in love with Silas, Lemon, wonderful Anna, the Dupree brothers (and their name-calling,) and even our feisty, hilarious, deceased Sophie. Oh, if we could all have a friend like her.

Now that I'm on the other side, I know a whole lot more. Like how Holden, Ashton, Ford, and Anna will all get love stories of their own. And I can not wait to share them with you.

But an author is never an island and I have some people to thank for helping me get here. So here goes:

Etta, for being the world's best brainstormer, cheerleader, and beta-reader any author could ask for. Half the ideas in this book are yours and I really, truly hope you finish your novel so we can co-write soon!

My daughter, Emma, who never fails to keep it real and keep me in check. I adore you. And you really are a kick-butt editor.

My other kiddos: Will, Cole, and Adelaide, for always believing in me and never treating me like I'm a hack even though you've seen me in sweatpants. Being your mom is, and will continue to be, the best thing I've ever done. (You too, Em.)

Beta-readers: Kenzie, Crystal, Natalie, and Mhairi. Thank you for all your comments and error-catching and for helping this story become its best. You guys rock.

Emily Faircutler, editor extraordinaire. Your work is invaluable. Thank you for making me look great.

Angelica Hagman at Purpose on Paper for the beautiful cover. You are a dream to work with. Seriously. So grateful that I found you.

Melanie Jacobson, an ever-faithful author friend who never tires of my questions and makes me believe that I am good enough to do this. You've always been a guiding light. Thank you.

And I will always give thanks to the One who loves and sustains me daily. He puts stories in my heart and words on my page. Without Him, I am nothing.

Here's to many more years of love stories and happily ever afters.

All my best,
Susan

Made in the USA
Columbia, SC
10 May 2025